To Jo for her unfailing help and encouragement

In memory of Darren Brown

Preface

Rhetoric is the art of persuasion that is indifferent to right and wrong: its only concern is to convince. (Plato: Republic)

"Why didn't England experience a full scale revolution?" This is a question that has been raised many times when reading of the events in England's Regency Period (1811 - 1820). The classic writings of Jane Austin portray a world of the handsome Mr D'Arcy and the Bennett sisters. This is a microcosm of society whilst the real world outside Pemberley House and the genteel society of Hertfordshire was vastly different.

This book is *not* a political treatise - it is a story using the background of a turbulent England that would eventually emerge as the dominant economic world power. Whilst this growth was happening there were towns and villages all around the country where there was massive deprivation.

This is the backdrop, *Rhetoric or Revolution?* is about fictitious characters from three of the strands of Regency Society. I have annotated events, laws and attitudes that have been extracted from the period. This is not my attempt to educate (far be it for me) but to remind and highlight the circumstances under which the characters would have had to live through.

It traces the formative years of the two main characters from what were called 'the lower sort' who work in stone quarries - Jasper - the protagonist - a big man in all respects, and his lifelong friend Robert who could be seen a Mr Everyman who rises to the occasion in an emergency.

A contemporary from their village, Charlie Heywood, becomes part of the growing bourgeois which would evolve into the Middle Class of the Victorian age.

The landed, aristocracy are torn between liberalism - Lord Charles Wareham, and conservatism - Lord Henry Olden (with a small l and c).

Right from the start - I would like to own up - I am not an historian. I suppose that is the wrong admission to make when writing about a period of two hundred years ago. I have researched as much of the facts as will make the story credible. It is not a book for study, but for enjoyment - giving a flavour of the time.

To set the scene I want to take away the glitz and glamour that can be a knee jerk view of the excesses of the bloated Prince Regent and his cohort. The following is a sample of what was happening outside the walls of the 'Brighton Pavilion'. These are some of the many events that could have been embryonic of a full-scale revolution:

- 1810: Prime minister Spencer Perceval is assassinated,
- 1811-13: The Luddites workers breaking looms and knitting frames,
- 1812: Riots of unemployed in Sheffield,
- 1815-6: The demobilisation (estimated at) of 300,000 soldiers and sailors after the Battle of Waterloo exacerbating already high unemployment,
- The Spa Fields 'Riots' attended by about 10,000 people. (Orator) Hunt spoke from the window of a public house; where he wore his white top hat, a symbol of radicalism and the 'purity of his cause'.
- 1816: The Ely and Littleport riots in May,
- 1817: The Pentrich armed uprising,
- 1817: the 'March of the Blanketeers' - hunger-march' to London from Manchester
- 1819: The Peterloo 'Massacre' where cavalry charged a peaceful demonstration killing women and children,

- 1820: The Cato Street conspiracy to murder the British Cabinet including Prime Minister Lord Liverpool,

The government had an Eighteenth Century mentality and its response was repression. The passing of The Six Acts proscribed meetings, the preamble stating 'every meeting for radical reform is an overt act of treasonable conspiracy against the King and his government'. This indicated a pre-supposition by the government that reform would lead to revolution.

In 1815 the Corn Laws introduced tariffs and other trade restrictions on imported food and cereals. The Corn Laws enhanced the profits and political power associated with land ownership. The laws raised food prices and the costs of living and hampered the growth of other British economic sectors, such as manufacturing, by reducing the disposable income of the British people.[1]

There is another backdrop for the Regency Period. The eruption of Mount Tambora was the most powerful volcanic eruption in recorded human history. Mount Tambora is on the island of Sumbawa in present-day Indonesia, Although its eruption reached a violent climax on 10 April 1815, increased steaming and small phreatic eruptions occurred during the next six months to three years. The ash from the eruption column dispersed around the world and lowered global temperatures.

The Thames had frozen over in an exceptionally cold winter of 1814. This was then followed by what was called "the year without a summer". when dust blocked out the sun and harvests failed. The characters in *Rhetoric or Revolution*

---

[1] They were not repealed until 1846.

are constantly getting wet from from rain and covered in dust - there was a reason for the inclusion!

The setting for the narrative centres around the gloriously named village of Langton Matravers on the Isle of Purbeck in Dorset. I have to declare an interest as whilst tracing my family tree to this village and visiting its museum it would appear that the name *Bower* was pre-eminent for most of the villagers. I have used places and names almost it could be said, indiscriminately. I must therefore emphasise that all the characters and events are purely the results of my own imagination.

The characters at this time were exactly the same as us but society had different values. To castigate men for their treatment of women and conversely women's acceptance of the status quo is not to be condemned in hindsight. In the same way today, ardent believers in their own faith would have different beliefs if they were born in the house, town or country next door.

When my characters espouse opinions that would be unacceptable to us today they do so to highlight how we now perceive situations as different. I do not identify myself with any such opinion and I have tried to articulate what a character at the time would say or believe. (Hopefully that will get me off the hook with my dear wife, Jo).

I bow to eminent historians as to reasons that history unfolded the way it did during this Period. I merely give a gentle suggestion that underlying the major events, ordinary folk in all walks of life want to live a life full of love, interest and always hopefully with humour.

Did these strands come together for the common good? Were they helped by the real power behind the throne?

My own humble opinion is that I am not miles away from what could have happened. Are we a country strong on rhetoric and protest, but weak when it comes to action except in self-defence?

There was no charismatic leader that emerged. I could say that the nearest was Orator Hunt. The following is an extract of his oration at Spa Fields (written in the 3rd person as I am quoting E.P.Thompson)

"He knew the superiority of mental over physical force; nor would he counsel any resort to the latter till the former had been found ineffectual. Before physical force was applied to, it was their duty to petition, to remonstrate, to call aloud for timely reformation. Those who resisted the just demands of the people were the real friends of confusion and bloodshed . . . but if the fatal day should be destined to arrive, he assured them that if he knew anything of himself, he would not be found concealed behind a counter, or sheltering himself in the rear."

[Quoted by E.P. Thompson, The Making of the English Working Class (Penguin Books, 1968), p.685]

He seems to be hedging his bets a great deal if asked to put his head above the parapet. - *Rhetoric or Revolution?*

If you the reader enjoys this book just a fraction as much as I have in writing it then you're in for a treat.

CHAPTER ONE

Death in a Quarry

'CRACK!' the silence in the quarry shaft is shattered. It was as if a canon had been fired underground. It's echo slowly dies until the oppressive silence returns broken only by the ever-present sound of dripping water.

'CRACK!' another sudden piercing sound is followed by an ominous cascade of falling loose earth and gravel.

'CRACK!' This time there is the ominous crashing of stone.

A young lad barely in his teens stumbles back against the stone wall. He catches his breath and remains motionless. A cruel silence quickly returns as he cautiously strains forward holding his tallow candle but the feeble light is soon overwhelmed by a wall of blackness. He stretches his eyes wide open as though they could capture more light,

Jasper is at the foot of a steep eighty foot ramp from the surface in a chamber barely six feet high. His older brother is working at the stone face two hundred feet away along the narrow underground lanes.

Jasper is already hardened by the dangers of working in the stone quarry, He enters under the lower roof of the lane grabbing a pickaxe with a four foot handle on his way. After only ten to twelve feet he crawls under a section where the roof has almost collapsed. In his rush to press forward the handle of the pickaxe jams between his knee and a protruding pillar. The stones seem to groan and he freezes as they settle and discard only a little gravel and a puff of dust.

Pillars are made by putting stones about one foot six inches square at the side of the lane, A similar slightly smaller stone is put on top and then another until they are wedged tight against the ceiling with clay packed in between to prevent them from moving. Every day, as the quarry is worked. the pillars sound like volley of muskets when stones split from top to bottom. The lanes are scattered with small piles of gravel and earth or some times partially blocked with broken stones. They are made with enough room to allow the dragging through of a four feet wide quarr cart.[2]

'CRACK!' This time the piercing sound is much louder and is followed by the crashing of an avalanche of stone. Jasper freezes and waits for silence to return before cautiously creeping forward until he is greeted with a total collapse of a pillar and its adjoining roof. After heaving and dislodging a couple of the larger stones he is able to squeeze through a gap.

He edges cautiously forward, then calls out as loud as he dare, "Ben, can you hear me?"

A few more feet; "Ben, shall I come through?" His voice quivers as his anxiety grows, unsure whether to keep going or get help from his father who is on the surface. Instinctively, he continues. Slowly crouching and crawling forward he has the mounting feeling of the whole mine enshrouding itself tightly around him.

Eventually he hears the scraping and scrabbling of stone.

Calling softly, "Ben, is that you?" he asks needlessly. Then a little louder. "Ben, are you alright?

After a few moments the muffled voice of his brother calls back. "Jasper, go back up to the surface."

Heedless of his elder brother's command he crawls forward until he is stopped by a wall of shattered stone. His feeble light shines on a narrow crack in the wall of rubble where fingers appear, then a bleeding hand. He can hear Ben's voice cursing.

---

[2] Low wooden cart with small wheels

Jasper sets his candle down and quickly starts to clear the rock until eventually a hole is torn open enough for Jasper to see Ben's head. It is encased in the usual stone dust and grime but he gasps when he sees blood spilling from several deep cuts. Ben gives a faint smile of encouragement and says quietly. "I told you to go back."

Jasper shakes his head. "The stone is loose on this side. We'll soon get it away." Their efforts resume at a frantic pace until enough space for Ben to make his escape seems just moments away.

'CRACK!' This time just a few yards behind Jasper. They both freeze and hold their breath. Ben stares at Jasper his eyes wide in a mix of anger and pleading and through clenched teeth he rasps. *"Jasper go back - now!"*

"No, we've almost made enough room." He renews his efforts at tearing away the obstructing stone. There is deep rumble and clay starts to cascade from the roof of the tunnel. Some extinguishes the candle and they are enshrouded in pitch darkness.

"Jasper go now." Ben shouts. "Think of Pa and Ma. Go NOW!" Another rumble as stones start to fall. Jasper is torn and hesitates. "NOW, Jasper - NOW."

Tears stream down Jasper's young face as he reluctantly crawls backwards until he can turn and scramble on his hands and knees through the crashing stone and clay until he is clear. Hesitating, he looks back down the shaft. "Ben? Ben!" The oppressive silence has descended again. After a further moments hesitation, Jasper reluctantly makes his way in darkness to the foot of the steep slope leading to the surface and slumps on the floor. His broad shoulders shake as he sobs.

From the Tomes' family quarry there is a short but steep downhill path leading to a cliff edge platform known to the locals as Dancing Ledge. Isaac Tomes has finished hauling stones on his horn-cart[3] to Dancing Ledge for storage until lowering them onto a boat to take to Swanage.

As he trudges back up the path he has a feeling of foreboding. The sight at the top of the slide confirms to him immediately something is wrong. Billy the donkey, whilst still attached to the capstan, has wandered as far as his yoke will allow and is idly grazing. There is no sign of Jasper who should have been driving Billy round, hauling one of the flat quarr Carts laden with stone up to the surface.

The steep slope called a slide has a smooth rock runway for hauling up the loaded quarr carts and wide steep steps to one side which lead down to the lanes. Dread churns Isaac's stomach as he expertly rushes down the slope to find Jasper at the bottom not moving, just staring ahead at the stone wall. Jasper had stopped sobbing and he is sitting numbly with his face set.

"Jasper what's happened?" Jasper doesn't answer. Isaac looks passed Jasper along the lane into the blackness. "Are you alright, lad? Where's Ben?" Jasper still doesn't speak. "Jasper - where's Ben?" Isaac almost shouts.

Jasper looks up slowly at his father. There is no emotion in his voice. "Some stone pillars cracked down in the lane - there…. there" he stammers "was a fall and Ben was cut off. " His eyes widened and his voice rises in desperation," I tried to get him out, " he stops, then with effort, his voice now quieter but void of any expression. "There was another fall. Ben told me to go. I failed. I failed to help get my brother out."

Isaac's eyes moisten as he fears the extent of the tragedy. He takes Jasper's arm and gives it a re-assuring squeeze. "I know you would have done all you could, lad. Go on, get

---

[3] Two wheel cart with no sides usually pulled by two men

back up to the surface." He gently turns Jasper around and nudges him back up the slide.

Isaac grabs a candle from the pile lying on the floor and rams it into an iron holder. His hands are shaking as he frantically strikes his flint until he has a flame. He crawls forward cautiously stopping frequently to shove to the sides debris from numerous small rock falls. Eventually his way is blocked by a more solid wall of broken rock and clay. Without pausing he starts tearing away at the rubble until he exposes a lifeless hand. He renews his efforts although he already knows they are in vain. Finally he is able to uncover his son's head but heaves at what remains of his beloved son's broken face.

There is yet another crack of stone splitting, and with a heavy heart he takes one final forlorn look at his son. The stone fall and the discarded debris had narrowed the lane. Like Jasper he is forced to crawl backwards before he can turn and make his way quickly to join Jasper on the surface.

Jasper, stops feeding Billy and turns expectantly to his father. Isaac shakes his head sadly. His mouth opens to speak but closes again without a sound. He turns his head to the white foaming sea, then slowly takes a few steps and stops . His blank stare neither sees nor his mind thinks.

Jasper drops Billy's feed and moves to his father's side. He stares quizzically then closes his eyes and with a barely audible groan slowly closes his eyes.

Man and boy remain silent as the wind, flecked with sleet, is driving straight into their faces. Nature and their grief at the loss of a son and a brother forces tears from their eyes..

Eventually Jasper turns to face his father and almost menacing says "This is not right. We risk everything and what for? Our whole lives are spent just so that we can survive." He catches his breath at the word survive.

"Aye lad, but there is no other way for the likes of us." Jasper was already as tall as his father and Isaac puts a hand on each shoulder and looks at him squarely in the eye. "You're my eldest now. I shall be relying on you to help me to support your Ma, and two sisters." He lowers his head whilst sternly holding Jasper's eyes waiting for a sign of understanding and agreement.

Then he straightens to his full height and says briskly, "We have much work to do to repair the quarry but that can wait until tomorrow. But now" he pauses "but now, we have to go to your dear Ma. She will be devastated."

"But it's just not fair …….." Jasper starts.

Isaac stopped him. "Jasper you have to be a man now."

Jasper stares straight back at his father then as if he has come to a decision, he shrugs and turns away and Isaac is sure he hears him mutter "One day…." The steely glaze had returned. Jasper would never weep again.

CHAPTER TWO

Real Power

"So you see my dear Coningsby, the world is governed by very different personages from what is imagined by those who are not behind the scenes." - Observation by Benjamin Disraeli (twice British Prime Minister) in his book Coningsby

In the heart of the City of London three brothers are sat around a large highly polished oak table. The walls of the room are lined with dark oak panelling and a roaring fire takes the chill off a cold afternoon. There are chairs around the fire but the brothers sit at the table; this is a business meeting.

The eldest brother Amit starts formally, "Shālôm 'alêḵem;. Firstly, our initial negotiations with the British Government have been completed. We will now be financing their campaign in Portugal and Spain. Arrangements have been made for the delivery of £10 million for the use of their Commander Sir Arthur Wellesley."

Grunts of satisfaction pass around the table.

He continues. "Britain's foreign policy is to prevent one country rule over the rest of Europe. The British government, has concluded an alliance with Russia, Austria and Sweden to form a European league. Their aim is for the French to relinquish a number of countries that they now occupy. The British offer is to pay an annual subsidy of £1,250,000 for every 100,000 troops that their allies employ in the field. I have indicated to the Prime Minster that we will be ready to assist Britain in anyway."

"Britain is already a very wealthy Nation and its trade is mainly with its Empire and other countries around the world. Since their Admiral Nelson's annihilation of the French and

Spanish fleets at Trafalgar they have complete command of the world's oceans. Although their existing trade is secure they have a entrepreneurial culture that will enable its economy to grow at a rate that will far outstrip any other country for the foreseeable future. Britain will be very rich and powerful and it is in our interests that we aid their growth." The others nodded with satisfaction.

"Now to the point of why I called a meeting today." He looked around the table knowing he had his brothers full attention. "The only situation that could jeopardise Britain's future is the current civil unrest. This must be stopped from becoming a full scale revolution as they had in France twenty years ago." He was about to be interrupted but held up his hand so he could continue. "I believe that we have a breathing space. The British are very patriotic, and they have a natural animosity to the French." He shook his head in despair, "They have been fighting with them off and on, for about eight hundred years. I believe therefore, for them beating the French is paramount and the people will accept suppression of their liberties until the threat of defeat has gone.

"You have obviously given this matter much thought." Solomon acknowledged.

"Quite. We are not here for a short time just looking for good profitable business. As our father has impressed upon us - we must make ourselves, indispensable. We must put ourselves in a position where the government needs to look to us for financial support and so that we influence events rather than leave them to chance.

I believe that unrest, riots and discontent to a certain extent are inevitable for the time being. But… and I must repeat and emphasise it is very much not in our interests for matters to get any further out of hand."

He paused again for effect. "I want to know everything about England. I want our Agents to cover the whole country. I want to know what each of the various classes are thinking."

Firstly, the largest, but least powerful and paradoxically where the threat for revolution will come from, the lower sort. I want to know about those labourers on the land and the workers in the mills and factories. I want to understand how long it is before they bind themselves for a full scale revolt. Or is not in their nature to follow that path." He paused and looked at his brothers sternly, " I believe that every man has a breaking point."

Secondly the class with the power, the Aristocracy and Landed Gentry. Do they all believe that repression is the only answer or are there some amongst them that see reform as essential.

Also thirdly," he added, "I want to know of any up and coming businessmen who create wealth through their own ingenuity and hard work. This middling sort, or should they be called the Middle Class, could become the most important part of this country's wealth."

He frowned as he looked from one to another. "These three classes are the bedrock of English society - two of which are at potential loggerheads. One has everything to lose and the other has nothing to lose. The emerging middle class needs both, for investment and for labour, for themselves to succeed." Another pause. "There are no guarantees. This country could go either way. Brothers, we know our own objectives, we need to ensure that this country takes the right path so that we may achieve them."

The dissertation is followed by silence as each brother digests Amit's conclusions. "There is no rush for the time being. We need a full understanding of the nation so that it can form a framework of our policies and actions in the future."

With that he declares their business at an end and speaks of domestic affairs.

CHAPTER THREE
Sunday Morning in Langton Matravers

Durlston Head, Isle of Purbeck, Dorset - August 1811

At Durlston Head fields drift away from the cliffs and as the sun sets, shadows fill the folds in the land like dark pools of water. On reaching the Headland the stillness of the countryside is broken by a cacophony of swirling birds as they swoop along the cliff faces. Often there is a swooping, squawking murmuration of starlings.

Jasper Tomes, now nineteen years old, sits with his friend Robert Bolson, on the dry stone wall that traces the cliff's edge . They had toiled in each of their father's. quarries all day and neither spoke for some time as they stared out across the English Channel.

Their reverie is broken by a sudden long whistle then a fast, falling trill of a Guillemot. Jasper straights up and watches it plunge down to the sea. He releases a deep breath and stretches his aching muscles from a hard days work. He turns and fixes Robert with a hard stare. "We need to move on." It was as though he was carrying on a conversation.

Robert briefly glances sideways then turns back to scrutinise the sea before saying quietly, "Don't worry we will."

They continued to sit for some time without speaking as close friends will as they forsake the need for constant chatter. Jasper starts again and repeats "We need to move on." as if he had not previously spoken.

Robert sat still and remained silent.

"When?" Jasper demands as if in answer. He says it more gruffly than he intended but he turns to stare at Robert waiting for an answer. Robert doesn't speak. "Robert, we worked the same today as we did yesterday. It will be the same next week. Every day. The same as our fathers. And their fathers? The same thing. What do we all have for our hard work? Nothing. Just about enough to feed and cloth our families, We get no chance to change - to do something else - different, exciting, seeing what's over that horizon." His voice had risen again.

"Alright my friend, but let's not talk about it now." Robert shifts uncomfortably. He agrees with Jasper, a life full of adventure would be much better than cuts, bruises and blisters from crawling underground in near total darkness. It was a big break though and it is a decision he always prefers to put off.

Jasper was becoming impatient for the lack of response. He carries on with what was becoming his pet subject. "We've seen those radicals when they come to Swanage. They tell us that it's through our hard work that this country is getting rich." Robert pulled a face and grunted in agreement.

"That last one, Cobbitt or Cobden.... whatever, said that men who had left their farms to work in the mills and factories are now being left without work 'cos machines were replacing them. I remember he said that they are revolting - smashing those machines."

Robert looked at Jasper frowning. "Do you want to get involved in all that? They'll get caught, put in prison then hanged or worse deported….. to Australia!"

Robert, dropping his head, closes his eyes and rubs a hand across his face. He looked up at Jasper, but says nothing at first. He then took a deep breath and turns to face Jasper. "What about our families. If we left it would be very difficult for them. Would they be able to survive without our help."

Jasper was ready for that problem. "For myself, you know we have had your Ma's nephew, Jimmy Corben with us for a few months now, he is ready to do his full share of the work."

"Are you sure? I heard that he's a little bugger. Didn't he release your donkey, Billy, one evening last week. You had to spend most of the next morning searching for it and work was delayed. I'll wager your Pa was not happy.

Jasper grinned   "Yes, Pa's belt across his backside will persuade him not to do that again."

"Would Jimmy be ready to take over from you though?"

"He'll have no choice. Anyway, you have three brothers to help your Pa."

"Well yes, but Peter is the only one old enough to take the full load of work," he paused, "I worry about Peter though." Then seeing Silas Winter the manager from the Crack Lane quarry approaching he quickly says "Jasper, it's not just as easy as you say. Our families have always worked down in the quarries."

They jumped down off of their stone perch and gave a cheery greeting. "Good evening Mr Winter."

"You're a pair of lazy young ruffians Sitting around here is not going to get your fathers' work done."

"You don't know the meaning of work. You just tell others what to do." They both chuckled but left it at that. Silas was a good man and they did not want to upset one of the men of the village lest their fathers' were to hear of it. They would then likely receive a cuff around the ear.

Silas gave a wry smile and carried on his way. When he was out of sight Robert looked at Jasper and could sense his frustration, 'It's Saturday, we'll be at The Ship tonight and we'll talk then."

Jasper grunted, "Alright." Then looking at the setting sun added,   "We had better hurry or we'll be late for dinner." They both scampered across the fields to arrive just in time for their meals.

* * *

Jasper and Robert lived in the village of Langton Matravers on the Isle of Purbeck a quiet backwater of east Dorset. The village itself was a community typical of many other rural villages in England, with communication to the outside world slow, and for many it was of no consequence. Most had never been far away from the village and almost none had been to a large city, let alone London. For generations the villages generally accepted his or her place in what seemed the natural order. On the surface life appeared timeless, almost idyllic, as the village seemed to never change.

The cottages in the village huddle together on Stonehouse Hill that leads down from the Crack Lane quarry and passes through the village on its two mile journey to Swanage. Most buildings in Langton Matravers have walls and roofs made of stone from the nearby quarries rather than the usual clay and straw, cob walls, under thatched roofs. St Georges church and The Ship Inn were central parts of the villagers' lives.

The quarrying of stones was the main source of work in the area. The parishes of Langton Matravers, Worth Matravers, Swanage and Kingston were honeycombed with quarry-mines as well as cliff-side quarries with their galleries and caves at regular intervals along the coast.

Most villagers still worked their own quarries as a family business although there were two large quarries owned by Lord Olden, the Crack Lane and Eidibury Quarries. These employed between twenty to thirty men in each at any one time. Other men in the village worked long hours in the fields for Tenant farmers who leased their land from the local aristocratic landowners.

This apparent peaceful serenity masked a hard existence eked out by both the men in quarries and the labourers. Their womenfolk also worked from dusk to dawn, usually through a succession of pregnancies.

Isaac and Ada Tomes had three children, their eldest son, Ben having been tragically killed in the quarry. Jasper now the eldest was followed by twin sisters just a year younger than him who were christened Eleanor and Ethel. The twins grew up without anyone really noticing as they were very quiet and shared their lives intimately together. The birth of the twins nearly caused the death of Ada and after two further miscarriages there were no more pregnancies.

Isaac's closest friend Joshua Bollson married Martha Cobden and they had a family similar to many others. Robert was the eldest sibling and Peter came two years later. They were followed by Dorothy, who everyone called Dot, then at regular intervals Walter, Thomas, Grace and Horatio. Martha also had an infant die in childbirth and another who died when just two years old. The last addition to the family they christened Horatio. There were huge celebrations when the villagers heard the news of Lord Nelson's victory at Cape Trafalgar. The news gave great relief as the fear of an imminent invasion by the French then receded. Joshua always had a twinkle in his eye when he was reminded that Horatio was born just nine months later.

Robert and Jasper, like their fathers, had become inseparable friends. Jasper started working underground when Ben was killed. Robert started soon after working in his father's quarry called Smokey Hole. They stuck to their tasks, tough as it was for boys of their age, but by the time they reached nineteen years old they were restless.

Jasper and Robert would meet for their usual Saturday evening in The Ship. After their discussion on their way home from Durlston Head, Robert knew Jasper would raise the subject of leaving the village again - but hoped he wouldn't. After quaffing a few beers, Robert's heart sunk when Jasper took his arm and steered them away from their fellow drinkers. "I hear tell that the King's Men will be in Swanage tomorrow.."

Robert frowned "King's Men? Do you mean the army?" Robert said cautiously. Jasper nodded. "I hear tell that if they offer you a shilling[4] and if you take it then it means that you have agreed to join the army. You can't change your mind." He looked hard at Jasper. "I don't think I want to join the army."

Jasper was persuasive, "Come on Robert, let's go to hear what they have to say. There's no harm in that, is there?" Robert was not convinced but reluctantly agreed.

The Tomes and Bolson families habitually attended the Sunday Morning Service at St. George's Church in the village centre. They were passive believers rather than devout disciples of the Church of England. It was an opportunity for the women to congregate together to catch up with local gossip. The men would feign interest but very soon this would be too much and they then gave their apologies for having to attend to some business which would entail sloping off to The Ship.

The Sunday that Jasper and Robert had decided to go to Swanage was no different from any other. When the sun broke free of cloud, despite the stiff breeze the temperature was pleasant. The multitude of villagers were in a generally happy mood as Joshua scanned the various groups, His surveillance was broken by a clatter of horses' hooves.

Many of the villagers doffed their hats or gave a brief courtesy as they recognised the sons and daughters of the local gentry who were out for their customary Sunday ride.. They were rewarded with a cursory acknowledgement from

---

[4] 1 Shilling = 5p: considerably more valuable at the time

the riders who then spurred their horses and without a second glance carried on their light hearted conversation.

Joshua looked back to Martha and put his arm around her shoulder and gave her a hug. "Our lives are very different to theirs. They seem not to have a care in the world." His attention returned to the groups around the church yard, some leaning forward and listening closely to a piece of scandal whilst the next would break out laughing. "`These are our friends and although life is tough they seem content as most have work and their children are fed and happy." His gaze rested on two or three couples who kept to themselves and spoke very little. He continued ""Life can be very hard for some. I understand from Robert that Jasper is unhappy and he can be aggressive at times"

Jasper was in conversation with Robert, and two other friends Charlie Heywood and Calvin Seagers who were lads from the village of a similar age. The four lads were friends but very different in their own way. Jasper, standing at least a head higher, dominated the group in both size and demeanour. He had a large long-limbed muscular frame with a long face with a crease in the skin between his eyes. This made it appear that when men looked up at him, which they had to do, he was looking down, appearing to scowl, which usually unnerved them.

Joshua's gaze shifted to his son Robert, who was leaning casually against the church's wall with his usual broad smile on his face. He was shorter than Jasper but his body was powerfully built from hours and days down the mine shaft. Square faced with regular features his strikingly blue eyes were shaded by a mop of blond curly hair. He drew the attention of many of the young girls in the area.

Charlie Heywood was speaking and they all glanced in the direction of Tess Edmunds, a pretty lass who lived next door to Joshua and Martha. She saw their look, went crimson and turned back to resume her conversation with her brother Ted and Joshua's eldest daughter Dot.

Charlie was shorter than his companions and he was quick in all he did, speech, movement and thought. He leant forward and spoke conspiratorially glancing at the unfortunate Tess. Jasper gave Charlie's arm a friendly punch on the arm whilst sporting the broadest of grins. Robert added another comment and they all burst out laughing.

Joshua shook his head in mock despair. "Lads of that age never change." He chuckled, "Those four lads have grown up together here in the village but they are so different."

Martha nodded. "Robert and Jasper, God willing will be like yourself and Isaac; friends no matter what happens." She frowned and added thoughtfully, "I do wish our Robert would assert himself more. Jasper can be quite dominating, all the lads in village look up to him already."

Joshua agreed, "I know what you mean. The other two are completely different. Calvin is older than the others and he's a serious young man. His Pa's not been very well lately and he has been taking on more and more of the work as Bailiff to Lord Olden. He's a big solid chap and he's getting that air of authority which must be coming from working at Olden Hall."

Joshua grunted but smiled as Charlie Heywood leant forward to speak conspiratorially to his grinning companions and they all started laughing again. "Young Charlie, I'm just not sure about him. He's friendly enough and if he's able to be, generous as well. He has worked very hard to help his Ma since his Pa was killed in that storm out in the Channel. He won't spend his life quarrying for stone, that's for sure." He paused then changing the subject added, "I think Robert and Jasper are off to Swanage this afternoon."

"Yes." Martha frowned but then quickly smiled as she saw Isaac and Ada Tomes strolling towards them. They were closely followed by their twin daughters who were talking quietly to each other. Isaac looked at Joshua and with raised eyebrows asking a silent question to which Joshua gave a slight nod. Both wives pretended they did not see the exchange.

After a few more moments of savouring the pleasant atmosphere Joshua took a deep breath, "It's time to go. I'll be meeting Isaac in The Ship as usual in a little while, but I will walk you home first.

Martha linked arms with her man. He was right, life was hard but agreeable. As they turned towards home the sun went behind a cloud and the stiff breeze made her shiver.

There were no clouds on the horizons of Charles Honsworth and Emily Pangborne. They passed by St Georges church without really noticing the nods and curtsies proffered to them by the villagers. Charles and Emily, both the offspring of powerful local families, were enjoying their Sunday morning ride. They had grown up together and they enjoyed an almost sibling intimacy. Joining them were Lord Olden's son, Henry, together with his soon to be bride, Henrietta Millborrow.

Charles was of medium build with a shock of dark curly hair and sideburns down to his chin. He was now twenty years old and his face bore a constant look of faint boredom tinged with disdain. Emily was a pretty girl a year younger than Charles. She had curly fair hair that peeped out from under her riding bonnet and a small figure that was, despite her age, only just now reaching womanhood.

After gossiping for a while they found that they had left their friends behind them. Charles reigned in his mount and pulled the bridle so he could turn to face Emily. He was an earnest young man and was a foil to the outward going Emily who did not hesitate to say exactly what was going through her mind at any one time. Her parents were not entirely happy that she did not display a more demure manner suitable for her station in life.

"Emily."

"Charles, you are wearing one of your serious faces. You are about to say something very profound aren't you?"

"My dear Emily." He hesitated so as to gather his thoughts. "Emily," he started again. "We have known each other for as long as I can remember. The only time when we didn't see each other constantly was when I was up at Oxford'"

"You are such a clever boots aren't you?" She frowned and then pouted, "All those books you read and told me about sounded so interesting. It's so unfair that Ladies are not allowed to go to university." She looked at Charles ignoring his irritation on being interrupted. She gave an unladylike giggle much to his discomfort. "I think you are going to say something very grown up."

"Emily," he started yet again. "My father has not been well." Emily gave a sharp intake of breath. "No, no don't worry. The doctors say he will be fine."

Emily breathed a sigh of relief. Charles' father, Lord Wareham, was like an uncle to her.

"It's just that as he had not been very well it made him think of the future. Well, I'll cut to the chase. Apart from Oxford I've spent most of my life down here in Dorset. To get more experience of the world he wants me to take a commission in the army. In fact he has already been in contact with Lord Olden's friends in the War Office and has arranged for the purchase of a commission in the East Dorset Regiment."

Emily looked alarmed. "Oh dear, does that mean that you will have to go away to that horrid war? I'm told it's quite beastly."

"No, the East Dorsets are mainly still based here in England." He stopped to look at Emily directly. "A number of the Companies are in Portugal but I have been assured that I will not have to do too much and if I so desire I will remain in England. I have been told that I will have to spend time with the Regiment for a few months at first."

Emily gave a small bounce in her saddle. "Well, that's settled then."

"Emily," he was in danger of wearing her name out as he hadn't finished yet. "It's just that I thought that we had a sort of understanding ." He hesitated. "I mean a sort of understanding about you and I."

Emily flushes. "Well, yes. I suppose....." she hesitates and a brief frown flits across her face. She then abruptly stands up in her saddle and looks over Charles' shoulder. "Oh look, here come the others. I'll race you to meet them."

She gives her horse's bridle a sharp flick and gallops off leaving behind a very frustrated Charles Honsworth.

CHAPTER FOUR

Committment and Consequences

After Morning Service, Robert and Jasper were anxious to get going to Swanage. They assured each of their parents that although they were both now nineteen years old, 'Yes they would be careful' and 'Yes, they wouldn't be too late'.

At the top of Stonehouse Hill they were joined by Charlie. "Are you two off to meet your army friends?" he joked.

"We're just going to listen to what they have to say, that's all." Robert responded quickly.

Jasper ignored the comment. "You said you were off to Swanage today as well. Any good reason?" Jasper wanted to sound casual but he was curious.

"Just business. Just business." Charlie raised his eyebrows giving an expression of innocence but couldn't hide a hint of smugness.

"I heard that you have been earning good money doing this and that." Robert was also curious.

Charlie relaxed. "Yes but it's been hard work. When Pa was killed he left Ma without a penny. As you know she used to traipse the four miles to Olden Hall every day where she was given odd jobs. She was just given the scraps." He looked directly at Jasper and Robert. "Literally the scraps sometimes from the table." He sighed. "It was tough."

"Yes, but I heard she hasn't done that for some time." Robert was concerned.

"No thanks goodness. I've been able to get work around the village. Occasional errands or whatever for Abraham Butt the blacksmith, the curate and also for Silas Winter at Crack Lane quarry. Anything to earn a Penny or two."

"I get the impression that you don't run errands these days, though?"

"No, although I still do bits and pieces for Silas. For some time now though, Isaac Gulliver has been giving me jobs."

Robert looked concerned. "We knew that, but Isaac Gulliver is not a man you should cross and you don't want to get caught by the Revenue Men."

Charlie smiled. "Smuggling has been going on for as long anyone can remember and Mr Gulliver runs all that trade on Purbeck now. To start with I acted as a lookout when they were making a landing. If you show yourself keen and reliable there's always work from him and he will treat you alright."

"I understand that you are out in the bay quite regularly."

"Yes, because Pa was a fisherman I told them I knew all about boats." Charlie chuckled. "Well, at least they believed me." He carried on. "They leave barrels suspended from buoys in the Bay. No-one can tell which are crab pots and which are supporting a barrel." He looked triumphant. "I've learnt to know the difference and I go out at night to check them and bring back any that are drifting out into the Channel."

They had reached Swanage and Charlie stopped and looked at his companions. "I've been able to save some money and today I hope I might be able to do some real business."

Jasper went to speak but Charlie held his hand up. "Sorry, that's all for now." He turned round and hurried ahead in the direction of the harbour.

Robert watched him disappear around the corner and shook his head. "One day he could make a fortune."

Jasper grunted, "More likely land up in jail. Come on let's get moving."

As they went through Swanage they saw several friends from both the village and Swanage going in the same direction. Turning the corner to the square in front of The

Harbour Inn they saw a crowd of twenty to thirty young men such as themselves, all listening, laughing and letting out the occasional gasp of disbelief. Three burly army sergeants impressively dressed in the King's uniform were holding court. Despite Robert's initial reluctance on the purpose of them being there he soon joined the other lads and became enthralled. They listened all afternoon to the sergeants' tales. They were promised that a life in the army would mean travel around the world and the opportunity to make untold riches. As young men, Jasper and Robert were filled with wonder. By late evening, and with the help of ale fuelled optimism, they were so carried away that they took the 'King's Shilling' and joined the army.

In contrast to Jasper and Robert, Charlie had a frustrating afternoon. He had walked round the crowd outside The Harbour Inn and went inside where he found the landlord, Seth Cobald looking out of the window with a satisfied grin on his face. Seth acknowledged Charlie as he came through the door and gestured towards a table by the window. Seth sat down so that he could watch what was happening outside. "The army is doing good business for me today."

Charlie smiled. "Business is always good for you these days, isn't it?"

"Yes it is. I will admit though that I'm lucky being in the middle of town and close to the harbour." He shook his head sadly. "It's not so easy for the landlords in the villages."

"So I've noticed."

"The French are helping as much as they can for people like Isaac Gulliver to land brandy, tea and other goods from across the channel." He chuckled. "One fisherman who has been over to Gravelines said that the French had set out a part of the town for the English. They call it Smugglers Town."

"Why would they do that?"

"I'm told that they will do anything that they think would be bad for the English. The landlords around here don't mind though, they are able to get what they need to sell, much cheaper. Otherwise, these days, they could go broke. I don't know what will happen when the war is finally over. Anyway, life is about seeing an opportunity and taking it."

Charlie was encouraged but hesitated and shifted in his seat.

Seth chuckled to himself 'The lad's nervous' Then encouragingly he prompted Charlie. "Come on, Charlie. It's not like you to be slow. Spit it out. You said you wanted to do some business with me."

Charlie went for it. "Gull Quarry, by Worth Matravers, is available for rent."

"What is your point? Why should I be interested? I'm the landlord of the Harbour Inn here in Swanage." He frowned at Charlie. "Also, why are you interested? You've never been underground in your life."

"Neither has Lord Olden, but he owns the Crack Lane and Eidbury quarries."

"Alright, what are you suggesting?"

"Gull is the smallest quarry that Lord Wareham owns. He has Estates here on Purbeck and all around the country. His Lordship is getting old now and his business is being left increasingly to his local Estate Managers. His Bailiff on Purbeck, Cyrus Claydon, is getting old and will do as little as possible. Gull is too small for him to be bothered about and he's tried to sell it. As there have been no offers he is willing to put it up for rent."

Seth was still frowning. "What are you suggesting, Charlie? I'm a landlord not a quarryman."

Charlie leant forward enthusiastically. "That's what you will remain." He took a deep breath. "Gull almost runs itself.

Ben Foster is a good quarry manager and his twelve workers have been there for some time and are reliable. They have good regular customers and the quarry makes a modest profit. Ben looks after his customers but he's too busy to make use of the opportunities there are for expanding the business." Charlie stopped with an expectant look on his face then his heart sank.

"I'm sorry, Charlie. You want me to take the risk of running a business I know nothing about. Where do you come in on this enterprise?"

Charlie was unabashed. "We could go in as partners. You will look after your business here in Swanage and I will run the quarry."

Seth chortled. "Yes but it would be a rather one-sided arrangement. I assume the money side will be my risk?"

One of the sergeants came through the door. "Mr Cobbald, my good man. We need more ale outside. If you would be so kind." He gave a large belly laugh, clearly enjoying his afternoon.

Seth rose from his seat. Charlie jumped up. "Can we talk some more about this Mr Cobbald."

Seth smiled benignly. "I'm sorry Charlie. You're a good, honest young lad but I don't think quarrying is for me."

"But…."

Seth put up his hand to stop Charlie. "No, Charlie. Look, I'm busy. You will have to excuse me." He turned to the sergeant. "Same again all round?" The sergeant nodded and Seth disappeared into the Tap Room.

Charlie slumped back down on his seat with a nagging emptiness in his stomach. After a few minutes staring at the floor he eased himself to his feet. He gave a returning Seth, who had more ale in both hands, a wave across the room, and left.

* * *

Jasper and Robert told the sergeants where they lived, "Just in case." one of the sergeants said with a stern look. They were then told to go to collect the minimum of what they may need before returning to The Harbour Inn at first light the next day.

They didn't linger at the Inn before eagerly almost running back up the hill to Langton Matravers. When Robert reached home breathless, he burst through the door taking his mother by surprise.

She spun round from the stove "What's got into you?" she exclaimed, then frowned. For some reason she felt a foreboding that made her stomach churn.

The remainder of the many pints of ale that had been plied down his throat caused him to spurt out expansively without thinking. "Jasper and I are just back from Swanage, and we met these men ………soldiers…they …… eh well we've joined the army and we're going to see the world." .

Martha's jaw dropped then almost vehemently said, "That Jasper! You always follow what he wants to do." She stopped, remembering that Jasper was the son of her husband's lifelong friend. She went to speak again but instead broke down in tears.

Joshua was outside getting wood for the fire when he heard raised voices. He hurried inside to be met by his wife in tears and his son looking at his mother in exasperation. "What's up now, boy?" he demanded. "What have you done to upset your mother?"

Robert did not know what to do it was all going wrong. He was about to start a whole new wonderful life and unusually for him he wasn't thinking of any consequences. He hated upsetting his dear Ma and he feared his Pa's wrath. He looked blankly at his father, "When I was in Swanage with Jasper." he paused then blurted out, again. "We have both joined the army." then naively added, "We won't have to go to the quarry every day anymore. We can make lots of money; that's what the man said." he stopped.

Joshua put his arm around Martha's shoulders and looked at Robert, his face darkened in rage, "You fool!" he shouted. Martha gave a loud sob. He lowered his voice and repeated, "You damned fool." Robert looked back and forth at his parents. He loved them dearly and the last thing he wanted to do was to hurt them. He thought of Jasper and the army sergeant, there was no going back.

"We've taken the King's Shilling." he said simply. "We can't change our minds."

A heavy silence descended on the room with Robert staring at his parents whilst his mother sobbed gently and his father tried to console her. Joshua eventually turned to Robert "You say you've definitely taken the King's Shilling" Robert nodded. Joshua didn't respond but fixed him with a steely stare as he thought hard.

Martha broke the silence, "Who's going to help your father in the quarry now?" she asked with a trembling voice.

Joshua turned to face his wife and putting his hands on both her shoulders said quietly, "He's nearly twenty now, he's a man. We can't stop him if he's leaving home, it's his life." Then glancing over at Robert he added, "Besides, once you've taken the King's Shilling there is no going back." He shook his head, "I just wish you hadn't been so rash and foolhardy" He gave Martha a squeeze. "You will go with our blessing, son." There was a catch in his voice.

Martha almost whispered "You don't have to do what Jasper says all the time." She stopped, bit her lip, then looked pleadingly at Joshua. "Is that it? Do we do nothing else?"

"Hush, my dear. There is no point. The die is cast." He glanced at Robert and then added, "Besides, we want him to come home when he's ready." There was a brief pause and after a deep intake of breath he straightened up, "Please look after yourself, son. The door will always be open for you." His voice softened and to Martha he said encouragingly, "Come dear, let's make this an evening he will look back on fondly. Go help him get whatever he needs."

Martha looked forlornly at the men in her life. Robert was still a child in her eyes. He was the baby she had cradled in her arms whilst he suckled her milk. He was the boy that had come home crying after he slipped whilst playing on the cliffs his legs and arms covered in cuts and bruises. Her boy was now leaving her, he had joined the army where some other mothers' sons would try to kill him.

She turned to speak to Joshua but stopped. His eyes were moist as he stared hard out of the window. She knew the inner emotions that he was feeling were the same as hers. He was a man though, and a man had to hide his inner turmoil and not show weakness.

She shook her head sadly at such stupidity but with a sigh and holding her smock to her nose disappeared upstairs.

When Robert's brothers and sisters returned home from the village green they were told he was leaving home and this brought more tears. The youngest, Horatio, did not understand and sat happily on Robert's knee. The evening passed with all concerned putting on a brave face. Very little sleep was had by anyone that night.

Just before dawn Robert lay staring out at the dark sky. Doubts had crepted into his mind as he looked around at the familiar dark shadows in the room. Everything around him was home; his life. He was leaving it, for what? He rolled over and lay still with his face buried in the mattress, dozing uneasily.

The cloud leaden sky started to lighten and as if it had prompted him to stir, he sat up on the edge of the bed and stared into the distance. Horses hooves slowly tapping their path up Stonehouse Hill brought him to the present. His thoughts wandered to the sergeants and he slowly recalled their tales until a mood of enthusiasm pushed away the dark doubts of the lonely night.

By the time he had gathered the meagre items he had been told he could take with him he was excited and desperate to get on his way.

The rest of the house had stirred and the family all eventually gathered outside the front door. The beer provoked insensitivity had evaporated. His enthusiasm remained but with a tinge of consideration for his family's feelings. Robert looked from face to face, took a deep. breath and smiling bravely. "I'm off, then." he said needlessly.

Joshua broke the mood by moving forward briskly and held his hand out to give his son a firm handshake. "Get going, lad. Peter will help me at the quarry. Just look after yourself."

Robert checked and looked hard at his father. He suspected he heard a hint of mordacity. He felt a pang of guilt, but he turned and hugged each of his family in turn. Peter stood back when Robert approached him. He had a look of reproach on his face. Peter hated having to go underground. The thought that this was to be his life with the family depending upon him from now on filled him with dread.

Robert hesitated, he felt genuinely sorry for his younger brother, "I'm sorry Peter. Please shake my hand before I go." There was an awkward silence as both looked at each other. Robert proffered his hand and almost reluctantly Peter shook it but immediately turned around quickly and walked away. Robert was sure that he heard a quiet sob.

Martha was torn. She hated to see any of her boys unhappy. Joshua went to her, put his arm around her and then gave Robert a grim smile. "Off you go lad. We all wish you luck. Please come back soon."

Robert stood and looked at each of his family. Then with a simple "Bye" he was gone.

As he made his way to meet Jasper outside St George's church his emotions were mixed but were gradually being overridden with the excitement of the new life that lay ahead of him. Jasper was already there waiting impatiently. "Ah there you are. Everything alright at home? " He asked.

"Not really. How about you?"

"Same. My Pa knows though that once I'm determined, nothing will change my mind." He looked Robert straight in the eye, "Come on, there's a whole world out there waiting for us." he laughed "Let's get going we don't want to be late for the sergeant."

This was going to be the time of their lives when excitement and adventure overruled everything else and they hurried down the hill to the rendezvous at The Harbour Inn. Little did they know of life in the army at a time of war. There would be the highs from the imposters of exhilaration and wonder which would be mixed with the lows of fear and horror.

Jasper and Robert's sudden departure was to have consequences for both their families. Each father had a quarry that had been in their family for generations and they depended upon the help of their eldest sons to help produce sufficient stone to bring in enough money for the family's survival. It was subsistence living from generation to generation.

When Robert left, Joshua and Martha exchanged glances as Peter had walked away without speaking to anyone. Martha called Dot over to her. "Take the others over to the Green, your Pa and I will want to have a talk."

Dot understood and called to the other children. "Come on let's go and play rolling the hoop. I say I can keep it upright longer than all of you." She went to take Horatio's hand but he darted off to grab a wooden spoon and a pan hanging over the fireplace. He then started to beat it like a drum.

"I'm going to be a soldier like Robert when I'm big. Can I Mama, can I?"

Dot looked at Martha who gave her a thin smile. "That's alright let him take them. Make sure you bring them back, mind."

When they had left the house felt empty. Joshua stared out of the window watching a cart being taken down Stonehouse Hill. Its driver walked alongside holding the horse's bridle and blew his horn warning anyone who approached him that he would be unable to stop with his considerable load should they cross his path.

As it finally disappeared from view Joshua let out a sigh. The distraction gone he had now to face reality. Martha moved next to him and put her arm inside his and gave it a squeeze. She put her head on his shoulder and following his gaze said quietly "Peter will have to take Robert's place at the quarry now won't he?" She paused, and pulling herself away looking up at her dear husband, she bit her lip. "You saw the way he behaved when Robert left. Do you think he can do it?"

Before Joshua could answer Peter came back through the door. He looked at his Ma and Pa. "You've been talking about me haven't you? You want me to go down into the quarry." He looked desperately from one to the other. "I can't. I hate it." He turned and faced the wall and gave it a kick. Without turning he said, "As soon as I go near the slide I get out of breath and start to shake." He spun around tears were welling up and his face was white and glistening with sweat. "I'm sorry. I've tried – I just can't help it."

Joshua stood looking at him then taking a deep breath he said. "You're eighteen now lad. When you are under this roof you have got to do your duty for the family."

"I know, but I have been taking reading and writing lessons from the curate. Mr Godbert says that I am doing very well and he thinks he can get me to work in Mr Cornelius Dearman's solicitors office in Swanage. He said that one day I could even become a chief clerk."

"That is as may be but you have to pull your weight now for the family. You're needed in our quarry."

Peter stood with a look of abject despair. Martha went to go to him but Joshua put a restraining hand on her arm and gestured for her to sit down. "Lad, everyone in this family has a duty to help to put food in our mouths and clothes on our backs. For folks like us there can be no passengers. I helped your grandpa as soon as I was able and thank the Lord when he went to his Maker your brother has been here to help me." He turned and stared out of the window and as if talking to himself, continued thoughtfully, "There are folks who say this should change. But how? I know no other trade than working in the quarry. Others in the village either work on the land or in the fishing boats and that's what we all do. There's no point ranting on about how it's unfair. We can't all live like Lord Olden." He looked at Martha as if to comfort her. "If anyone around here wants to start trouble then I for one won't go with him."

He drew himself up to his full height and said in a louder sterner voice. "So it's now your turn lad, to do your duty for your family."

There was a moment's silence then without looking at either parent Peter rushed out of the door and slammed it shut behind him.

Martha looked at Joshua. 'Why do things have to be like this?'

Any further thoughts went as the door burst open and Horatio came in crying and holding his bleeding elbow. "I was winning, I made the hoop roll the most then I tripped as it ran away from me" He gave another sob as if to emphasise his ill luck with the game and his injury.

Martha spread her arms to welcome him. "Come here, let me have a look at you." She took a cloth that she used for cleaning the stove and wiped away the mud from his cut elbow. "Now, now my little man if you're going to be a soldier you will have to get used to being wounded....." She stopped abruptly and looked across in anguish to Joshua.

They stared at each other for a moment then Joshua collected himself. "It's late. There's much to do today at the quarry without me having to go down the slide." He left and walked slowly to the quarry deep in thought. He spent the day clearing stone that had been brought to the surface and prepared for it to be lowered to his boat. He worked automatically carrying out tasks that had been part of his life since his childhood.

His spirits were low when he arrived back home that evening as dusk was falling. He gave Martha a perfunctory kiss on the forehead and went to sit on his chair by the fire. Martha watched him for a moment then said brightly in an effort to break his mood, "Your dinner is ready. The children have already eaten and I've sent them to bed."

Joshua grunted but tried to smile "Thank you dear." He looked back at the flames in the fire and without looking up, said. "I won't be able to bring enough stone to support us all from the quarry on my own." He looked up at Martha. "Peter has got to take some of the burden and do Robert's work." He paused then gestured toward the stairs. "Is he upstairs?"

"No he hasn't come back yet."

Joshua went to sit at the table and ate his dinner in silence. When finished he stood up. "I'm tired. It's been a long day - it's time for me to get some sleep." He looked directly at Martha. "When Peter comes back tell him he's coming with me to the quarry in the morning. I think I may be able to work a way to get the stone to the slide and Peter can then haul it to the surface. Then we can both lower it down onto the boat and he can take it round Durlston Head to Swanage."

"Will you be able to do all the work in the lane?" At your age?"

"I'm afraid it looks as though there is no alternative." He gave her another kiss "Good night my dear. Tell Peter to be ready at first light." Martha watched his back as he trudged up the stairs and shook her head. She knew that her man was to take on work that would fast become beyond his capabilities. She did not know yet the full consequences.

CHAPTER FIVE

Success and Reality

Charlie Heywood was looking to the future but it didn't appear to be very promising. He was now twenty years old and he was beyond doing odd jobs around the village. He had tried to increase the amount of work he did for Isaac Gulliver but all he was mainly used for was as muscle power to hoist barrels and chests from the beach to wherever he wanted them stored. Charlie realised there was no full time or long term future in that sort of work. Mr Gulliver did pay him for going around to some of his customers to drum up more business after a shipment had been landed but Charlie knew he had to start making his own way now.

He had been forced to use some of the money he had saved and as he sat on the wall in front of St. George's church late one afternoon he was deep in thought. He had a feeling of desperation growing inside and had been totally deflated by Seth Cobbald's reaction to his proposition about Gull Quarry. 'Why wouldn't he take him seriously?' What do I have to do to convince him that it is a sound idea?' He turned to look up Stonehouse Hill when he heard people approaching in the distance. It was Ted Edmunds coming home from Crack Lane Quarry. He had been joined by his sister Tess who worked as a housekeeper and maid for Bill Hancock and his wife the local baker.

As they neared Charlie, Tess tried to pull her brother away showing an obvious shyness. Ted carried on and Charlie heard him mutter "Don't be daft, come on." As they reached Charlie, he hopped down off the wall, "Afternoon to you Ted." then turned and added with a playful flourish "and to you Miss Edmunds." He gave a sweep with his hand and bowed his head. Tess went crimson as she was wont to do.

Ted chuckled. "You have a good life, don't you Charlie. Whilst we have been working all day, you have been sitting here on the wall whiling away your time."

Charlie felt that emptiness in the stomach. 'If only they knew.' He gave them a broad grin and tapped his nose knowingly. "You've got to have a nose for business in this life."

Ted laughed. "Whatever happens, we all know good ol' Charlie will be alright." He took his sister's arm. "Come on Tess, I know you want to stay to talk to Charlie but we have to get back home to help Ma." Tess showed her embarrassment again but they both hurried off.

Charlie watched them go. He felt a fraud.

He didn't move for some time as his mind raced. Then he closed his eyes and said softly to himself. "Right, they think I'm clever, it's time I showed them that they're not wrong." He dropped his head, deep in thought for some time until finally he said out loud. "Right, Mr Seth Cobbald, you want a proper deal from a grown-up. You will have one."

Charlie spent the next two weeks hurrying from place to place meeting with people until he was satisfied that he had a proper plan in place.

Eventually, when he was ready he made his way to Swanage to meet Seth Cobbald. He had picked a Wednesday afternoon as he knew it would be quiet in The Harbour Inn at that time. The fishermen would have finished their drinks after selling their morning's catch and the businessmen would making their way home as it as half day closing.

Seth Cobbald had cleared away the debris from his midday business and was relaxing. He sat at his usual table by the window where he could see everyone who went by through the square. He was contently puffing away at his pipe and sampling a glass of brandy just delivered by one of Gulliver's men.

Charlie briskly walked through the door. "Good afternoon Mr Cobbald. Can I speak with you, please?"

Seth smiled and with a friendly wave of the hand invited Charlie to join him at his table. "You're a persistent young devil, aren't you? I think I know why you're here."

With all the preparation he had made, Charlie was convinced he could answer any question that Seth could throw at him. He took a deep breath. "Mr Cobbald."

"Mr Heywood." Seth responded with a teasing grin.

"I take it Mr Cobbald, you would be interested in any business venture that was to make you a profit?"

Seth chuckled. "What can I say? No I'm not?"

"Also Mr Cobbald, I take it that any venture would have to have no, or a minimal amount, of risk."

Seth chuckled again. "You could say that. Go on Charlie, spit it out."

"I have some money that I can contribute to the cost of the rental of Gull quarry. I have spoken to the Bailiff of Lord Wareham's Estate and he won't accept just my commitment to finding the balance. He wants someone else to put some money into the business as well."

"I'm not surprised." Seth interjected.

Charlie pressed on. "I have also spoken with Ben Foster the quarry manager and he has given me the names of people who buy the stone from Gull. Providing the stone is delivered on time and is of the right quality they have each given a commitment to buy a certain amount of stone over the next six months. Ben says that they have been giving that service for years and there would not be a problem."

Seth took his pipe from his mouth and tilting his head back blew out a long cloud of smoke into the air. After a few seconds he squinted and looking down he pointed the stem of his clay pipe at Charlie. "Good so far. The only problem would be that I know Gull makes a profit but that would be swallowed up by the rental that would be paid which is a cost that does not exist at the moment. The whole exercise would gain me, eh us, nothing."

Charlie's heart leapt as he realised that despite Seth dismissing the idea originally, he had obviously been asking questions of his own. "Very much so, it would be pointless. However I have asked the existing customers, who else in Swanage buys stone. Well anyway, to cut a long story short, I was able to meet with Mr James Tyler who is the son of Samuel Tyler the largest supplier of stone in London. After speaking with Ben Foster, I was able to give Mr Tyler a very good price for prepared ashlars[5] and he would be prepared to give us an initial six month contract." Charlie hesitated and checked for Seth's understanding. "As you know there is more profit in finished stone." Seth nodded and Charlie added. "At the end of that period it has been agreed that we will talk again to Mr Tyler."

Seth was impressed, there was certainly more to Charlie Heywood than just an odd- job lad from the village. Seth was starting to warm to the scheme. "Alright Charlie, what is the deal?"

Charlie looked Seth straight in the eye without blinking. "Mr Cobbald, I ask you for a proportion of the rent and I will make up the rest. The existing business from Gull will provide sufficient profit to cover both our costs. The additional profit from Mr Tyler's business will be shared between us in the same ratio as the amount of rent we each pay. I will also during this time pursue other business here on Swanage and I will look to see if it is possible to sell directly to London based companies. Obviously not those in direct competition to ours here in Swanage."

---

[5] Sawn building stone usually square or rectangular

Charlie stopped to let his words sink in.   Then he sat forward. "Mr Cobbald, there is a risk in any business venture but I believe that all reasonable points have been met."   He stood up and thrust out his hand. "Do we have a deal?"

Seth laughed and waved for him to sit down again. "Charlie, you're going to go a long way.   I'm definitely interested but I'll need to think about it."

Charlie's hopes sank.   Now was the time to get the deal, whilst Seth's enthusiasm had been raised. "Mr Cobbald, I will come back with a copy of all the figures and agreements with Lord Wareham, the local businesses, and Mr Tyler. If they all back up what I have proposed to you today, do we have a deal?"

Seth didn't move and didn't speak.   There was heavy silence. Charlie instinctively knew it was time to shut up — not to speak. For what seemed an eternity the only sound was the ticking of the old wooden clock in the corner of the room.

Suddenly Seth stood up and thrust his hand out. "Charlie, yes we have a deal."

Charlie sprung out of his chair and they shook hands. "Thank you very much Mr Cobbald, you will not regret this. I will come back next week with all the papers I have promised."

Seth moved round and put his arm around Charlie's shoulders. "You're a good lad. I think that this will be only the beginning for you."

It was not long after Jasper and Robert arrived at the Harbour Inn that they realised that the friendly and expansive sergeants that they had met the previous day had another side to their nature. Thirteen young men from Swanage and the surrounding area congregated in front of the Inn talking excitably about what lay ahead. Their voices quietened as they heard the sound of marching feet and orders being bellowed out. The sergeants appeared with three men who it was obvious were there under duress. As they came closer, Jasper whispered to Robert, "Those two are the Bailey brothers. Last I heard of them they had been sent to jail again."

Robert whispered back, "The other one is Charlie Cooper. This is the first time I've seen him sober."

Before another word could be spoken the largest of the sergeants bawled out "Right you scum, form a single straight line!" He shouted so loudly that without a thought the new recruits scrambled to do as they were ordered. "Call that a straight line. God help us, we've got the worse dregs in the British Army."

The door to the Harbour Inn swung open and Seth trying to sound formal, announced "Mr Cornelius Dearman Justice of the Peace for the town of Swanage is inside waiting to carry out the King's business." As the Sergeant approached him he lowered his voice, "You had better have is Fee. He's not happy having get here on Monday morning at this hour."

The Sergeant turned to address the assembled volunteers. They blinked in frightened astonishment at the change in their drinking friends from the previous day. "Right. One at a time . You first, and pointed at Charlie Cooper who seemed totally unaware of where he was and stood with a slack mouth in total confusion. "Follow me." Charlie was marched in and several minutes later was out again still looking totally bemused. Then one at a time, the Bailey brothers were wheeled into, then out of, the Inn.

Next it was Robert's turn. Without time to think he found himself attempting to stand to attention in front of Mr Dearman who, without initially looking up, demanded. "Name?"

Robert blurted out "Robert Bolson, sir."

"Right, you are about to become a soldier in His Majesty's British Army." He fixed Robert with stare that also betrayed his boredom with the whole business.

"Repeat after me: 'I Robert Bolson by this oath do swear to faithfully defend His Majesty and His Heirs and successors. against all enemies. I also promise to obey the authority of all Generals and Officers set over me." Robert duly repeated, phrase by phrase, his oath of allegiance.

Without a chance to gather his senses, his next instruction was barked in his ear from point blank range. "Right, Private Bolson, turn and rejoin the rest of your squad."

Jasper was next although the instructions given did seem to be an octave lower. Once all had been duly sworn into the army they were brought to order again at an attempted straight line.

The two brothers were scowling and looked as though they would make a break for freedom at any moment. Sensing their mood the sergeant continued in the same belligerent manner, "You lot are in the army now. You will follow orders at all times – without question." He paused, glaring at each one in turn, "Anyone who thinks they can change their mind and wants to leave," he paused again, for effect, "will be shot for desertion."

Robert gulped; this was not why he had joined the army. Jasper looked straight ahead with a steely stare.

Jasper and Robert spent the autumn training at the East Dorsetshire Regiment's barracks. They were assigned to 'B' Company and were issued with the traditional red coats. It was left to their colonel to obtain their uniforms although these were not the same as other regiments they still were given the standard cylindrical 'stovepipe' shako hat. Their lives quickly became centred around cleaning their kit and obeying orders on the parade ground.

They were not to see the sergeants that had so beguiled them back in Swanage. Instead Sergeant Parker, a veteran of service in India and Ireland, became the centre of their lives. After learning how to march up and down they practiced endlessly how to carry out the essential battle formations of squares and lines abreast. A great deal of time was spent on maintaining, firing and re-loading the muskets that they were issued. They had to achieve a firing rate of four shots per minute. The slightest mistake or perceived slowness was deemed unforgivable and fear of their sergeants and officers was instilled into them. They soon learnt that automatic obedience to orders was the only option. Life in a training camp of the army was always done at a frantic pace at the double and discipline was tough.

Although life underground in the quarries was tough, the Dorset countryside by comparison was quiet with life at a sedate pace. Langton Matravers seemed a very different, distant world.

The two young men were determined not to be overwhelmed. Unfortunately others that had joined with them could not make the change. Charlie Cooper to put it bluntly was a drunk. The hard life was too much for him and it broke him. Early in October Jasper realised he had not seen Charlie for days and he asked Corporal Reynolds who was in charge of their unit if he had been taken sick. Reynolds looked Jasper directly in the eye "Don't you worry soldier, he's gone." Reynolds did not explain and made it clear he was not to be asked for details.

On a cold overcast day late in November the entire regiment was ordered onto parade at first light. Sergeant Parker brought the men to attention then advised them that 'B' Company had been assigned a new Company officer.

Captain Charles Honsworth sauntered onto the parade ground on his white horse and sat casually watching them. He gave his usual characteristic appearance of being bored and disinterested in the whole affair

Despite his outward demeanour, inside Charles Honsworth was a mixture of disillusion and despair. After his albeit brief conversation with Emily Pangborne that Sunday morning as they rode through Langton Matravers he was convinced ahead of him was a life of bliss with the person he had realised he loved. He followed his father's wishes and had taken the commission purchased for him with the East Dorsets.

He bought the finest uniform that his London tailor could produce. He was anticipating that Emily would be dazzled by his dashing appearance and would consent to being his wife without delay. After just a month, during which time he was introduced to his commanding and fellow officers, he believed that it was now time for him to discuss his intentions in regard to Emily with her father, Lord Pangborne.

He made the short journey to Pangborne House and casually trotted up the carriageway and dismounted. He was met immediately by a groom from the stables. He handed the bridle to the groom and turned to face a footman who had rushed forward from the House. Barely looking at the man he told him to inform Lord Pangborne and Miss Emily of his arrival.

The footman frowned fleetingly, but escorted Charles inside to wait in the Drawing Room. Charles became a little irritated and indeed surprised when he was left waiting for at least fifteen minutes. Eventually the Butler, Rawson, who he had known since he was a boy, appeared obviously feeling awkward and embarrassed.

"Ah, Rawson. There you are. Is Miss.." he stopped as apprehension built inside him. "What's the matter man? Is there something wrong?"

Rawson cleared his throat; he was definitely uncomfortable. "Sir," he started, "I'm afraid Miss Emily is not at home."

"What? Where is she? Is she alright? There's not been an accident has there" Charles was alarmed.

"I believe that she is in excellent health. However I'm afraid that she is at Lord Serrell's house with her parents, Sir George and Lady Pangborne." He coughed again, his discomfiture very evident. "The family are all there on the occasion of the announcement of Miss Emily Pangborne's imminent marriage to Lord Serrell's son."

"What?" Charles' mouth continued to move but he was speechless. He frowned, spun round, brought his fist down on the back of a nearby chair then spluttered. "That cannot be true. Miss Emily and I have an understanding. It is she and I that are to be.." he stopped again.

Rawson wished he could speak openly. He hated to see the distress on the young man's face. He shook his head sadly. "I'm terribly sorry to inform you that the parent's of the recently betrothed couple have made all the arrangements. The matter is settled."

Charles remained staring at Rawson. The butler wished it had not been his duty to tell such news that he was aware would be so devastating. He had always liked the young man.

Finally Charles spoke. "The matter is quite settled, you say?"

"Yes, Sir. Quite settled."

Charles strode up and down the room slapping furniture on the way, not knowing quite what to do. After some minutes he turned and stared at Rawson, for a moment his eyes almost glazed. "I bid you good day, Rawson." He spun on his heel and stomped out of the house in a daze. The groom was just returning from the stables when Charles confronted him. "My horse man, where is it?"

"It's - it's in the stable, Sir. Shall I get it for you, Sir?" He stammered having been confronted by such an agitated gentleman.

"No, I will get it." He brushed aside the startled groom, found his mount still being warmed down by one of the stable lads and it was still saddled. He grabbed the reins, mounted in one movement and galloped off back down the carriageway at the horse's full speed.

His mind was racing. 'Why? Had he done something wrong? Could he change the impending course of events?' After a while he realised his horse was starting to blow and he reined it in to a walk. One thought remained 'Why is it that the person that you love is the one that is able to hurt you the most?'

Charles spent days avoiding company as he foresaw a life in front of him that was to be empty. Several weeks passed before he came to a decision. In a cursory conversation with his father, Lord Wareham, and his mother, he informed them that he would re-join his regiment and would seek a posting abroad if that was possible

It was thus that Captain Honsworth sat in front of the men now under his command. After walking his horse up and down the front rank he turned his mount to face the assembled parade. "Men, I look forward to leading you as you do your duty for your King and country. I am pleased to tell you that we will soon be leaving these shores and we will be facing our enemy, the French. We will see danger but I'm sure that you will not fail to stand firm." After this brief speech he turned to Sergeant Parker. "Carry on Sergeant. I understand that you have other business today." He saluted Parker then walked his mount to the side of the parade ground to watch events unfold.

After returning the salute Sergeant Parker looking even more stern than usual, strode up and down in front of the motionless ranks. He did not speak but his eyes seemed to penetrate the soul of each soldier in turn. Eventually he stopped in front of Robert who stood stock still concentrating on a distant tree that was being buffeted by the cold wind.

Sergeant Parker put his face inches from Robert's. "Soldier – steady - stay where you are. Right soldier, give me your musket sling." The order was bawled out so violently it made Robert jump and in an effort to comply he dropped his musket. There was no sympathy. "You cretin, soldier. Pick up your musket and give me the sling." Robert scrambled to carry out the order as quickly as possible and disconnected the two inch wide and yard long leather strap and gave it to the sergeant.

Parker took the sling and striding up and down the assembled parade gave an occasional flick so that the sling snapped in the air. He stopped, confronting the stony faced muster. "We do not take kindly to thieves in this regiment especially when they steal from their fellow soldiers." He paused for effect. "You are about to witness what happens to such low-life." Akimbo

He spun round and barked out in the direction of the nearest hut. "Corporal Reynolds, bring out and prepare the prisoner." Directing his next order to the parade. "Parade, stand at – EASE."

The simultaneous clap of hands on muskets and stamping of feet signified their training had been successful. One of the Bailey brothers, George, appeared and was marched at the double to stand at attention before them. Two halberds[6] were brought forward and jammed into the ground, forming a diagonal cross. "Corporal, fasten the prisoner." George Bailey was stripped to the waist and strapped by his wrists and ankles to the halberds so that he was standing with his feet and arms outstretched.

Satisfied with the preparations, Parker turned to face the regiment again. The silence could be cut with a knife. "In this regiment we sling-belt vermin." He thrashed the sling on the ground. "As this scum has stolen from his comrades, it's only right that his comrades should punish him." He scanned the faces frozen in front him. "Soldier this is your sling-belt. Do your duty."

Robert was aghast and didn't move. "Soldier at the double." Robert lurched forward and took his sling-belt from the Sergeant. "Give the prisoner thirty lashes." He took a step towards Robert. "If I just think that you're going soft and not using your full strength – you will be next."

There was no movement in the ranks, the parade ground was totally silent. Robert slowly moved toward George Bailey trying not to allow his hand to tremble. As he neared the prisoner he could see he was shaking and it was not from the biting wind on his bare back.

Robert tried to shut his mind to his task in hand. Each blow left a red wheal across the back and when a blow re-struck the same wound the skin would split and blood seeped down his back. After all thirty lashes had been administered Robert stopped, exhausted, and just stood with his arms hanging by his side. The prisoner was dragged from the parade ground barely conscious.

---

[6] Two handed pole weapon. It forced the prisoner to stand like the Vitruvian Man with arms and legs spread out

Sergeant Parker came back to Robert's side and his tone softened as he spoke directly to him so that the front rank could barely hear. "Well done lad, you've done your duty. Take your place back in line and after parade Corporal Reynolds will issue you with enough rum for a good night."

The parade was dismissed and Jasper turned to Robert and put his arm around his shoulder. The scars on George Bailey's back were physical; Robert's scars were in the mind.

Jasper tried to be supportive. "Come on, I heard the sergeant, let's get that rum and this evening the army can go…" he stopped as the sergeant marched passed.

"On your way soldiers, on your way."

That night as Jasper and Robert sat drinking the rum until Robert went quiet, deep in thought. Jasper studied him for a while. "What's going through that mind of yours? You can't dwell on today. That bastard got his just deserts."

"No, its not just about today." He looked carefully at Jasper. "We joined the army with our eyes wide shut. We were all mesmerised by those Sergeants in Swanage but what we have been through in these last few months is not why I left Langton Matravers."

"We have to do this. We can't fight the French without knowing what to do."

"What about seeing the world and making our fortune. You say fight the French? Have you ever met a Frenchman?"

"I know where you're going with this." Jasper grimaced.

Robert ignored Jasper's remark. "Does a Frenchman have horns? Has one ever raped any women from the village?"

"No, of course not."

Robert stopped and again didn't speak for a while. Jasper just sat watching. He would let his friend have his say after his experience earlier in the day.

Looking Jasper directly in the eye, Robert started, "We're sitting here at the start of a totally different life to that in the village. We know life's hard and uncertain there ... you know, your brother Ben...." he stopped.

Jasper gestured for him to carry on.

Robert shook his head slowly, "Here in the army we have even less control over our lives than we had back home. Take today for instance and what about when we meet the French?"

Jasper interrupted "Taking the fact that we are here anyway, what are trying to say?"

Robert thought for a moment, then looked again at Jasper painfully, "Oh gawd, I don't know. I suppose I should just shut up and get on with what we've got ourselves into."

"That's a good boy." Jasper playfully being sarcastic

Robert half smiled then his face resumed a serious look. "One of us is going to be killed. The odds are totally against us both surviving." He turned to face the wall behind Jasper and as though addressing an audience asked. "Which one would the world want?"

Jasper was not to be dragged down. He recognised the trauma his pal had gone through and it was now time to pull him out of his mood. "Well you're fun to be with tonight. A right bundle of laughs. Come one, you silly sod, Let's get this rum down our throats."

Robert let out a sigh. "I'm sorry Jasper ignore me. Whatever we may think now, we have made our bed and we have to lie in it. There is no point in dwelling on the past, or the future." He frowned, "If you know what I mean." He raised his tin mug. "Fill me up again. Let's drink to the future."

Jasper did as he was bade. "That's more like it."

The cruelty of the British military punishment code Wellington supported to the end of his life. Later in the war, the more draconian punishments were abandoned and the offenders were shipped to Australia instead.

CHAPTER SIX

Posted Abroard and First Action

"Join the Army and see the World!"   Those were the words that rang in the ears of the raw rural recruits from Dorset.

The punishment parade was traumatic but Jasper and Robert stuck to their resolve to make the most out of an irreversible commitment to the army.   It was with eager anticipation therefore when a week following the parade their Regiment was sent to Portugal. They were to be part off a large deployment of troops to reinforce Wellington's Peninsula army.

After sailing into the mouth of the River Tagus and leaving Lisbon they had marched through a rugged and inhospitable terrain. From north to south ran ranges of great undulations with peaks that straddled deep valleys, gullies and wide ravines.   Interspersed amongst these natural barriers were a number of fortifications that had been recently built or were in the latter stages of completion.

B company were Stood Down from their morning's march near one of these sites. There was a unit of British Engineers with local Portuguese soldiers so Jasper and Robert with a couple of others strolled over out of curiosity to find out what was going on.

As they approached, one of the engineers called out to his mates. "Look out, here comes a bunch of virgins." Turning to the newcomers. "You mind you don't let those soft pink faces get burnt."

A couple of friendly expletives were thrown back in return. Robert looked at the soldier who had spoken. "What are you doing. What are these buildings we've seen on our way up here."

The engineer laughed. "Don't you know what a fort is when you see one?" There was a ripple of laughter behind him. "That's a fort and there's over 150 forts and redoubts in this area now."

Robert was impressed, and asked innocently. "Why?"

The soldier grunted. "You probably don't know it yet if you've just arrived but there is a town called Torres Vedras not far from here and the mountains run from there to Lisbon. With all these forts we've built in this mountainous countryside it makes it almost impossible for an army to get through and take Lisbon." He finished and glanced over to his mates with a look of pride.

The raw recruits were all impressed. Robert as self appointed spokesman asked. "Are you sure?"

Another soldier sitting on a large boulder, drawing on his pipe, laughed. "Sure? The Crapauds…"

"Crapauds? Who are they?" Jasper interrupted.

"Crapauds.. the French. They were sent packing earlier last year. One of our officers told us their Marshall Messéna came with an army of over 60,000 men. They spent six months here in what we've been told was the coldest winter local people can remember. Beyond these Lines the Duke ordered that all crops, livestock and shelter be brought to Lisbon or destroyed. Eventually the French were forced to retreat with their tails between their legs. The officer said that it's thought they had lost about 20,000 men mostly through starvation or disease."

The newcomers were impressed but any further conversation was cut short when the sergeants started calling the Company to order. The march was resumed until they reached Pero Negro.

As dusk approached Jasper and Robert fixed bayonets and dug them into the ground together with their muskets and ramrods and then tossed their blankets over their weapons to create a tent. With a joint sigh and grunt of satisfaction they both collapsed to ground and sat leaning back against their packs.

They disregarded the slightly damp ground from the morning rain as they surveyed the surrounding terrain.

Robert spoke first "You can see why the Duke made this his headquarters a couple of years ago. You can see for miles around."

Jasper nodded, "I've been chatting to that guy, George, who joined us when we landed in Lisbon. He was with the headquarters group, with the Duke himself, but for some reason he asked for a transfer away from them." he shook his head. "Odd, I would have thought that would be a cushy number."

Robert frowned. "He doesn't look as though he's had a rough life, not like like the rest of us."[7]

Jasper agreed. "I know what you mean. Anyway he gave me a good explanation of the reason for this site. Interested?"

"Yes go on."

"Well, looking down from the fort here, you can see how the natural lie of the land makes it an easily defensible position because of the slope that the French would have to climb up, and we can also control any movement on the road below."

Robert peered over into the distance. "Yes. I can see that but most of the redoubts and forts we've passed are on much steeper hills. Our cannon would be virtually useless because

---

[7] George, Prince of Wales, (future Prince Regent then George IV) married a Mrs Maria Fitzherbert secretly on 15 December 1785, and – as both parties were well aware – against the law. That is Fact. What isn't and purely the Author's mischievous speculation is that she had a son by The Prince, and that it would have been called George BUT, if true, he would have been in his early twenties in 1812.

they could not be depressed enough for them not to overshoot any path at the bottom of the hill."

Jasper shrugged not knowing the full reason for why various forts were placed in their positions. "Suppose they would be even easier to defend. Whatever. Ask George, he'll know." With that he closed the conversation by shutting his eyes in an attempt to doze off.

Jasper's attempt at a nap after passing on what he had learnt about the nearby fort was interrupted by the sound of a chuckle from Robert. He opened one eye and saw Robert was grinning.

"What's got into you?"

"So far so good'"

"What does that mean." Jasper responded, frowning.

"I really enjoyed the trip over here on the Bellerophon. Shame so many of the others were sea sick most of the way.* He grinned. "To think that ship was actually in the Battle of Trafalgar. One ol' sea dog I was talking to said it took a hell of a beating but was able to take two enemy ships out of the battle. He stopped and stared, trying to picture the scene. He carried on enthusiastically. " When we landed we saw the city of Lisbon. George, told me it has been re-built on the hill since it was totally destroyed by an earthquake and tidal wave 50 odd years ago. Did you notice all those pure white building and red roofs - it looked fantastic."

Jasper nodded appreciatively and chuckled himself. 'Seems as though George knows all about this country.

Robert warmed to his subject. "The surrounding countryside is so different to home. No acres of fields and hedges. You can see that during summer it must get really parched and dusty.

"………… it's always hacking with rain at home."

Robert ignored the comment. "Then not far from Lisbon we went through all these mountains where they've built the forts." He paused, "Jasper we wouldn't have seen all this if we had stayed down the mines.

Jasper grinned. "We said we wanted to see the world."

"There's something else. I heard a couple of sailors once in Swanage; someone said they were Dutch, and they were talking in their lingo. Since arriving in Portugal, and on our way up here, I haven't understood a word the locals are saying."

"That may be because they were talking Portuguese?" Jasper grunted with heavy sarcasm.

"I know, I know. It's just that – well let's face it neither of us have been any further than Poole. It just seems so strange."

Jasper laughed. "You'll say next that even the children have learnt to speak Portuguese."

"Alright. I was just saying, that's all." He laughed as well and threw a discarded sock at Jasper.

Sergeant Parker overheard their conversation as he was making sure that all was in order with the erection of the nearby tents. He strolled over to them and signalled for them to stay where they were as they had started to struggle quickly to their feet. The Sergeant was more relaxed with his troops now that they were off the parade ground. The fine wrinkles around his eyes showed that beneath the gruff and aggressive veneer there was a ready smile and even a hidden kindness. "The dust and language is not all you'll find different. You may think that a hot summer's day is uncomfortable in England. You wait until the sun beats down in the middle of the day when we move inland away from the sea and these hills.

Jasper and Robert looked at each and grinned. "This is more of what we were expecting when we took the King's Shilling. It will be better than freezing our butts off when we were underground in pitch darkness."

Sergeant Parker grunted and shook his head. "You might wish you were back there after a few months out here." He shook his head again and walked off to his own quarters.

One thing that didn't change from when they were in the barracks back in England was the continual drilling and musket practice. To form squares, lines abreast and fire four rounds a minute was engrained into them. They were soon though to learn that there is a dark side to a soldier's life.

As Spring approached the Regiment were decamped and marched across Portugal until they came to the impressively fortified town of Badajoz. Veterans in other Regiments that had been in Portugal for some time told them that the stronghold held the key to any advance into Spain. They were also quick to dispel any ideas of a short and glorious storming of the town. They had already twice been marched to the walls and each time had been repelled with heavy losses.

The town dominated the surrounding countryside with a massive cathedral soaring from its centre.

There was no time for B Company to think of what lay ahead. The night they arrived they were detailed to move forward in total silence to guard the working parties that were digging communication trenches in the flat marshy ground in front of the town. The sentinels on the ramparts heard nothing and the night finished with the Company in good spirits.

The second night did not go so well. B Company lay prone on the ground with muskets ready. Sergeant Parker moved along the line of his men making sure that they were all in position and alert. Despite his necessarily tough exterior he knew that many of his charges were raw and probably fearful of coming under fire for the first time. A nod here, a wink there, gave as much reassurance as was possible.

Jasper and Robert lay quiet but pulses were racing as they were aware that they were in range of the French. Jasper kept his eyes steadfastly staring at the dark and foreboding walls towering above them. As the sergeant passed by them Jasper tugged Robert's sleeve and in a soft whisper said, "That ol' bugger's alright really."

They remained still. There was just the faint noise of shovels dislodging sodden turfs and briefly eyes flicked skywards as a Petrel flapped passed on its way to its nest as if on an inspection on what was beneath its flight path.

Robert's heart suddenly hit his chest like a hammer blow. A chill ran down his back, as without moving, he felt totally disorientated. The roar of hundreds of muskets opening fire simultaneously had broken the silence. All around him there followed a hail of screams, some cut ominously short.

Sergeant Parker scrambled down onto the ground next to Jasper. He turned to speak but his mouth moved noiselessly then his head slumped forward gently as if he had fallen asleep. Jasper was about to move towards the still figure when there was a shout from Corporal Reynolds. "Fire at the ramparts. Keep their heads down."

The next hour was spent with volley following wilting volley being fired until the defenders took discretion rather than valour and eventually the diggers and their guarding infantry were able to withdraw in good order having completed the night's work.

Fifteen men were killed that night, including Sergeant Parker, and their bodies were left where they fell. A few days later Captain Honsworth could see that they were becoming an obstruction to the trench digging squads. A party of men were detailed to creep forward just before first light and drag the casualties back out of range of the town defenders and they were left unburied some fifty yards from the camp.

In the days and nights that followed the Regiment was kept busy by moving forward to counter sporadic forays from the French as they tried to undo the work being carried out beneath their defences. A week after Jasper and Robert's first baptism of fire the English artillery batteries began their assault. The bombardment on the walls continued relentlessly for days until there were three breaches.

Some old hands in other regiments started to cheer. Robert looked at Corporal Reynolds, but before he could ask, Reynolds said. "We should be so lucky. It is supposed to be that if a practicable breach is made then the defending occupants will ask for terms and retreat rather than waste unnecessary lives." He grunted. "The storming of a fortress is not the same as a battle where we expect casualties. If we have to storm that - "he nodded towards Badajoz "even with breaches, the number of us to be killed or injured is going to be awful. " He cursed then added. " I don't think those crapauds are in a generous sort of mood." He then turned to look up at the defences and his eyes narrowed with what could be seen as a mixture and hatred.

"There's more to what you just said isn't there?" Jasper asks carefully.

Reynolds paused, looked at Jasper quickly, then staring up at the town again, replied, "This is the third time we've been here and we've lost too many men for this god forsaken place already. I've been told that's it's the locals, the Spanish, who are supporting the crapauds. Without local help they would have withdrawn by now." He swore again. "If I get my hands on any locals ………. God help them."

Jasper nodded without commitment and moved away. Robert moved beside him. "What was that all about?"

"I not sure, but I've heard comments about the Spanish helping the French. I don't know if its true but some of the lads are really wound up about the locals." He shrugged and fell silent.

Their thoughts were interrupted as the regiments were deployed to various assault positions. Then there was a long pause during which there was silence. Some offered silent prayers, others motionless, stared ahead with unblinking eyes and ashen faces. They were not to know what was being discussed about their immediate future and indeed if there was to be one.

Then suddenly orders started barking out up and down the lines. The army commander for the siege General Picton, had decided that as there was no proper response from the defenders the breaches were enough for a full-scale storming of the town. He was to take part in the assault and had it passed down the line that their was a guinea for every soldier that survived the capture of the fortress. The storming of the breaches then commenced.

The East Dorsets followed behind the Forlorn Hope[8] and A Company but had to halt and were crammed in the ditch below the ramparts. They had to wait for ladders to be brought and were showered in musket balls and small exploding devices made with glass bottles as well as burning coils of rope coated in tar, pitch and oil. Two men next to Jasper were caught in a rope coil and screamed in agony from the scalding and scorching.

Jasper and Robert witnessed the appalling carnage taking place in front of them. Thousands of British troops were killed and maimed in the fury of the respective assaults. Bodies piled up in the breaches as the attackers slowly made headway up through the breach in the wall.

---

[8] A group of men first sent in through the killing zone of a defended position - the risk of casualties were very high

The order came for B Company to join the attack. They rushed forward into the fray and their minds numbed as they fired then thrust and cut with bayonets. They had no rational thoughts, their minds and bodies reacted with senseless aggression to whatever appeared in front of them. At one time a wounded soldier clung onto Robert to prevent himself from falling backwards which would have meant certain death. Jasper grabbed Robert by the. tunic which caused the soldier's grip to break causing his death but saved Robert from joining him. They scrambled up the ladder immediately behind Captain Honsworth who, showing no fear, harangued them to follow him.

The ladder had jammed into an embrasure which was manned by the French defenders. Captain Honsworth pistol in one hand and sword in the other reached the foot of the opening when an enemy officer took aim - fired - and missed. Captain Honsworth immediately gave his assailant a back slash with his sword across the knees. As he toppled forward Honsworth thrust the point of the sword into the man's stomach and yanked him forward so that he hurtled down into the ditch.

The Captain leapt through the gap followed by his men and with bayonets fixed most of the defenders were summarily cut down whilst the remaining few rushed for safety towards the town gate. This was half blocked as they fought each other to desperately fight their way through one at a time.

A group of about 50 men with Captain Honsworth stood staring around gasping for breath, their eyes still wide open from their frenzy. They were jolted by a roar and spun around to see the figure of General Picton appearing at the embrasure waving his gun and sword.

"Well done men! Well done!" Picton roared. He staggered has he waved both arms in the air. Blood was oozing through the crutch of his breeches - the red matching the vertical stripes at the side seams.

He quickly surveyed the scene as more men poured over onto the parapet behind them. Seeing Captain Honsworth he repeated, "Honsworth, well done sir. I want you to secure this area and wait for further orders." Looking around again he paused and squinted at Jasper. "What's your name soldier"

"Private Tomes, sir!" Jasper snapped to attention but failed to salute as he was holding his rifle in his right hand.

"At ease soldier. I saw you at work back there. Very good."

'Thank you, Sir."

"You obviously know how to handle yourself and I think your mates appreciate that." He glared around as if anyone might have the temerity to disagree. "Right, Tomes you are now promoted to Chosen Man. Take six men and clear that gateway into the town. Check that the are no Frenchmen skulking in that area of the town wall. Then wait for further orders."

"Yes, Sir". Jasper spun round, gestured to Robert and 5 other men from his company to follow him and they made their way quickly to carry out his designated orders.

Jasper and his group soon cleared the entrance to the town. They made short sorties into the town in the vicinity of the gate to make sure there were no hiding Frenchmen. They waited until the early hours of the morning and it soon became obvious that all was not well within Badajoz. They could see from their position what was just a few hours previously – a well-organised, brave, disciplined and obedient British Army, fuelled with only with an impatience for victory. With the ensuing carnage followed by success came mass looting and disorder as these redcoats turned to drink and it would be some 72 hours before order would be completely restored.

As dawn was approaching Jasper decided that as they had no orders to the contrary they should return to camp. As they made their way along the parapet it revealed the horror of the slaughter all around the curtain wall. Bodies were piled high and blood flowed like rivers in the ditches and trenches.

Unsure which way to go they slipped into a narrow street and all was calm around them. A figure suddenly appeared in a doorway and the man next to Robert spun around and fired without hesitation. Robert saw the figure jerk backwards and it lay like a rag doll on the ground with her dress now covered in blood.

As they went further they passed many genteel houses that were filled with men who were pillaging and what could not be carried away they would just destroy. This would seem slight when passing what appeared to be a baker's shop the door was suddenly thrown open and the figure of a naked man was catapulted onto his knees on the cobblestones. He was followed by three pairs of glazed eyes, slack mouthed men who kicked him back to the ground when he tried to get up.

"Where's your money? NOW!"

The poor man's mouth quivered as he sobbed "I have none. I have only what is my house."

Robert moved forward "Hey, leave the poor sod alone. It's obvious he's not got anything on him."

"Stay there. This is our business. If you know what's good for you, stay there." He raised his musket level to Robert's chest.

"If he's got nothing, then he's no use to us." One of the other two swore, and before anyone could move picked up the poor man and threw him head first down a draw well in the middle of the street. That was enough for Jasper and with the butt of his musket, he rammed it into the side of the head of the man threatening Robert. He turned to the other two and with all his force thrust his boot into one man's groin. The other had seen enough and scarpered as fast as his legs could take him.

A scream came from the house from where the man had been thrown out. Without further thought Jasper and Robert rushed inside to be met by an horrific scene. An old lady was clasping a sleeping baby to her bosom. She was crying and pleading with a soldier bearing over her. They spun round to the noise of a whimper and were faced with a semi-naked younger woman - no doubt the mother of the baby - her clothes torn off her spreadeagled body on a bed. Three men stood over her with only one thought in their lecherous heads.

For a moment all stood still. Then with a yell and with the same frenzy as on the ramparts Jasper and Robert tore into the four men in the room. It was short, within moments four soldiers found themselves battered and bruised on their knees in the street. They saw their erstwhile compatriots already there on the ground. One was not moving with the side of his head a caved-in and the other was still in a ball crying for his now useless manhood. Jasper appeared at the doorway and that was enough - all four tore off down the street.

Robert went back into the house. "Bolt and barricade this door and then hide upstairs until all this dies down." The old lady nodded silently and gratefully. Robert left and wished them from his heart all the luck there could possibly be in this hellhole of a place,

Jasper and Robert were numbed. As they left the town they saw one atrocious scene after another. Homes were broken into, property vandalised or carted away, Spanish civilians of all ages and backgrounds killed or raped. They saw one British officer shot as he tried to bring one mob to order.

The two lads from Dorset were incensed with the killing of so many of their comrades who had become friends, but there was within them an innate sense of what was right. They were not alone and a trickle of men started to move back to their camps outside of the town. Very little was spoken as men just sat around and Robert in common with a number of others was physically sick as he recalled the horrors that he could never have imagined.

The day after they had returned to camp Captain Honsworth was moving around what remained of his Company. He was trying to assess, before the full headcount was carried out, how many he had left under his command and their condition both mentally and physically. When he saw Jasper he stopped and went over to them both. 'It's alright stay where you are." he said when he saw them struggle to get to their feet. "How are you both? Any injuries?"

"No, Sir. Well, just a few scratches but no problems."

Captain Honsworth looked from one the other thoughtfully. "You were both drafted to Portugal in January?" Without waiting for an answer he looked at Jasper and carried on. "I believe I recognise you. Where are you from?"

Jasper responded strait-away. "Langton Matravers, Sir,"

"Ah yes, quite so. quite so. My part of the world." He paused again obviously he wasn't happy about something. "So, we're all new to this." He gestured to Badajoz then carried on again without waiting for a reply. *Not good. Not good."

Jasper and Robert remained silent. It was not their place to have a conversation with an officer.

Honsworth turned and stood looking at the battered curtain walls and swore as he saw scavengers already stripping the piles of bodies of any valuables and clothing. He started carefully as if ordering his thoughts. "The laws of war which, vague as they are, at least suggest it's legitimate to surrender once our artillery had made those breaches. Their Governor, General Phillipon, refused. Given the enormity of the task facing our men, I don't begrudge them their feelings of anger …. a desire for revenge." His voice rose. "Thousands of men needlessly slaughtered…….." He stopped as if collecting himself. Looking at Jasper and Robert he carried on briskly. "However that does not justify ……" he paused and then in a businesslike manner, "Sir Arthur Wellesley is appalled at their behaviour and he has already ordered the rounding up of the worst offenders. Many will be flogged as punishment and a gallows has been erected."

Honsworth gave them a nod "Carry on men. Get some rest. This war is not finished by a long chalk. There is much to do." He went to leave, then having remembered something, turned to Jasper. "Your promotion to Chosen Man is to be confirmed. The paymaster will be informed." At which he strode off,

Robert looked at Jasper and grinned for the first time for several days. "I suppose I have to call you Sir now."

"Piss off." was Jasper's response.

Ignoring the advice Robert chuckled and mockingly chided Jasper. "You have constantly moaned about how unjust it is that us of the lower sort never have any control over our lives. Now you've started up the ladder to the Ruling Class."

"Alright, alright have your fun." Jasper nodded in the direction of Badajoz." You said yourself; how many crapauds have we met? how different are they to us?"

Robert shrugged his shoulders, the humour having gone from the moment.

Jasper carried on, "You and I don't fully know why we're here. We're told it is to save Portugal from the French. A few years ago Admiral Nelson annlhihated a combined fleet of French and Spanish ships." He grunted. "A whole number of the British Army has just ransacked a town and done god knows what to the Spaniards in the town. By the way, Spain is now on our side - there were Spanish regiments here to storm the town. Yet we take it out on the local Spaniards. The French are the occupiers of Spain and we're told they do the most awful acts on the Spanish. Have you heard the word Guerrilla, no? well it's what the Spanish call their local bands that carry on their fight and do the same to the French." He stopped, screwed his eyes as he looked to sky and growled, "God, what a mess."

Robert was taken aback. Not knowing how to respond. He just said quietly :There's nothing we can do about it."

'That's the point!" Jasper stormed. 'That's the point. We don't have a say in any of this. We're just told to kill or be killed." He stopped and let out a large breath. 'Sorry, mate. Look I'm going for a walk." He gave Robert a large friendly slap on the shoulder and half smile and walked off into the trees away from the scene of horror behind him.

Fatal Ambition! say what wond'rous charms
  Delude mankind to toil for thee in arms?
  When all thy spoils, thy wreaths in battle won:
  The pride of power and glory of a crown;
  When all gives, when all the great can gain,
  Ev'n their whole pleasure, pays not half their pain!
                    Nicholas Rowe, Poet Laureate

CHAPTER SEVEN

Survival

By the Spring of 1812 Joshua had been carrying out the grindingly hard work alone underground at the stone face for over six months. Martha was increasingly more anxious as he was being worn out and was ageing rapidly. Joshua's body, at over fifty years old, was still strong but he was loosing his stamina and was more liable to mistakes and injury.

The effort of pushing the laden Carts back to the slide after a session at the stone face was straining his body to the limit. It was only a matter of time before something was going to break.

Peter worked diligently on the surface but was not oblivious that these daily exertions were taking their toll on his Pa. He was a gentle soul and in other circumstances he would be well liked and popular. Quarrying though was a harsh business and he knew that he was seen as a weakness in his family. He desperately wanted to impress his Pa and would offer to do any work he was asked to do. He did try going down the slide but panic set in almost as soon as the darkness and confined space engulfed him

It was a paradox, Joshua was torn between the love of his son and his feelings deep down that Peter was letting the family down. The rest of the village would think the same, and he would defend Peter, but it saddened Joshua that he felt less of him.

Early on a Sunday morning Joshua called Peter down stairs. "Peter, get yourself ready now.I know it's the Lord's Day but I need to under-pick a large stone so that we can get it to Swanage tomorrow with all the rest that has to be loaded. We need the money as soon as possible." The task ahead of picking out the clay around the stone was going to be long and laborious. He was not going to allow Peter to lie in bed whilst he was hard at work.

Walter joined his brother and Pa, and they walked to the quarry in silence. As soon as they arrived Joshua gave Peter a sharp glance. "Don't go wandering off. Be ready as soon as I call you to bring the Cart to the surface." He looked quickly around. "After you've lowered the Cart, there's plenty for both of you to do. Walter, you're old enough now to help your brother." He went down the slide, waited for the Cart to be lowered then crawled along, dragging the Cart behind him to the stone face

Peter told Walter to gather some of the smaller stones then told him to go over to the capstan. "Listen out for Pa. As soon as he is ready to come up, call me straight away."

He grafted away as quickly as he could until Walter shouted over to him. "Pa is there, he's ready to come up."

Joshua had under-picked and wrenched a massive stone free and onto a Cart. He then pushed and shoved it along the lane to the bottom of the slide. He was by this time exhausted but grabbed the chart's rope immediately to tie the stone securely in place. It wasn't.

Peter hitched Drummer, the donkey, to the capstan and cajoled it to its appointed task of using its full one donkey power to pull the heavy-laden Cart to the surface. This was a job done countless times by Peter, Robert, Joshua and all their forebears but today fate took a hand. As the Cart almost completed its seventy-foot journey, the extra large stone got caught on a protruding stone on the slide wall. Drummer was jerked to a halt. Peter cursed and gave Drummer a smart smack on its hind quarter. The poor animal lurched forward and the sudden movement dislodged the stone free of its rope on the Cart and it started careering down the shaft.

Peter, without thinking grabbed the rope, flicking it free from Drummer. A Quarr Cart is heavy and Peter was taken by the sudden snatch which freed it from his hands and he fell backwards onto the ground. The cart teetered near the surface but being heavier than the chain it also started to descend downwards.

Peter was immediately up on his feet and threw himself at the fast disappearing rope. He wasn't quick enough. The cart continued downwards gathering pace.

The noise of the stone hurtling down the shaft warned Joshua and he had just enough time to throw himself back against the wall to avoid being hit by the errant stone. He was battered by chips and smaller stones that had been dislodged on it's journey but was unscathed.

Dazed, he looked up the slide just in time to see the Quarr Cart gathering pace after its erstwhile load. In desperation Joshua was able to thrust himself against the wall again. but not totally clear. The Cart crashed, shattering on the lane floor spewing its parts, stones and its trailing rope in all directions. Joshua was this time battered to the floor and stayed there

Silence followed with just the odd dislodged pebble bouncing down the seventy-foot void. Peter at the surface pulled himself together and venturing cautiously down the first few yards of the slide, called out. "Pa, Pa are you alright. In God's name, please answer."

All remained quiet, as Joshua lay still.

Peter kept calling. Walter seeing what had happened was in tears and pleaded with his big brother for assurance. "Is Pa alright? He's not hurt is he?"

Peter didn't reply; he was devastated. His first frantic concern was for his Pa. He then thought that everybody was going to blame him. His mind was crowded with different emotions as he thought he must be evil that at such a moment he was concerned about what other people were going to think about him.

Joshua stirred but he was still too stunned to move or even cry out in pain. He would say afterwards that 'the Lord giveth and the Lord taketh away'. The Lord gave by sparing his life as the large stone missed him; He then took it away as the crashing Cart smashed into him.

Quarriers are tough men and Joshua, despite his years, was as tough as any. He had to be practical. He turned to face up the slide but stopped and winced from a pain in his arm, which he realised immediately was broken. Ignoring Peter's distant calls, with one hand steadying himself on the stone walls, he started slowly to limp up the steps of the slide. Waves of pain from his arm and some of the deeper cuts stopped him several times.

Quelling his own fears Peter met him halfway. His first reaction was relief, but was shocked when he saw his father's condition. Slowly together they made their way to the surface. Joshua's right arm was hanging loose but at an obvious unnatural angle. His clothes were torn and there was blood oozing from several cuts, one large one just below his right eye.

Joshua stood, stooping whilst taking deep breaths.

His sons stood waiting in trepidation of what he was about to say.

Joshua grimaced in pain then spoke sternly, "Right, I'm going to need your help to get home." He looked up the steep path to the cliff top. "Two hands are needed to be able to scramble up the path. Bring that other Cart over there and I'll sit on it and you two will drag me up to the top." He paused and looked hard at Peter "If you know what's good for you lad, avoid too many bumps on the way. He then lay himself on his back on the Cart as gingerly as he could but had to close his eyes as another bout of pain racked his body.

Despite Peter's determined efforts, Joshua was jolted and bumped painfully as they slowly dragged him up the cliff path.

Joshua limped home through the village just as Sunday's Morning Service had finished. The whole village saw Joshua painfully making his way to his cottage with his two sons in close attendance. Isaac Tomes rushed forward and put Joshua's sound arm around his shoulder and virtually carried him the rest of the way home. Martha closely followed. She turned to Peter, "In the Lord's name what's happened?"

"It's all my fault. Pa shouldn't have to go underground anymore – but….." his voice trailed off.

They reached the cottage and a bruised and bleeding Joshua was eased into his chair by the fireplace. Martha asked needlessly "Are you alright, my love?"

Isaac took control. "Martha, I think it best that he should be washed so that we can see exactly where he has been cut." The door had been left open and young Ted Edmunds and Bill Tubbs hovered in the doorway. Isaac spoke to Ted, "Lad, find a stout piece of wood." Speaking to Martha, "We need to straightened Joshua's arm as much as we can. Find some cloth so we can bind the wood around his arm."

Grateful for Isaac's authority, Martha busied herself by getting a bowl of warm water and then disappeared upstairs to find some binding cloth.

Peter remained in the background looking distraught. Dot came in followed closely by the rest of the family. She kept them out of the way whilst at the same time putting her arms around the weeping Walter and Horatio.

Under Isaac's direction, Joshua was cleaned and bandaged. When they had done all that they could, Joshua looked around the room giving a weak smile of thanks. He tried to raise himself in his chair but collapsed back letting go an expletive and holding his arm whilst he winced in pain.

Martha crouched on the floor by him gently holding the hand on his unbroken arm.

All this drama was too much for Peter. He had tried his best, he had worked as hard as he could, but whenever things went wrong he knew he was going to be blamed. He looked at each of his parents but Ma was too busy fussing around her dear husband and Joshua was sat with his eyes closed giving out the occasional wince of pain. Peter turned and stumbled out of the house not sure where he was going or for what reason.

Joshua briefly opened his eyes and looking around he said weakly, "Has Peter gone? It's not his fault, I have been too hard on him."

Martha looked at the doorway. "I hope he doesn't do anything silly. I don't think I've seen him in such a state."

Isaac sensed there was nothing else that could be done at this point. He saw Ted, a quiet lad who lived next door, following Dot's directions and carrying out errands, trying to help wherever possible.

Isaac was surprised to see Bill Tubbs had continued to stand by the door but he also noted that he didn't offer to help in any way. After a while Tubbs approached Joshua and said bluntly, "You're not going to be able to work for a while, and your Peter won't be any help." Joshua didn't reply. "You won't be able to feed yourself and all the family for a while yet."

Martha looked aghast at Tubbs. Joshua shook his head. "Look here Tubbs, I don't need you here at the moment." He went to gesture for him to leave but the movement caused another spasm of pain.

Tubbs carried on unabashed. "You need to have less mouths to feed and I know how you can."

Isaac stepped forward and took Bill Tubbs by the scruff of his neck and turned him around towards the door. "Look young man we don't want you here." He then manhandled him to the door and he said quietly "Bugger off – and do it now."

Tubbs scowled. "Only trying to help." He received a smart push in the back that propelled him outside. As he reluctantly moved away he left a parting comment. "Joshua Bollson, you will be glad of my help in the end."

Joshua survived his injury but it was several months before he was able to go underground again. He was fortunate at first that there was stone which had not been shipped round to Swanage. He was able make much of it into polished ashlars and then sell these sawn, finished building stones for 5 shillings[9] each. Purbeck stone was often referred to as Purbeck Marble as it was able to be polished to appear like true marble and could be used for decorative purposes. Peter helped and although he was there every day he had retreated into his shell and there was a reproachful look in his eyes.

Eventually Joshua had to go back down the slide, but the hard grind of working underground every day was becoming too much for him. As the months passed the amount of stone he was able to bring to the surface was reducing such that he was struggling to support Martha and the children.

Each evening he would come home, have his dinner and collapse exhausted in his chair. The food that Martha was able to produce was barely sufficient to sustain the hard labour that Joshua had to carry out. She made sure that nothing was thrown away. Any meat she was able to buy was boiled with some vegetables, bones, barley, oatmeal and grits. She would also add to the pot any food left on a plate – which was becoming less and less.

---

[9] 5 Shillings = 25p

One evening Martha had been to Swanage during the day and had acquired some fish. When this meal was finished, the bones, heads and the remnants from the plates were put into the liquor that had cooked the fish.

Martha put Joshua's meal on the table and he looked up at his wife with a pained expression. "Is there enough for the children?" He had been taking less for himself but he feared it would not be long before the children would be close to starvation.

Martha put a re-assuring hand on his shoulder "Yes, dear. Don't worry we'll survive." Joshua could see the anxiety etched on her face. "I have put a crust of bread into the pot that is stewing with the food from yesterday. It will attract the fat and swell out the bread. It will be good healthy food for you to take to the quarry tomorrow."

Joshua smiled weakly. He loved his dear wife and felt deeply sorry that he could not provide for her and the children properly. He also knew that matters would only get worse. His thoughts were interrupted by loud banging on the door.

As Martha opened it, Bill Tubbs strode passed her without a comment and stood before Joshua. Joshua frowned and asked bluntly, "What do you want?"

"Thank you for such a warm welcome." It was as though Tubbs was privy to Joshua's previous thoughts as with heavy sarcasm he said. "Look, it's obvious you're struggling and I can help."

Joshua was not convinced. "How can you help? I don't see you as an angel of mercy."

"Well that's where you're wrong. You have a big family and one less mouth to feed would be welcome, wouldn't it?"

Joshua frowned, "Go on, what do you mean?"

'What I mean is that I would be willing to take your daughter, Dot, and make her my wife."

Martha who was pottering around the room gave a sharp intake of breath.

Tubbs continued unabashed. "I'm a good catch for her. I'm strong, in good health and I've got regular work at the Crack Lane Quarry. I take home 15 shilling[10]s every week." He looked round at Martha and back to Joshua then as if playing his trump card said, "Also when my Pa died last year he left me Hollow Cottage and Ma has gone to live with my sister in Wareham."

Joshua just stared at Tubbs without replying straightaway. Tubbs shuffled his feet awkwardly. "Well? It sounds good to me. You will have one less mouth to feed."

Joshua shook his head slowly. "Do you realise you have never once mentioned that you love Dorothy."

"Let's not get sentimental about this, I've known Dot since we were children. Hollow Cottage needs a woman about the place and she's grown into a good sturdy lass." He paused and looking at Joshua there was a hint of a smirk on his face. "I can promise her food, clothes and a roof over her head. Can you?"

Joshua eyes flashed "Get out!" he shouted and got up from his chair with obvious ill intent towards his guest.

"Alright, alright. I'm leaving but the offer's still there. How about asking Dot?" He turned and walking out of the door did not bother to close it.

Martha hurried over to Joshua's side and squeezed his arm. "He's such a nasty man. I was hoping that Ted Edmunds was going to pick up the courage to ask Dot to marry him."

"So was I, but that's up to Ted. Ted is a grown man now and he has to make that decision. Besides I will not have it be

---

[10] 15 Shillings = 75p

known that I was trying to marry off my daughter because I am not able to support my family."

Martha understood but shook her head sadly at the way that a man's pride came before anything.

As the scene had unfolded they were unaware that Dot was sitting on the stairs listening to every word.

"Watch out below!" Isaac Tomes came sliding down the path to Joshua's quarry.

Seeing his old friend, Joshua greeted him with a warm handshake. "What brings you here today?" He paused and frowned, "Not bad news I hope."

"No…. No." he stopped. He frowned then took a deep breath, then continued. "Look, we're old friends." He nodded in the direction of the quarry shaft "It's not easy for you is it?"

Joshua didn't speak. He wouldn't admit he couldn't cope and he would normally have taken offence.

Isaac looked over in the direction of Peter who was glumly loading stone onto the crane for lowering down to the boat. "Peter's not filling Robert's place." He said rather than asking.

There was a crash and as both men spun round to the noise. Peter had thrown a hammer and wedge to the ground and was storming down to the boat. Both men watched in silence for a moment then Isaac said, "I'm sorry he must have overheard me. That was stupid of me."

Joshua was a loyal father but Isaac and he knew each other too well for him not to be honest. He grimaced to acknowledge Isaac's comment but then added, "Peter's alright he works hard here on the surface. Don't worry, I'll speak to him when he comes back." He stopped and in an effort to change the line of conversation asked Isaac. "It's not easy for you either now that Jasper has gone. How are you coping yourself? I understand that James is a lazy so-and-so." Isaac didn't answer. Joshua continued, "We both know it's getting very difficult for both us, so why have you come here today?"

"I've been thinking." He stopped, chuckling as he expected a friendly jibe, "Yes I know that's new for me. I've got some ideas, which may help us both. Can you meet me in The Ship tomorrow evening? It's the middle of the week, it won't be too busy and we can have a talk."

"I'm always for a meeting in The Ship." He stopped and frowned. "I can't really afford it."

Isaac, his errand accomplished, gave Joshua a friendly clap on the shoulder. "Same for me but don't worry I've a few pennies for a couple of beers. See you tomorrow evening then." With that he turned and scrambled back up the cliff path.

Joshua stood for a moment thinking about what had been said before shrugging his shoulders and walked over to the cliff edge. There he saw Peter sitting on the lower ledge staring out towards the sea.

He was slightly miffed at his churlish behaviour in front of his friend, although this was typical of Peter at the moment Joshua was beginning to fear that Peter might do something rash. He didn't know what, but he was concerned. Joshua took a deep breath. "Peter, come back up here. Stop sulking and help me go back down the slide."

As Joshua made his way downwards, there was just the sound of the creaking rope and the occasional bumping of the cart on the side of the slide. He brooded on the fact that maybe he was being too harsh on his son. Peter was becoming more and more remote and when, even his family tried to speak with him, he wouldn't answer or snapped back at them.

Joshua shook his head. What could he do? His son was grown up now he had to pull himself together and act like a man.

Thoughts of Peter were overtaken as Joshua applied himself to his day's work. Evening came and as usual he trudged his way home exhausted. He would have welcomed company but Peter went on ahead without waiting for him.

After making a detour via Abraham Butt's forge to arrange for Drummer to be re-shod he arrived home and found Martha with a look of concern talking with Dot.

He sensed immediately something was in the air. Looking from one to the other he asked with a frown, "What are my two ladies talking about?"

Martha started to speak but was cut short.

"No Pa. I was just telling Ma I am going to get married." Dot blurted out. "I heard Bill Tubbs asking you for my hand in marriage the other evening. Well," she paused, "I saw him today and said I would be willing. I am now betrothed to Bill Tubbs."

Despite his tiredness, Joshua exploded. "What! You cannot be serious. To Bill Tubbs? What about Ted? I thought you and he….." he stopped.

"Pa it's for the best. Bill can provide for me and we can live in Hollow Cottage as soon as we are married. We grew up together in the village. We know each other well." She paused and looked down. "Besides, it will also help you and Ma."

"That's not the point. It's you that's important."

"Pa, you know life's not like that for us. We have to do what we have to do." She hesitated and glanced in the direction of Peter who was playing with his meagre meal at the table. "Since Robert left you have not been able to replace him and the family could starve before long."

Peter crashed his fist on the table. "It's all my fault again. I know you all think I'm a burden! Well it's time that I wasn't." He jumped up from the table his chair falling backwards as he did so.

"Peter, that's enough of that. Sit down and be quiet." Joshua shot back at him.

"No. I've had enough." Peter then stormed out, which was the catalyst for Martha to burst into tears.

Joshua went over to her and putting his arm around her gave a deep sigh. "I don't know what I'm going to do about that lad." He said quietly almost to himself. He then looked back at Dot. "You can't marry that man, Tubbs. The family will survive – somehow."

"I don't think it can and besides Bill was very pleasant to me when I saw him today. He even promised to pay me for my upkeep here until we do get married. Pa it's done. I'm betrothed to him."

"Is there nothing I can say to persuade you not to marry him? Once you are married, your life is his with no exceptions. That is as it should be but we wish it was not Bill Tubbs."

"Please, you gave Robert your blessing when he left. Ma – Pa, can I now leave with your good wishes as well?"

Martha still had tears in her eyes as she went and gave Dot a long hug. "Of course you have them. We both love you dearly and we understand your reasons for your sacrifice."

"Thank you, Ma." She gave Martha a kiss then went over to Joshua, and reached up to kiss him on the cheek. "I'm going to bed now. It's been a long day." As she left the room Martha could see her eyes welling up with tears of her own.

Martha looked at Joshua but did not speak. Neither did Joshua, he just stared into the fire. He was the head of the family and he was failing them. Eventually he hauled himself back to the present and rose wearily from his chair.

"I'm going to turn in now.   It's another long day tomorrow."   Martha went and reached up to give him a kiss which Joshua returned with a rueful smile. Martha watched her dear husband trudge up to his bed then slumped down in his chair by the fire. After a few moments she shivered with a deep sob and buried her face in her hands.

Joshua collapsed onto his bed but there was a long restless and sleepless night ahead of him.

He met Isaac the following evening as arranged at The Ship. He was surprised that it was more crowded than usual for a weekday. He saw Isaac sitting next to young Calvin Seagers who had recently taken over as Estate Bailiff for Lord Olden upon the death of his own father from a fever. As Joshua sat down Isaac turned to Calvin "You don't mind if we have a chat do you.   It's not private but we have some matters to discuss."

"Of course not, go ahead, would you like me to move."

"No of course not."   He turned to Joshua just as George Tupe, the landlord, brought over two tankards of their usual beer. "Joshua, let me cut a long story short. You can't cope much longer at your quarry without help.   Whatever your loyalties to your son, Peter is not much help." Joshua went to speak but was stopped. "I am the same. Jasper has gone and James is going to go back to his Pa who needs him now." He grunted, "I wish him the best of luck at getting any work out of him." He shrugged, "With just the two girls I will have to do it all myself – and I can't."

"So we're in the mire. Why are we here then? To drown our sorrows?"

"No… but it's not a bad idea though."   He said grinning. "We've known each other all our lives so I ask could we work together? You know work just one of our quarries."

Joshua thought hard and long then gave a sigh. "Good thought but it wouldn't work."

"Why not?"

"Each of our quarries can only provide enough stone to support one family. Myself with Robert, and you with Jasper, brought in enough to support - just - our own families. If we got together we get the same amount of stone from just the one quarry but what we made would be spread over the two families."

There was a long pause. Isaac sat back in his seat disappointed and breathed quietly "Damn, I know you're right. I was just hoping this might be a solution."

"Also, we're not getting any younger. How much longer can we go underground? In the past, the sons of the family would take over."

Neither spoke for some minutes.

Their silence was broken by a quiet cough from Calvin Seagers. "Excuse me for interrupting but I may be able to help."

They both turned and looked at Calvin frowning. "Pardon? What are you going to do, go down to the stone face?" Isaac grimaced but gave a friendly smile, "I don't think so."

"I'll ask you both one question. Each of you has a quarry that has been in the family for as long as you can remember. Would you give that up to work for someone else?"

"What do you mean?"

"I mean, would you give up your own quarries and work for Lord Olden at the Eidibury Quarry? Let me explain. As you know, the same fever that took my father to the Lord took a number of people around here. It mainly took elder folk a few of which worked at Eidibury. They did the lighter work on the surface rather than go down to the stone face.

They also drove the wagons down to Swanage. These are jobs that you could do for years yet."

"Sounds good, I suppose." Joshua said slowly and carefully, then sat back in disappointment. "Jobs on the surface don't pay very much. I've heard that Lord Olden is an old skinflint and he doesn't spend money when he should. Would it be enough for us?"

"It's not for me to say. You are right, it won't pay the same as those men who go underground . I think that you would be better off though."

Isaac frowned, "How?"

"You will take home what you are paid. You will not have the cost of maintaining your equipment and boats. Your donkeys cost you money to keep them fed and shod. Also, as you will be working on the surface, a major cost for you at the moment is the sharpening and replacing of your tools. All these costs will disappear." Calvin sat back satisfied that he had made his point but added one final shot. "You can also forget about the worry of finding buyers for your stone. Portland Stone along the coast is a strong competitor to the stone from Purbeck; that will be Lord Olden's problem from now on."

His audience was stunned. It was as though they had been given the opportunity to take one swift bound and they were free of worry.

Joshua hesitated. "My quarry has been in my family for years. I would be the last in a long line to work it."

Calvin was not to be denied. "Does that matter? Times are changing, more and more men are becoming employed. You might not have heard but factories are opening all over the country and employing hundreds of men in each." He paused to close his offer. "Come on you know it makes sense. Unlike many men you will have the surety of work for despite Portland Stone there is a growing need for Purbeck Marble in the new cities."

Joshua looked thoughtful for a few moments as they both digested what Calvin had proposed. He then had one last question. "It would be a shame if our quarries became derelict. Would we be able to sell them?"

"To be quite frank, I don't know." Calvin paused and looked at Joshua and Isaac in turn. He then asked the question to which there was only one answer. "You have to ask yourselves, 'Can I carry on as I am at the moment'?'"

Joshua looked at Isaac who nodded, then stood up and offered his hand. "Calvin, you don't know how much I, - I think I can say we, appreciate your help. Thank you very much, if there is any way we can return your kindness in the future you can rest assured that we will do so."

"That's business. If I can help anyone from the village, I will. Now, sit down. Let's have a drink to seal the deal. Oh, don't worry, this is on Lord Olden which I think I can put down on his account as a business matter."

The deal was sealed in style. The two old friends left Calvin with more thanks and handshakes and were in happy frames of mind as they made their way home.

Joshua didn't speak for a while then clapped his arm around Isaac's shoulder. "You know, before this evening I couldn't see a way out of trouble. We've both now got work that will support our families. I am afraid it is too late to stop Dot marrying Tubbs but I'm sure he's not as bad as he first appears."

Isaac grunted. "Let's hope so for Dot's sake."

"Yes." Joshua said simply. A few moments silence was broken as he continued. "I've also realised that Peter won't have to work at our quarry anymore."

"He's a strange lad, your Peter."

"No, not strange." Joshua was defensive. "In fact he's a bright lad. It's just that he won't go underground. I don't understand his problem."

"What is he going to do now then?"

"I'm not totally sure. He has had reading and writing lessons from the curate. Walter says that he could get work for him in Mr Dearman's office in Swanage. I'll speak with Walter after Service on Sunday."

"That'll cheer the lad up."

They reached the crossroads by the church and stopped. Joshua turned to Isaac. "This will be a weight off Martha's mind. She has been very worried about what was going to happen to the family. She will be relieved that Peter should be happier from now on as well."

Isaac nodded. "Let's hope so." He took a deep breath. "We are both going to be busy for a few days whilst we close down our quarries. In case I don't see you before," he thrust his hand out to shake Joshua's "here's to life as one of His Lordship's workers. I'll see you at Eidibury next Monday."

On arriving home Joshua thrust open the door happy to be able to deliver good news. He was stopped in his tracks. Dot was crouching on her haunches grasping her weeping mother's hand. They both looked up as he came in the room the beaming smile on his face disappeared instantly. "In God's name what's up?"

Dot gave her mother's hand a squeeze and looked up at her father. "Some men were meeting a boat down on the beach under Austell Head. They found Peter at the bottom of the cliff." She stopped, not wanting to say the awful news. "He's dead."

A funeral is a time when a village gets together to help the bereaved at their time of sorrow. There were however, not very many people at the church for Peter's funeral. The families of Bollson and Tomes were all there as was a somewhat reluctant Bill Tubbs as a putative member of the family. He stood at the graveside but his gentle rocking movement belied the fact that he had been an early visitor to The Ship. When the curate had finished the service, Tubbs was heard to mutter without too much effort to keep his voice down, "Good, that's done; back to the Ship."

Dot caught her breath with a sob and moved closer to her mother. Both Joshua and Isaac turned and stared at Tubbs who stood his ground. He stared back belligerently at first until Isaac made a move in his direction.

"I'll leave you lot to it." He said hastily as he retreated, stepping on gravestones on his way.

Isaac shook his head sadly. "Not a pleasant man." He lowered his voice. "Is Dot quite resolved on the matter of marrying him?"

Joshua nodded quickly. "Yes, I'm afraid so, although I've told her it's not necessary. Let's not talk about that now. Please come back to the cottage, Martha will make tea for us."

"Thank you. I have a gift that I think you will appreciate."

Joshua looked at him enquiringly, then said, "Come on. Let's get moving it's starting to get cold."

At the cottage Martha and Dot busied themselves with making the tea and laying out some bread on the table. "I'm sorry I can't offer you anything more."

"Don't be silly Martha. Isaac and I are fine, aren't we dear." She said looking at Isaac.

"Yes, of course." Isaac said quickly, then delved into his bag, which he had left on a chair by the door, and with a flourish produced a bottle of brandy. "Charlie Heywood is a good young lad. I saw him yesterday and he said to pass on his apologies for not being at the church today. He gave me this so that we can have a drink on him and to toast Peter's life."

Joshua smiled grimly. "He's a credit to his dear mother.

Martha brought over a couple of mugs, which Isaac filled generously with the brandy. After solemnly toasting Peter, Isaac looked carefully at Joshua. "How are matters with yourself?"

"We'll be alright. The money from the work at Eidibury Quarry will be a lifesaver. I mean that; Martha can put food on the table again." He looked thoughtfully out of the window. "It was disappointing not to see more people at the church."

Isaac put his hand on Joshua's shoulder. "You mustn't feel guilty about Peter. You did what you could and you always stood by your boy. Most of those in the village did not understand his fear of going underground. To them going down into the lanes is a way of life. It was seen as a weakness, which overshadowed his other strengths. He appeared to be an intelligent lad."

"I still feel that I should have been more understanding." He took large gulp of the brandy and glanced across the room to where Dot was in serious conversation with her mother and Ada. "Dot believes she is committed to marry Bill Tubbs. I know she did that just to help the family." He sighed. "First of all we lost Robert, the Lord knows where he is now. I pray to God that he's still alive. Then Peter, and……" his voice trailed off. "…. now Dot decides to leave to marry that Tubbs.

Isaac didn't speak for a moment, then put his arm round Joshua's shoulder. "Come on old friend. I know that today is not a happy day but let's remember we both now have work that will feed and clothe our families. Here's to the future." He raised his mug of brandy and took another long draught. "Let's join the womenfolk."

* * *

The marriage of Dot and Bill Tubbs was delayed so as not to be too soon after Peter's funeral. When it did take place it could not be called a joyous affair. On Tubbs side only his mother and sister with her family, were in the church. The Bollson and Tomes families were there in force, together with the childhood friends of Dot from the village. Ted Edmunds made his apologies to Dot and did not attend. The church ceremony finished and all concerned congregated again, this time in The Ship.

Drinks were taken and toasts given but unfortunately Tubbs made a few toasts too many. His behaviour became progressively more boorish and most of those present wished Dot all their best wishes and gradually the room emptied. Dot's Wedding Day was not turning out to be one of great joy. After all the guests had left she left quietly with her parents and went back to their cottage.

Her hopes of a quiet night were crushed when in the middle of the evening she was startled by a, frankly not unexpected, loud and insistent banging on the door. Upon cautiously opening it she stepped back quickly as Bill Tubbs intent on a further assault connected with empty space and staggered into the room.

"I'm told my wife is here. Ah, there you are. Come with me woman, you don't live here anymore." He grabbed her by the wrist and they left with Dot almost being dragged along in his wake.

Dot's wedding night was horrendous as the marriage was consummated. Bill Tubbs was inept and aggressive in the marital bed and his rough handling made Dot scream, as her virginity was taken. His male climax finished, he promptly rolled over and loudly snored in a deep sleep. Dot lay weeping in the dark, barely moving so as not to stir her new husband.

That night was enough to produce a daughter which Dot, without any interest from Tubbs, had christened Nancy Martha. Without any consideration for his wife, Tubbs was persistent in the marital bed even through the latter stages of her pregnancy. It was inevitable that Dot was very soon become pregnant again. Within a year she gave birth to another daughter which she had christened, Annie. Tubbs showed no delight in the birth of his two daughters as he wanted a son in his own image and he not having one was Dot's fault.

Joshua and Martha would see Dot and their granddaughters every Sunday at the Morning Service and she would sit with them. Bill Tubbs never attended as he usually slept through the morning as the ale from the previous night worked its way through his body.

Martha noticed that Dot would often have bruises on her face and trembled to think of how many were on the rest of her body. One morning she couldn't ignore a black eye and after the Service she asked in full knowledge of the truth. "Is your husband beating you?"

Dot looked down and there was a catch in her voice as she said. "Don't fret Ma. It's my fault I must learn to become a better wife."

Martha touched her sleeve gently. "There's always a place for you back with me and your Pa."

Dot smiled weakly, "I'll be alright, Ma." She then gave Martha a kiss on the cheek and left.

Joshua had heard the conversation. "You be careful, my dear. She's Tubbs' wife and he has his rights."

CHAPTER EIGHT

Eventual Success

Charlie was feeling good. Since taking on Gull Quarry he had been able to double sales to Gull's existing customers and had satisfied James Tyler on his contract which had been renewed after the initial six month period. During these months, Charlie had overseen all deliveries. As he was always available he was also able to take additional orders even before the other quarries knew the business was on offer. As a result the Quarry was flourishing. Ben Foster, the quarry manager, had taken on more men and Charlie ensured they were all paid at a good rate. He had also noted that Ben was still fairly young and was ambitious. Charlie kept that in mind.

Charlie and Seth Cobbald met each month to confirm sales, monies received and payments that were due. Now, some eighteen months since the start of their venture, they were due to meet as usual on a quiet Wednesday afternoon. Charlie had already begun to realise that although Seth was pleased with the extra money, his heart was not in the venture. It was time to tackle the subject with Seth head-on but he didn't want to appear to be pushing him aside.

Seth was sitting at his usual table by the window puffing at his clay pipe. "Good afternoon to you Seth," he had dropped the Mister Cobbald, "how's business here?"

Seth smiled. "It's good, I'm having to take on another lass to help serve the drinks. I'm not as young as I used to be, you know."

Charlie grinned. "None of us are getting any younger, that's for sure." He paused, it was time to put his cards on the table. "Seth, I get the feeling that this quarry business isn't filling you with much enthusiasm."   He studied Seth. "I'm right aren't I?" He waited for an answer.

Seth stared out of the window for a few moments then he turned back to Charlie. "I'll be honest with you, no."   He held up his hand as if to parry any protest. "Don't worry, I entered into an agreement with you - and I will honour it."

Charlie was sympathetic. "I know you will, Seth."   He paused. "The business is doing very well.   It just needed some hard work to get all the extra orders that are coming from London and other places."   Now was the time to make his offer. "Seth, I would like to take over the entire rental."

"Can you afford it?"

"Yes. Well, not all of it immediately, but during the course of the next year."

Seth didn't speak but stared into the distance deep in thought. After a while, during which Charlie had kept quiet, Seth looked Charlie straight in the eye. "Alright if you can pay the entire rent then I will gladly step aside and let you take over the whole business."

"Are you quite sure?   I don't want you to think that I'm trying to get rid of you now that I can cope on my own."

Seth grunted and with a smile said simply, "I was hoping that you would want to do this at some point in the near future."

"Thank you." Charlie said quietly.

Seth grinned.   "You're a persuasive blighter and you convinced me to go into the business when that was really the last thing on my mind." He put his hand up again. "I grant you everything you said has happened to the penny - and more. I'm reaching the time in my life though when I want to sit back.   It won't be too long before I will want to sell The Harbour Inn.   Molly will then be married to a man of independent means." He laughed.

Charlie reached forward to offer his hand. "Thank you again Seth. I will never forget that you helped me to get started." He then added enthusiastically. "There is a large contract available next year for me to supply James Tyler with more stone than the Gull quarry can produce."

"You can't take the contract on, then." Seth looked worried.

"I've already spoken to a number of the family quarries and I will be buying from them to meet the delivery dates."

Seth sat back chuckling. "I've said it before, you're a bright young man, you'll go far."

"Thanks. James has promised that if the contract is met properly, and it will be I can assure you, then there will be a large bonus in it for us."

"Us? I won't be involved."

"No that's true but one thing I have already learnt is to recognise those who you owe a debt of gratitude. I wouldn't be getting a bonus at all if you hadn't helped me at the beginning. It will be over and above the normal profit and we will share it half and half."

Seth shook his head slowly and said quietly. "You're a good man Charlie. A good man." He took a deep breath and sat upright in his chair. Turning to the Tap Room he called out. "Molly, two large glasses of brandy."

Charlie sat back and clasped his hands behind his neck. He was satisfied that he had acted properly. Business was good when all parties were happy.

Molly came out with the brandies. She was a short, square woman with large hips that supported a spotless white apron. Her now white hair still kept curls which peeped out from under her white mop cap.

"Thank you Mrs Cobbald." Charlie took a long draught from his glass and let the warming liquor tumble down his throat. He inspected the glass as he twirled it with his fingers. "This is good stuff." He looked at Seth with a twinkle in his eye. "I wonder where you got it from."

Seth grinned. "You know darn well." He looked concerned. "I understand that you are more involved with Isaac Gulliver these days. I don't mean by keeping a look out when there is a landing. You be careful, young man."

"Don't worry. Isaac is alright. He's not as tough as people think." He paused then lowered his voice. "It won't be long before he wants to sit back as well, as you say, as a man of independent means. Shall we say I'm just helping him by taking over the chores so that he can ease his way to a quiet life."

Seth just shook his head and looked at Charlie with renewed admiration.

May 1812 to June 1813

The mood in the Regiment after the storming of Badajoz was somber. even the old veterans of campaigning in Portugal and Spain were quiet.

Only a matter of days after the siege had been lifted a garrison force was left at the city and the army was on the march northwards. At the end of the third day they were halted and dismissed for the night on the banks of a river. As Jasper settled down for a quiet smoke on his pipe he looked across at Robert. "This must seem like a daft question but: What's got into everyone?"

Robert grunted, "I think that's bloody obvious - Badajoz."

Jasper. "Yes, alright. What I meant was - Why? Is it the number of men killed. I know we lost over 30 in our Company and add the injured that left just about half our full number active. Or is the mood because of what happened in the city after the crapauds had surrendered."

Robert shook his head "Dunno." Obviously not wanting to talk, then changed his mind. "It doesn't help that we haven't been paid for five months."

Corporal Reynolds was sitting close by. "It's some or all of those reasons. You'll notice though very soon everybody will be back to normal. You would land up in the Bethlem Hospital[11] very soon if you did't move on."

Changing the subject, Jasper asked Reynolds. "Do you know where we're going. I've noticed a few men have been drafted into our Company and the whole army is getting bigger."

Reynolds sat up as he noticed a few other men starting to take an interest in what he was about to say, "I've spoken with Sergeant Hollins. This is the first time we've been in Spain for three years and we have information about the movement of the French. Our army has about 48,000 men mainly British but quite a few Portuguese and Spanish and we're looking to catch the French near the city of Salamanca."

"That will be another battle then?" Robert asked quietly.

"That's why we're here, lad." To show the conversation was at an end, he turned and settled down for the night.

Corporal Reynolds was right. The Allied army was able to catch up with the French near the city of Salamanca. The British commander, Sir Arthur Wellesley, brilliantly outmanoeuvred and inflicted heavy losses on Marshall Marmont's army.

The news of the Battle reached the Prince of Wales, now the Prince Regent, and he created Wellesley Viscount Wellington and commander of all allied forces in the Peninsular.

---

[11] The word "bedlam", meaning uproar and confusion, is derived from the hospital's nickname. Now a modern psychiatric facility, historically it was representative of the worst excesses of asylums in the era before lunacy reform

Wellington split his army; one Division was sent to lay siege of the town of Burgos, while the remainder were able to enter the Spanish capital of Madrid.

Jasper and Robert had never seen a large city before except for Lisbon briefly but which was small in comparison to Madrid. They took the opportunity to sightsee and it wasn't long before Robert was able to say again 'this is why we joined the army'.

They sauntered the wide and magnificent streets and watched numerous processions of monks and priests. It had spectacular sights for two lads from a quiet country village. There were public exhibitions of fireworks in the Plaza Mayor which they viewed with some circumspection after the events of the previous five months. They toured the length of a two mile long Promenade with waters sprouting from ornamental fountains which freshened the air. There were statues, planted trees and large vases containing fragrant flowers.

Their whole visit to this majestic city was awe-inspiring and it happily numbed some of the traumas of the previous few months.

Jasper and Robert were raw recruits when they arrived in Portugal just eight months previously but the next year was to season them into hardened veterans.

Wellington ultimately withdrew from Burgos and re-deployed back to Ciudad Rodrigo on the Portuguese border where he spent the winter reinforcing and training his army.

In contrast, Napoleon withdrew 15,000 soldiers from Spain, as he had to reinforce his army, which had been decimated by the disastrous Russian campaign. He left his brother, King Joseph, in nominal command of the French armies in Spain. Napoleon told his brother that Wellington would remain on the defensive. Napoleon was wrong.

Campaigning on foreign soil could mean days of marching in torrential rain turning roads and tracks into glutinous mud which sapped strength and stamina. In contrast, in the Spanish summer, exhausting heat would be too much for many men who would collapse by the roadside with fever.

During the winter months when the troops were stood down at Ciudad Rodrigo Jasper and Robert experienced the endless boredom of the repetitive routines of army life. Each day began with the drummer beating a long roll on his drum before sunrise. The Company then washed, dressed and ate, before starting the day's business. They were drilled repeatedly on battle routines and musket practice.

Fire & Reload — four rounds a minute : Form Line Abreast : Form a Square.

Drinking seemed the only off-duty recreational activity available. As well as appeasing boredom, drink also provided a means of escapism. When soldiers are cut off from civilian society, their behaviour reflects their lives of habitual violence, together with the physical and mental strains. There was also within the British Army a sense of superiority together with brutality towards not only their enemy, the French, but also towards the Spanish and Portuguese, their supposed allies.

The lads from Dorset were not slow in enjoying a drink. One such night a half dozen men from the Norfolk Brigade, themselves obviously drunk, didn't notice Jasper who was laying on his back, head resting on his pack. One of them tripped over him, staggered a couple of yards, then spun and kicked Jasper's thigh. "Get out of my way, you pillock."

Jasper leapt to his feet and his assailant's friends saw his size. "Come on, Bill let's go. We've got more brandy we need to finish."

Bill was too slow. Jasper would normally have left the matter but he had consumed a few brandies as well. One quick step and he caught Bill flush on the jaw which was enough for him to take no further part in the proceedings. There followed a scuffle until Jasper caught another man with a glancing blow which was enough to put him on the ground. This deterred any further interest from the Norfolks who made a swift withdrawal dragging their groggy comrades with them.

When they had left Robert inspected his bleeding knuckles and felt a swollen lip. He chuckled "Well thanks for that, Jasper, you're as bad as the rest of them around here."

Jasper looked at Robert and grinned then became serious. "No I'm not and nor are you." He frowned then continued. "We both like a drink and we will still have a few but we can't let ourselves be ground down to their level."

Robert nodded. "Yep your right. I've been thinking lately, we joined the army to get away from Langton Matravers. After the last year I'm not sure if we made the right decision or not. Whatever. Our sole purpose now is to survive. For how long I dunno, but we'll know the time when we can or if we want to move on."

They both knew that there was no more to be said. It was one of those moments where a pact has been made between two friends.

They still had the winter to endure and when off duty they would smoke, drink, and gamble as they saw fit. Some men would chat about home life and their thoughts of the future, although others would never talk of either.

Private George Fitzherbert was such a man who always kept in the background. He had wavy dark hair that he ruffled forward at the sides His locks framed a soft skinned face which matched what were once soft hands that had surely never had to labour during his young life. He was also obviously educated which drew Jasper and Robert to spend hours talking with him.

One such night the conversation turned to life back in England. Jasper soon brought up his hobby horse and espoused his opinion. "Life is unfair for us that do all the work. We work all the hours that god gives whilst Lord Olden sits on his arse in Olden Hall never lifting a finger. There's no justice in that."

Robert grinned. "He's off. If you're not careful he'll go on for hours."

George shook his head. "You are right Jasper. the ruling class and the mass of workers are ignorant of each other's habits, thoughts and feelings as if they were inhabitants of different countries."

"You see, George agrees with me." Jasper looked at Robert triumphantly.

"Ah, but what's the answer." George said then paused and Jasper remained quiet. "Look what happened in France. Do you want to storm Olden Hall, drag out his Lordship and hang him from the nearest tree?"

"Well, no." Jasper replied slowly.

"Some would." George said emphatically. "I think they're in the minority. I believe that there must be some sense of a middle way."

"Do you know what that is?" asked Robert.

"I've got ideas. I've some books stashed away in my pack that are very interesting. Ah." he paused. "Can you read?

"No." Robert said defensively.

"Right, whilst we're here, I'll teach you how to read and write."

"Really?" Jasper said cautiously.

"Yes. It's said that knowledge is power. It will also make the evenings much more interesting rather than getting blind drunk."

As if on call their conversation was brought to an end when a great drunken brawl broke out in the camp.

In May 1813, Wellington launched his final offensive in Spain by marching his troops from northern Portugal over the mountains into northern Spain. Wellington's army was supported by an extensive and efficient commissariat, which made the advance across the barren mountainous region of the north-west of Spain possible and which the French did not believe feasible.

Wellington also ensured his supply lines were not overstretched. The Royal Navy now commanded the seas which enabled him to move his base from Lisbon in Portugal to Santander in north east Spain.

The French commanders were unable to obtain reliable information on Wellington's movements or even communicate effectively with each other. This was due to the operations of the all-pervasive Spanish guerrillas, while Wellington was well informed on French movements by the same guerrillas.

King Joseph was unsure what Wellington was planning. Reports were coming in of activity from the direction of Bilbao and Joseph could not rule out the prospect of an attack on Vitoria from the north.

The French decided to make a stand around Vitoria and Joseph put his trust in the arrival of reinforcements from Pamplona. The decision was influenced by the need to cover the substantial convoys of valuables, cash and official documentation in Vitoria.

The main French army marched onto the Vitoria plain and took up defensive positions behind the River Zadorra. Wellington carried through the attack and after a fierce battle, the division under General Picton managed to break into the centre of the French and break through their defences. The majority of fleeing French were allowed to escape towards the Pyrenees where they met their advancing reinforcements which were too late.

The French suffered 8,000 troops killed, wounded or captured and lost all their 150 guns, except one. The British suffered 3,675 troops killed or wounded, the Portuguese 921 and the Spanish 562.

The British 1st Division commanded by Lieutenant General Thomas Graham had been deployed to the north flank near Vitoria. As the French started their general retreat those in Vitoria were attacked by the 1st Division. French morale collapsed and they ran for it

3,000 vehicles were crammed into the area of Vitoria, filled with goods that had been removed by King Joseph's army, together with herds of livestock. There were also crowds of civilians attempting to escape the collapse of the French regime in Spain. Joseph is said to have abandoned his coach and escaped on horseback.

By 7.30pm the French had been pushed out of Vitoria and were pursued by the majority of the Foot Battalion and the German Legions on the road to Pamplona. In the melee of battle, sections of the East Dorsets in close support of the Hussars were separated from the main force in Vitoria.

Many British soldiers turned aside to plunder the abandoned French wagons, containing "the loot of a kingdom". There was extensive looting by troops who were now no longer available for pursuit of the enemy.

Jasper and Robert were amongst the chaos until at one point Robert was nearly crushed by a coach as it was upended by its horses being cut free and galloping off. A pile of satchels and bags collapsed over Robert and as he pushed them away one split and its contents of gold coins showered over him. A Hussar seeing what happened charged over and snatched the bag and then was away from the scene.

Jasper was about to react but saw other comparable luggages piled up seeping similar contents.

Jasper took one quickly, made sure it was full spun round to Robert. "Quick follow me." Without waiting he dodged into the doorway of what was now an empty villa.

Robert joined him, breathless. "What's up? What have you got there?"

Jasper didn't reply and just open the bag and showed the contents to Robert.

"My god!" Before he could say any more Jasper noticed two soldiers from a brother Company stop and look at them. He looked them in the eye and took a pace forwards

One of them shrugged, then pulled the sleeve of his mate. "Come on. there's plenty more." and they run off.

Robert looked around, saw a wooden staircase. "This way." He charged up the stairs, saw another and they made their way onto the roof. Jasper was almost behind him, having paused to grasp a bottle of brandy he had seen in a cupboard.

Below them in the streets there was pandemonium. Every Frenchman who had been in Vitoria had flown from the distracted British enemy together with all the inhabitants who had disappeared leaving their homes to the ravages of war. There was nothing for the two comrades to do but watch.

So it was that the most conclusive battle of the war in Spain and Portugal was overseen by the lads from Dorset sitting on two chairs that had been left on the roof. They had seen no direct action themselves having followed the Hussars the sight of which was enough for the remaining French. They sat in the evening sunshine with their legs on the stone parapet swigging from a bottle of brandy.

The battle was of wide significance throughout Europe. The Emperor Napoleon was already reeling from the catastrophe of the Russian campaign. Vitoria helped to show that his dominance of the continent was coming to an end. By December, after detachments had seized San Sebastián and Pamplona, Wellington's army was encamped in France.

The magnitude of the day was of no consequence to Jasper and Robert. They stayed on the roof until the light was fading and the scene had quietened down. They were able to hide the satchel discretely and made their way back slowly to where they had been deployed.

On their way Robert nudged Jasper and nodded to an area thick with trees and bushes. "There's no rush to get back, let's have a good look at what is in the bag."

Finding suitable tree stumps they sat down and Robert wrench open the bag. He was awe struck. Delving his hands into the bag he let coins run through his fingers. "This looks like pure gold to me. It must be worth a fortune."

"Aye, fantastic." Jasper was equally overwhelmed with enthusiasm. "You're right. The Lord knows how much that lot is worth." Then regaining his composure. "This will be great for us when we get back to England." He grunted. "Whenever that might be."

Robert grinned. "Over the last couple of years we've not much chance to say that those Sergeants back in Swanage were right after all. We have made our fortunes." He threw a handful of coins in the air.

Jasper laughed ruefully. "Did we ever doubt them?" He then became serious. "We know that we're not the only ones to get our hands on some of the French horde but we must keep this to ourselves. This may be the point in our lives which gives us a chance to truly achieve something different." He paused and grunted with feeling. "That's if we survive this goddam war." His mood brightened. " As far as I'm concerned, we've earned this - it's ours and we keep quiet about it."

On reaching their camp the general mood was one of the usual relief and celebration tinged with regret of friends killed or injured. As usual much alcohol was consumed followed by many sore heads in the morning. No officers or NCO's were in the mood to search those under their command, especially as many had been able to garner their own treasure.

Jasper and Robert were to spend the remainder of their service ensuring that their 'French Booty' was not stolen by their comrades or confiscated by an over zealous officer.

Charlie Heywood had braved the winter weather for a meeting in London. He was not sure of the reception he would receive but after a deep breath he knocked on the door of Jack Winbow, a shipping agent in Southwark. The door was opened by a clerk who Charlie greeted with a friendly smile. "Good day to you, sir. Mr Winbow is expecting me. Charlie Heywood is the name."

The clerk looked doubtful, but gestured Charlie to wait in a small room next to the front door. It was a plain room with white washed walls and two wooden chairs either side of a plain rectangular desk. Charlie remained standing and gazed out of the window. After ten minutes the clerk re-appeared. "Mr Winbow will see you now. Follow me."

Charlie was led up the stairs to an office which overlooked Great Surrey Street. In contrast to the room he had just left, there was dark oak panelling around the walls that were covered with mainly maps of various regions around the world. Jack Winbow sat behind a large impressive desk and gave Charlie a welcoming smile as he entered but remained seated and did not proffer his hand. He indicated for Charlie to take a seat.

"Good day Mr Heywood. I understand that you have a business proposition you would like to put to me."

Charlie was nervous, but was able to hide it well. "Good day to you Sir. Yes, I believe you have in the past conducted business with Isaac Gulliver."

"That is correct."

"Mr Gulliver has decided to retire from, eh, importing. I have worked for – with Mr Gulliver since I was a boy. He has suggested that now that he no longer wishes to continue to trade, that I should contact you. To do business, I mean."

Jack Winbow looked at Charlie with interest. Isaac, who he had dealt with for years, had written to him about Charlie Heywood. He had written that he was impressed and that he should give the young man a chance. "That is all very well Mr Heywood but this is a business where goods are paid for before delivery."

"I am in a position to do so - if the price is right."

Isaac Gulliver had also written that Charlie was from a poor background. Jack Winbow gave an encouraging smile. "How pray, are you able to find the necessary finance?"

Charlie relaxed. He was comfortable in dealing with his host. "I have a business quarrying stone, Gully Quarry near Swanage. I have recently become the sole owner of that business having just paid the final instalment to Mr Seth Cobbald who was my fellow investor in the venture. I have today, before coming to see your good self, met with Sir John Soanes' business manager. I have supplied stone to his business before. I have now concluded a contract to supply stone for a number of projects that Sir John has in hand here in London."

"Well done, Sir. I congratulate you."

"Thank you. It is a contract that will last for at least three to four years. I have received an initial payment for the first delivery of stone which will be delivered within the month."

"Will this be sufficient to purchase a full shipment? I do not deal in the odd barrel or two."

"Yes, it is a goodly sum. That is not all. A local man of rank, agreed through his Bailiff, will invest in the shipment, as will a local man of the cloth." Charlie then added with a grin. "Mr Cobbald has also agreed to re-invest the money I have just paid to him."

Jack Winbow sat back in his chair. He smiled at the thought that Charlie has persuaded Seth Cobbald to give the money straight back to him. Isaac Gulliver was right, this young man is impressive. He leant forward. "That is one side of the matter. Have you obtained customers that will be paying for the goods when you deliver to them?"

"Yes I have. I would prefer to be discrete on that matter. Suffice to say, that I am assured of payment up front so it will not be a concern to yourself."

Jack Winbow paused, deep in thought. He then suddenly stood up, walked around his desk and thrust his hand out. "Sir, it appears that we will be able to do business." He shook Charlie's hand warmly. "I have another appointment now across the river in the City which I must keep. Can I ask that you return tomorrow at the same time? I will have then prepared for us to discuss the details of a shipment and how it will be collected by your good self."

"Thank you Mr Winbow. I shall return tomorrow."

A look of mutual respect passed between the two men of business. Charlie left the building with a spring in his step. He thought to himself that he would remember this date in 1813 as the prelude to exciting times. He was right in more ways than one.

Northern Spain - April 1814

Wellington's army reached France in December but there were still many costly engagements, in casualty terms, to be won. Wellington remained with the Reserve. unusually delegating command to Lieutenant-Generals Rowland Hill and John Hope. Marshall Soult was finally defeated at the Battles of the Nive, a series of engagements near Bayonne. The East Dorsets, not for the first time in Spain suffered heavy casualties and they were kept in reserve with Wellington. At one of these engagements both Jasper and Robert were injured but fortunately both were cuts which time healed.

As Winter turned into Spring the marching continued whilst the heat of southern France rose. On Easter Monday their march, which yet again appeared to the troops, to be going nowhere was called to a halt when a party of officers galloped to meet them. They were shown the way to Wellington's senior staff quarters. Wellington could be seen to be stoically watching whilst the others were in animated conversation.

To the soldiers, the stop was a welcome relief from the midday sun.

A grove of pine trees with the backdrop of the shimmering Pyrenees in the distance providing a refreshing shade. The only sound was the low sighing of the wind amongst the pines and the ever-present buzzing of flies. The swarms of multicoloured butterflies were ignored by the soldiers as the men spread out, lolling in various positions. Most of the them just dozed, welcoming the respite from the daily trudging along dusty uneven tracks. Their reverie was briefly broken by a rusty brown and red coloured bird squawking overhead in an attempt to distract any attack on its nest. No-one had the desire to talk.

The gloss of life in the army had gone for Jasper, Robert and any survivors of their comrades that had landed in Portugal. They had all experienced the fears and triumphs of an interminable succession of actions against the French. These had been interspersed with long periods of the tedium of marching, musket practice and drilling.

Robert swatted a fly that persisted on buzzing around his head and casually rolled over onto his side. He saw Corporal Reynolds being spoken to by Sergeant Hollis. The Corporal saluted then spun around and ran over to the men under his command. "Men, great news! Napoleon isn't the crapaud's Emperor any more. It means the war is over."

Reynolds expected his news to be received with a wave of enthusiasm. One of the new recruits fresh from England jumped to his feet and give an elated punch in the air "Bloody great." He stared around at his comrades like the Corporal, expecting a similar expression of joy. They were both disappointed, as the veterans of many campaigns remained lounging on the ground. Private Benn a scrawny and dishevelled reprobate eventually raised his unshaven, scarred face and gave Reynolds a hard stare. He stopped picking what was left of his teeth, spat out a dislodged morsel and growled "At last. What happens to us now in this godforsaken country?" The Corporal was miffed. He stood briefly with his hands on his hips looking at his troop, then turning on his heel he grunted "Sod you then." and moved to find his own patch of grass to stretch out on.

Jasper watched Reynolds stride off and for a few minutes said nothing but appeared deep in thought. He eventually turned slowly to Robert. "If this war is over, they won't want so many of us poor bloody soldiers. If you were given the chance though would you want to sign on for a permanent life in the army?"

"No!" Robert shot back, "Absolutely not!"

Jasper chuckled, "Don't beat about the bush. I assume you've thought about this then and you've had enough?"

"YES!" Robert turned to face Jasper squarely. "Look, we wanted to see the world and have adventure away from the tedium of working in our father's quarries. We've replaced one life of tedium with another. Instead of blisters on my hands and knees, I've got them on my feet. We spend most of our time blindly obeying orders and we never know whether tomorrow will be our last. You can keep this life of adventure, and as for me I've seen enough of the world."

Jasper smiled at first at Robert's tirade but found that he was also nodding in agreement. He had escaped from the drudgery of the quarry but he was still not master of his own destiny.

Robert stood up, looking into the distance he saw the officers delightedly clapping each other on the back. Wellington remained still. Robert turned to look down at Jasper. "There are moments that I cannot get out of my head. As you know, I am still physically sick when I get another bout of the shakes. I've thought I was about to die - or worse - many times. I can't forget that crapaud at Badajoz taking dead aim at me with his musket. The second I saw him, thank the Lord, one of our riflemen blew half his head off." Robert put his head in his hands covering his face.

Jasper sat quietly watching his friend. Robert suddenly took his hands away showing his eyes reddened with tears. "Then at Vitoria I killed a man who was doing nothing but guarding a wagon. He must have been the same age as my young brother Peter. The look on his face was fear and pleading but I mindlessly thrust my bayonet through his throat."

Robert spun around, walked quickly away from the grove and as he stopped his shoulders could be seen to heave as he was violently sick. The silence had been broken but the other soldiers watched dispassionately as the scene took place. Private Benn who was lolling against a tree nearby nodded his head in the direction of Robert and muttered to Jasper, "What's got into him then? He looks like he's blubbing."

Jasper jerked round, "It's none of your business. You just keep your trap shut." Jasper stirred as if he was about to move in Benn's direction.

Benn jumped up, "Alright. Alright." He moved quickly away and growled at some of the other men, "God, don't get between those two." Jasper heard the comment but ignored Benn and watched Robert.

At this point Sergeant Hollis walked down the line of lounging soldiers kicking feet and barking out, "Get up and get into line - NOW!" He approached Jasper, hesitated, decided against giving Jasper's foot a kick and planted a particularly hard blow on the next man. He said over his shoulder, "Private Tomes get your mate into line at the double."

The Regiment found out later, that whilst they were being held in reserve, there had been one last battle at Toulouse the day after Napoleon had abdicated. On hearing this news George Fitzherbert gratuitously reminded everyone that the battle had been totally unnecessary. He then added that there had been a high number of causalities which had been all for nothing.

This was enough to enrage Jasper who growled out, "Bloody waste of lives."

All fell silent and the rest of the day was spent marching and nobody in the Company knew where they were going or why.

They never usually did, but even the gleeful officers could not have foreseen what was soon to unfold.

The Regiment marched northwards after the news reached them of Napoleon's abdication until they were diverted west. They spent the winter billeted near Bordeaux and feared that they were about to be sent to America. England was at war with America but the rumour came back that both sides found it unnecessary and they settled their differences by Treaty.

Most were lucky to be billeted in local houses in Bordeaux. Jasper, Robert, George and a Norfolk lad, Tom Faulkner were put in the house of David and Anne Laure and their young son Emile. They were well looked after and in contrast to army food their first supper consisted of shell-fish and roasted chestnuts, to which was added a plate of pickled olives. This was washed down with copious amounts of red wine from the Bordeaux area. The only bed was the one used by their hosts and so they lay their blankets on the floor and slept soundly. Upon rising early they found their hostess busily preparing breakfast similar to supper with the exception of a glass of brandy each instead of wine.

As they wintered in their billets in Bordeaux the four men became good friends as did their hosts. The fact that peace had been declared did not stop the daily routine of army life continuing:

Fire & Reload — four rounds a minute : Form Line Abreast : Form a Square

As winter was drawing to a close it was rumoured that they were going to be sent home. After much hugging and cheek kissing and with promises they would return some day they left and were to make slow progress northwards. They reached Calais with the expectation that they would be embarking for the short trip across to England any day. They didn't and they waited.

In the middle of March the mood changed. Suddenly officers were looking concerned and training was intensified. They were eventually moved south with the knowledge that they were again under the command of the Duke of Wellington.

On an overcast and wet day in June they encamped just south of the city of Brussels. The East Dorsets Regiment, were ordered on parade as they were about to be addressed by their Company Commander, Captain Honsworth. The Regimental sergeants barked their orders and the men scrambled to line up. Robert shot a quick glance to Jasper, "What's this all about?"

"Don't know," was Jasper's hurried response, "I will tell you one thing, they look worried. Sergeant Hollis said that there was something big brewing."

The Regiment stood motionless as light spots of rain began to fall. After some time, Captain Honsworth trotted slowly passed them on his immaculately turned out white horse. Despite his usual look of faint boredom mixed with disdain he was nevertheless well respected by his men. As he rode by them it was as if he were out for an evening ride in the Dorset countryside.

His mount tossed its head, gave a short snort and pawed the ground impatiently as Captain Honsworth turned to face his troops. "Men, you have fought bravely for your country and you have done well. We are one of the Regiments to have gained glory in Spain and still be with his Grace, the Duke of Wellington, here today. He has told me that I am to inform you that he is proud to have you under his command. You are veterans and you will have, as the Light Infantry, the honour to be the left flank of the Regiment in battle."

There was a low rumble of satisfaction. To be in the centre of the battalion's deployment could mean certain death. A call was heard from the middle of the ranks "God Bless his Lordship."

Men at the rear were craning forward to hear the Captain as he continued, "Old Boney has escaped from his exile and has raised an army filled with his Old Guard." He paused to let his words sink in, then spoke raising his voice, "What this scoundrel does not know is that he will be facing you men that have beaten his armies many times before. You have out shot them and out fought them time and again." There was a growl of approval. "We are also joined with our brave allies the Dutch and Prussian armies. We have the largest army to take the field since these wars started a generation ago. Tomorrow you will have the chance to thrash the blaggard." He stood in his stirrups, drew his sword and waving it in the air, roared "Are we going to thrash him, men? Come on let's hear you. Are you going to give those Crapauds the beating of their lives."

Before he had finished, the entire Company was cheering, waving hats and muskets and shouting, "We won't let you down." "God save the Duke of Wellington." "God save the King." "We'll give it to those French bastards."

Captain Honsworth, still waving his sword, kicked his heels, and his mount cantered away with his oratory leaving his Company craving to get at their enemy.

Robert spun around to Jasper, his eyes wild with the fervour of the moment. "This is it. Now is the time to beat them once and for all."

Jasper was a little more circumspect, "Aye, whether we like it or not, it looks like we have got ourselves into one hell of a battle." He looked in the direction of the departing Captain Honsworth, "I'll say one thing about our good Captain, he's a 'Come on' rather than a 'Go on officer." He paused, his brow furrowed. "He does seem as though he doesn't really care what happens to himself. It's as though, at times, he would almost welcome death."

The Sergeants started to move amongst their men. Sergeant Hollis was a bull of a man. His shaven head was on a neck as wide, and it seemed to join his head directly to his shoulders. He grabbed Jasper by the arm, "Tomes you are promoted to Corporal until further notice. Corporal Jenkins is sick and will not see active duty again. You will take his place."

Jasper went to speak but was cut off by Hollis. He put his face inches from Jasper's "Be quiet Corporal. I won't hear any nonsense. You are here to serve your King and country, there is no back talk on this." He stood back, "You know Jenkins' men, get them to fall in. We are going to the Gemioncourt farm buildings in front of Bossu Wood. The Duke has given orders that the French must be stopped from moving through the cross roads over there at Quatra Bras."

Jasper had fought against moving up the ranks, which his stature and natural authority had made many times seem inevitable. After several months in the army it had appeared to him that there was nothing to be gained from promotion but it was obvious that now was not the time for argument.

Robert had heard the exchange with Sergeant Hollis. "Well done, Jasper," then added with a grin " - or should I say Corporal. Not before time."

Jasper briefly frowned then looked passed Robert to the rest of his command of men who were now waiting for his orders. After a moment to collect himself he gave his first order. "Right: form a column of four and when I give the order we will march to our position." The men being veterans of many campaigns accepted Jasper's new authority immediately and fell in line. Jasper looked at them for a moment then in a quieter tone spoke, "As the officer said, tomorrow you will be serving your country. When you get back to England make sure they will be proud of you and what you have done. The best of luck to you all?" Then louder, with authority he barked out, "Now forward March!"

After an hour they arrived in position and camped down for the night. There was torrential rain all night typical of that on the north European plains in June.

Surprisingly. there was no movement from the French in the morning and the Allied forces were given time to take their positions. The rank and file know nothing of the overall tactics and strategy of a battle. Some may remember small events but would not be able to recall in what order they occurred or at the exact moment. They followed orders and they tried to survive as most often chaos surrounded them. The East Dorsets took their allotted position with the many nationalities being deployed to prevent the French taking command of the crossroads.

Whilst they held their position, cavalry of both sides rode back and forth. The French bombarded the allied positions around 2.00 in the afternoon and then launched a concerted cavalry attack on the Dutch artillery. They were turned back and then advanced again. The Dutch cavalry charged the French artillery battery but were themselves then driven back.

An English artillery battery was attacked by French Lancers but it was, again, driven back. Dutch cavalry galloped passed the East Dorset's position then minutes later galloped back seemingly unscathed.

Whilst all this activity was frantically taking place, there was the constant thudding of artillery as an undertone to the entire day. The battlefield was sometimes shrouded in thick billowing smoke which would then clear to show in stark detail the running and riding back and forth of men who's lives hung in the balance by the vagrancies of chance.

At one point French skirmishers foraged forward to the East Dorset's positions and were driven back by volleys of fire from a detachment of the Rifle Regiment.

Jasper watched dispassionately as the battle seemed to pass them by. He knew though that their time would come and he had to make sure that his men were ready.

He thought their battle was to start as a Dutch Calvary troop passed close by the Dorset Regiment. They must have been recruited locally as they were heard calling to each other in French and being mistaken for the enemy someone in Jasper's Company opened fire. Captain Honsworth realising the error in the confusion roared out, "Cease Fire!" Sergeants in each area echoed his order immediately, "You heard the officer, Cease Fire!" One added, "Don't worry lads your time will come."

Then it was their turn. French artillery fire was directed at their positions. The purpose of such a bombardment was to decimate enemy ranks as much as possible before a frontal attack. It was also to break the formations and the spirit of the impassive ranks who remain steadfastly at their posts. The earth shook and the noise was frighteningly deafening. At one moment Robert glanced across to his right just as a group he had chatted with last night were suddenly converted to a mess of limbs and blood. His mouth was dry but he had been here before. There was nothing he or his fellow comrades could do. Robert was a veteran of such scenes and he trusted that his officers would take the right action at the right time. He had no influence on his fate. As he stood in line abreast he knew that any minute could be his last but he was outside of the control of his own destiny.

They all did believe that given the chance they would beat their enemy, so they stood fast. They would not dishonour their Regiment or Country by turning and running. Robert concentrated on the peaceful field of wheat spread before him and tried to think of the quiet fields surrounding Langton Matravers back home.

The bombardment suddenly ceased and as they peered forward through the smoke they could hear chanting. A breath of wind cleared the smoke and revealed columns of French infantry lined fifty abreast marching steadily towards them. As they drew nearer, the chant of "Vive l'Empereur!" "Vive l'Empereur!" "Vive l'Empereur!" became hypnotic.

Captain Honsworth called, "Sergeants get your men in lines of four." All the endless training and practice made their response to command instinctive. At the order they spread in lines four deep in front of the advancing French columns. "Soldiers, front line - kneel. Take aim!" this was echoed down the line. Another order was barked out, "Wait for it. Wait for it." The three French columns got nearer and nearer still chanting, "Vive l'Empereur!" "Vive l'Empereur!"

Robert knelt frozen in his place. He was hemmed in. He had nowhere to go. 'Come on, give the order to fire?" he desperately whispered to himself, but his experience kept him still. He heard Tom Faulkner next to him curse, "Sod it." He quickly looked to his side and saw that Tom had wet himself but he remained staring fixedly ahead. When the French column reached twenty yards from the English line the order finally came, "FIRE!"

A crashing volley dug into the first rows of the French columns and they crumpled to the ground. "First line re-load, Second line, FIRE!" Another volley thud into the French infantry who were now scrambling over the bodies of their fallen comrades. "Second Row re-load." "Third row - FIRE!". "Third Row re-load." " Fourth row - FIRE!"

The French still came on, their tactic of advancing in columns having proved so successful in campaigns all over Europe. It enabled them to attack quickly and once they reached their enemy they would drive a wedge through the opposing ranks from which they could create panic and force a retreat.

There was a major drawback that the English had exploited in Spain. Columns abreast meant at any one time they were limited in the number of muskets firing at the English. The English arrayed in four lines before them and with their constant practice were able to fire at least four rounds per minute. In addition, the English army's morale was high and they did not turn in the face of a French advance. This meant that continual volleys were pouring into the advancing columns. The volleys were repeated time and again until the ground in front of the English lines was packed with blooded dead and dying French infantry. The French wilted then retreated.

Immediately orders barked out, "Hold your lines. Hold your lines." Previous battles had shown that the French could use this as a tactic and as soon as their enemy broke ranks, the French Cavalry would charge into them. Foot soldiers are no match for mounted cavalry and there would be a massacre.

Robert looked at Tom Faulkner, neither spoke. Their faces were both deathly white and Tom was shaking. Robert's lips were trembling and he felt he was about to be sick.

After some minutes the eerie quiet was broken with shouts of "Prepare to receive Cavalry. Company form squares. Form Squares." Robert and Jasper went through another drill they had performed hundreds of times before. The Company formed squares of men all facing outwards. Jasper and Robert were in a front row kneeling with their bayonets jammed forward. This wall of steel would meet the advancing horses. It was the only way infantrymen could defend themselves against a cavalry charge as no horse will try to go through or even jump such an obstacle

The sight of the approaching French cavalry was awesome. The breastplates gleamed in the watery sunlight now breaking through, and the horsehair plumes on the helmets were whipping in the wind. The advancing charge seemed irresistible as the horses' powerful muscles rippled under glistening coats and hooves gouged the earth beneath them. Robert knew he was about to die.

The French were experienced and executed their charge with skill. A square next to Robert's Company broke as a stricken horse fell through the line on one side. French cavalry immediately streamed through the gap. It was a death sentence. The square broke completely as foot soldiers were attacked from front and back. Caught in the open the Company was annihilated. Long swords plunged into faces, necks and bodies with horrifying ease.

Captain Honsworth remained in the corner of their square. Although he appeared perfectly composed with an air of thoughtful boredom, his face was white. As Cuirassiers reached within twenty yards of his rigid square he barked out the order, "Sergeants, Commence Firing!"

Instantly a roar from Sergeant Hollis came from immediately behind Jasper and Robert - "FIRE!" The seemingly irresistible force was met with a withering volley of musket fire. The air filled with the dull, metallic ring of musket ball penetrating heavy breastplates.

Captain Honsworth's Company maintained discipline and their fire was well-directed and brought men and horses down resulting in confusion in the French ranks. French officers bravely did all in their power to re-organise their men and they charged again. English rifle fire was directed at the officers and they were cut down.

There are times that could be said to be pivotal in men's lives.

A French cuirassier, his eyes blazing, desperately drove forward at the English ranks. Within just a few feet away from the kneeling Jasper, his horse reared in terror away from the bristling bayonets. Shots into the magnificent beast killed it instantly. Its momentum carried it forward and it collapsed onto Tom Faulkner. The rider leapt forward and plunged his sword down on Jasper's head. Robert instinctively drove his bayonet upwards into the falling Frenchman and dug deep into his body under his armour through his groin.

Then from a deafening confusion of charging horses and volleys of musket fire everywhere went still. The silence was broken only the screams and whimpering of men and the pathetic neighing of dying horses. The French had been driven off and a cease-fire had been given. Captain Honsworth was still astride his horse but his right arm hung useless at his side, covered in blood from a French musket shot. Oblivious to any discomfort he gave the order "Sergeants get the men back into line abreast. Wounded to the rear."

Robert by this time had spun around to tend to Jasper who was bleeding profusely but was still conscious. Tom Faulkner was scrambling out from beneath the French horse. He was cut, bruised and winded but otherwise unharmed. "Tom, help me with Jasper." Sergeant Hollis seeing their efforts said crisply, "Right lads, get him with the rest of the wounded. The doctors will need help after this. Stay there and do what you can to help them."

There were carts being loaded with casualties and Robert and Tom quickly got Jasper onto one. A few more shattered bodies were loaded and they then went as escorts to the field hospital in a nearby village.

Robert and Tom worked around the clock helping the doctors and medical orderlies. There was little they could do in many cases. Two days later they were swamped with more casualties as the greatest battle of all took place close to where they were in the village of Waterloo. Streams of the wounded were being brought back and at one point Robert hurried over as George came through the door nursing a blood soaked cloth around his hand. "Good god, what's happened to you?"

George snorted. "Not sure really, I was in the thick of it and was about to reload when, it must have been a musket ball, but suddenly my hand was covered in a mass of blood. Strange," he frowned, "it doesn't hurt."

A doctor was hurrying passed but seeing George stopped, looked quickly at George's hand "You've lost two fingers." He pointed to an orderly. "Get him to put a suture on that and get it bound up." He looked at Robert. "It will hurt, probably very soon. Give him brandy from this house's store." The Doctor was about to move on but said to George. "There's a lot worse than you here. Once you been seen to, your help will be needed."

Before moving to get treated, George frowned with concern. "I saw you and Tom carry off Jasper. It didn't look good. How is he..... he is alive, isn't he?"

Robert looked down. "He isn't good at all. He hasn't regained consciousness yet." He shook his head. "I thought he would be the one to survive this sodding war. Not me."

Robert was in the field hospital station where Dr Arthur Bell was the main surgeon in charge. The station was hampered by a lack of proper facilities. Even Robert with an untrained eye could see there was a lack of medical supplies, and fresh, clean water. As it had poured with rain the night before the whole area was sodden.

Robert couldn't tell how effective the regimental surgeons were in alleviating suffering. As there were so many men to treat, Dr Bell took the view, fearing infection followed by almost inevitable death, he would amputate limbs immediately. He would not pause to give a thought of whether they could have been saved. Unfortunately in the majority of these cases there was still infection or the patient would die of shock from the amputation itself.

Robert helped with holding down the amputees and was also given the task of helping with bloodletting in an effort to stop gangrene. Unfortunately, even though the doctors insisted on persevering with this treatment he noticed very quickly that the wounded man very often developed rapid, shallow breathing and cool, clammy skin. Death would follow very soon. There was no time to show emotion before there would be a call for him to rush over and help somewhere else.

Thankfully, many of the locals, especially the women, helped care for the wounded. Many of the wounded were left in the streets because the houses commandeered could not cope with the numbers of men needing attention.

One thing that Robert and the other two would each never forget was the silent heroism of the greater part of the sufferers. There were many stories they could tell of the bravery and fortitude in the face of pain. One instance filled Robert with national pride when Lord Raglan was brought in with a shattered arm. He told the doctor "Do you duty, man!" Not a sound then came from his Lordship's mouth until his arm was amputated. He then called out in his usual casual voice, "Soldier. Don't carry away the arm until I have taken off the ring."

A week passed as Jasper lay semi-conscious and delirious from a high fever. He had been able to dodge the main weight of the thrust from the sword but his right eye was badly damaged. His brain had not been harmed but the open wound across his skull had become infected. Their was little Robert or anyone else could do apart from trying to reduce his fever.

Jasper's innate strength helped him to survive and after a week he finally regained consciousness. Robert saw him stirring and was immediately by his side. Jasper managed a weak smile, "God, I feel awful. What happened?"

Robert grunted, "You got in the way of a French Cavalry officer." Robert looked away into the distance then added without any satisfaction in his voice, "Don't worry, he won't be doing that again."

Neither spoke for a moment, then Jasper said quietly, "Thanks."

Robert smiled briefly "That's what friends are for." He looked up as Tom Faulkner walked passed and gave him a thumbs up sign. Turning back to Jasper he grinned, "Incidentally, not that you had much hair left in any case, they've shaved your scalp."

Robert looked around to see if he was needed anywhere. All appeared quiet, so he lowered his voice and continued, "You may not think so right now but your wound may be the luckiest thing to happen to you since you joined this goddam army." Before Jasper could ask why, Robert carried on "There has been one helluva of a battle a few miles from here whilst you have been lolling in bed." He grinned, "Thank the Lord, the crapauds has taken a helluva beating. One of the doctors has told me that he thinks Napoleon has been captured." He gave Jasper's hand a tap "In any case old friend your army days are over." He looked around to make sure that they were not overheard then almost whispered, "Also our kit is safe and nothing is missing."

Jasper nodded, "Well that's good at least."

Jasper's wound looked horrific with a cleft having been gouged across his skull reaching his right eye, which was now sightless. The disfigurement across the socket was such that at the suggestion of Dr Bell he put on a black eye patch. Robert looked at his life long friend and saw a big man with a dark tan from his three and half years in the Spanish sun, shaven head and black eye patch. He was an intimidating sight.

It took two weeks following the battle before all the wounded had been treated, with survivors being sent to larger hospitals. Finally its was a day to clear up and wash down the field hospitals. Limbs and other body parts were buried and corpses were left outside the village of Waterloo for disposal by the burial parties from the battlefield. Floors were scrubbed as much as possible but any other cleaning or debris were left to the locals.

At the end of the day Robert, Tom and George were lounging on some farm equipment with Jasper propped on a bench by the house door. Each had tin mugs containing generous drafts of brandy acquired from a local cellar. Tom nudged Robert "Look out, officers coming." He peered closely at the figures. "Yes, better watch out I heard Dr Bell talk with that other guy earlier. He's The Duke's main Doctor, Sir James McGrigor."

As the officers approached Dr Bell was heard to say, "Yes Sir, its was horrendous. I'll be quite frank with you my clothes were stiff with blood and my arms were weak from the exertion of using my knife." He paused "Excuse me, Sir James."

"Quite alright. Carry on Arthur."

Dr Bell addressed the four lads. "You four men are to rejoin your Regiment. They will based back at Calais." He nodded to Jasper. "Take some means to carry your comrade here, he's not fit to walk very far yet. Make sure the locals look after you on the way, they should be friendly enough. Take your time your Regiment won't be back there themselves yet."

He went to resume his conversation with Sir James, but stopped and looked hard at each of them. "You men did a tremendous job doing what you could do for fallen comrades. On behalf of them and us thank you very much."

Sir James grunted. "Yes, so I've heard. Its been a bad business. Bad business." He moved forward and shook the hand of each of them. The officers turned and resumed their briefing.

Left on their own, the remnants of the East Dorsets raised their mugs and drank a toast - to themselves. The next day they started their trek, not march, slowly back to the coast.

"Next to a battle lost, the greatest misery is a battle gained."
Duke of Wellington: surveying the battlefield after Waterloo

CHAPTER NINE
Control Planing

British defence spending in 1815 alone amounted to £73 million (the equivalent of £266 billion at current values), creating huge debts owed to the bankers who had loaned the money. Some of the UK's current debt dates back to war bonds originally issued in 1815 (Guardian, October 2014)

"This remarkable coup could only have been achieved by a complex series of dealings, many of which were encased in a secrecy which cannot now be penetrated."In only 5 years (1810-1815), Nathan Rothschild became the main banker for the British government and the Bank of England.

The three Bankers settled down at the oak meeting table and the eldest indicated he was ready to start. Although it was a warm late summer's day and they were on the 1st floor the window had been pulled shut to ensure that they were not overheard.

Amit casually strummed the table to indicate he was about to start. "It is now a couple of months since the defeat of Napoleon at the Battle of Waterloo. He chuckled. "or as the Prussians call it of the Battle of La Belle Alliance. and the French - Mont Saint-Jean." A gesture with hand indicated he was serious once again. "It has been an excellent period for us as we followed our financing of Wellington in the Peninsular with his campaign cumulating at Waterloo. Also I am please to report that our brother Nathan enabled Napoleon's escape from Elba and. the funding of his army. Nathan conducted our funding through the Eubard Banking House of Paris."

Solomon intervened. "Excellent progress. Also I'm pleased that our business through the London Stock

Exchange after Waterloo was more like substantial rather than satisfactory." (See below)

Amit lowered his head with a self-congratulatory smile. Resuming in a serious manner. "Previously stated civil disturbances have increased and the price of food has risen to a very high point, as a result of several bad harvests. The problems with labour will be further exacerbated by the imminent demobilisation of about 300,00 soldiers and sailors"

He shook his head. "I'm afraid the Government is not responding in a helpful way. It is about to pass a Bill, The Corn Laws, which will in effect keep the price of food high so as to protect the British farmers. Also in response to the increasing unrest it has also passed a Bill, The Six Acts, three of which are expressly to quash insurrection rather than deal with it."

"So do we expect matters to get worse."

"Possibly or even probably. However, the British do not naturally 'Revolt'. They will moan, they will march and they will also at times riot. Only twice has there been full scale rebellion. Once was 400 years ago. It was called the Peasants Revolt. It was caused by tax increases; the peasants didn't pay tax, it was a Middle Class Revolt. Then 150 years ago there was a full scale Civil War. This was Parliament against the King. Members of Parliament cannot be called peasants or working class they were again almost mainly from the Middle Class. Out of that Civil War came what they call The Glorious Revolution of 1688 and signing by the King of The Bill of Rights. Just to emphasise the point let me read it to you"

"It stated that. "it is illegal for the Crown to suspend or dispense with the law, to levy money without parliamentary assent, or to raise an army in peacetime, and it insists on the due process of Law in criminal trials." For the Crown now read Government.

Also in the last century we have had what has been called The Enlightenment. This has seen a period of huge change in thought and reason. We have had centuries of custom and tradition being brushed aside in favour of exploration, individualism, tolerance and scientific endeavour in tandem with developments in industry."

Amit was now in full flow. "As I have said before, this country over this coming century will see the emergence of an ever increasing Middle Class. They will be entrepreneurs, men who will see opportunities and not accept the status quo. They will be from the poorest classes and over time will bring in reforms. The existing ruling class will be forced to concede to changes in society. Britain, despite its current problems, will become the wealthiest country in the world. A position it could hold for a hundred years."

There was silence as Amit's words were digested. He stood up and walked over to the window and stared outside. He turn round and with earnestness in his voice. "Our family has retained the philosophy of our father that we must endeavour to control a country's money supply. The richer a country becomes the more control is in our hands."

He went back to his chair. "It is imperative for us to identify and then encourage, support and of course finance enterprising individuals around the country. So far we have a few such men. A couple in London, one each in the north east, Manchester, Dorset and Birmingham. These men must be aware of local issues and investment opportunities that will quell any discontent amongst the lower sort by providing security for new and existing local industries."

He looked from brother to brother. "Also," he stopped and gently laid his outspread hands on the table to emphasise his final point. "They must be far-sighted enough to embrace the very real revolution that will transform this country…and the rest of the world - transport!"

* * *

[1] *An apocryphal story says that the Rothschilds, knowing that information is power, stationed a trusted agent near the battle field. As soon as the battle was over their Agent quickly returned to London, delivering the news to the Banker 24 hours ahead of Wellington's courier.*

A victory by Napoleon would have devastated Britain's financial system. Rothschilds stationed himself in his usual place next to an ancient pillar in the stock market and began openly to sell huge numbers of British Government Bonds.

Reading this to mean that Napoleon must have won, everyone started to sell their British Bonds as well. The bottom fell out of the market until you couldn't hardly give them away. Meanwhile Rothschilds began to secretly buy up all the hugely devalued bonds at a fraction of what they were worth a few hours before.

2

CHAPTER TEN
Escape and Romance

Langton Matravers - January 1815

Bill Tubbs wasn't as clever as he thought. He was having an adulterous affair with a woman in Swanage and he wasn't subtle enough, or cared enough to keep it a secret.

Ted Edmunds had kept at a discreet distance since Dot had married. The day she found out about Tubb's affair she passed Ted on Stonehouse Hill. He saw her eyes were red rimmed, obviously from tears. He stopped her as she tried to hurry passed him. "Dotty, what's up?"

"Nothing. Nothing." She tried to escape from his concern.

"No, please tell me." He pulled her gently aside into a small footpath where they couldn't been seen.

Dot burst into tears. Ted put his arms around her and she buried her face in his chest. "Is it about Tubbs and that woman in Swanage?"

Dot looked up and sniffed as she nodded.

"He's a bastard – oh sorry, I didn't mean to swear." He looked into Dot's eyes, he knew he loved her. It wrenched his stomach when he thought she would be his wife if he hadn't been so slow. "If I could get you away from him, would you go?"

"Ted you're so kind. But how? I don't know if I dare."

"My cousin lives in Winchester and she has been a housekeeper in a solicitor's house in the town. Her husband has lost his job and they are going to go to America to start a new life over there." He held Dot's look. "I'm sure that I could get you to replace her."

"What about the girls? I couldn't leave them with that man."

"I will get my sister to tell them your husband has died and you are looking for work. Winchester is fifty miles away. No one there knows anything about a small village this far away."

Dot stood staring at Ted. "Ted, how things could have been so different."

Ted's own eyes started to water. "What has happened - has happened." He paused, "At least for now anyway. Dotty I will make arrangements. I will get word to my cousin."

Dot stood staring into space then she made up her mind. "Yes please, could you."

Ted did not let Dot down and a week later, whilst Bill Tubbs was working at the Crack Lane quarry, she slipped out of the village making sure that no one saw her. Ted had found out that Charlie Heywood was going to London on business. Charlie had bought a light four wheel Phaeton carriage that was drawn by a single horse. He was more than willing to let Dot and her children join him and they crammed on board. He left them in Winchester on his way through the town.

The solicitor and his wife, Hugh and Mabel Lambrick were a friendly couple and as they were childless they were more than happy for Dot to move in with the two girls in the servants quarters. Dot settled into a comfortable, albeit hard working life. She was pleased to realise that she would not wake with that feeling churning in the pit of her stomach warning her of impending misery. Over the ensuing months, memories of daily beatings, and being forced to do her wifely duties in bed, began to fade.

September 1815

Charlie Heywood took a final draft of coffee. He idly gazed around at the hive of activity that was normal for the Gloucester Coffee House in Piccadilly. Although it was still early in the morning, travellers were gathering to board their coaches bound for various towns and cities around the country. Everyone appeared to be set on his or her own mission and there was much hurrying and scurrying about. Charlie had already identified his Mail coach in its scarlet and black livery. It had its mailbags piled on its roof, and luggage for some of his fellow travellers was being loaded in a rear compartment.

Charlie took his watch from his waistcoat pocket and frowned. He had agreed to escort the sister of the owner of three cargo boats that plied their trade between Swanage, Poole and London. Over the last few years he had come to know Ambrose Tillson very well. It was a reciprocal business arrangement – Charlie had negotiated a keen price for transporting the stone from his quarry whilst Ambrose was assured of this regular business. The guard on Charlie's coach blew a shrill commanding note on his horn and then bellowed out his invitation. "All passengers for the Winchester and Poole mail coach board now, please."

Charlie looked anxiously at his watch again, shrugged and moved to embark.

There was a sudden shout and a flustered lady emerged from the throng followed by a wheezing manservant straining under the weight of her luggage. "Is this the Mail Coach for Poole?" She was able to breathlessly ask. "Please wait."

The guard puffed out his chest in self-importance. "Hurry along please The Post Office is always on time and will wait for no one."

Charlie stepped forward for this was obviously the lady that was to be in his charge. "Hold those horses my man." He gestured to the manservant. "Put the luggage in the back," then to the lady. "Miss Edith Tillson I assume." He gave a slight bow of the head.

"Oh dear, yes. Are you Mr Charles Heywood?" She could hardly speak as she gasped for breath.

"At you service, Ma'am" Charlie proffered his arm so as to assist her to climb aboard the coach

"Thank you Mr Heywood." She embarked and rather inelegantly sat back in her seat.

Charlie stepped into the coach. "The name is Charlie, Ma'am." He gave a friendly re-assuring smile. Edith Tillson mumbled another thank you and looked down to study her hands folded on her lap.

Charlie looked around at the three other passengers who had already boarded. One had a constant superior scowl, another in uniform just casually watched in amusement the seeming chaos outside of the Coffee House. The other just sat, sweating, in his corner seat looking out of the carriage window, obviously with his mind elsewhere.

The coachman bellowed to all within range. "Make way, make way for the King's Mail." There was a crack from his whip and the four horses moved forward with such enthusiasm that three passengers were almost flung forward in their seats whilst the other two were rammed backwards.

The coach careered through the crowds with the guard giving blasts on his horn if it appeared not everyone was aware of their approach. It wasn't long before London had been left behind. It is not a trait of a travelling Englishman to break into conversation with strangers even when thrown together in close proximity. The first hour passed in silence with each having their own thoughts to reflect upon.As Charlie bounced in his seat he smiled to himself as he thought with a certain pride and certainly satisfaction over the last two years. His first landing of a shipment of brandy had gone like a dream. Jack Winbow was paid exactly as arranged. The ship carrying the merchandise was met by a group of men from Charlie's quarry who were grateful for the extra money and the distribution to the pre-arranged buyers was completed within the week. He had turned in a very good profit all within a month from start to finish.

Jack Winbow was pleased that the business was completed without mishaps and regular shipments then followed. Word soon spread and Charlie had become known as a trusted organiser who knew his business well and could be relied upon. Charlie was now the man to contact for business along the Purbeck coast.

The carriage gave a violent jolt over the newly constructed road which provided the occasional pothole. He looked across to Edith Tillson and mouthed, "Are you alright?"

Edith nodded and looked down quickly again at her hands. Charlie idly scanned the other passengers and as was his habit, he pigeon-holed them. The man who had the superior scowl, he judged as a professional man. Charlie came to the silent conclusion that he was probably a solicitor. The uniformed gentleman was obviously a man of the sea – not a captain but certainly an officer.

Charlie's smile faded when he studied the third man. To say he was portly would give him too much dignity. He was fat. His waistcoat was stretched above his stomach to reveal his undershirt which itself was barely kept tucked into his trousers. All his clothes had seen better days. The man sat staring out of the carriage window and Charlie noticed a doleful look in his eyes. It was obvious that tragedy or ill-fortune had reduced this man. Despite the early hour he took continual swigs from a brandy bottle that he was clutching as it rested upon his thigh.

Another jolt came just as the brandy was being raised again. The man missed his mouth and brandy trickled down his chin and onto his waistcoat. It also splashed the dress of Edith Tillson. Charlie leant forward offering a clean handkerchief that he quickly produced from his topcoat pocket. Edith took it but looked embarrassed preferring not to be the centre of attention.

As Edith wiped the brandy from her dress, Charlie looked at her more closely for the first time. She was dressed in a sombre dark dress with an equally non-obtrusive top coat and bonnet. She was young, possibly in her mid twenties, slightly on the plump side. Her face with the modern fashion of Rose Lip Salve on her lips was quite attractive. Her hair was pulled back into a tight bun.

"Thank you, sir – eh Charlie." She quickly finished wiping her dress, and returned the handkerchief. "Most kind."

The perpetrator of her discomfort tried to apologise. "I am most dreadfully sorry Ma'am. It's just the coach jolted ….." He stopped as he realised he was saying the obvious but would get no sympathy from his reluctant fellow travellers. "Oh heck I'm sorry." His voice trailed off. He went to take another swig but stopped and tried to concentrate on the passing scenery but quickly closed his eyes in anguish.

Edith saw his discomfort and like Charlie, she recognised that the man was down on his luck. "That's quite alright, sir. It was a mishap and there's no harm done."

Charlie was taken with Edith's kindness and he felt that this was the opportunity to make conversation. He was after all her escort for the journey. "Your brother told me that you have been in London for a few years. Are you returning to Poole just to visit Ambrose or is this a permanent move?"

Edith hesitated, she felt awkward that she should be discussing her private life and the conversation would be for the others in the carriage to overhear. "I have been the Companion of a titled lady for three years. Unfortunately she died recently and there was no employment left for me." Her eyes flicked to the other passengers regretting that they now knew her situation.

She was relieved of further discomfort as the coach gave another lurch and a belch was forced from the drinking man. The solicitor used his favourite expression of a superior scowl whilst the naval officer issued a reprimand. "Sir, control yourself. There's a lady present."

There followed a period of uncomfortable silence. Charlie decided to try to relieve the tension, by turning to the naval man who he deduced would know the details of their journey. "I understand that our journey will be broken by stopping for the night at The Kings Head, in a small village called Hursley just passed Winchester. I believe the accommodation should be satisfactory as it has only just been built."

He was rewarded for his efforts at conversation with a grunt of agreement. "So I believe, sir."

As they pulled up outside The Kings Head a group of twenty to thirty men were on the village green shouting and waving their fists. On a makeshift platform of a tree stump a better dressed man was obviously provoking his audience to their anger.

The solicitor shook his head. "There's more and more of this unseemly behaviour."

The navy opined that they should be clapped in irons and given a good lashing. He looked at Charlie. "The lower sort need to be reminded of their place." Edith looked away but Charlie smiled inwardly. 'Little does he know of my upbringing. Glancing at Edith he recollected her brother Ambrose saying that his father was an ordinary fisherman as well.'

After the overnight interruption to their journey all five travellers climbed on board the coach hoping that the time to Poole would pass quickly.

After a couple of hours, Charlie judging that they were nearing their destination, smiled encouraging at Edith. "It will not be long before you will be back home." Edith smiled weakly in acknowledgment and not a little relief. Charlie felt drawn to make one further statement. "I have to visit Ambrose next week on business. We will no doubt meet again then after this journey is over."

The obvious advance was greeted in turn by; a superior scowl, bored indifference and a swig of brandy. Edith blushed and said nothing.

November 1815

Charlie casually strolled along the quay in Poole taking in the bustle of ships being loaded and unloaded to and from the line of warehouses. One of the larger towns in Dorset the magnificent houses and public buildings were proof of the prosperity enjoyed as a result of its north Atlantic fishing trade.

The first week in Novemmber had brought a bright day with puffs of white cloud scudding across the sky in obedience to a chilling wind. A sudden gust whipped open Charlie's top coat which he hastily re-fastened. He espied Ambrose Tillson who was supervising the unloading of fish from Newfoundland. "Good Morning to you Ambrose. Busy as usual, I see."

Ambrose quickly finished giving instructions to one of his men, then spun round to respond to the greeting. "Ah, Good Day to you Charlie." They shook hands and Ambrose indicated that they walk along the harbour in the direction of the Custom House. On the way they both acknowledged various greetings from other merchants, ship-owners and businessmen.

After a few moments Charlie looked at Ambrose interestedly. "The landing of fish from Newfoundland has been going on for years. I've noticed recently though that it does seem to be quieter here these days. Is there a problem?"

"Yes, very much so." He frowned. "It's quite serious. It has been since last year, when the war ended. Our trade across the north Atlantic had flourished especially all through the war. Portugal, Italy and Spain relied upon their supplies of dried fish provided by us Poole merchants. Our navy made sure that all other ships were stopped from this trading. Peace has meant that the French and Americans could now fish the waters and take over many of the other services we provided. Within a few years many of the merchants could cease trading and face ruin.

Charlie was concerned. "You're one of an elite group, what they call 'merchant princes of Poole' aren't you. Can't you all do something together to stop the decline?

Ambrose grunted. "No, not really My business goes back over a hundred years but the fish business - the 'merchant prince of Poole' as it used to be will stop with me."

"Charlie tried to be encouraging. "Come on you will keep going and then when you have children they will take over from you."

"No…..no., that won't happen." Ambrose looked slightly embarrassed. He took a deep breath. "I have seen it coming. Businesses like yours, that are supplying stone merchants in London, and others around the country are fast growing. It will become my main trade." They maintained a brisk pace in the cold wind and upon reaching Lilliput Street turned away from the harbour in the direction of Ambrose's residence. "Of course, I will keep a couple of fishing boats that catch cod way out across the Atlantic. That trade will never entirely go away."

They arrived at Ambrose's front door and a man servant was in immediate attendance. As they passed through the hallway into the Library, where Ambrose conducted his business, he turned to speak over his shoulder, "Stephen, please bring some coffee for Mr Heywood and myself." He

144

gestured towards a chair away from his desk and Charlie sat down.

Ambrose glanced at a couple of invoices that had been placed on his desk. He grunted and muttered to himself, "Bannister must be joking if he thinks I'm going to pay at that rate." He shook his head then went to sit alongside Charlie. "Before we speak of business, can I thank you for your kindness in escorting Edith on her journey from London."

"That was a pleasure, sir. May I ask, how is Miss Tillson?"

"She is very well." He paused, there was a twinkle in his eye. "Edith has asked that when you next called whether she may thank you herself." His twinkle had developed into a grin. "In fact, I'm sure that she has instructed Stephen to inform her the moment you arrived."

Charlie felt a sudden lightness of the heart, something he had not as yet experienced. The door opened with Stephen carrying a tray of cups and a coffee pot. He was closely followed by Edith who nearly overtook him as he crossed the room.

Looking directly at Ambrose she said rather unnecessarily. "Dear brother, Stephen tells me we have a guest." Charlie and Ambrose both rose to their feet. "Ah, Mr Heywood, it is indeed good to meet you again." She gave a curtsy and despite her outward bravado there was a slight blush to her cheeks.

Charlie noted Edith had again applied the fashionable Rose Lip Salve. Charlie found that he was quite taken by her appearance.

Edith continued. "I was most grateful for your Company on the coach."

"Ma'am it was a pleasure." Charlie responded gallantly. This was followed by a short silence as neither of the erstwhile travellers knew where to go with the conversation.

Any awkwardness was avoided as Ambrose, with his grin even wider, intervened. "Charlie, we have here in Poole a most delightful and active music society. We have the next recital on Monday. Edith and I would be delighted for you to join us. That is of course if it would amuse you, and of course if you do not have a prior engagement."

Charlie had that feeling again which was most disconcerting for such a man of business. Without hesitation, he replied. "That is indeed most kind sir. I would be delighted to accompany you. Next Monday is quite free." Charlie made a mental note to get a message to his quarry manager to cancel their weekly Monday evening meeting.

Ambrose gave a satisfied nod. "Well that's agreed then. If you would kindly meet us here at six in the evening it is but a short walk to the recital room." He looked at his sister with a fatherly stern look. "Now Edith, Charlie and I have business to discuss which I'm sure would be too boring for you."

Edith gave a momentary frown but a smile immediately returned. She turned to Charlie and gave a deep curtsy and bowed her head. "Mr Heywood – Charlie, it has been a pleasure to meet you again and I look forward to next Monday."

Charlie was confused by his feelings but responded with a bow of his head. Edith rose, glanced at her brother, a filial look of gratitude passed between them and she turned and swept out of the room.

She left both men smiling albeit with each having differing thoughts. Ambrose then spoke. "Charlie, please be seated. We have much to discuss. You say you have a new contract for a supply of more stone to James Tyler in London. You have done well as he is now the largest stone merchant in the country."

The morning then passed with discussion of quantities and timetables until both men parted company satisfied that they had conducted mutually beneficial business. When Charlie left and walked back towards the harbour he decided he was definitely in a good mood.

January 1816

"Damn!"

Charlie picked himself up. "Would you believe it?" He looked down to see his knees caked in slush and his gloves were sopping wet. It was the first week in January and heavy snow had fallen across the south of England. Charlie was at the door of Ambrose Tillson's house.

The evening spent at the Poole Music Society's monthly recital in December had proved so pleasurable he had agreed to return for the next Meeting. Charlie had already made up his mind to suggest, if it was not too forward of him, to make it a regular arrangement.

Charlie had determined to be in Poole for Monday in each month but the snow had delayed him and he was late. The weather had made the journey across country horrendous and because he had tried to hurry he had slipped over in the snow.

Charlie was brushing himself down as the door opened. Ambrose appeared and immediately looked concerned. He moved forward to take Charlie's arm. "Are you alright Charlie? ."

"I'm so sorry to be late Ambrose, the weather is awful."

"That is perfectly alright, please do come on inside" Ambrose started to guide Charlie through the doorway.

"Thank you, but please, I'm perfectly fine. I fear that it is only my dignity that is wounded. Landing on one's hands and knees is always discomforting. There is only the light from your windows to see where to step, it's difficult to keep one's balance."

Charlie removed his gloves and they were taken by the ever attendant Stephen. Ambrose solicitously ushered Charlie into the Drawing Room where there was a roaring fire. Charlie looked down again. "No harm done. I'll dry myself in front of this welcome fire, if I may." He faced the fire spreading his palms forward then rubbing them together, "It is bitterly cold outside, it's good to be inside. It's a few years since we've had so much snow but it does always seem to catch everyone unawares."

Ambrose joined Charlie at the fireside and proffered Charlie a large glass of brandy. "This will warm the inside as well."

"Much appreciated, I must say. Your good health, sir." He raised his glass then paused. "I believe a toast to the new year would be in order."

Ambrose smiled in agreement and retrieved his glass from the drinks table. ""Here is to the year -1816. May it bring us all good luck." They each took a large draft and Charlie could feel the welcome warming sensation go down and he gently beat his chest with his fist.

The door suddenly burst open and Edith entered appearing very upset. She went straight to Charlie. "Stephen tells me that you have had an accident. Are you hurt?"

Charlie had a further warm feeling this one not induced by the brandy. "I'm quite well. Your brother has given me the proper medicine." He raised his glass.

Ambrose intervened. "I believe, in view of the late hour and the weather outside, our visit to the recital be should cancelled this month. We will miss the start of the recital in any case."

Edith looked disappointed, then her face lit up. "I shall instruct cook to prepare a meal for us all and we shall spend the evening at home." She thought for a moment then turned to Charlie. "I shall also tell Stephen to prepare a room for you. You cannot go out again in this weather."

Charlie waited for Ambrose to give his approval of Edith's plan.

Ambrose smiled. "Of course. That is an excellent idea."

"Most kind. I shall not impose upon your hospitality long in the morning as I have to go back to Swanage for a meeting tomorrow morning."

Edith spun around saying as she left the room, "That's settled. I shall speak with cook and Stephen."

When they were left alone once again, Ambrose took a more serious tone. "I know that my sister looks forward to this evening with much anticipation." He looked directly at Charlie. "We are both men of the world. I am In Loco Parentis for Edith. As I believe you are aware, her mother died of a fever shortly after she was born and very sadly our father died soon afterwards."

Charlie looked down in polite acknowledgement of past tragedies.

Ambrose continued. "I do all in my power to ensure that Edith is not hurt in any way. May I ask you what your intentions are in regard to my sister?"

For once Charlie was on the back foot. He was a man of business and was totally unsure of himself in these situations. He found himself making an admission that he had not prepared. "I find Edith's company most agreeable." He paused to give himself time and he further surprised himself. "I am not so sure of matters of the heart as opposed to those governed by the head. However, I do know that, with your permission, I would like to call upon Edith more often." He paused again. "It is only three months since we first met of course, I do not wish Edith to feel as though I am rushing her into commitments she may not wish to make."

Ambrose chuckled. "I do not think that you should worry on that account."

"I thank you then Ambrose. As I say, with your permission I will call upon Edith whenever I can and we shall see in the fullness of time what becomes of it."

Ambrose's chuckle became a short laugh. "It is indeed good that you do not carry out your business affairs with such impulsiveness."

Charlie looked embarrassed, then almost as a parry to the intrusion on his own thoughts he looked at Ambrose. "Do you have someone that you are visiting?"

Ambrose looked away quickly, then said quietly. "No, I have not met....." he faltered, "anyone - a lady as yet."

Charlie looked sharply at his host and was about to speak when Edith returned. "All is set, we shall dine in half and hour. Stephen is also preparing a room." She went to her brother and linked arms with him as she looked at him enquiringly. Ambrose's relaxed demeanour returned, and he gave her a reassuring nod.

Stephen had placed an extra few candles in the Dining Room as well as stoking up the fire all of which helped to lighten the dark corners of the room. Outside there was no movement in Lilliput Street. The good people of Poole were staying out of the cold and not venturing on to the dangerous snow that was under foot. Inside, the room was quiet apart from polite conversation as they ate a meal of jugged hare with potatoes followed by Apple Dumplings. The evening passed pleasurably for all as the conversation ranged from the serious to sometimes, flippant.

Edith was good company and Charlie began to realise that there may be more in life than the next business deal. As the talk flowed without his immediate need for input, his mind wandered to where the evening, and his conversation with Ambrose earlier, would lead. He was not inexperienced in respect of a physical relationship. He had spent time with the daughter of one of his customers in London but it was a casual affair in which neither party saw or wanted more than a brief dalliance. He had started to wonder whether he would ever meet a woman he wanted to be with for the rest of his life.

As Charlie looked at Edith he felt an attraction as she seemed to be able to participate in the discussion and most certainly had opinions of her own. The attraction was also not just of the mind.

"Charlie, you are very quiet. I trust the meal was satisfactory or is there something else troubling you?" Edith was worried. Was she being too forward?

"No, not at all. The meal was delightful. In fact a veritable feast compared to that which my Ma was able to provide when I was a lad. God Bless her." He straightened himself in his seat as he realised he had come to a decision. "I was just considering that business will be bringing me to Poole quite often. With your permission Ambrose, I was thinking that if your time allowed, Edith, we may take a stroll along the harbour some times and I could possibly call upon you of an evening?"

Ambrose was quick to respond before Edith could speak for herself. "Charlie, you are most welcome. I'm sure Edith would be delighted to meet with you."

Charlie's reaction was a pleasant inner feeling of delight. The evening proved to be a success and Edith went to her bed that night in a merry mood.

CHAPTER ELEVEN

London Life

Autumn 1815

The four erstwhile recruits from the field hospital made their way uneventfully and pleasantly to Calais. The local people were happy that their homes had stopped being used as a route for various armies marching across northern Europe. Billeting at various places they were able to spend many pleasant autumn evenings enjoying the local wine and brandy.

On one such evening George was lounging on a pile of sacks appreciatively sipping a glass of red wine. Looking across to Jasper and Robert, similarly on comfortable perches he asked casually, "Have you enjoyed my attempts to show you both how to read and write."

"Yes. Thanks it's been really interesting. I've enjoyed them." Robert responded.

"And you Jasper?"

"Oh yes, very much."

"Will it help you when you're out of the army.?"

Jasper frowned and said, "I hope so. Even just for the enjoyment of reading. The trouble is there aren't many books that we could afford to buy let alone know which are interesting."

George grinned and turned gesturing in the direction of their kitbags and raised his eyebrows, "That shouldn't be a problem. At least not for some time. I didn't mean that though, enjoyment was not the point."

Jasper ignored the gesture. "What is the point? "How will it help us."

"Well, you're now able to read Notices on walls or shop windows. If someone wants you to sign a contract you'll know what it contains. Remember you had to sign with a cross when you joined the army. You'll also find newspapers to read in coffee houses - if you ever visit them and cheap pamphlets are always on sale."

"That's true." Robert nodded

'Alright, fair enough. To be able to read will be useful I'm sure. Getting to the nitty gritty though it won't help us to earn money." Jasper paused, and the others knew what was coming next. "When we get back to England it will be the same old thing."

Tom who usually kept quiet at these times, spoke up. "A few of the lads that joined us before Waterloo said it was almost impossible to get work of any sort, let alone anything you might enjoy."

George frowned and held up his hand "Wait, before you say anymore," he went over to his kitbag and pulled out a book and handed it to Jasper. "Try to see if you can make any sense out this book. If you find it difficult in places." He stopped and raised his hand. "Sorry I'm not being rude. It's called The Rights of Man by Thomas Paine. He wrote it just after the crapauds had their revolution."

"Thanks." Jasper took the book carefully and with almost reverence opened it to the first page.

"Don't start now. When you're on your own and can concentrate." George thought for a moment. "The first part is really Paine arguing against a British member of Parliament, Edmund Burke and his support of the French Revolution. Skip that and go to the second half. If you come across anything you don't understand, read that bit again then press on. Just try to get a general grasp on what he's suggesting."

Tom was pleased he had been able to contribute to the conversation for once, reached over behind him and turned back with a bottle of wine in his hand. "More important than all that stuff. More wine anyone?"

All agreed more wine was necessary and it was duly consumed for the rest of the evening. The conversation rolled around any amusing events that had happened whilst they had been in the army.

Over the next few weeks Jasper's head was stuck in the book whenever he could get the time.

Eventually one evening the four friends were billeted in the outhouse of a farm. The good farmer had supplied a meal and told them to help themselves to as much wine and brandy they may need. With the meal consumed and wine replenished twice, Jasper suddenly stood up and went to his kitbag to retrieve George's book.

"That was really good." he said with satisfaction.

Robert grinned. "Did you really understand it? I saw you frown loads of times and go back a page…or two, and re-read bits"

If Jasper smiled wryly,. "Yes, well, there were so many people I've never heard of, but they seem so important." He looked at George with a triumphant look on his face. "Besides that, he says what I have been saying all the time. It's us who do all the work and we never get a say on who rules us."

George looked straight a Jasper. "What does he say then?"

"Right, hold on I've written down a few things. Not only have I read the book …of sorts anyway," he looked at Robert, "but I've written down a few things to remind me." he said with satisfaction.

"Carry on." George said encouragingly.

"First; why do the King, the aristocrats and land owners rule the country. Only they can vote for a government and they will look after themselves. The rest of us - the majority -

have no rights and our opinions are ignored. Most Laws they pass are meant to keep us from changing that system.

Next, so who pays most tax? Not those who pass the tax laws. Why can't tax be evenly spread across the whole country.

The King is the oldest son of the previous King. Our King is mad and his son is…is"

George helped, "the Prince Regent."

"That's it, the Prince Regent; it's said he spends fortunes on himself and his friends. After him has he got a son? If yes, will he be any better?" He stopped as George choked half way through a swig of wine. Jasper carried on, "He could be like any of us." Another choke from George.

Robert, "Blimey. Is that it?"

Jasper looked around sheepishly after his tirade. "Sorry, there's more. Paine is right, every man should have the right to vote and then Laws would not just look after the rich. And as well, "he pounded the table with his fist." The rich should pay most tax and should look after the poor." He looked across at George. "Have I got it right?"

George said nothing for a few moments. He then said carefully. "Well yes. More or less. There's quite a bit more to his book, but he probably wouldn't disagree with what you've just said."

Jasper stopped, took a huge breath and asked, "Do you agree with him?"

"Yes and no. What he says is right but I can't see the changes he wants actually happening. Look I'll leave it to you. You think about it and make your own mind up about it. How will you make changes back in Langton Matravers. Don't forget I asked you once what you would do with Lord Olden …..and the Countess."

George looked hard at Jasper and finished on a serious note, "There could well come a time in the future when you'll remember all this and may be tempted to do something you might regret." Jasper frowned, and George finished by saying, "Just remember; will you want to right a wrong? or will your actions be a catalyst …."

"What?" Jasper interrupted.

"…the reason to cause unforeseen events to take place that will spin out of your control."

Robert felt for his friend, he was troubled and frustrated and almost out of his depth. Robert agreed with the gist of what he had said but it was a dream. He couldn't see himself sharing a meal with the King, or was it? - The Prince Regent. At that thought, he stopped. and his eyes went wide open, and he turned to George.

His next thought was stopped when Tom's stomach suddenly rebelled against his last mouthful of brandy. Tom jumped to his feet, spluttered "Sorry" and dived into the adjacent bushes.

George sat back and took a deep draft of his brandy and thought to himself 'What have I done? He thought of a barrel of gunpowder - had he just lit a fuse?' He thought of the great English poet Alexander Pope who said 'A little learning is a dangerous thing.'

January 1816

After finally rejoining their Regiment at Calais they had to wait a month before they were disembarked into the barracks at Tilbury Fort in England. They were not given any information on what was to happen next, Ten days after their disembarkation their frustration was growing day by day and men started to drift away from the barracks - desert.

Finally, on a cold, bleak late January day the Regiment was assembled into its Companies on the Parade Ground. Light rain with flecks of sleet was driving diagonally through the air and the stiff breeze tugged at their tunics and made their eyes water. There was silence as the sergeants stood them At Ease. Robert gave an involuntary shiver as the cold ran down his back. He idly wondered whether he was catching a cold as the back of his throat felt dry.

No one saw a signal but a chorus of orders were suddenly barked out bringing the parade to Attention. The former Captain, now Major Honsworth, casually rode forward to address the men. The empty right sleeve of his uniform was tucked into the front of his tunic. He walked his mount over to Sergeant Hollins and spoke in a manner that none else would hear. Hollins turned and quickly looked behind the assembled Regiment. He straightened even more, if this was possible, and responded with an immaculate salute. "Yes, Sir!"

Major Honsworth turned his mount to face his troops and ran his eyes across the ranks. Slowly he raised his head as if he were to speak to the ranks at the rear and started his address; first to the left, then to the right – never directly to the front..

"Men you have served England well. Some of us will bear the scars of our service to the end of our days." He paused then went on, "His Grace the Duke is aware that we have all suffered the terrible loss of old friends and comrades. He is proud of you as he is reminded that nothing except a battle lost can be more melancholy than a battle won. I have been told that he knew not what effect you had on the French, but by God you terrified him." There was a ripple of laughter and murmurs of approval.

"It remains for His Grace to say that the war is ended and he," the good Major paused, "and I, thank you for your courage and determination. It is time for you to go home, your time in the army is finished. When you are dismissed today you are free to go as you please." He brought his left arm up to salute his men then wheeled his mount away.

Sergeant Hollis faced the parade. "Men, three cheers for Major Honsworth, Hip! Hip!" The three cheers were given and the good Major was gone before the third had died away.

Sergeant Hollis addressed the men. "Right: When dismissed get your back pay from the Paymaster." He turned to the rank with Jasper, Robert, Tom and George. "Private Fitzherbert, on the order, you are dismissed immediately and you will make your way at the double to," he paused to clear his throat, "ahem, a group of gentlemen waiting to the rear of the Parade Ground."

Sergeant Hollins then turned to address the waiting Regiment. He paused as if to prolong the moment, then, one last order "Parade: Right Turn: Dismiss!"

The parade obeyed the order, which was their last in the service of their King. There was an initial silence as men stood wondering what to do next. They gathered around in groups with a growing mixture of excitement and confusion.

'Where should they go? What should they do now?' Confusion. Many had spent years where the future was not in their hands, never having to make a decision on what to do next themselves.

The lucky ones would return to their homes where there was a warm welcome and work waiting for them. Most soldiers in the East Dorset Regiment were like the hundreds of thousands of soldiers and sailors that were arbitrarily de-mobilised after the Declaration of a secure peace. These men were to find that their old jobs no longer existed and there were no other spaces to be filled in the crowded mills and factories. For countless old soldiers the army had been their lives and they had no other home, to be summarily dismissed was bewildering

Jasper caught Sergeant Hollis by the arm, as he was about to march passed, "Sergeant, what happens now?"

"Go home lad.   Go home" was the Sergeant's crisp response albeit a frown did cross his own face briefly.

"Is that it? After all we've been through?"

"Yes *Mister* Tomes." with the emphasis on Mister. "That's it."   With that he spun on his heel and marched off to his quarters

Jasper and Robert stared at the back of the departing Sergeant until he was out of sight.   Robert looked with concern at Jasper. He could tell that he was boiling inside but before Robert could try to placate him, Jasper exploded.

"I don't believe it. We've been through four bloody years where we have risked our lives - faced death. We've been told our country needs us, that we must not let down those back home, and they will be proud of what we have done for them."   he waited for Robert to agree, but he was looking down studying the ground.

Jasper turned and kicked a tin mug that had blown across the parade ground, so hard it caught one of another disgruntled group of men on the ankle. Jasper shrugged his shoulders and turned away dismissively.

"How dare they!" His tirade was not to be denied. "Look at me" he pointed to his head and eye patch. Not just me - what about you Robert? How long will you have the shakes and nightmares? Good God, I just don't believe them. We're just fodder to them." He spat out an oath, went to speak again then stopped.

Tom interrupted, gesturing to the other side of the parade ground, "Who's George with."

They looked and saw two high ranking officers and a very smartly dressed gentleman. About a dozen troops were standing to attention within about ten to 15 yards.   George was talking in an animated way to the three men and was obviously getting very irate.

Robert looked hard at the civilian gentleman whose clothes on closer inspection would be called dandified. He was waving a kerchief arrogantly to dismiss any comments that came from George. Robert was reminded of a picture in an officer's quarters he had seen at some time. The man in the picture was a young man whilst the gentleman talking to George was putting on weight, in fact he was already fat. He had greying dark wavy hair that was ruffled forward at the sideburns. He was an older, fatter version of George and of the man in the picture.

On seeing Robert, Jasper and Tom, George broke a restraining arm from one of the officers and hurried over and re-joined his friends. After a gesture from an officer he was followed by two soldiers who halted just five yards away and they each held the latest Baker rifle across their chests ready for instant use.

Robert was about to speak "Who is…". Before he could go further George cut across him. "I know what you are thinking - don't." He paused looking around the group. "It looks as though this will be goodbye. I have no choice but I have to go with those men."

Jasper, still fired up, spoke aggressively. "No you don't. We can sort those guys out." Robert noticed the two soldiers tighten the grip on their rifles.

"No!" George responded almost shouting. Then more calmly, "Apart from anything else they're hand picked - the best. No, Jasper this is not one you, or I, can win." He looked at Robert. "Don't try to make any conclusions, Those are powerful men. The most powerful." He emphasised. "Matters are what they are." He moved and shook each warmly by the hand. "I really have appreciated and valued your friendship through the last few years. I sincerely hope that life will be good for you." He looked over his shoulder and saw the dandy getting agitated. "I must go. Jasper one last thing: stick to your principles but don't go too far. Everyone in life has to answer to someone else. Always ask yourself is there a better way."

He then spun on his heels and strode back and straight passed the waiting officers and the gentleman. There was a very grand coach waiting, he wrenched a door open and slumped back into a seat. The officers looked at each other but the dandy ignored them and went to the coach, he paused, looked at the handle for a moment then petulantly pulled the door open himself and flopped down into a seat opposite George.

Jasper gave another heartfelt oath, screwed his eyes and shaking his head he strode off in the direction of the quayside. Robert knew when Jasper was best left alone. As he was unsure what to do next, he stood still and watched Jasper pacing up and down.

Tom Faulkner was lost to what had happened in the last half hour. "That's it then." he said flatly. "What the bloody hell do we do now.

Robert looked skywards, then at Tom "In God's name don't you start."

Tom looked over at the back of Jasper. "He looks as though he could take the whole French army on by himself. He's a frightening man when he's roused.

Robert said simply, "Yes he is. Just leave him alone. He's right though, we are being let down."

Tom agreed, "The pay that I've got coming won't keep me going more than a few months." He looked at Robert and squinting his eyes said, "It's not the same for you two is it?" He paused looking in the direction of Jasper, "You've got some loot stashed away, haven't you?"

Robert hesitated then said quietly, "Tom, you've been a good friend - especially when it got tough. Yes you're right we've got booty from Vitoria." He looked quickly at Jasper who by now was standing still staring across the River, "I'm sure that Jasper will agree that when we've swapped it for cash, there will be some for you."

Tom's face broke into a wide smile. "Thanks - very much - both of you." he said hesitantly. "That'll be very welcome."

Robert clapped Tom around the shoulder. "Right, come on then there's no point hanging around here. When we were on the boat coming back to England I spoke to a couple of lads that come from London. They gave me an address in Southwark, which is just over the river south of London. We should be able to convert what we've got into something we can use."

Robert paused then quickly said, "Wait here for a moment." He trotted over to Jasper and Tom saw him talk animatedly for some minutes as Jasper appeared to just listen. Jasper looked in Tom's direction, then nodded. Robert disappeared along the quayside to return ten minutes later and gestured for Tom to join them.

Jasper gave Tom a friendly smile, "Don't mind me. Robert says there's a boat going up river to the barracks at Greenwich. Apparently it's not far to walk to Southwark from there. We'll go get our back pay then meet back here in an hour."

It didn't take them long to collect their kit and other personal effects. The Paymaster gave them what they were due and that was it - they were discharged from the army. Jasper shook his head slowly in disbelief again at the callous way they had all been treated. The conduct of the army on this day, which was at the behest of the establishment, would leave a deep scar inside Jasper. It would fester and Jasper was not alone in his anger.

From the jetty the three now ex-soldiers boarded the boat that was to sail up river. Robert, eager as ever, asked the boatman. "Is it far? We've not been to London before. I was saying to my friend Jasper here that I'm sure it's probably much bigger than Swanage."

The boatman laughed, "I could tell you're not from these parts. You'll be like virgins let loose in a whore house. I've sailed into Swanage and you could fit that small town into London many times. You will soon understand how big it is when you stand on the bridge that goes over the river. To reach the fields outside of London you will have to walk about four miles to Clerkenwell in the north. If you went west it's about five miles to a village called Chelsea, and then to the east it's three miles until you get to the countryside at Bethnal Green. Believe me, the City is enormous. That's not all. There are too many people in even this vast area and many of them it would be better to avoid. The streets are packed with...... " he paused and smiled, "..but enough. I wish you the best of luck."

Jasper chuckled at the description, "I'm sure we'll be able to cope."

Arriving at Greenwich, Robert paid the boatman for their trip then asked, "We have to go to Southwark, which is the best way?"

"What might interest you is to go up that lane there onto Blackheath where you can join the road from Dover. As you've not been to London before you'll get a good view of it from there."

They followed the boatman's advice and very soon reached the top of the hill that lead to the Heath and there they stopped in awe of the sight before them. After some minutes Robert broke the silence, "Just look at that. We've been through Lisbon and Madrid and other cities but ...."
He stopped and more silence followed as they took in a sight like nowhere else in the world. A panorama of tightly packed houses that stretched into the hazy distance surrounded countless church steeples. Occasionally a larger building

lorded itself above its neighbours. Robert was almost breathless "It goes on for miles and look at all that dusty haze. Every chimney has smoke drifting into the air. The flag is just hanging there in a cloud - does the sun ever shine through?"

Tom caught Robert's sleeve, "Look down on the river. It's completely full of boats. Over there look, at the docks. You couldn't get anymore ships in there, and how do they get out with all those blocking the river?"

Jasper was the first to collect himself and bring them back to their task in hand. "Let's get going. Robert you were given an address in a Horseshoe Alley, which is apparently near the Anchor Brewery in Southwark. It can't be that hard to find."

After the walk down the hill they reached the buildings in Southwark. Eventually they tracked down the house and Jasper banged briskly on the black door causing some of the paint that was peeling to slither to the ground. There was no response. A second, louder volley had some success. The door creaked open a few inches to reveal a squinting pair of eyes and a voice rasped, "What do you want? What ever you want you can't have it." The door then slammed shut again. Jasper was not in the mood for nonsense. He gave the door a blow with the heel of his hand and kick with the sole of his boot, which were of sufficient power to dislodge the hinges of most doors.

"Open up or I'll have this door down. We're here to do business."

The door opened slowly and a small indiscernible figure stood in the gloom against the wall and gestured for them to go up the rickety staircase in front of them.

They entered a room where a thin hook nosed man sat behind a table and kept out of the light. "What do you want?" he rasped.

"We're told that you will be interested in buying French gold coins."

"Maybe."

Jasper reached down into his kit bag and pulled out a hessian sack. He shoved the open neck of the sack under the dripping nose of the man.

After a few moments hook nose said dismissively "Alright I might be interested in giving you something for all of it - just 'cos I'm in a good mood." Despite his stated good mood there was not the hint of a smile and his eyes glinted in the gloom.

After much hard bargaining, an exchange was finally agreed for their 'French Booty' to be changed into money they could spend. Business was completed begrudgingly by all concerned and they left without handshakes or satisfaction expressed by either party to the deal. Until they turned the corner of Horseshoe Alley they kept their expressions of growling dissatisfaction. This tactic they had agreed would help get the most for the hoard whilst carrying out the negotiations. As soon as they were out of sight all three gave a whoop of joy and hugged each other. They knew it was nowhere near the true value but it was more money than any of them had ever seen.

Their first port of call was The George, nearby in Borough High Street. Until the ale took full effect Robert was uncomfortable with the feeling that they were being watched. It was obvious to the other drinkers that they were fresh out of the army and they had money. They were three veterans from Spain and Waterloo but the size and sight of Jasper discouraged any brave would-be footpad. An evening of good drinking was rounded off in a room rented upstairs for the night. They took it in turns to stay awake to ensure no-one tried to relieve them of their new found wealth whilst they were asleep.

The next morning as they ate their eggs, bacon and bread, Robert asked Tom, "What will you do now?"

Tom seemed content. "I've decided to make my way back home to Norfolk. I grew up in the small seaport of Wells. I might be able to get some work on the harbour loading grain onto the ships. There was always work available there when I was a lad." He looked at his erstwhile comrades, "How about you two?"

Jasper answered, "We're going to stay here in London." He glanced at Robert then continued, "We are going to try making our way in the world without having to go back underground in a stone quarry." He then gave a laugh, "First though, we are going to enjoy ourselves. We've got enough money that we don't need to rush into anything."

That was it. An hour later, Jasper and Robert shook Tom warmly by the hand; they paused looking at each other as if there was something else that had to be said but then parted company.

Jasper watched the departing figure of Tom then said "I've had a word with the landlord here at The George. He say's that if we need lodgings then we should contact a friend of his who is the landlord of The Brewers Tap near Moorgate. He should know of a place that we could rent."

Robert was ready to move. Grinning at Jasper he said, "What to do now, old friend."

Jasper rubbed his hands gleefully in anticipation, "We go out of this courtyard, turn right and over the Bridge. Then we're in London - then who knows what's ahead of us."

They were in a buoyant mood, both eager to drink in the sights, sounds and atmosphere of this incredible city. Strolling up Borough High Street they came upon London Bridge which was disappointing as it did not provide London with an impressive entrance. Robert looked around as they started to cross the river. "I don't think we should stay on here too

166

long, this decrepit old bridge doesn't look as though it will last much longer."[12] He glanced at Jasper. "Do you know, since we left The George you've had a permanent grin on your face."

"Robert, do you realise until now our lives have not been our own. Four years ago we let the army become our masters and we've had sergeants or officers barking orders at us - we were drilled into not thinking for ourselves. Before then, as soon as we were old enough we had the daily grind of working in our father's quarries. We were given no other choice." Jasper smiled widened, "Now if we want to turn right or left at the other side of this bridge, it is our decision. If we want to watch boats sail down the river then we can spend all day doing so until we get bored." He gave Robert's arm a friendly punch. " We can also spend all afternoon drinking good ale, it's up to us."

Robert was pleased for his friend "This is what you wanted, isn't it?" He hesitated to say more and Jasper noticed his concern. "I know what's on your mind. There's a subject I know you don't want to think about. Alright, neither do I at the moment but sooner or later we will have to consider what we are going to do when the money runs out." He evaded a couple of scruffy urchins that were dodging their way through the crowds. "We've enough money for months yet so let's enjoy ourselves first."

The Bridge was packed and as Robert turned to look where he was going he nearly walked into a man wearing a pointed floppy hat and loose fitting smock. He was brandishing a long staff and Robert staggered to avoid him and ricocheted over one of the flock of sheep the man was marshalling over the bridge. Robert crashed to the ground and several sheep

---

[12] The 'old' London Bridge was demolished after a new one was opened in 1831

vaulted over him.   He looked up at the man who was scowling "Oh, Lord I'm sorry."   Robert gasped whilst clambering back to his feet.

The man growled with no hint of an acceptance of the apology, "Look where you're bloody well going." He carried on his way without stopping and was heard to mumble to himself, "Sodding soldiers, they think they own the road."

Jasper laughed, "I don't think you made a friend there. So much for a heroes welcome home."   He looked down at himself. "I think that when we've found somewhere to camp down, we had better get some different clothes to these old uniforms."

"You're right."   Robert looked in the direction of his antagonist. "He was a miserable old devil wasn't he?"

Jasper shook his head still smiling. "Come on let's get moving. We've got to find somewhere to kip tonight, I don't feel like camping down on the streets."   He paused as he squeezed passed a man sporting two large baskets full of bread. "If we did we'd probably get trampled to death."

They continued northwards through a maze of streets and were forced to ask their way several times. It usually took a second or third attempt as they were constantly ignored as people carried on without a glance in their direction.

A couple of times Robert was sure he fleetingly saw a familiar face.   "Jasper do you feel as though we're being followed?"

Jasper looked around, "I know what you mean but with all these people how would you know?"

Eventually, they finally found Finsbury Square with Chiswell Street on their left.   At the other end was their destination, The Brewers Tap, where as they walked in they were immediately greeted with a cheerful welcome. "Good day to you lads, what can I get you?"

Robert was relieved to find a friendly face, "We're looking for a Mr Tom Wilson. Do you know where we can find him?"

"Look no further lad. You've found him." Tom Wilson roared.

Tom Wilson was a portly man with large, white, side whiskers framing a florid face centred by a veined purple nose. His chins always had several days stubble and with all this hair below his brow the top of his head had given in and was completely bereft of any fuzz at all. The sleeves of a beer stained shirt were always rolled up to his elbows and the rest of his attire was protected by a similarly beer stained leather apron. His face was cheery and his customers were greeted by loud belly laughs for the slightest reason.

The Brewers Tap stood between Chiswell Street and Grubb Street. As if to be fair to both thoroughfares, its door divided them on the corner. It was a modest establishment with wooden clad walls around which were benches and large solid wooden tables. Sawdust was scattered on a stone floor. The pervading smell was of hops from a brewery next door and Mr Wilson's tap room. During the winter this smell mingled with that of a large fire that was fed with logs retrieved from the fields north of Clerkenwell. As the Ale House was next to Mr Whitbread's brewery, customers could be sure of unadulterated ale.

Tom Wilson was a straightforward soul and he sold ale. Simple as that. That did not mean though that he was simple himself. The bluff exterior betrayed a shrewd mind and he knew which of his customers were trouble and who were not.

Tom took to Jasper and Robert as soon as he met them. He could see they were honest lads and seeing their uniforms, unlike many others, he was proud of men that had served their country. He soon realised that any apparent generous lifestyle was temporary; Tom was shrewd enough to recognise their working man's background.

"Can we have two tankards of your London beer? We're told it's very good." Jasper asked expansively.

Tom chuckled "Very good of you to say so. Two of Mr Whitbread's finest coming up."

Tom gestured for Jasper and Robert to sit at the table adjacent to the tap room, he then disappeared through the door to return moments later with two beers held in one hand. He sat down and joined them.

"Well lads, what can I do for you or were you just looking for the finest beer in London?' He roared with laughter, "Well lads what is it?"

Robert was first to respond. "The army decided that it didn't need us any more. First of all now, and most important, we need somewhere to stay. Do you know of anywhere?"

Tom chuckled, "It's your lucky day. My cousin owns some houses just around the corner in Grubb Street just twenty yards from here. He rents out rooms and I know he has a few empty. They're nothing grand, but I suspect that you won't be spending much time there in any case." He looked at their uniforms, "You'll need some other clothes. There's an area not too far from here where they make clothes for all the toffs. Go to 54 Peticote Lane[13] it's near a big market called Spittlefield. - don't worry I'll tell you how to get there. Say I sent you and Samuel will sort out good clothes that some milord has forgotten to pick up, changed his mind or hasn't paid for his previous orders."

"Tom, we can't thank you enough." Robert looked at Jasper, "I think we've fallen on our feet." He turned back to speak to Tom just as a pretty young girl walked passed and ran her hand across Tom's shoulders without stopping and

---

[13] Petticoat Lane

went into the tap room. "Yes, Tom if ...." he faltered as his eyes followed the young girl.

Tom chuckled, "Oh, I'll introduce you to her next time you're here. That's my daughter, Sarah."

Robert blushed, "I'm sorry .... I didn't mean to...." he flustered, "Yes, as I was saying, thank you very much for all of your help."

Tom always kept an eye on the rest of the room and had noticed a weasel faced man who had slipped in and sat by the door just after Jasper and Robert arrived. Seeing that Tom had looked at him he quickly turned away. Tom leant forward and lowered his voice. "There are people in this city who can't be trusted, and should be avoided. Look out for yourselves all the time." He took a deep breath and stood up, "Have another beer on me if you want, but I have work to do. I'll no doubt see you soon." With this he brought the conversation to an end.

Jasper and Robert declined the offer of a drink and went quickly round the corner and soon arranged for modest lodgings at No. 4 Grubb Street at 2/6d[14] per week. This was much more than they could have afforded if it was not for the proceeds from the Battle of Vitoria.

The next morning Robert rolled over onto his back, stretched his hands under his head and stared at the ceiling. Daylight had just fought its way through the dirt and dried rain on the window panes. Jasper was still fast asleep and chose this moment to let out a large snort of snoring as if in a greeting.

Jasper and Robert had woken up in many places when in the army. Whether beside a track at the Lines of Torres Vedra, in a trench under the walls of Badajoz, a Bordeaux farmhouse

---

[14] 2/6d = 13p

or in a barn in northern France, when they woke up they always had things or do or places to go.

Not this morning,

Robert looked around the room he would now call home at least for the foreseeable future. It was a large room with two wooden beds; he occupied one on the wall across the room to the door. Jasper's frame was just about contained within the dimensions of a bed on the wall opposite a window overlooking Grubb Street. Under the window there was a small table and two old chairs with cane bottoms.

At the bottom of Jasper's bed was a doorway to a small room containing two chests each with three deep drawers. A small window had, under its sill, a cupboard with a double door which opened up a space for storage and on top there was a basin and ewer for washing. The window looked down on a yard. which contained a stand pipe for water and a communal privy for the building.

As civilians, replacing their uniforms was a priority. Robert was in no rush but after half an hour he decided it was time to stir. On shuffling passed Jasper's bed he gave it a stout kick, mumbled "Morning" and carried on to the basin and ewer for a quick wash.

When finished, Jasper was sitting on the side of his bed, eyes glazed staring at nothing in particular. "Just going down to use the yard - then to get some clothes - yes?" Robert was half way down the stairs before Jasper could respond with a stifle yawn and "Yep."

Tom Wilson's directions to Peticote Lane were straightforward enough and in distance it was not too far, less probably than a couple of miles - no problem?

'Back down Chiswell Street over Finsbury Square, onto Crown Street to the main thoroughfare of Bishopsgate Street, turn right and it's down one of the roads on your left.' Robert chuckled, "Same distance from home to Swanage, turn right out of The Ship and keep walking until you're there." It was a different journey.

What Tom did not tell them is that as soon as they left The Brewers Tap they were rejoining a city that seemed to be in chaos. Once they had crossed Finsbury Square the streets were narrow and filled with a teeming populace. Everyone is attempting to hustle and bustle to reach their myriad of destinations in the quickest possible time.

Crossing a street had to be negotiated between coaches and carriages as well as heavy wagons laden with produce from the nearby countryside. These were on their way to the specialised London markets scattered around the city

Countless number of costermongers[15] carts and stools blocked alleys and sometimes roadways. Robert was dug in the stomach when he didn't anticipate a coal heaver thrusting back his shovel with no thought for others around him. Robert cursed but found he had to raise his voice to be heard. The host of people, the horses pulling carriages and drays heaving their wagons of ale and the costermongers calling out their wares for sale, it was an ear numbing cacophony.

Stables, essential to service the legion of horses, seemed to be at every corner. All the splendid thoroughbreds or the wretched carthorses had one thing in common. They had to release their manure where and when it was necessary. The stench to the uninitiated was almost overpowering.

It was crowded - it was noisy - and it did stink to high heaven ,but the visitors from sleepy Langton Matravers were enthralled.

After a couple of wrong turns they found Spittlefield Market and then close by Peticote Lane, then number 54. In the doorway stood a short, round man. He was wearing a waistcoat which was open and displaying the top of his

---

[15] Street sellers

trousers that his braces pulled over his stomach. A tape measure hung round his neck and he peered out of very strong glasses. "Good morning gentlemen. I'm Samuel. What can I do for you today?"

Robert introduced themselves and said that Tom Wilson had suggested that they come to find him.

On hearing Tom's name Samuel leapt forward and greeted them with open arms. "Welcome, welcome He is a very good man, Mr Wilson."

Robert pointed to their clothes, "As you can see, we've been in the army and we've just arrived back in England from the war."

"Ah yes the war, such a terrible business. terrible…". Samual said nasally, and shaking his head in despair. "And you boys, are you alright?" Looking at Jaspers head and eye patch he shook his head again. "Tsch, tsch such a terrible business." He moved between them and linking arms and pulled them further into his building. 'But you're here, you're safe." Then the smile slipped slightly. "Let me see how I can help you, my boys"

Jasper spoke for the first time. 'We don't want anything fancy. We just want to replace these uniforms with clothes that will last."

"Ah, good I have some really good clothes - made for a gentleman - really good clobber"

Jasper and Robert took their time. They did quickly spurn the offers of the fancy dandified outfits originally meant for the 'toffs' .

Jasper chuckled. "Some of this stuff would suit that guy who took George away. Anyway, clean and sensible is what we need. Let's get on with it."

"Jasper we haven't had to buy clothes before. The army directed us to what we had to wear. Before that it was 'hand-me-downs' or something Ma had bought for me."

They did have the problem they didn't know what they actually needed. Jasper was even more difficult as he had to find clothes of his right size. He was particularly pleased to find a pair of moleskin trousers ('they've got some wear in them') that fitted him. Braces and waistcoats were essential as were top coats and hats. Jasper found a long, black, serge coat and decided upon a squat bowler hat. He was conscious of the fact that the cleft across his scalp attracted attention.

Robert preferred a dark brown jacket that reached halfway between waist and knees. He kept to a regulation flat cloth cap. This was quickly to regularly slip to the back of his head leaving a mop of blonde hair falling over his forehead.

Samuel went out to his back room and produced an old canvas ditty bag which were issued to sailors to store their kit. Jasper and Robert crammed all their new clothes into this bag and with grateful thanks paid Samuel. They did not have a clue whether they had value for money but felt that although Samuel wanted their business, he would not cheat them, especially having been recommended by Tom Wilson.

Job done they strolled around to Spittlefield Market. The market traded from a collection of sheds and stalls, doing its best to cope with London's need for fresh fruit and vegetables. They stood for a few minutes watching the heaving Market Place just drinking in the atmosphere.

Jasper started grinning. "I never ever imagined places like this." They ambled around, squeezing and pushing their way through the crowds. Eventually Jasper looked at Robert. "We could do with taking this bag back to our rooms."

Robert nodded. "Yep, and then I think it will be time for a mug or two of Tom's fine Whitbread ale." Then as an afterthought, "and get something to eat."

They took their time getting back to their digs. On their way it started to become increasing obvious that London had a dark side. Encroaching on The Market and Peticote Lane were the slums and hovels of the London workless, homeless and destitute eking out an existence.

Their mood had quietened by the time they had made their way back to their digs. This was not to last for long. They stowed the spare items of clothing in the two chests of drawers. Once all chores were completed Robert stood in the middle of their indoor empire and with a broad grin said, "Well, what do think? This will do for me."

Jasper returned the grin with enthusiasm. "Me too." He gave another brief look around and with a satisfied look on his face said. "I think we promised ourselves some Whitbread ale. We must also thank Tom.."

"Agreed! Let's go."

As they walked through the door of The Brewers Tap, which they quickly shortened to Brewers, they were met with a roar of laughter from Tom Wilson. "I thought I might see you again before too long. Two pints, lads?"

"To start with please." Jasper responded with a grin.

Tom indicated for them to sit at his table next to the Tap Room and disappeared in there to pour their drinks. Tom brought out one for himself as well and sat next to them. He lowered his voice to indicate a more private conversation. "Well lads. What's it all about? What brings you here and where are you from - I can tell from the way you speak you're not London lads."

"No, we're from a village called Langton Matravers but we joined the army and have spent the last four years in Portugal, Spain and France."

Tom gave a slight nod of the head to indicate his respect. "They no longer need you now that Ol' Boney has been trounced."

As if suddenly ignited, Jasper thumped the table. "Thats right. Without warning…. off you go."

Robert interrupted "Ahem, Jasper, not now."

Jasper looked at each at the table and deflated. "Sorry, Tom. A soft spot."

"I can tell. I don't want to get in the way when you're really cross. But carry on."

Robert continued "Well that's basically it. We've done our bit for King and Country and we're now in London. We want to enjoy ourselves at first but sometime in the future we will have to think of the future…"

Tom looked straight at them. "What are you going to live off in the meantime?"

"That's not a problem…." he started but then stopped.

Tom looked from one to the other. He took a deep breath and started slowly "Look lads, you can tell me what it is. I'm well known around here. I've been here for years and I not going anywhere soon."

Robert looked at Jasper who nodded almost immediately. Robert instinctively looked over his shoulder before lowering his voice. "Tom, there was a certain battle in Spain in which the cra… French took a good going over. They made it hot foot away and left their baggage train. Well this baggage contained a king's, no several king's fortunes. Put it this way, we took our share."

Tom sat back and let out a roar of laughter. "Quite right too, lads." He rocked forward grabbing his flagon and raised it. "Here's to the departing French." He then stopped, quiet again. "Where is it? Is it safe?"

"It was originally in the form of gold Two Franc coins which were called Napoleons. In Spain and France we sewed some into the seams of our uniforms and the rest we stuffed them into our kit bags. It was safe enough. Anyone seen poking their noses around the baggage whilst the rest of the regiment was in battle formation would be shot without warning. The first thing we did when back in London was to change them into English money. We know we got a bad deal in the exchange but its still more money that we could have imagined."

Tom raised his eyes in appreciation and looking from one to the other he said with total sincerity "You've had to be tough. Here's to you lads. Well done." He stood up' "You deserve another drink." He turned, disappeared and was back almost immediately this time with a tray holding three beers and three large brandies. "Right, here's a toast to you and to the future." Three large gulps of ale preceded the downing of the brandies in one go'"

The three sat for some moments in silence before Tom resumed on a more practical tone, "Look lads, you don't want to carry it around all day. Where is it now?"

Jasper indicated the hessian bag on the floor between his legs. "Never leaves our side."

All three turned around as a soft voice said, "What are you three up to?' It was Sarah. Jasper and Robert rushed to stand up but Robert slipped and fell backwards onto on his backside, on the floor. Sarah squealed with delight. "Oh please sit down, its only me." Then looking at Robert added. "On the bench."

Robert's face went scarlet. Tom relieved his embarrassment by turning to Jasper and saying quietly, "I've the perfect place for your sack to be securely kept. Down in the cellar there is a small hole cut into the wall that's big enough to hold that. If anyone was to get into the cellar they wouldn't see it, and even if they could they wouldn't be able to open the door."

"That's great Tom. Much better than lugging it around."

The lads spent the next couple of weeks venturing as far as Smithfield Market, St Paul's and Covent Garden. At the end of each day they would return to The Brewers Tap which quickly became their base camp.

One evening, Robert and Jasper were sitting at each end of a long bench and were talking to those immediately around them. Robert grinned with satisfaction, he was in a good mood and called across to Jasper "The guys here were just saying that Samuel Johnson lived in the house next door to our rooms. Apparently he wrote a book that has the meaning of every word in the English Language." Then almost by way of explanation he finished, "Grumpy ol' sod apparently."

Sarah was walking passed and saw Jasper looking at Robert, shaking his head and laughing. With a slight frown she asked "What's up?"

Robert answered hurriedly "Oh, hello Sarah. Nothing's wrong. I've just been talking to some of your regulars." Gesturing to his fellow drinkers. "I've said that we've only been here a few weeks and there are so many fantastic places to see."

Sarah looked around the company. "Yes, and these gentlemen I'm sure, can help you with your travels. She looked around the table and gave a slight courtesy by way of a mock salute. "Most of them are on the stage or writers of some sort or another. They used to print the Grubb Street Journal." She received a volley of self-deprecatory smiles or nods.

Robert half nodded to indicate that he was still listening then carried on. "Well anyway I was telling them of all the places we've seen already here in London. Trouble is, it seems that anyone who lives in London, isn't interested on what is here in front of their eyes.

Sarah chuckled, "You're probably right. Mind you they're not all men of leisure, like yourselves."

Jasper from across the table raised his glass, "I don't have a problem with that. Your Good Health gentlemen. "Sarah stood back for the salutation to be given and received. "I'm going to have a short break. If you need anything you know where to find me." At the Tap Room table she flopped rather than sat down. Robert hesitated, looked around his company, then stood up and mumbled "Excuse me." He went and stood over Sarah who was studying a nail. He repeated himself, "Excuse me."

Sarah looked up quickly frowning for being disturbed as soon as she had relaxed. The frown disappeared immediately she saw it was Robert. "So sorry, I didn't realise you needed another drink."

"No. No. I'm fine for the moment, thank you. Please stay where you are."

He paused awkwardly and Sarah gestured for him to sit down next to her. He cleared his throat and asked, "Do you like working here?. I mean for your father and having to deal with some of the drunken types that come in here?" Sarah shrugged and gave him a friendly smile,

"Yes, I don't mind." She paused and looking out of the window said quietly, "My mother died from a fever soon after I was born so I feel that I should take her place for my father."

Robert looked down at the table, embarrassed. "I didn't mean to pry. I'm sorry."

She put her hand on Robert's, "Don't be silly, you're not." Then as she turned away she added "I'm glad that you will be coming in here now." then she bit her lip hoping she had not been too bold. She hurriedly stood up and greeted a new customer as he came through the door.

Tom had watched the last couple of moments, standing by the cellar door, his face relaxed at the encounter. Tom's daughter was a reminder of the love that he had lost. He had never married again as it would have seemed to be a betrayal. Sarah who at just twenty years old was a cheerful girl with a slight figure and bright blue eyes. Her blond hair was usually pulled back into a fashionable tight bun and the clothes she wore were sensible for the daily chores she carried out willingly for him. Although the model of proprietary her sparkling conversation betrayed an inner depth and a desire for fun rather than the mundane.

Jasper also saw Robert's brief encounter and moved over to join him and was met at the same time by Tom. Jasper grinned at Robert and if it had not been for Tom, would have teased him on his attempt to engage a lady in conversation. Tom saw, and understood all the undertones and smiled inwardly then said "Right, where are you going tomorrow?"

Robert looked across at Jasper and raised his eyebrows, seeking agreement. Jasper nodded and said, "We've been down through Smithfields meat market a couple of times and we had a good look at St Paul's Cathedral. Alright, done that. We wondered what was in the other direction."

Tom sat thinking for a moment. "Ah I know, you've seen St.Paul's and that's over a hundred years since that was built. Try looking at an impressive building of a different type, one that was only finished just before the war. Somerset Place[16] it's right on the river. Afterwards call in on a good friend of mine. Harry Pack, he owns the Cheshire Cheese just off Fleet Street which you have to go passed."

Tom, grinned and gestured to the table that they had both left. "You could very likely see one of the guys from over there. The Cheshire Cheese always has its fair share of writers. Dr Johnson, "they both nodded to confirm they knew who he was talking about, "was a regular in there. There is a saying that he called 'a stroll down Fleet Street' as 'a visit the Cheshire Cheese.'"

Jasper and Robert looked at each and came to an instant agreement. "Thanks Tom, perfect." Jasper paused then said

---

[16] Somerset House

more quietly, "I had better get a top up from our French friend in your cellar."

The weather the next day was warm with the sun trying to burn through the layer of smoke and dust. They made casual conversation without too many interruptions until they reached the bottom of Ludgate Hill and carried on to Fleet Street. They were then confronted by what seemed a wall of traffic and people.

Visitors to London are inspired by the grandeur of parts of the city but it is the population as well. The world is represented there in a few square miles. Everywhere there was a confusion of people, the very rich and the destitute. Londoners mixed with those from abroad. There were the nobility and gentry, well-to-do merchants, household servants, city officials and law officers, vagrants, pickpockets and prostitutes.

Men and women hurried to and fro bent on their own pursuit of pleasure or business concerns. All lived, worked, traded, and ate, drunk and begged in the same crowded streets. Life was at a pace unlike anything they had experienced in the village of their youth

They stopped as Fleet Street widened into The Strand. "It must be here somewhere. Tom said they're building a new bridge over the river around about here."

Jasper gave Robert a nudge, "They've knocked down a few buildings over there and that will be a new road to the bridge.' They moved forward. "Yes that's the new bridge and it looks almost finished to me."[17]

"It does...... wait on, that must be Somerset Place there." Robert pulled Jasper's arm back and pointed at an enormous

---

[17] Waterloo Bridge built 1807 to 1817 and named in commemoration of the Battle of Waterloo.

white stoned building. A man in a frock coat, waistcoat and top hat used his cane to ease them out of his way. Robert quickly moved aside, Jasper more slowly. "What's that building, sir? " Robert asked as politely as he could.

The man paused, looked at both of them with disdain and went to move on his way. He relented as he called over his shoulder, "That is Somerset Place. It's no place for the likes of you." He then disappeared into the ever-moving throng.

Jasper grunted, "I've noticed since we've been in this city, everyone's a stranger, nobody tries to be friendly - they seem to be in their own sweet world."

Robert was becoming frustrated "This is really impressive but we can only see part of it. That side over there butts straight onto the Thames.."

Jasper nodded in the direction of the river., "Come on, this way. They're all busy doing what they have to do on the bridge. We can get far enough to have abetter view." Which they did and were able to admire the magnificent structure in all its glory. They were able to spend time taking in all the views from their vantage point. The new bridge was on a major bend of the River Thames and gave views from the City of London in the east, to Westminster in the west.

"Oi! You two, what are you doing here?"

Jasper grinned, "I suppose we should make a move." He gave a cheery wave. "Just on our way, sir." He then turned and they strolled off the nascent bridge.

The man made a step in their direction, took in his options and decided he had done enough and went back to the centre of the site.

Robert was in a happy mood and looking at Jasper, chuckled. "You won't find many buildings like this in Swanage." Robert looked to his right and said, "I remember seeing The Cheshire Cheese on our way here. Time to take up Tom's suggestion?"

He turned and nearly walked into a thin scruffy man. Robert looked at him and frowned, "Do I know you."

'No." was the snapped reply and a weasel faced man scurried away.

Jasper looked at Robert and shook his head, "Looks familiar, but can't say I know him. Anyway let's go."

Around the corner in The Strand, weasel face met with another man who had obviously been waiting for him. The other man was tall and dressed in clothes that had seen better days. His skin tight trousers barely reached his shoes and his waistcoat was a stranger to the top of them. His long black frock coat would not meet across his stomach despite his skeletal frame He was a bald man although wispy strands of lank grey hair overlapped his ears down to his collar. His thin wrinkled face sported a large hooknose that he continually wiped with the back of black woollen mittens.

"Well what have you found out about them?"

"Since you paid them for what they brought back from Spain, they've moved into rooms in Grubb Street that Tom Wilson of The Brewers Tap found for them. I can't tell, if they've got anymore to trade or just have the money you paid them."

The tall man grunted.

"I think they have recognised me. I let them in to see you at Horseshoe Alley and they have bumped into me a couple of times since I have been watching them."

The tall man grunted again, "You stupid sod." He stood staring at the weasel face. A full minute passed before he finally made up his mind, "What they had was good merchandise. If they have any more it will be at their lodgings. Get a couple of men from over the river – Mad Jack and Horse will be good. Follow them back to – where did you say? – Grubb Street?" He spat out his orders without pausing for an answer. "Don't be too pleasant when you introduce yourselves and then lean on them so that if they have anything else to trade they will be glad and relieved to hand it over. Oh, and don't forget the money I have already given to them."

Weasel face nodded with a malicious grin. "It will be a pleasure."

The tall man looked down at his crony with disdain and almost repulsion. "Get on with it! Bugger off and don't waste time." He leant forward and putting his hook nose inches from the weasel face, he sneered. "Don't let me down or you'll be sorry."

He kept his face thrust forward for a moment to emphasise his point then straightened up, turned and melted into the crowd.

He left his trembling underling wiping spittle from his face.

In The Cheshire Cheese, oblivious to their intended fate, Jasper and Robert sampled an array of ales, beers and in particular the local London favourite, Porter. As the day wore on Robert began to have a sense of foreboding. He tried to shrug it off but eventually said to Jasper, "Do you have a feeling that something is about to happen? Not something pleasant?"

"Not really. Why?"

"Oh, I don't know really. Just me being daft, I suppose."

"Look, these people may think of us as country bumpkins," he looked around the other drinkers, "but I don't see any here that could face ol' Boneys army."

Robert nodded cautiously but the bad feeling would not go away. They spent the rest of the afternoon and evening in The Cheshire Cheese until inevitably, they eventually made their way back to Grubb Street.

* * *

"Enjoying your meal, lads?" Jasper and Robert had very quickly became firm friends with Tom Wilson who acted like a benevolent uncle. "Had a good day?

"Yes - very good. Thanks for directions to Somerset Place yesterday … and The Cheshire Cheese is a great place. We'll certainly call in there again."

Tom chortled, "Now don't go giving my ol' pal Harry too much business."

Jasper grinned then asked, "We were talking about what to do tomorrow. We haven't been towards the west end of London, yet. Any suggestions?"

"I've been thinking about that. You may like to go over to Soho Square where there's a new place that's been opened called Soho Bazaar. It has been converted from a warehouse and it might interest you as it's run for the benefit of old soldiers. What they don't sell isn't worth having, I'm told." He shrugged his shoulders, "You may be interested - you may not. It's up to you."

Robert looked at Jasper, "Sounds good. You up for it?"

Jasper grinned and nodded, "Sure, why not."

Sarah brought them two more Whitbread beers. Jasper saw Robert and Sarah look at each other and excused himself. "I want to have a quick word with Tom about our money.

As he stood up Tom noticed the weasel faced man dart out of the door.

Jasper noticed as well. "Who was that who just went out?"

Tom frowned, "I don't know he's not a regular but he has been in here a few times lately. I'll ask around to see if anyone knows him." Tom looked over to Robert. "Enjoy yourself tomorrow." He then turned and disappeared downstairs to the cellar with Jasper.

The next day saw rain teeming from the sky until mid-morning. Not wanting to waste too much time and having spent three years in the vagaries of Portugal and Spain's weather they decided to wait until it eased.

The lads were starting to get used to Tom's directions and the way to squeeze through the ever present throng. The day warmed up as the rain stopped and they casually strolled westward along High Holborn until eventually they arrived at Soho Square. They didn't have to look for the Bazaar for long as the large building in the corner of the Square was attracting the crowds with the Square itself now filled with carriages. As they entered the building they were struck by the high ceiling which covered an enormous interior space. Underneath was a legion of stalls containing, as Tom said, everything that could be imagined.

They were about to advance to mingle amongst the throng when Jasper stopped in his tracks.

"What's up Jasper?"

"I've just realised who we just walked passed. Come on let's go back and have a word with him." Jasper moved back to the doorway where a familiar uniformed soldier was standing up straight and almost to attention. "Hello Sergeant Hollis. I didn't expect to see you again."

Sergeant Hollis was startled out of his reverie. He was the same man that had governed their lives, and who had commanded their total obedience. Now however, there was something lacking in his aura of invincibility, he had lost a little weight and his uniform hung on him more loosely. Although smart he was not now immaculate.

The good Sergeant looked uncomfortable. "Eh, hello lads. I didn't expect to see you either." he cleared his throat and looked around as though seeking to escape.

Jasper was intrigued, "What are you doing here? Why aren't you with the East Dorsets."

"I'm the same as you, lad. As soon as they paid me at Tilbury Fort I was discharged. Twenty years I had served with the regiment."   He stopped and bit his lip and looked into the distance then added with almost disgust 'Then I was told they didn't need me anymore. That was it." He paused again, "The army was my life."

Jasper and Robert both shifted uneasily.   Jasper was the first to speak. "What are you doing here?"

"There are some officers that are good men. Our Major Honsworth, or should I say Lord Wareham now, is one of them. I am, ..er,.. in his service."

Jasper persisted, "What are you doing here though."

Sergeant Hollis wanted to get away, but nevertheless answered,   "This here….um...Bazaar, as they call it, is intended to help the widows and daughters of our brave lads that were killed in the war."

"It just goes to show that the toffs do think of us poor foot soldiers." Robert was naively impressed.

Hollis grunted, "Well yes, some do. Lord Wareham, is one of them.   This Bazaar at least helps a few of the womenfolk.   Lord Wareham is most particular though, the ladies at the stalls have to be good decent women and dressed in a modest manner."

"But what do you do?" Jasper persisted.

"I make sure that no riff-raff get in here."   He looked passed them and stood up straight and thrust his chin out. Jasper and Robert spun around to see they were being approached by what was obviously a gentleman of good rank. They recognised immediately the familiar look of slight boredom and disdain and also that he had the right-hand sleeve of his frock coat tucked into his pocket. "Lord Wareham, good day to you sir." Hollis crisply announced.

Lord Wareham bowed his head in acknowledgment, then looked at Jasper and Robert. "Do I know these men?"

"Yes, your Lordship. They were in the East Dorsets. This is Private Bollson and Private....er, Corporal Tomes, sir. They were at Quatra Bras with us, sir." His Lordship looked them up and down, and noted Jasper's scar and eye patch. "It seems we have something in common to remember that day." He bowed his head again, then concluded with, "Good man, good man." He turned and casually walked away calling over his shoulder, "Hollis follow me, there are some people I need you to escort out of here." Then he was gone with Hollis in his wake.

Jasper and Robert just stood looking after them feeling as though they had been summarily dismissed - again. Jasper shook his head and with quiet anger in his voice said, "No matter what you say, the milords and their kind don't give a fig for us. One day they will get their comeuppance."

Robert tried to break the mood. "Come on let's have a look around." Striding forward with Jasper almost reluctantly in tow he started to take in the different merchandise on offer. After just a few minutes he gaped in wonder, "Have you ever seen so many different things for sale. In just those few stalls, there's hats, lace, shawls and toys. Oh, and look over here, there's a shop selling prints." Robert strolled over and flipped through a number of prints showing the Prince Regent and some members of parliament.

Jasper was interested and chuckled at a print of an enormously bloated Prince of Wales. "The fella that did these has certainly got something against the Prince."

The stall holder overheard. "Are you interested in any of them? The artist is James Gillray - he died last year. That small one there has been here for some time. You're likely looking lads you can have it for 2 Shillings.[18]"

Jasper brought Robert back to earth and taking his arm guided him away, "Thanks very much but what do ex country, ex army lads like us know about that sort of thing."

---

[18] = 10p

Robert was not to be denied and spent a further hour inspecting the stalls. His attention then drifted to watching the mass of people meandering around. After a while he turned to Jasper, chuckling, "Do you notice that all these fops, dandies and rakes who are lording themselves, they never seem to buy anything."

Jasper chuckled, "Yes, I've noticed that." He looked around then shook his head, "Look I think I've had enough of this. Tom mentioned that we may be interested in The Shakespeare's Head which is not far from here. I think we should have a look at what it has to offer." He then added as if in justification "We were late getting here because of the rain and it's a good walk back afterwards to the Brewers."

Robert grinned, "Alright, it seems like a good idea to me."

As they left the Fair they met Sergeant Hollis gripping two decoratively dressed women by the arm as he escorted them brusquely to the door. "This type think they can find customers amongst decent folk." The response from one of his captives was in a language reminiscent of their days in the army.

Once outside in the square they walked passed Lord Wareham who was helping a lady into a carriage. The Lady's attire displayed that she was in mourning. She was wearing a dress of a heavy black material together with a black crepe veil. She had pulled back the veil and showed her white, delicate face.

The Lady safely aboard, Lord Wareham closed the door and as he turned he came face to face with Jasper and Robert. Robert went to bid him 'Good Day' but was cut short as his Lordship walked passed them and climbed into the carriage on the other side.

Jasper watched Lord Wareham's carriage depart. "Typical, I thought I'd become invisible. We'll probably never see him again anyway, he can go to hell. Come on, let's go." They made their way towards Great Marlborough Street, and as directed by Tom, on the corner of Carnaby Street they found The Shakespeare's Head. It met with their immediate approval. A large room was dominated by a long wooden table lined by benches. In the corner mirroring the meeting of the two roads outside was a large fireplace. Good ale was being served and it was not long before an enjoyable afternoon was in prospect.

Jasper and Robert may have been inseparable but that didn't mean that they were always at each other's side. Jasper became involved in a conversation with a garrulous man who introduced himself as George Wombwell. Wombwell owned a travelling Menagerie[19] with, he claimed, animals from all over the world. Although not particularly interested in animals, Jasper was fascinated by the man's obvious showmanship.

Robert meanwhile was casually watching the other patrons whilst feeling very content with life. So content that he didn't realise that one tankard of Porter was being swiftly followed by another. After a while a young woman sidled up to him.

"I haven't see you in here before." she said with a smile whilst touching his sleeve

"No, we're... " he pointed at Jasper, "not long out of the army."

The girl giggled, "Oh, I love a soldier."

"No we're not anymore..." he started.

She placed her finger on his lips and with sparkling eyes said, "I would wager you were at least a Captain."

Robert flushed. She was pretty and so friendly Robert became quickly smitten with her to the exclusion of anyone else around them. She introduced herself as Daisy and said that she should have met her uncle here at The Shakespeare's

---

[19] Zoo

Head but he hadn't shown up, and she was alone. Feeling instantly sorry for her he offered to buy her a drink and to keep her company until her uncle arrived. Very soon Daisy moved up close to Robert and he felt his manhood stirring as she began to run her fingers through his hair and pressed her thigh against his. After a few more minutes she whispered in his ear "Robert, let's go back to my room. We can be alone there."

Robert who had consumed many ales by then, had no thought other than how his charm and good looks had bowled over this pretty young thing. Robert might have been naive about the young girl's motives, but he was excited as he quickly realised that the evening ahead would end with him in bed, having longed for sex.

Robert stood up without any further encouragement, and in a slightly stilted manner stood back with a gesture for his conquest to lead the way. "Milady," he said grandly, "I am at your command. Please lead me to your bed ... oh no I mean - sorry," he flustered, "I mean your room."

Daisy laughed and took his hand.

George Wombwell was still beguiling Jasper with his plans for making his Menagerie even more famous. George, as a showman, could see that Jasper, with his distinctive appearance could be a great asset to him. Also his undoubted strong nerve and muscle would be very useful in helping to control the wild animals. They were interrupted when Robert brushed passed being led by the hand by a young woman. Robert had a sheepish grin on his face as he waved at Jasper with his fingers.

Jasper had already seen this young girl chatting to other men in the room before she homed in on Robert. He called Robert back. "Where are you going with her?" he asked, almost needlessly.

Robert grinned again, "A man has got to do what a man has to do."

"Hah," Jasper chuckled, 'You soppy sod. I hope you've got some money left from today's pot." He nodded across to the impatiently waiting Daisy, "It will cost you."

Robert stood frowning not comprehending Jasper's point then the truth hit him. "Do you mean...." he looked at what he believed was his night's conquest. He had thought his charms were to give him a night of passion. ".. you mean," he repeated, his jaw dropped, "...she's a tom? "

Jasper shook his head despairingly, "Good God Robert, we've seen enough of her type on our travels. I'm sure the poor girl has a sad story to tell but you won't get a night of passion, I would imagine money up front, a 10 minutes quick grope and then you're on your way." He glanced at Daisy, "Poor girl certainly, but she'll be back here afterwards for her next customer."

Daisy had walked back to grab Robert's arm. She stared at Jasper and snarled, "Why don't you bugger off. He can look after himself."

Jasper shrugged and gestured towards the door, "It's up to you mate. You do what you want. I'll still be here when you get back which will be before I need to get another drink." He looked down at his half empty tankard.

Robert was horrified. He snatched his arm away from Daisy, unconsciously wiping his sleeve. "You bitch." he stammered.

Daisy wasn't going to waste time. "Your problem...please yourself. There are plenty of others." She looked at Jasper and sneered, "Make sure he's in his bed nice and early and he says his prayers." She then spun round and flounced across the room and plonked herself on the lap of a surprised youth who looked barely old enough to be capable for what she had in mind for him

George Wombwell had watched this exchange with bored amusement. When Jasper turned back to continue their conversation George had a proposal. "Would you like to do some work for me?"

Jasper was surprised by the question, "Doing what? I know very little about animals and in any case I'm not sure I want to work for someone else again - or at least not yet."

"I need some muscle for when I'm getting ready for a show. Would you," He looked at Robert who was starting to doze and chuckled "and your mate if he's not too busy with the ladies, like to give me a hand?"

Jasper thought for a moment, "Yes, but only when you have something big coming up."

George was disappointed at the lack of enthusiasm. "Alright let me know where I can find you. The Bartholomew Fair is due to start in a few months and I will need some help when I set up my Menagerie."

"We could be interested. If you leave a message any time at The Brewers Tap in Chiswell Street then we will get it." He then rose and took Robert's arm, "Come on Mr War Hero, a good walk across town will help you to wake up." Then giving George a nod, he left with a rather unsteady Robert.

It was late evening by the time they reached Grubb Street. Although the fresh night air had worked well on Robert, as they stood at the door, Jasper made sure that he would be able to climb the stairs to their room. "If you're alright, I think I will have one more. I noticed Tom Wilson was still open for business."

Robert nodded, mumbled he was off to bed, and pushed the door open. He slowly climbed the stairs to their first floor room but frowned when he saw that their door was ajar. He was sure he had shut it when they left that morning. Either tiredness, or the ale dispelled caution, he lent against the door and he walked straight in. One pace inside the room and he felt the simultaneous sensation of hitting his head on a solid beam and his teeth clunking together. He collapsed to the floor completely dazed.

"Go easy don't kill him. We want him to be able to talk."

Robert felt himself hauled to his feet then thrown on to the bed where his head took another blow when it collided with the wall. His vision was blurred but he could just make out two large figures with a small one who even in his dazed state seemed familiar.

The smaller figure came over to him and gave his foot a kick as it hung over the side of the bed. "Where're you keeping your money and the other stuff?"

Robert's vision and mind began to clear. He shook his head in an attempt to clear his mind further, but stopped as that just increased the pain.

"What do you mean no? Horse, remind him to show respect and answer us properly when asked a simple question." One of the large figures in the background moved towards the bed.

Jasper had watched Robert go through the door and being satisfied that he couldn't come to any harm walked the short distance to The Brewers Tap. Tom Wilson was just turning out the last of the evening's drinkers and Sarah was clearing up, straightening the tables and chairs and sweeping the floor. Tom seeing Jasper coming through the door feigned exasperation "Jasper, you'll be the death of me – I'm fair worn out, its been a busy night."

Sarah looked passed Jasper and frowned. "Where's Robert?"

Jasper chuckled. "He's alright. Shall we say he is feeling very tired. He's gone up to the room. Tom, join me in one of Mr Whitbread's best before you close?"

Tom shaking his head but smiling broadly disappeared into the Tap Room. Sarah still looked worried. "Are you sure Robert is alright?"

"Don't worry Sarah, he's fine." Tom returned and put two tankards on the table by the Tap Room door, and gestured to Jasper to sit down. Jasper was grinning, "Tom, your daughter seems very concerned about my old mate."

Tom raised his eyebrows and gave Sarah a mock stern look.

"Oh Pa, don't be silly. It's just that when I went outside a little while ago to collect some glasses there were three men hanging around outside Robert's building. They looked as though they were up to no good. There were two big men and a little weasel faced man. I didn't pay much attention but when I looked in their direction again they had gone but I'm sure the door to Robert's building was just closing."

Jasper and Tom stopped drinking and stared at each other.

Robert was not a man to look for trouble but he could stand up for himself, and he was a man to be feared when aroused. He had spent his youth in the tough environment of the stone quarries and then for over four years was in the army and was in the thick of a number of bloody battles. He was not a softy.

Under orders from weasel face, Horse moved forward to the bed where Robert was still sprawled but was desperately trying to regain his wits. As soon as Horse lent forward to grab Robert he was caught by a kick that was delivered into his groin with as much force as Robert could muster. The foul breath of the thug coughed out and Robert leapt up grabbed him by the top of his jerkin and hurled headfirst onto the wall behind the bed. The pain in Horse's groin was the last sensation he ever felt as he lay perfectly still.

Weasel face, and his remaining mugger, Mad Jack, stopped in stunned silence. Robert did not stop. He spun around and grabbed a wooden chair and swung it round with such force that the wood splintered as it gouged into Mad Jack's face. The wounded thug sunk to the ground his nose broken and totally stunned.

Weasel face panicked and tried to make a rapid exit. Unfortunately for him Robert was between him and the door and he sunk cowering on his haunches with his hands in front of his face. "Please, I'm sorry. I'm just following orders."

At this point the door flew open and Jasper burst in on the scene of bloody carnage. He looked around and saw a large figure laying on the bed not moving as if asleep without a physical mark on him. Crumpled on the floor next to the door was a groaning figure covered in blood with his nose bent out of shape. The third intruder, a whimpering little individual, had Robert standing over him so that he dare not move.

Robert turned around and upon seeing Jasper relaxed. A sloppy grin appeared on his face "You took your time getting here. We've had guests."

Tom and Sarah then appeared breathless in the doorway. Sarah seeing Roberts's bruises ran to him. "Are you alright? You're not badly hurt are you?"

"I'm fine. Don't worry." He felt a surge of pleasure that Sarah was so obviously concerned about his well being. He then looked around and viewed the scene. "I know this little runt. He was at the door of the house where we exchanged our French booty in Southwark. He's been following us."

"It's not my fault. I was told to come here." The crouched figure bleated.

"Who said you could speak. Shut up."

Tom Wilson had by this time moved over to inspect the still body on the bed. "This one has had it." He thought for a moment. "This was not your fault and I'll be bound that this crew are wanted for other such blags. The best way now will be to report this to the Magistrate. He can then deal with them." He nodded in the direction of the lifeless form. "He can also dispose of him."

Tom Wilson was now in charge of the situation. "Sarah, take Robert back to the Tap and make sure he's not badly hurt. Jasper, you stay here and look after our two friends here. I don't think they will try to get away. I will go round to the Magistrate and his men can take care of them. I know Justice Peak, there shouldn't be any problems."

Robert then left with Sarah solicitously holding his arm. One step in the direction of the live culprits from Jasper was enough to convince them that their best option was to stay still. Tom Wilson then attended to the details and the incident came to an end.

CHAPTER TWELVE
Regency London

November 1816

Dot Tubbs was happy to have settled down at College House in Winchester. The Lambricks could be mistaken for an aunt and uncle. Mr Lambrick was a busy country solicitor although his black austere clothes could easily see him being mistaken for the local undertaker. He was a tall thin man with a fringe of hair around the back of a hairless dome. This crowned a pale drawn face that had spent years pouring over dusty old legal transcripts whilst he left the running of the house to his wife, Mabel.

Mabel saw her role as being supportive of her husband, whilst he remained the master of his house. As she had not produced any children, she believed their marriage should resemble a friendship, with she and her husband as companions. She was similarly tall and thin with her hair tied back fashionably into a bun. Her face, although thin and pinched, could break into a ready smile for anyone she liked.

Dot became fond of both her employers and although she saw little of Mr Lambrick, Mabel Lambrick would regularly have polite conversation with her. One particular day, Mrs Lambrick stopped Dot from leaving the room after she had brought her afternoon tea.

"Dot, are you happy here? Do you miss your home?"

"I'm very happy here Mrs Lambrick."

"But do you miss your home?"

"I always think that home is where you wake up, where you eat and where you live with your children." Dot hesitated remembering that Mrs Lambrick did not have children, but she was relaxed by an encouraging smile. "The house where I used to live is just a pile of stone, it has no feeling for me."

Mrs Lambrick was rather taken aback by Dot's dismissive tone. "What about your family?"

"I miss my Ma and Pa, and brothers and sister, especially the youngest, Horatio. He is a little scamp." She smiled remembering the scrapes her youngest brother got into.

"Are you the eldest?"

"No, my eldest brother, Robert is in the army. We haven't seen him for years. I pray each night that he is alive and well." She frowned then added, "I had one other elder brother." She paused again and busied herself pouring Mrs Lambrick another cup of tea.

"You say, 'had'. Where is he now?"

Dot took a deep breath. "He was killed in an accident. No one knows quite what happened."

"How sad." Mabel felt sorry for this young mother. She could tell there was a story within her. It was as if she was stifling blackness deep within herself.

"Emily". A name so familiar but Lord Wareham's honour had told him he must forget. His heart would never truly do so.

He saw that so familiar profile looking one way and another. A Lady in a modicum of distress obviously, looking for a carriage. He hurried over "Emily. I never thought…" he stopped, "…I would ever see you again." He looked up and down the square but there was no carriage making a movement towards the Bazaar doorway.

He indicated for Sergeant Hollis to come to him. "Hollis get the coach man of Miladies carriage and tell him that her Ladyship is being escorted by…." He looked over at Emily, "…an old friend."

Charles saw his own carriage which was waiting close by and obstructing others. A quick flick of the wrist and it was in front of him. "Emily may I offer you a seat in my carriage?"

Emily was being rushed and confused but surprisingly to herself, agreed without hesitation. It was when he rushed round to assist her into her seat that he brushed passed Jasper and Robert. The sight of them around the battalion for four years and even the exchange of views after the relief of Badajoz were not in the forefront of his mind.

Once into the seats and the door closed, Lord Wareham turned to look intently at the Lady that he once believed would become his wife. "It's Lady Serrell now?" He hesitated "May I say how pleased I am to meet with you again"

Lady Serrell frowned as Wareham sat beside her. "Those men seemed to know you."

"They were in my regiment in the war. Brave and honest fellows."

"Ah the war – a terrible business. I was told that you had taken a commission as your father had wanted. I am so glad that you have returned although I fear not totally unscathed." She tried not to stare at Lord Wareham's empty sleeve. "It has been some years since we last met in Dorset. Meeting you today is such a surprise." She was flustered and hesitated, then added, "I thank you so much for offering me your carriage to take me to my London residence. It is now in Portman Square."

Lord Wareham lent forward and called to his driver, "Bateman, take us to Portman Square."

Shrouded in her widow's weeds, the only sign of Lady Serrell's pleasure, which she would not admit to, was a slight flush that came to her cheeks. "Since my late husband was killed, I have seen it was now my duty to help the respectable widows and daughters of those brave men who were killed in the war. I am most gratified to hear that you were supporting Mr Trotter who created this fine Fair."

"Quite so." Wareham paused then having decided to advance rather than retreat, he gently placed his hand over those of Lady Serrell as they were clasped in her lap. "You still dress in a full mourning manner. Is it not time to come out to at least half mourning?"

Lady Serrell quickly took her hands away. "Sir, my husband was killed barely a year ago. It would be most unseemly for me to yet dress in any other way."

Lord Wareham took his hand back and they sat in silence for a few minutes as their carriage turned into Oxford Street. A gentleman does not press his suit too hastily but a few years in the army, and facing death, had convinced him that a bold advance is always preferred to hesitant inaction. He cleared his throat with a slight cough. "We grew up on our country estates in Dorset and I was most surprised when your family and that of Lord and Lady Serrell's announced your betrothal to the late Lord Serrell." Lady Serrell kept silent.

Wareham had started so he was not to be denied. "In the circumstances as they are now, I would be pleased to call upon you next week."

Lady Serrell's eyes softened as she recalled their youth. Those happy days ceased on her marriage to the Lord Serrell. She had been a respectful and dutiful wife and had carried out what was expected of her when his Lordship made his demands. It was not however a marriage made in heaven. The infrequency of Serrell's demands and the fact they spent increasing amounts of time apart meant there were no heirs to the Title. Eventually his Lordship took a commission in the army, he was sent abroad and he never returned.

The news of his death had truly grieved her and she assumed that her life would now be that of a lonely widow. When it became known to her that her present companion in the carriage had been wounded she was surprised to find herself so alarmed. She was however cognoscente of her position in Society.

"Lord Wareham," she started, straightening her back so as to emphasise her dignity, "a widow should show her respect by being in full mourning for at least three or four years. It would be most decadent not to remain so for a decent period before changing to half mourning attire." She looked at Lord Wareham and despite her pronouncement on her condition there was a look of tenderness on her face. "However, we are old friends and I believe it would still be appropriate for us to meet from time to time."

She had finished and she turned to watch their progress through the carriage window. If Lord Wareham could have seen, he would have noticed there was a small tear in her eye.

The rest of the brief journey was rather stilted. Both were pleased that the chance meeting had taken place. Each also knew there was so much more to be said between them. There was something there - whatever it was, it could go no further. The nonsense and formality of manners and etiquette prevented any further advances.

Upon arrival at Lady Serrell's house Lord Wareham jumped from the carriage and took her hand to escort to her door. He repeated that he was so glad that they had met again and bade her farewell. Its was like a fine meal, it was to be savoured for the moment, another course would have been an indulgence and spoiled it.

Lord Wareham's experiences in the army, in addition to a few years maturity, had transformed him into a confident and outward-going young man. When he received the news that his father had died at Christmas 1813, not unknown for officers from a certain class, he returned home. As his father's death meant that he had inherited the family Title and all it's Estates he had to settle any outstanding affairs of the Estate. Within six months he was recalled in time to be at the Battle of Vitoria.

When Napoleon had initially abdicated Lord Charles had returned again to England and promptly visited all his properties to ensure that they were being run in a proper and profitable manner. He spent the year until Napoleon left Elba visiting his properties. Where necessary he dismissed workers who had been taking advantage of his father's loosening control on affairs. He also dispensed with those who he felt were just not up to the tasks in hand, but to his credit he ensured that they were not left destitute.

He was aware that the world was changing and he brought in younger men with energy to implement improvements where he thought it necessary. Once he was satisfied that matters were in order, he left the management to those men he had employed.

He returned to the Regiment in May 1815 in time for the action at Quatra Bras. He recovered sufficiently from his wound and was back to full health to fulfil his final military task which was to dismiss the Regiment at the Tilberry Barracks.

His energies had already turned to wider affairs. The Wareham title had ownership of the local Dorsetshire borough constituency, and he used this to become a Member of Parliament. The Earl Grey was an old friend of the Wareham family and he was soon sitting on the front bench of the Whig party. His travels around the country to his Estates had made it clear to him that there were problems in the country and that Parliament had to address and reform.

His energy began to be recognised by others in Parliament and he was soon seen as the man to watch. Unfortunately he would come up against his old commander, whom he still very much respected, the Duke of Wellington who was a complete reactionary to any change.

Lord Wareham felt his home to be in Dorset although he spent a great deal of time at his Hanover Square address. When he did think of Dorset he would frequently remember his childhood days and the times that Emily Pangborne, now Lady Serrell, and he were left to play together.

After escorting Lady Serrell home to Portman Square Lord Wareham took her at her word and two days later was back there to present his card and request that her Ladyship grant him permission to visit.

Lady Serrell was slightly taken aback, but upon her instructions the footman ushered her visitor to the Drawing Room door. "Lord Wareham, your Ladyship." He paused then coughed politely. "Would you like me to send your maid to sit with you?"

Lord Wareham frowned. He knew this flunky was quite correct and doing his job properly but it irked him nevertheless. He was pleasantly surprised and pleased when Lady Serrell said, "That's quite alright Bates. His Lordship and I are childhood friends and we do not need to be accompanied."

Bates face was impassive as he responded. "As you wish milady." Wareham was sure that beneath the mask he saw a look of disapproval.

Wareham watched as Bates shut the door behind him, then turned and smiled. "I am most happy to see you today. I thank you for your permission to visit."

Lady Serrell bowed her head as a brief recognition of his gratitude.

Wareham started to speak again, "Lady Serrell......" he was stopped in his tracks.

"Oh Charles, for goodness sake can we forget about all this formality. I am sure my reputation is ruined by allowing you in here without my maid." She patted the chaise longue beside her. "Please sit down, Charles."

Charles was surprised but readily sat down. "Lady.... Emily, I am so glad we met at the Bazaar. May I be so bold as to say that I often think about the days in Dorset when we were young. My recollection is that the sun always seemed to be shining."

"Yes indeed. They were happy days." Emily looked wistfully into the fireplace. The re-united childhood friends then passed the time remembering escapades, fun and adventures they had spent together in Dorset.

Eventually they ran out of memories and Charles stopped and looked at Emily for a moment. "I thought that you and I would always -." He hesitated. "Forgive me, it is just that when I took the commission I was assured that my service in the army would be in England so that I would only be away for some three months. However when I returned to Dorset you had become engaged to Lord Serrell. I was devastated and that was why I asked to be posted to Portugal with the rest of the regiment."

Emily looked down and studied her hands folded in her lap. "I had no choice. The marriage was arranged and as you know us ladies quite frequently have little to say in the matter." She reached out to touch Charles' hand. "It was not a blissful marriage." They both sat looking at each other and neither spoke.

The clock struck four and broke the silence. "Emily I must depart. I thank you from the bottom of my heart that we have be able to speak like this today. I do hope that you will give me the pleasure of visiting you again very soon."

"Oh, of course Charles, but we must be discreet."

Charles looked into her eyes and gently raised her hand and kissed it tenderly without averting his gaze.

"Charles." She stopped as a flush came to her cheeks. She reached for the bell as Charles rose to leave and the footman appeared almost immediately as if awaiting a distress call from his mistress. At the door Lord Wareham turned and bowed his head. "Your Ladyship." Then he was gone. Anyone observing His Lordship cross Portman Square would have discerned at slight skip in his step.

All the vigour he displayed in his public life he also now applied to his private life. His chance meeting with the object of his unrequited childhood affection, Emily Pangborne, now Lady Serrell, aroused old feelings. A part of him that had been deadened by her marriage to Lord Serrell was now making a lazarian revival.

Within a week of his visit to Emily, London society was rife with gossip when it learnt of the shocking news that Lady Serrell had entertained Lord Wareham in her Drawing Room without her maid being present.

The scandal was further inflamed as the couple met regularly and were once seen on their own at the opera in Convent Garden. Suffice to say that the Lord and Lady cared not a jot for old-fashioned formalities. This was a new century and as far as they were concerned they embraced their own new 19th century ideals. Lord Wareham's experience in the war and now in public affairs and Emily's innate intelligence provided a basis for a fulfilling relationship. Although there was an underlying physical attraction their shared interests made their time together a rewarding experience.

It was not long before Charles realised that he had to make a decision.

* * *

"Scandal? Damn them, sir." Lord Henry Olden showed slight amusement when a recollection came to mind. "You no doubt recall when Wellington was threatened with some tittle tattle nonsense of an affair?" He paused for effect. "His response, Sir? Publish and be damned!"

Lord Wareham laughed. "You're absolutely right. In fact, I do believe that as is the way of London Society, the comings and goings of myself and Lady Serrell has already become stale gossip. It is very kind of you and Henrietta to invite Emily and myself to join you at Vauxhall Gardens next week. I only asked in case Henrietta is anxious about idle talk."

Upon Lord Wareham's return from service abroad he soon met his old friend from his youth in Dorset, Lord Olden. The four, that had met on Sunday mornings for a ride, resumed their friendsships as part of the post war West End Society.

Lord Henry had married Henrietta Millborrow who had provided him with a daughter. Lord Henry Olden was a die hard Tory from the old school. Although too young to serve with William Pitt, he carried on Pitt's policies of repression and opposition to reform. It was a friendship between the Liberal Lord Wareham and a Tory from the old school. It was a true friendship, as they could argue their points of view strongly against each other, then within minutes be sharing a glass of brandy.

The four were to meet at Lady Serrell's Portman Square house. The Olden's arrived early and decided to wait for Charles and remained seated in their large and rather staid Landau carriage.

Lord Wareham had decided upon his two-wheel Curricle carriage today which was the height of fashion as it was deemed sporty by the younger set. He drew up outside Emily's house and he leapt down and bounded up the steps to announce his arrival.

.

Lady Henrietta chuckled. "I do believe that I have not seen Charles so jolly in ages."

Lord Henry smiled. "Yes, I'm pleased. It was a terrible shock for him when Emily married Serrell. I never did like that chap but he died in the service of his country." He paused and looking out of the carriage window added. "However, it was arranged by old Lord Wareham for the best of reasons."

Lady Henrietta gave her husband a quick glance then looked down quickly. There was a frown, which verged on being a scowl.

Emily appeared at the doorway in a noticeably bubbly mood. She wore a fashionable high waisted brown dress with short puffed over-sleeves. A wide brimmed matching brown hat was perched slightly to the back of her head revealing her blond curls. She had draped over one arm a patterned shawl. Charles had not commented that, contrary to her first comments to him, she had forsaken her widow's weeds some time ago.

They decided they would use the Olden's four-wheeled carriage, which had two seats opposite each other with hoods at each end which could provide protection against the seemingly constant rain this summer. As Charles and Emily approached the carriage he raised his arm for Emily to use to climb aboard. It was unseen by the other passengers, that as she did so she gave Charles' arm a surreptitious squeeze which gave the urbane Lord a momentary start.

When they arrived at Vauxhall Gardens and alighted from the carriage, Emily despite her Ladylike demeanour was in sparkling form. "There are so many things to see. I must see the tightrope walkers and I here tell there is a concert later."

Charles was so pleased that Emily was happy. He touched her hand lightly before saying. "There will be a hot air balloon ascent soon and before the concert there will be a firework display."

Lady Henrietta smiled. "You two go off and look at whatever you wish. Henry and I are anxious to see the Turkish Tent."

Charles took his watch from his waistcoat pocket "We'll meet you at the Turkish Tent in say two hours." Lord Henry checked his watch likewise and each gave a slight bow of the head. He proffered his arm to his wife and they sauntered off similarly glad to be in their own company.

Emily went to grasp Charles's arm but took his empty sleeve in error. "Oh dear, I'm so sorry. I didn't mean to – Oh dear." She stopped flustered, her face crimson.

Charles laughed. "Don't be silly, so I have one arm. Does that offend you?" He looked her straight in the eye.

Emily dropped her eyes, and then with a flutter of the lashes almost simpered. "Of course not. I'm proud of you." - another flutter of the lashes. "My soldier man'" She added playfully, flirting with him to cover her embarrassment.

Charles made a gallant gesture to move around her so that she could take hold of his remaining arm. He then escorted his wide-eyed companion through the crowds as they made casual conversation on their sightseeing tour.

After a while they came across one of the many unlit shaded paths. They both knew that these were used by couples wishing to be away from the crowds. With a brief glance he guided them both down the path until they came across a seat. Charles indicated whether she would like to take a seat to which she readily agreed.

He took her hand. "Emily, can I speak plainly?"

Emily was slightly nervous. "Please Charles, always do so."

"I am so pleased that we have met again and I cannot keep back my true feelings for you."

Emily was alarmed. "What do you mean?"

"My dear, I love you. I realised that I have loved you ever since we used to take those Sunday morning rides." He paused then knowing he was at the point of no return, continued. "The day that you were at Lord Serrell's House for the announcement of your betrothal to Lord Serrell I came to ask your father for your hand in marriage myself." Emily went to speak but Charles held his hand up so that he could continue. "I was distraught. I could no longer stay in the Country whilst you were married to someone else. That is why I requested a posting abroad."

Emily started to weep. "Oh Charles."

"Please do not distress yourself. We have found each other again." He squeezed her hand. "We are adults. We have our destiny in our own hands. I have my Estates as do you now. There is nothing anyone can gainsay what we do." He held Emily's eyes. "Emily will you consent to become my wife? Will you become Lady Wareham?"

Tears streamed down Emily's face. "Charles. Yes, Yes. I am also happy that we have met again. I thought that my life was destined to be as a dry old widow. Yes I will marry you." She flustered. "Oh, I'm so sorry. I don't mean that is why I will marry you."

Charles lent forward to kiss Emily gently but as soon as their lips met there was a movement behind him. Spinning round he saw two men edging their way towards him. He leapt up and faced them. "I don't know what you two ruffians are up to but I don't like the look of you." He strode towards them displaying his natural authority and a total lack of fear. It never occurred to him that it would not have been a contest of two against one man who had only one arm. They fled.

He turned back to Emily and took her hand as she stood up. "My dear, this is not the place to linger. I believe that it's time to re-join the others."

Lord Henry and his wife were already outside the Turkish Tent when they arrived. "I am most sorry. I hope we have not kept you waiting."

"Not at all. Unfortunately Henrietta is feeling unwell and we will not be staying for the concert."

Charles gave Emily a quick glance. "I think we will leave now as well. It has been a wonderful day though."

As Charles and Emily strolled ahead of their friends, Henrietta nudged her husband and whispered. "Did you see how flushed Emily was when they came back and she has been crying." She gave a knowing grin. "I think they will be telling us some news before too long."

Henry smiled then his eyes widened as Henrietta continued. "I also have some news for you. The reason that I have been feeling rather unwell lately is because there will be a further addition to the Olden dynasty.

Sir William Blackstone KC (late 18th century English Judge): "By marriage, the husband and wife are one person in law: that is, the very being or legal existence of the woman is suspended during the marriage, or at least is incorporated and consolidated into that of the husband. /// The chief legal effects of marriage .... that even the disabilities which the wife lies under are for the most part intended for her protection and benefit: so great a favourite is the female sex of the laws of England."

Lord Wareham's carriage drew up outside No 23 Portman Square. He had spent the day meeting with some of his fellow members of the Whig Party. Until the carriage stopped his thoughts were on the increase in civil unrest that was spreading in the towns and cities throughout the country.

Some of his colleagues feared the worst but entrenched opinions of the majority of the House still rejected any idea of reform.

His thoughts on these weighty matters dispersed as he stepped down from his carriage. They were replaced by a feeling of anticipation that rose within him whenever he was to meet his beloved Emily. He glanced to the centre of the square and noted that Lord Henry Olden's carriage had already arrived as had a grand Barouche carriage that was waiting on what were its obviously august passengers.

'Ah good, the Olden's have already arrived' he thought and chuckled to himself. 'Good 'ol Henry, always punctual - the bastion of the proper form.' He knew Lord Henry would hate to see the tongues wag further if Charles was to arrive before him and he would then be alone with Emily. Lord Wareham and Emily's whirlwind romance, and now their subsequent betrothal had returned, if only briefly, to be the centre of attraction of London's society. Lady Serrell's husband had fallen at Waterloo just two years previously and some would say that there was an unseemly haste for her to fall head over heels in love so quickly.

Charles had heard some of this gossip and had dismissed it. He cared not a jot for this chatter as he was not going to lose his dearest Emily again.

Once inside, as Charles entered the Drawing Room the conversation stopped, and all eyes moved upon him. He was pleased that Lord Henry had been able to persuade his father-in-law to also be present. Henrietta's father was The Right Honourable, Chancellor of the High Court, Sir William Millborrow one of the senior law officers in the country. The grand carriage outside no doubt belonged to him. Sir William was a large impressive man wearing a dark cut-away coat and breeches that met knee length stockings. Dark eyebrows seemed to meet over piercing blue eyes that produced a natural deep frown. With his bottom lip thrust forward his entire appearance produced the effect that he was studying one's very soul. It was a stare that had terrified prisoners in the dock and he would show no compassion when donning the black cap to pronounce a sentence of execution.

Charles had met Lord William on a number of occasions and knew that his razor sharp mind had not dimmed with the passing years. He also knew there was a mutual respect between them. Charles paused as he entered the room and bowed his head in greeting to each group. "My Lords – Ladies."

Emily who was sitting on a chaise longue with Lady Millborrow jumped up to meet Charles. She restrained herself to curtsey in front of him and when she rose proffered her hand. Charles took it and kissed it. "My dear Emily."

The hiatus as the couple looked at each other was broken by a polite cough. The reactions to this little scene varied with each of the onlookers. Lord Henry looked slightly embarrassed and was keen to resume a conversation on the business in hand. Sir William had turned and was viewing out of the window his team of horses with his carriage. Lady Millborrow had a slight frown as she recalled some of the talk that had centred around the couple. The final viewer, Lady Henrietta looked on benignly with an encouraging smile on her face.

Charles appeared to be oblivious to the differing reactions to his entrance. He exchanged glances with Emily then addressed the assembled company. "I do thank you all for being here today. As you know Lady Serrell has consented to be my wife. As my father is no longer alive and lady Serrell is a widow," Emily looked down to feign sadness. "we will decide forthwith on any arrangements."

Sir William cleared his throat. "My daughter has told me that you would like me to offer my opinions on any legal or financial issues." He looked slightly aggrieved "You will appreciate that having spent many years on the King's Bench, I have not looked at such matters for some time." Once having made the point on his status, he continued. "I do know a very good solicitor which I will be most pleased to instruct to finalise any agreements."

"I thank you Sir William. I trust that as there are no impediments to our marriage, the whole affair may be settled without too much fuss." Charles was anxious that the infamous long arm of the legal profession would not drag out what should be a simple case. "If there would appear to be any delays, I'm sure that you will be able to overcome them."

"Quite so. Quite so. However everything must be carried out properly." He looked at Charles and nodded towards the butler who was standing dutifully by the door. Charles responded by addressing the patient man who was jolted to the present finding he was the centre of attention. "Thank you Bates. That will be all for the moment. We will ring when we require you."

"Lady Serrell, all your father's Estates have passed to your younger brother, Is this correct?"

"Yes Sir. He is however only fourteen years of age."

"Yes of course, however he is the male heir." Having set that matter aside, Sir William continued. He was in control. "Your late husband had no brothers. What were the provisions made for you upon his decease?"

"My father drew up an Agreement before our marriage whereby his entire Estate was to be left to myself."

Sir William raised his eyebrows in surprise. "There are no other male relations in his family?"

"There is a cousin that I believe lives in Scotland."

"Your late husband however was party to the Agreement leaving everything to yourself.?"

"Yes Sir."

"Most unusual. All the lands and wealth to pass to a Lady." He shook his head in mild disbelief. "Although I have heard of such cases before."

The tone of the conversation was increasingly irritating Lady Henrietta. "Papa, you speak of us Ladies as inferior beings."

"My dear, it is the law."

"Quite so and we must all obey the law. Would it not be fair then that half the people governed by these laws should have a say in what these laws shall be?"

"Men are made for public life; Ladies for private. If you were to elevate a woman's place it would be contrary to the Bible and contrary to God's plan for women."

"Ahem." The father and daughter dialogue faltered and Charles interjected. "I do not believe this is the time or the place to discuss such matters." Charles looked from one to the other to emphasise that the line of conversation was at a close. "If we now return to Lady Serrell and myself, I believe our affairs should be straightforward." He paused as if to offer someone the opportunity to comment. There was silence although Sir William was seething inside as his own daughter had confronted him and he had lost control of the discussion.

Charles continued. "I would appreciate your advice Sir William. Unless if I have misunderstood matters, all of Lady Serrell's properties and assets pass to me upon our marriage. Is that so?"

"Of course." Sir William responded firmly.

"To spell it out simply. There is no necessity for us to involve lawyers and such like. Under the law our two Estates merge to become one."

"Yes under Statute…"

"I do beg your pardon but I don't want to go too deep at this time. Is the matter as I have just stated?"

Sir William went to speak again but then just replied simply. "Yes."

"Excellent. However I am anxious that the future Lady Wareham," he smiled at Emily, "should receive the usual small allowance per annum that she may spend as she sees fit."

"My God!"

"If she requires, or suggests any major item of expenditure she has only to ask, then I should be able to accommodate her."

"My God!"

Lord Henry was getting increasingly angry and embarrassed by his wife's behaviour. "My dear I do believe that we should let these matters be discussed without intervention."

Lady Henrietta sat bolt upright, tight lipped and her hands clasped tightly in her lap. She just stared at her husband. This was not the meeting that Charles had planned. A silence fell over the room with just the sound of the clock making its rhythmical advance. The clatter of a large carriage passing by directly beneath the Drawing Room window stirred Lady Henrietta to say softly. "As you wish my dear. I am at your command."

Emily had remained in the background but she seized the moment and moved alongside Charles, taking his arm. She was not going to have a discussion on her wedding taken away. "That's all settled then. Let's talk about the wedding. Dearest Charles, I would love it to take place here in Mayfair, at St. George's in Hanover Square."

"Then there it shall be. We have to arrange for the banns to be read over three weeks which can be tiresome. Charles Manners-Sutton, the Archbishop of Canterbury, has a son that has just been appointed The Speaker of the House of Commons. He has been the Judge Advocate General and you must know him well Sir William. Could you speak with him and arrange for his father to issue a Special License, it would be so much more convenient." Charles thought for a moment. "It would also be most agreeable if the Archbishop could carry out the Service."

Sir William was pleased to be brought back into the conversation. "I will see what can be arranged. The Archbishop is very amenable I cannot foresee a problem."

"I think that concludes the arrangements. Fortunately weddings do not attract large congregations and as most of our relatives are in the country we have just a few relatives here in London who will attend. I hope that you Sir William and you Lord Henry will do Emily and I the honour of being present."

Both men acknowledged their acceptance of the invitation. Lady Henrietta said softly to herself. "I assume that means us Ladies as well." This was met with a large sigh from her husband who promptly turned away and starting talking with his father-in-law. Charles joined them after giving Emily's hand a squeeze.

Emily then asked her two Lady guests which of her best Sunday dresses she should wear. She did point out that she would just *have* to buy a new bonnet.

Lady Henrietta remained quiet as she realised that the room had reverted to type. The men were deep in conversation with weighty matters, whilst the Ladies spoke of more trivial things.

'Why does it have to be like this?' Lady Henrietta determined that no matter how long it may take, she would take at least one small step to change this absurd unfairness.

In February of 1817 the Olden's held an evening of dancing to be followed by dinner. There were twenty people invited and

Lord Wareham and Lady Serrell were special guests in view of their impending marriage.

To ensure a bright atmosphere Lord Henry spared no expense by adorning all the rooms in a myriad of candles. Lord Henry's Butler, Burford, acted as the Master of Ceremonies and introduced dances about to be played by the professional musicians.

The dances were lively and the evening was a triumph with Emily dancing the Scotch Reel and her favourite La Boulangere with great enthusiasm. Charles was a proficient dancer and overcame with skill the problem of only having one arm.

Lord Henry was not so relaxed whilst dancing. If the truth be known he would have preferred to have taken the role of an interested and benevolent bystander. As a good host he went to speak with his father-in-law, Lord Millborrow. "Sir, are you not dancing this evening?"

The mighty law lord grunted and haughtily responded. "Dancing is in itself a very trifling, silly thing. It is however, one of those established follies to which people of sense are sometimes obliged to conform. They should be able to do it well. I am afraid, sir, I cannot do so - I will therefore decline."

Henrietta seeing her husband and father talking together, she joined them. After a moment so as not to appear to rudely interrupt, she took Henry enthusiastically by the arm. "Burford tells me the next dance is a Quadrille. Dear husband, I insist that you join me." Henry allowed himself to be cajoled into the dance and he did admit to himself that he found it enjoyable.

Once the Quadrille had finished, after a nod from Henry, Burford announced with a flourish that Dinner was to be served. The gentlemen escorted the Ladies into the Dinning Room and Emily made sure that Charles was her escort by immediately placing her hand on his proffered arm.

Lord Henry surveyed the table and gave a grunt of approval as his guests took their seats and were confronted with several courses with a multitude of dishes in each. Their eyes roamed across, amongst other items, a tureen of soup, meat, game, pickles, jellies, vegetables, custards and puddings.

Once all were seated, conversation suddenly ceased as the Head Footman entered the room, with Burford in close attendance. There were gasps all the guests saw the Footman was carrying aloft a large silver tray of crushed ice on top of which was an enormous pineapple. Emily squealed in delight followed by all the other guests giving an appreciative applause. Holding up a hand and shaking his head in mock embarrassment, "Please, please. Gentlemen and Ladies it is nothing."[20]

A comment voiced all the guests appreciation. "I say Henry old chap. That must have put you back a pretty penny."

"Not all, it is for all of my guests but in particular for our Guest of Honour and his soon to be, Lady Wareham.' There was another pause to allow a further ripple of applause. Then Henry gave his Coup de Grace, "I have told Burfield that it is to be fully served tonight. None to be sold on."

Lord Henry's stock in London's extravagant Society was sealed.

It was a cheery scene around the long table which was adorned with shining silver cutlery and sparkling, highly polished glasses.

---

[20] The pineapple was a huge status symbol. It had become a sign of hospitality and of generosity. Pineapples would be the centrepiece at dinner parties, not eaten but viewed, almost revered. Some would even rent a pineapple for an evening.

The conversations were sparkling and Emily was in an effervescent mood as she sat between Lord Henry who as the host was at the head of the table, and Charles who was to her left. Once all had settled following the presentation of the pineapple Lord Henry supervised the serving the first course of Asparagus Soup.

When that was finished Lord Henry called. "Burford." His butler was immediately at his elbow. "I think we are ready for the main courses to be served."

The remnants of the soup course cleared away and Henry carved the larger joints of mutton, beef and turkey. The gentlemen of the party served themselves from the dishes in front of them, and then offered to serve the lady to their left. If a dish was required from another part of the table, Burford directed one of the Grooms to fetch it. Guests were not expected to try every dish on the table!

Henry looked round the table with smug satisfaction. The serving staff stood back as the diners reached forward and placed food on their plates. All present thoroughly enjoyed the repast, and the conversations flowed with wit and banter mixed with the occasional pompous statement.

When the main course was cleared a small dessert of salad and cheese was put in its place until that was cleared in favour of the next course. Burford went to Lord Henry side and announced for all to hear, "My Lord. We have; Fowl with skewers garnished with crayfish, olives and black truffles, a ragout of forcemeat balls, sweet breads and mushrooms, roasted duck and a haricot of mutton."

Whilst Henry kept a solicitous eye on the food being brought to the table, Charles and Emily chatted about the latest opera they had attended in Covent Garden.

Henry was pleased to see a particular favourite dish of his, a fricassee of veal with hard boiled yokes of egg, laid before him. However, he noticed a slight grimace from Charles.

"Charles, is there a problem?"

Charles gathered himself. "No, no please it is not important." He felt an explanation was in order. "It is just that this fricassee is known as a French dish." He patted his empty sleeve. "I bear no regard for the French, and as well, the late Lord Serrell fell against them at Waterloo."

A voice was heard to mutter across the table. "I would have thought he would have been grateful for that."

Charles dismissed the comment. "Henry, it is of no importance."

Henry was anxious to gloss over any potential awkwardness. "Burford, move that dish to the other end of the table." He hesitated and then said quietly to his Butler. "Put a serving on my plate in a moment."

Charles lowered his head briefly in recognition of Henry's good manners.

Lord Henry gazed around the table in anticipation of a wave of approval. He was not disappointed.

Emily looked lovingly into her beloved's eyes and with almost a simper she asked, "Charles have all the arrangements been made for next month at St. Georges?"

Charles smiled. "Yes, all is ready. As you know I have been away on important business on one of my estates in Norfolk. However there will be no further delay as Henry has seen to it that His Grace, the Archbishop, has issued a Special Licence." He paused and looked enquiringly at Henry. "I do believe though that there may be a problem with His Grace conducting the Service. Is this so, Henry?"

"Yes, I'm afraid he will not be able to attend."

Emily looked alarmed. "Henry, pray what is the problem?"

Henry was re-assuring. "There will be no problem. It is just that His Grace is now getting old. He has arranged for the Bishop of Lincoln, Pretyman Tomline, to officiate."

Charles intervened. "That seems a strange choice. I have had some disagreements with Pretyman Tomline in Parliament. He is intransigent in his stance against the emancipation of Catholics. It is something that will happen in the not too distant future whether he likes it or not." Charles frowned. "There are enough problems in the country without making too big an issue about the inevitable."

"Quite so. However he will shortly be appointed to the Bishopric of Winchester. The Archbishop thought it appropriate considering that most of yours and Emily's Estates are within that Diocese." He chuckled. "I did hear that you and he had had some differences. It maybe an opportunity for you to persuade him to see sense."

Charles laughed. "Thank you for the sentiment, however he is set in his ways." He shook his head sadly. "Unfortunately there are many in Parliament who do not see the dangers that could lie ahead in other matters as well."

Emily gave Charles' arm a friendly tap in admonishment. "Tsch. This is not the time for such talk."

As the water ice was brought to the table Charles placed his hand on Emily's and looked at his host. "Henry, Emily and I are grateful for this evening it has been thoroughly enjoyable."

Henry acknowledged the thanks with a smile and at this point he decided to underline his triumph of the evening. He rose to his feet and announced that he would be pleased if his guests of honour partake some pineapple followed by each of those present. Burford leant over and spoke quietly in Henry's ear. Henry then re-addressed his guests: "I have just been informed that to accompany the pineapple we have some, Parmesan Ice Cream and an alcoholic punch."

The room was filled with calls of "Bravo! Well Done! Good Chap, never fails. Thank you!"

Burford moved discretely to Lord Henry's side and whispered quietly. "Cook was told to prepare a simple meal. May I say that it has your approval?"

Lord Henry was relieved that the evening had progressed so well. "My compliments to Cook. I am very happy."

When all was finished the ladies retired to the drawing room to gossip and embroider and chat for about an hour. The gentlemen remained in the dining room enjoying their Port.

The party broke up, quite late in the evening.

CHAPTER THIRTEEN
Pivotal Decisions

"Jasper we need to have a talk." Tom Wilson was obviously serious as he didn't wait for Jasper's response but turned and sat at his Tap Room table. Robert looked at Jasper with a frown and a silent 'what's that all about?' Jasper shrugged but would not be intimidated, so took his time to walk over to join Tom.

As Jasper sat down, Tom took a moment before speaking, then "Look Jasper, I'm not you Pa and even if I was…. you're your own man now. You can do what you want."

Jasper felt Tom's awkwardness but responded sharply "Go on Tom have your say."

Tom took a deep breath. "I understand that you have met Francis Place a few times.

"Yes, why."

"Francis is a good man and he sees much that is wrong and he wants to make changes - he wants to reform."

Jasper nodded in agreement. "Robert and I told you that when we were in the army we met a guy called George Fitzherbert and he lent me a book - it wasn't easy to totally understand but it was all about the unfairness, and how things should change - yes reform. Tom, look around London, the milords will spend what is a fortune to you and me for a dinner, whilst 100 yards away in St Giles, for instance, people are destitute and starving."

Tom held his hand up. "Yes, alright. No it's not fair. The big question is how is that going to change?" Jasper went to speak but was stopped by Tom's upraised hand again. "Francis Place is a reformer. He is a law-abiding, working-class self-improver who works and agitates for change within the law."

"What he says is right."

"Yes, but," Tom leant forward to emphasise his point, "not all of those so-called agitators are like Francis Place. There are many that carry out dirty schemes that are not the same as Francis' temperate methods." Tom punched the table. "Jasper don't be naive and don't get drawn into the violence of those radicals. Apart from rioting in the streets and the breaking of windows, their brand of protest uses underground methods They will use extortion and libels to vilify and undermine the ruling order of politicians, peers and princes alike." He paused and kept his hard stare at Jasper. "What do you get by violent destruction of law and order? You get revolution and mayhem which ends up with the innocent people suffering in the end."

They both sat back neither speaking, and just looked at each other.

Finally Tom spoke softly, "Jasper, I will just say that you could find yourself being drawn into something from which there is no escape. There may come a time in your life when you have to make a choice. Just be careful its the right choice."

Neither spoke until Jasper replied in an even tone, "I understand." Silence then, "Thank you."

Tom saw Robert looking across the room at them and he gestured for him to join them. When Robert sat down he looked from one to the other and asked earnestly, "Is there some wrong? What's the matter?"

Jasper grunted with a smile. "I have just had my arse kicked. No, not now. Don't worry we'll speak later." Glancing at Tom, he then added. "There is no problem."

Robert looked at Tom for a moment then said brightly, "Sarah says that you have something that might interest us."

"Oh, yes. George Wombwell has been in here, and asked whether you two were still willing to earn some quick money for a few days work. If so, could you meet him in the Square next to the St. Bartholomew Hospital in Smithfield.   You won't be able to miss him"

Robert looked at Jasper and shrugged his shoulders "Why Not? Could be interesting.

Jasper took a deep breath glad of the change of subject. He grinned "Just make sure we keep out of the way of the lions - if he has any."

Wombwell was a little surprised but expansively greeted them and they spent several days helping to set up his Menagerie for the forthcoming Fair. Apart from the awful weather the work was not too onerous.   The set up was completed ahead of schedule and they were rewarded by George with a bonus.

Despite a complete soaking by getting caught in the latest cold downpour of rain and sleet, after drying off and a change of clothes they were in high spirits. An evening of warming up at the Brewers with some extra cash was in prospect - what could be better?

When they arrived at the Brewers there was a jolly crowd shrouded in a smoky, flickering haze with the ever present dust accumulating on coats and furniture. Many of the old regulars were there, as were a few from The Cheshire Cheese that had become acquaintances from their evenings spent in Fleet Street.   Progress through the crowded room was slow with nodding at, or grunting a 'ello here or there and the odd quick follow up from a previous joke.

Tom Wilson was in a cheerful mood in anticipation of a busy and profitable evening ahead. A sweeping gesture guided them to their usual table next to the Tap Room.

As soon as they had sat down, Jasper gave Robert a dig in the ribs. "Didn't take long."

Robert turned round, frowning.   "What do you mean ....Oh. Hello Sarah."

'That's very nice. At least I'm glad to see *you*..both."

Robert flustered. "Oh dear, I didn't mean to be rude, I didn't see you."

Sarah relaxed. "Sorry, no it's alright. It's just that you're a little later than usual."

Robert quickly started, "We've been…" He heard Jasper cough beside him but he refused to look in his direction.

Jasper interrupted, with a huge grin. "I'll leave you two to it. I can see the level of conversation will be well above my head." Sarah looked down embarrassed. Jasper continued. "There's Jeremy Hornsby over there. I've got the dates he wanted for the Barts Fair from George. Can I leave you two alone for a moment or two.' Another grin and he turned away.

"Don't mind him, Sarah. You know what he's like."

Sarah smiled. "Would you like your usual Whitbread?"

"Yes, please but don't hurry. When you're ready. Eh……" he stalled. "It's busy isn't it?"

"Yes."

"Are you working here all evening?" Sarah replied, "Yes, until we close."

"Oh good." was his lame response.

They both looked at each other, neither knowing what to say next. Finally Sarah shrugged her shoulders but gave Robert a smile. "I must get on or Pa will not be pleased."

Robert watched her disappear into the Tap Room. Jasper had witnessed the exchange, "You are such a beau – you nearly swept her off her feet.

"Oh shut up" Robert said giving Jasper's arm a friendly punch. Chuckling he added, "I was just being friendly." Jasper roared with laughter.

After that night the gaucheness between Robert and Sarah slowly slipped away and they spent more and more time talking. The conversations between them lengthened until, with her father's approval, she would sit down and join them at their table. The two of them would talk and laugh at each other's jokes no matter how trivial until it got to the point increasingly where Jasper would leave them alone and join some of the other regulars.

It became obvious to Jasper, as a friend, and to Tom, as a father, that a relationship was growing. Robert for his part would be anxious to return to the Brewers Tap by late afternoon instead of spending evenings away from what he was now starting to feel as home. Sarah found that when Robert appeared in the doorway her heart almost skipped a beat. She would stand on her toes give the biggest smile that she could and even give an unnecessary wave across the room.

Tom was pleased that they showed the true innocence of two young people growing together. There's was not a brutal relationship spawned out of convenience or necessity. Nor was it a minuet where the couple danced round to the music of manners and formality.

Tom could also see that Robert was appalled and at times incensed by the deprivation that was for all to see in the great city of London. He did not bear it though, with the bitterness and with such frustration that was likely to boil over with Jasper. Robert's attitude was reform and change similar to Francis Place. He hoped that Jasper would not take the destructive road of rebellion that was just under the surface in London,

Tom could see that Robert was quieter and more thoughtful than Jasper. Being Sarah's father, he knew that these qualities would be attractive to his daughter. He was quite happy to see the friendship grow although he did have some reservations.

* * *

Late one afternoon in August, Sarah was waiting for Robert to arrive. She sat at her father's table next to the tap room watching the door. Her face lit up as Robert and Jasper came through the doorway and Robert immediately made his way over to her.

She stood up and said brightly, "Pa doesn't need my help in here this evening. I thought that as it's such a nice evening, for a change, we might go for a walk. We could go up to the Clerkenwell fields by Wenlock's Farm."

"That would be lovely. Yes let's go straightaway. I have wanted to have a talk with you - alone." Sarah's face flushed and she looked down to the floor. Robert took her hand then stopped and looked quickly over to Tom Wilson who has watching them both with a benign smile on his face.

"Go on the pair of you. Have a lovely evening." He then put on a stern face. "Now you look after her, mind."

"Thank you, sir." Robert said quickly and holding Sarah's hand started towards the door. He then remembered Jasper who had been left standing in the middle of the room. Robert grunted, "Sorry, Jasper. It's just ……."

"Oh go on. Don't mind me." Jasper chuckled and added, "Enjoy yourselves. You'll know where to find me when you get back."

The young couple disappeared through the doorway almost hurrying so as to be alone. They soon slowed to a stroll and unusually neither spoke very much. The occasional conversation flitted between several banal incidents that had happened at The Brewers' Tap. Each knew that the occasion was more than a simple walk. After about fifteen minutes strolling up City Road they turned into Shepherd's Walk and when they reached the stile that lead to the path to Islington village, Robert stopped.

"Sarah, I have something to ask you." Sarah's heart jumped, but before she could speak, Robert looked at the stile, "Come on, let me help you to sit up on here." Anxious to resume their conversation, Sarah was seated on the stile before Robert could get to her.   Robert's courage seemed to desert him. He had reached a point quicker than he had anticipated and in his hesitation he fell silent. Even the usual evening birdsong seemed to pause in anticipation.

As if to break the uncomfortable moment Sarah nodded towards Wenlock Farm, "Do you miss living in the country?"

Robert frowned in slight confusion at the change of topic, "Eh, yes, I suppose." Then collecting himself he added more firmly,   "Yes, but I'm glad that I came to London – to Moorgate – to Chiswell Street."   He smiled awkwardly, "Otherwise I wouldn't have met you."

Sarah was a confident young woman but knowing where Robert was leading, she blushed. "Thank you." She said quietly.

"Sarah you know how I feel about you. Every day I look forward to when we can meet. I believe my life would not be worth living if we couldn't be together." Robert went to get onto one knee, realised that as Sarah was sitting on the stile he wouldn't be able to reach her hand he straightened up again. Robert could contain himself no longer. "Sarah, I love you – will you be my wife?" He finally blurted out.

Sarah leapt off her wooden throne and threw her arms around Robert's neck, "Yes, yes of course I will. I love you too." Robert pulled her to him and the feeling of her body pressed against his stirred his whole being. He was not a virgin but this was new – it was different.   Sarah felt his excitement but could not stop the moment. Her body relaxed and became pliant, melding itself to his, reshaping itself to fit his contours. They both knew what each wanted but before they reached that point of no return, Sarah suddenly stood back.

"What's up my love?" Robert was desperate not to have upset his future wife – had he been too impulsive?

Sarah touched his cheek tenderly, "Nothing's wrong dear it's just that we shall have to ask my Pa's permission and I know that he is concerned about you."

Robert was stunned, "I – Jasper and I, have always got on so well with Tom."

"He likes you both very much. He's said once he thinks of you as his sons. He's worried about the future though. He's worried that you haven't started to think of what you are going to do with your lives yet. He wants to know what you intend to do when your money runs out."

Robert felt his stomach churn. It was time for the future to be faced but it wasn't just his own future that he had to think of now. He had to give assurances to Sarah's Pa which he knew he couldn't. He turned away from Sarah and stared into the distance.

Sarah caught his sleeve, "I'm sorry dearest Robert, Pa will not allow us to marry without you having work. When Ma died he was left alone apart from me – his only daughter. He is frightened that once he has gone I could become like some of those poor women you see begging – or worse, on the streets."

Robert looked Sarah in the eye, "I love you, Sarah. I couldn't live without you. Somehow – someway I'll find work."

Sarah felt sorry for Robert but whatever the problems that lay ahead she would stand by him. "My love, it's time to go home. We'll speak to Pa when we are ready. We shall keep this our secret but for now let's just be happy that we know that we love each other." She then almost whispered through clenched teeth, "….and we will get married."

They made their way back into London and their mood lightened, happy in the commitment they had given to each other. Robert' stomach was still churning though.

A boisterous scene met them as they entered The Brewers' Tap and Sarah gave Robert's hand a squeeze, "I'll go help, Pa. It looks as though he's been doing good business this evening."

Robert walked over to Jasper who was holding forth to a number of the regular drinkers they had both befriended over the months. Jasper was in the middle of a yarn that Robert half recognised as an incident that happened whilst they were in Spain. With Jasper's embellishments the truth was left in storage as the story unfolded. At the climax even Robert who knew the reality found himself laughing along with the rest of Jasper's audience. Jasper by this time had consumed a good portion of Tom Wilson's cellar and Robert was in that uncomfortable position of not seeing the humour in a further succession of jokes that were, to Robert's sober point of view, just not funny. He bade Jasper, Good Night and left with much on his mind.

"The weather is as bad as you.?" Robert spun around to see Jasper sitting up in bed back against the wall. Robert had woken early, and having washed and dressed was stood staring out of the window. The sun struggled to shine through a hazy sky but he barely noticed as his eyes were glazed whilst he was deep in thought.

"What?" Robert half turned around but stopped "Oh, you're awake. Sorry I was miles away." Then grasping the sarcasm in his remark. "It's not raining anymore." He responded half-heartedly.

Jasper gave a slight sigh that was tinged with exasperation. Since Robert had proposed to Sarah, for the first time the bond between them was proving to be increasingly difficult.

As Jasper had watched Robert standing at the window for some minutes he had come to a conclusion. Without speaking again he got out of bed and carried out his morning routine, When he had finished Robert had not moved. The time had come for matters to be brought to a head. Little did he know this day was to be a pivotal day in both of their young lives.

He went over to Robert and gave hime a friendly push in the back to gain his attention.

Robert started "What?

Jasper, in a tone that was not to be contradicted, said, "Robert let's take a stroll down to the river."

"Why?"

"To look at all the boats."

"What? Why?"

Jasper sighed and shook his head. "Forget the boats. I'm just getting fed up with talking to myself; you and I need to have a talk." Robert frowned but Jasper ignored his hesitation and strode to the door. "Come on, let's get moving."

Without another word they were threading their way through now familiar streets. Robert was still distracted, and there was none of the usual banter. The jumble of buildings on the banks of the Thames were divided by old wooden steps that led to the mud and stones exposed by the tide. Tilted rows of boats had sunk onto the shore awaiting the bobbing dance of the next tide. Jasper looked up and down river and went to the nearest boat and leant against it. He pulled out his clay pipe and lit it.

Robert picked his way over the stones to a boat a few yards away and Jasper fixed him with a stare. After a few moments Jasper, not for the first time, sighed. "For God's sake Robert, I know what's troubling you but you've got to make your mind up what you're going to do."

Robert was irritated. "Thanks friend." he said sarcastically, then relented. "Look, I'm sorry, it's just that……oh you know…." He left the sentence hanging. Jasper remained silent but continued to watch Robert. After another few moments of silence Robert took a deep breath, and started carefully as though he wanted to set his thoughts in order.

"Jasper, since we were discharged from the army we've had a great time in London." He paused and chuckled. "That's apart from when I had some unwelcome visitors." Jasper smiled and nodded encouragingly. Robert took another deep breath before continuing. "I've now reached a point in my life where I want something more. Jasper, I'm in love. I've told you that Sarah and I want to get married." He brought his heel back to kick the side of the boat he was leaning on "….but we can't."

Jasper, although he knew the answer, said simply. "Why not?"

"Sarah is more precious to me than anything else, but I can't meet the demands that Tom has made before he will allow us to get married."

"Why don't you get married anyway?"

"Sarah would never go against her father and quite frankly I don't want to make an enemy of Tom. He wants to make sure that Sarah does not land up destitute on the streets. He knows that my - our - money will run out sooner or later."

"Are you saying that you are going to get work here in London?"

"That's part of the problem. As we were walking here today how many ex-soldiers did we see already half-starved on the streets. Why should I be any different to thousands of others. What work is there for the likes of me? So, if I don't find work here, then I will lose Sarah."

Jasper drew a deep breath. "Go back to Langton Matravers and get work there."

"There's no guarantee of me finding work and without that guarantee Tom will not allow us to marry." He raised his voice. "Whatever I do; stay in London or go back to Langton Matravers - I lose Sarah!" Robert slunk his shoulders and looked at Jasper. "If I was to go back to the village in the hope of finding work would you go as well?"

"No."

"Then I am in danger of losing the two most important people in my life."

There was another period of silence before Jasper spoke but this time with a softer, friendly tone. "I'm sorry old friend, but I can't give you an answer." He paused then continued, "Don't give up though, we'll - you will find a way, and I promise you, I will do everything I can to help."

Jasper suddenly stood up and looked at his pipe that had gone out a while ago. He shrugged and tapped it on the hull of the boat. "Come on we won't find the answer down here, let's go back to Brewers. I could do with a drink – and so could you." He put both hands up as if surrender. "Alright, I know that's not the answer but we've cleared the air. I know that Sarah has noticed that we've not been our usual selves lately. The last thing you want now is for Sarah to get worried - which will irritate Tom."

The day had become warmer by the time they reached the brewers Tap. The shafts of sunlight that streamed through the open door contained a multitude of speckles of drifting dust. Tom rose from his tap room table and cocked his head in anticipation of their order.

"Two tankards of your finest, Tom." Jasper enthused.

Tom chuckled, "Good day to you lads. Two ales coming up." As Tom returned from the barrel clenching the mugs of ale in one hand he noticed Robert, who was the keeper of their joint purse, counting the coins more carefully than had been his custom. Tom put his hand on Robert's to restrain his payment "No, no - not this one. These are on Mr Whitbread's account next door." he said with a knowing wink.

Robert hesitated, "Are you sure, Tom? We'll take no charity."

"Don't think your ale is free from now on. It's a fine day - enjoy." He paused, looking hard at each in turn. "Come and sit down. I would like a word with you both." he put on a rare stern face and they followed him without question. Once they had settled with their host, Tom lowered his voice. "Look lads, you're having a grand time since your army days and by God you deserve it." After a short pause he raised his eyebrows then asked, "The French booty is going quick, isn't it?"

Neither Robert nor Jasper spoke. Tom asked again in almost a whisper, "Well?"

Robert was the first to speak. "You're right, it's going much quicker than either of us thought. We've a few more months before it runs out, though. So no reason to get too concerned yet."

Tom Wilson grimaced and looked questioningly at them both. "Have either of you thought of getting work. He concentrated his stare at Robert.

Jasper gave a deep sigh, "I know, but what can we do? We know how to dig stone, march, or - " he laughed, "or kill."

The humour was hollow and was followed by silence. Tom sat waiting for a proper answer until he caught sight of his daughter, Sarah on her return from the market in Covent Garden. He gave her a broad smile then turned to look directly at Robert. "Sarah has told me that you and she have talked about the future. She knows that I will not permit you to marry her unless you have the long term means to properly support her."

Tom fixed Robert with a look that made him shift uncomfortably in his seat as the dilemma he faced was again brought home to him.

Tom addressed them both; "There's nothing for you here in London now." He paused, then said slowly, "Would you be willing to go back home if it meant you had work?" He let his words sink in. "It would mean going back to the quarries."

Jasper slammed his beer down on the table and strode over to the open doorway. He saw where the conversation was going and he knew he was going to be dragged back to the old life. It seemed the past years had evaporated in seconds. He stood staring at the crowds streaming passed. He grimaced as he saw the thin, wizened and unhealthy appearance of the majority of them. Most of the inhabitants of what he was told was the greatest city in the world did not share in its good fortune. London was noisy and full of life and opportunities, but it was also brutal. Langton Matravers was unchanging, quiet and predictable.

It was some time before he spun around and re-joined Robert and Tom who were watching him anxiously. "We've broken free from the past." Jasper spoke as though there had been no pause, "We've earned the right to join in a new future. Look, I hear tell that there are marvellous new inventions and engines and manufactures that are making men fortunes. They say that we are on the verge of an exciting new world that has opportunities that could make our purses full of gold."

Tom dropped his head and kept his voice quiet "Aye you're right, we hear of men who have ideas and are now as rich as the grandest milord in the country." He looked up at Jasper, "But my friend, where would you start? What else is there new to invent?"

Robert nodded despondently in agreement,

Jasper looked at both Robert and Tom then thumping the table he took a huge quaff of ale and clenched his eyes shut in frustration.

Robert looked at Jasper cautiously, "We both have our own lives. You're my dearest friend and will be always." He looked at Tom, then back to Jasper, "Sarah and I want to get married, and I will do whatever it takes to make that happen."

"I'm sorry if this is difficult for you Robert, but you know my feelings when it comes to Sarah's future." Tom smiled encouragingly as he knew that what he was about to say was not going to be easy for either of them. "I have a proposition to put to you – to you both." He looked down to gather his thoughts; his proposition would also mean some heartache for himself.

"Do you remember Charlie Heywood? Well, he came in here about a month ago." Jasper opened his eyes and frowned. Tom chuckled, "Since you left to join the army, he has done very well for himself. He was in London to see Jack Winbow one of his business contacts and they met here. Shall we say that Mr Winbow is in the business of receiving shipments from abroad? Well anyway, I buy some brandy and wine from Jack – he's able to sell to me at a good price." Tom raised his eyebrows in an attempt to look innocent. "Well anyway, we got talking and the way he talked sounded familiar. I asked him and he said that he was from Langton Matravers. Of course, I told him about you two, and without going into details, what you were doing in London." Tom paused and looked thoughtful, "Charlie is a very shrewd man. He understood straightaway that your time here might be difficult unless you eventually found work."

He let what he had said sink in. "I got a message last week through Jack that you can get work back in the Crack Lane

Quarry." he paused, "It would mean you have to go home immediately. The work won't always be there for you."

Jasper felt he was on a runaway horse which he couldn't control. "No! We can't give in now." Jasper shouted, as he started to lose his temper. Other patrons in the room began to look worried as they saw this fearsome man in a rage.

"You just calm down, lad!" Tom equally raised his voice. He would not let anyone shout at him. He was master of his domain.

Jasper sat back quickly and collecting himself said quietly, "Sorry Tom."

"That's alright Jasper, but losing your temper doesn't solve anything."

"Yes alright but look I … we can take up George Wormwell's offer to work with him. He has said that he wants us to join his menagerie permanently." In an attempt to lighten the mood, he added with a chuckle. "He means to help with the animals not join them."

Tom smiled briefly, but he was not to be denied. "I'm sorry but that's not good enough. Jasper, I can't keep you from doing whatever you want. The trouble with Wormwell's business is that it could finish tomorrow – or next week. I know he has other business interests and he will look after himself first. Also Robert, I know that you aren't happy in the way he treats his wild beasts and Sarah feels the same. Could you live your life knowing what was happening to those creatures." He stopped; he had made his point.

Tom studied both young lads in front of him. He felt sorry for them. They had both wanted to break with the past but the facts of life were pulling them back. He could see that Robert would accept his fate more readily as he hoped for a future with his darling daughter. Jasper, he was not so sure about, his future hung in the balance. Jasper was not a man of business like Charlie Heywood. Tom shook his head slowly;

he just hoped that of all the possible futures in store for Jasper, he would be able to hold his head high.

Tom continued. "Robert, you will have to make a choice it's either stay with Jasper and ultimately lose Sarah or you go back to Langton Matravers with my daughter and my blessing." He took a deep breath and sat up straight. "That is my decision. It is now up to you Robert."

Robert did not take long to respond. He had been given a lifeline from the turmoil that he had been living with since proposing to Sarah. He glanced quickly at Jasper then nodding to Tom, "There is no decision, Tom. Sarah means everything to me." He looked back at Jasper, "I'm sorry Jasper but I have to go back home." The two lifelong friends sat looking at each in silence. Robert finally brought it to an end by adding softly, "I'm sorry."

Jasper smiled, "You have to do what is best for you." He then sat back, "What's the matter?"

Robert looked distraught. "It can't be done. If Sarah and I are to be married we will have to make arrangements with the church. St. Lawrence's round the corner in Guildhall is the nearest one and it will take weeks to arrange to see the vicar and get him to read the Banns. None us know a Bishop to get a special Licence. By the time everything has been settled, the work at Crack Lane quarry will have gone."

Tom held up his hands to calm Robert down. "I could see this was going to be a problem. Robert I have an answer but it may not be what you want."

Robert frowned in some confusion. "If it solves the problem, then it's what I want."

Tom took a deep breath. "Times are changing. People do things now that they would never of dreamt of doing in the past. There are values that we accept now that our forebears would never have accepted."

Robert became impatient, "Come on Tom. What is it?"

"Don't get married. Go back home with my blessing. Go with Sarah."

'What? You can't mean that."

"I do. You would be surprised how many people in this city live as husband and wife but have never been married in church – to each other, I mean."

"You mean this – you wouldn't mind?" He thought for a moment then said, "That's all very well here in London but back in Langton Matravers people would never accept us living together – unmarried."

"Don't tell them. When you go back, tell them that Sarah is your wife. Why would they ever suspect anything different? Look, this isn't what I hoped would happen but the happiness of my daughter comes first – before anything."

Robert sat in almost disbelief at how the conversation had gone. "If you're sure Tom? Will Sarah accept living in sin with me?"

"Grow up Robert. What's sinful about living with the woman you love? The only people that would see it as sinful would be narrow-minded bigots. Don't worry about the church – I don't think you would be able to find me a clergyman that hasn't sinned." Tom was vehement. Robert was slightly taken aback by the forcefulness of Tom's outburst. It occurred to him that there was probably a reason for his strength of feeling but he was certainly not going to ask him.

Robert's mind raced, events were happening too fast and other problems sprang to mind. "Where would we live? I don't know what has happened at home with my Ma and Pa whilst I've been away but I'm sure they won't have room for us or be able to afford to feed us as well as the rest of the family."

Tom had obviously thought through the whole situation. "I'm not a wealthy man but I can give you what you can call a dowry for Sarah. I will let you have enough money for you to live off it for a few months. As far as somewhere to live Charlie said there is a cottage in the village that has been empty for months. Did you know a Gabriel Woolley? Well anyway, unfortunately this Gabriel's wife died a while back and he's now living with his son. It's a place called Fig Cottage, do you know it?"

"Yes, it's near St. George's church. Poor old Mabel, she and Gabriel had been married for years." Robert looked at Jasper who was staring out into the street. "He used to spend most of his time in The Ship when she was alive I expect he almost lives there now."

Sarah came out of the kitchen and went to lean on Robert and put her arm across his shoulder. Unseen by Robert she looked at her Pa and raised her eyebrows as if asking a question. Tom gave a slight nod as a way of saying yes.

Robert looked up. "Sarah your Pa and I have been talking and he has come up with a solution whereby we can get married…" He hesitated. "…at least we can be together." Robert frowned, he realised that he had agreed to a plan for he and Sarah to live together outside marriage and he hadn't asked her how she felt.

Sarah gave him a encouraging smile as if she was reading his mind. "Don't worry, Pa wouldn't have suggested it to you without making sure that I would agree."

Robert heard Jasper cough. He realised that Jasper had been quiet all the time that Tom and he were talking and he suddenly felt very guilty.

"I'm sorry Jasper; it's all been about me sorting out my life. What are you going to do?"

"I'm not going back." Jasper knuckled his temples and studied the table. He eventually looked up and took a deep breath, "I was expecting something like this to happen and I really am pleased for you both." A look of sadness flitted across his face but he continued, "It doesn't surprise me about that rascal Charlie, I'm glad he is able to help." He looked from Robert to Tom and said quietly, "You are really a good man Tom. I hope Robert understands how much." He shook his head. "This is my opportunity to break away from a life in the village. I want to better myself and being in this city will give me the chance to be more than just one of the working sort."

Robert took a deep breath. "Take what's left of the French money. If you want to stay in London, to give it a go, then there will be enough for just you to live on for a while." He chuckled and looked at Tom, "I'm sure our Host promises that despite how good his ale may be, he won't let you give it all to him."

Jasper smiled at Robert, "I will take you up on your kindness." At that he suddenly got to his feet. "Look, you have plenty to talk about with Tom. George's Menagerie is at The Bartholomew Fair. I think that I'll go there now and have a talk with him."

Tom looked up at Jasper "I'll tell my cousin that you will still need his rooms round the corner – for the time being at least. I assume you would like me to still keep what's left of the booty in my safe store in the cellar. Just let me know when you need some of it."

Jasper nodded at Tom, "Thanks." He then turned with the intention to shake Robert's hand but was beaten to it as Robert rushed forward and held Jasper in a sincere hug. They both stood back, each slightly embarrassed with such a show of emotion. Jasper was the first to recover "I will see you before you go. I do wish you the best of luck my friend." He turned to go, but stopped, "You never know I might be buying Olden Hall when I get back home." Robert held out the purse containing the balance of their day's money, which

Jasper took and quickly turned and walked out into the sunshine and was gone.

Robert whispered under his breath "Good luck old friend."

Tom seeing what seemed to be the breaking of a lifelong union, put his arm around Robert's shoulder, "Come son, there's much to talk about before you go."

Leaving The Brewers Tap and Robert behind him Jasper strode purposefully down Chiswell Street, but he had only just reached Barbican some hundred yards away before he stopped. Big men rarely show any feelings to others. The busy throng passing him by saw only a large, ruddy-faced man with an awesome scar and black eye patch standing motionless. They gave him a wide berth careful not to brush against him lest they attract his displeasure.

'This is stupid' he thought. Jasper was in turmoil. 'I should see sense and go back with Robert to a safe existence in the Dorset countryside.' he told himself. "I must be daft to try anything else." This time aloud causing several passers by to cast curious glances in his direction. He turned and looked back in the direction of The Brewers Tap, then muttered aggressively to himself, "No, move on. Langton Matravers is the past. Here is the future." He turned again moving this time without pausing in the direction of Smithfield where the Bartholomew Fair was in its second day and was in full swing.

As he reached Smithfield, the crowd and the noise increased and he merged into the throng. He strolled between the various sideshows of musicians, wire-walkers, acrobats, puppets, freaks and prize-fighting booths. A Mr George Richardson, his name proudly displayed along the top of his stand offered theatrical delights that he loudly claimed were the better of any in Drury Lane. Jasper passed young lads with their lasses on their arm. He smiled as one romantic asked his beloved to choose from a rich display of tempting sweetmeats, apples, oranges and nuts but she was so taken with the choice, her lover chose for her.

All around were an abundance of ways of relieving all and sundry of their money. Small stalls had freely available oysters and fruit, as well as inferior kinds of cheap toys and other articles which were of trifling value. There were prizes for impossible feats but just as busy were the many pickpockets whose deft trade was skilfully executed.

There were as many ladies as men and a great many of these ladies were of dubious virtue. They were keen to offer a quick dalliance to a rich young gentlemen whose thoughts were too constrained below their waists.

It was becoming a rare hot day at the end of a summer of awful weather. The sale of liquid was doing a roaring trade even for those who declined the temptation of the many nearby ale houses. An ample supply of chalk and water was baptised as milk and there was ginger beer and soda water for those more discerning. The hot weather did ensure the consumption of alcohol and fights were common amongst drunkard brawlers, often arguing about futile bets.

Jasper saw George Wombwell as he was barking for passers-by to come to see his wild beasts.

"Hello George. How's business?"

"It's good. I had a problem last night though, when my elephant went and died. Uriah Atkins has a small menagerie on the other side of the Fair. He found out mine had died and put up a notice *"Come and see a live elephant."*

"That's sad. Your elephant was one of the big attractions." Jasper stopped when he saw a large notice on the entrance to Wombwell's menagerie

'COME AND TOUCH A DEAD ELEPHANT'

Jasper laughed. "You must be joking"

"Not at all. Nobodies allowed to get too close to the animals including the elephants. Now, here they can actually touch them, they can feel an elephants skin." He laughed. "They're flocking in." He nodded towards the entrance. "See what I mean?"

Jasper shook his head in mock despair. After a few more minutes he looked around. "I'll come and help you at the end of the day but I want to have a good look around first."

Jasper happily lost himself in the colourful crowd of voyeurs. After a while a prize-fighting booth caught Jasper's attention as he saw one hapless youth emboldened by too much drink and urged on by his equally drunken friends tried to take on the resident pugilist. Over-confidence and arrogance by the old fighter allowed the youth one lucky blow which caused the enraged veteran to land several blows with his bare knuckles that would leave lifelong scars.

The promoter of the booth, Jack Broad, a small man with a loud coloured frock coat, rushed forward to stop the one-sided affair. "Bad luck sir, I thought you might have him there." he said none too convincingly pushing the youth towards his stunned friends. He grabbed his fighter by the arm and whispered "Look, I've told you. Don't punch these lads too hard Len, or you'll drive them all away. They're only novices."

Jack Broad started his patter again. "Come on you brave fellows, who will take on Mad Len Blackman. Be able to put your toe to the line after five minutes and win five shillings. Come on lads, a shilling a minute, it's good money. Just sixpence a try." His hectoring voice soon gathered a crowd. Jasper was incensed at the treatment of the poor lad. He also thought any way he could add to the French's money would be good. With his size and fighting experience in the army he knew he was a fearsome opponent in any one-on-one contest.

He stepped forward, "Here you are, here is my sixpence. I will take on the boy basher." Some of the crowd cheered when they saw the size of Mad Len's next opponent, others jeered when they saw he had only one eye. Jasper looked at the pugilist who was moving to place his foot on the line scratched in the dirt and felt an initial pang of pity. Mad Len squared up to him with a battered and scarred face, of indeterminate age, which carried a permanent scowl. His white hairy body was now turning to flab as a result of advancing years and too much alcohol. His days were numbered and he resented it.

Jasper recalled the treatment handed out to the poor youth and placed his toe resolutely on the line. Jack Broad announced to the crowd that each fighter if he was to be knocked to the ground would have thirty seconds to come up to the scratch line, or be announced the loser. He then turned aside to his fighter, "Now remember Len, take it easy this man has only got one eye."

Without any further notice Mad Len stamped his boot on Jasper's and threw a swinging bare fist into Jasper's good eye. Jasper went straight down into the dirt amid howls of derision from the crowd.

"Take him back to his ma."

"Country bumpkin, no match for a London man."

"He won't get up."

"Go on hit him again."

Mad Len moved forward and placed a hefty kick into the side of Jaspers ribcage. "Get up you coward. "he growled.

Jasper's head was ringing, he was sucking in air as a result of the kick to his body and the swelling around his eye was blurring his vision. He squinted up at the sneering face of his adversary and all the pent up frustration and anger in him exploded. He leapt to his feet and without any pretence of avoiding further blows to himself tore into his hapless opponent. Blow after blow thudded into Mad Len's face which fast became covered with the blood pouring from his nose, eyebrows and split lips. Jasper stood back and with a final charging blow threw an uppercutting blow with all his strength into the body of Mad Len's just below his heart. His training from the army had become instinctive.

Mad Len eyes widened then rolled back and he collapsed to the ground. He lay completely still as the derision of the crowd turned upon their erstwhile champion. The prone body remained perfectly still and the crowd began to go quiet. Jack Broad rushed forward and bent over his man. He turned his head towards Jasper and said evenly "He's dead."

Pandemonium broke out amongst the onlookers who to a man dispersed, putting as much distance between themselves and the protagonists. Jack Broad and Jasper were soon almost alone in the area around the booth. Jasper, his head still ringing, was gently flexing his bruised and swollen hands whilst gasping to get air back into his lungs. "Come on," Broad rasped, "Help me get him into the back of the booth." Between them they dragged the body out of sight and threw old sacks and rubbish over it.

Broad caught hold of a young urchin who had been watching the whole affair from the corner of the booth. "Here lad, a penny for you. See that big man over there in the top hat? Run as fast as you can and tell Ned Bullen I have a disposal job for him." He gave the youth a cuff around the ear, "And be quick about it lad, or you'll be sorry."

Jasper was a spectator to a scene in which he had the starring role. Broad looked at him intently "Where did you learn to fight like that?" then with a nod towards the scar that was now livid from the exertions of the fight he added, "Army or Navy?"

"Army ......Spain and Waterloo." Jasper responded almost vacantly, whilst looking in the direction of the booth and the pile of rubbish. He had just killed a man. He had killed men in battle but he had been trained to look upon them mindlessly as the enemy. It was kill or be killed. He had now killed a man who didn't have a gun or bayonet.

He realised he had acted on impulse. It was not the money, five shillings is of no real consequence. He could see that the man was a bully, who beat, usually drunk young men with too much bravado for their own good. He had killed for his country but this was different. Had the army and war, killed a piece of himself inside that he would react without remorse?

Broad saw his look "Don't worry about him. He had no-one who will miss him" he grunted and added, "'Except for the landlord of The Market Gate where no doubt he owed a pretty penny." He took Jasper's arm and led him away from the booth that was now deserted apart from its macabre secret. He continued "People are getting unhappy around here about what goes on at this Fair these days. We have to be careful. There will be some questions being asked."

Two men in filthy and sweat reeking clothes, appeared and snarled aggressively "Mr Bullen says you have a job for us, gov." He glared at Jack then Jasper and added "He wants paying up front."

Jack Broad was totally undaunted, "You mind your tongue, else I'll have it cut out." He then threw a purse at the larger man. "That will be enough for Ned Bullen .... and don't think that he won't know how much I've given you. Now get on with your work." He turned to Jasper and grunted "Old Father Thames will have a new resident tonight'"

He led Jasper away until they reached the meat market of Smithfield. When he was sure that they hadn't been followed, he stopped. He looked hard at Jasper and for once felt a rare compassion for a man that would always demand respect but was still young and now out of his depth in the big city. Maybe it was the knowledge of the danger this man had faced in his King's service that made him want to help the young fellow. Broad shook his head at his own softness and resumed his usual brisk tone. "You are a man to be noticed and you need to get away from here. Do you have anywhere you can go?"

Jasper held Broad's look whilst his mind raced. Finally he dropped his head to stare at the ground and sadly said "Yes... back home. I left my friend and his girl at The Brewers Tap just a few hours ago. They will be making their way back to Dorset in the morning."

"The Brewers Tap? Come on, I know Tom Wilson, he's a good man. Now quickly we will take the back streets to Chiswell Street."

Without protest, Jasper allowed himself to be led back to where he had left Robert in what seemed a lifetime ago. Robert leapt up when Jasper appeared in the doorway. He looked back and forth from Jasper and the small man in a brightly coloured frock coat, who was obviously on a mission. Broad made his way straight over to Tom Wilson and the pair disappeared into the tap room in earnest conversation.

Robert approached Jasper, "In the Lord's name what have you done to your face?" Then noticing Jasper was still flexing his knuckles, "You've been in a fight" he said rather than asked.

Jasper, looking to where Tom and Broad had disappeared, simply said, "Yes, but not now. We'll have plenty of time to talk."

Tom, with his visitor, came out of the Tap Room and went over to his desk where he retrieved a small purse. He gave it to Jack Broad. They shook hands and turning to leave, Broad called across the room to Jasper "Look after yourself lad, and good luck." With that he left and ended a brief and traumatic encounter in Jasper's life.

Tom looked at Jasper with a wry smile. "I'll get Sarah to clean the blood off your face." He looked down at Jasper hands, "You might have a problem holding a full tankard of beer with those for a few days." He grimaced, "Jack Broad told me what happened. He's right it would be best for you not to be around for a while. It will probably all be forgotten within a week but we don't want you tempting the hangman's rope."

He faced Jasper and Robert and put a hand on a shoulder of each of them. He studied them for a moment He could tell that they saw the future in different ways but each with some frustration. "Lads, you have lived life more than most men already. You had to work from a young age for your fathers and for four years you fought for your King and country." He chuckled, "You have also spent time savouring the delights of this fine city," He raised his eyebrows and shook his head, "and no thanks I don't want to know the details."

He walked over to his table and gestured for them to follow. "Look, this is the beginning for you both. You are only twenty-four years old and eventually you will look back on these times as a only a part of your lives. You have proved that you are both fighters; and I don't mean just with your fists." He looked hard at Jasper. "Jasper, you will stand up for yourself and anyone else you think has been badly treated. Jack Broad told me about you taking on 'the boy basher' as you put it. Now stop feeling sorry for yourself and get rid of that bitterness."

He looked back at Robert. "As for you young man, don't you dare think your life is over as you will be settling for married life - especially as it will be with my Sarah! You have shown that you will stand up for yourself and your fellow men will admire you for it and will follow you."

Tom paused then broke into a broad smile and sat back, "Life doesn't come to a grand climax. It's a series of episodes and events. I know that you've got many adventures and scrapes ahead of you both. Life will not be dull." He stood up, "Now if you'll excuse me I have to make some arrangements." He gave one of his belly laughs, "Good Lord I envy you. Go with my blessing you've got much ahead of you."

Tom was a good friend to have at times of trouble. By the time it became dark he had arranged for a brewery dray to be waiting to take all three of his charges out of London at dawn the following morning. Every father knows he will lose his daughter to another man eventually, but this had happened to Tom quicker than he expected. His emotion at the loss of his beloved Sarah was evident by the tears in his eyes but he gave Robert a long, warm hug. He said that at least he was gaining a son and made Robert promise to look after her properly. He then made sure that they had sufficient money that when the brewer's dray got them to Kew they could ride in a coach from there to Winchester, and then on to Poole, and home.

It was not an easy journey as emotions were mixed. Happy anticipation of the future contrasted with an air of frustration and not a little trepidation.

At the end of the journey, broken by the overnight stop near Winchester, the coach finally reached Poole late in the afternoon. It disgorged its passengers and rattled off leaving them and their bags on the quayside. They looked around not quite sure what to do next when Jasper saw a familiar face. He called across to a man climbing off his boat onto the quay. "Captain Jenkins, it's good to see you.

Jenkins squinted in the evening gloom then his face lit up. "Robert Bollson, Jasper Tomes is that you?"

"It most certainly is."

The good Captain rushed forward and shook each warmly by the hand. "My god it's good to see you back again.

Heavens preserve us, you've grown into fine young men." He hesitated looking at Jasper with his scar and eye patch. "Is everything alright with you son?"

"Jasper chuckled dismissively. "Oh that." He said looking up with his one eye." It was just a scratch. You ought to see the other guy."

Sarah was standing aside when Jenkins realised she was there. "Who's this lovely young lady?"

Robert moved to Sarah's side and put his arm around her. Without a pause he was proud to say for the very first time, " Captain Jenkins, may I introduce Sarah, my wife"

"My dear, it's lovely to meet you" He turned to Robert. "You ol' dog. You've got yourself a rare beauty, lad."

Sarah blushed, but she also felt an inner warmth as she saw her man was remembered, and so well liked, though he hadn't been seen for so many years.

Jasper was anxious that they finished their long journey. "Captain, I see you still have The Pride of the Bay. Would you be going back across to Swanage?"

"I am – hop on board and we'll get going right away."

The journey across the Bay passed with much conversation about where they had been and what they had done. In the way of such casual recollections, only the good times came to mind.

Once they had landed in Swanage, Jenkins left them with further warm handshakes all round. The weary three were worn out but the final walk up to the village became easier as they recognised familiar surroundings. Upon reaching the church, Jasper and Robert turned to look at each other. Although they were to work and live in the same village and still drink together in The Ship, they were about to break a bond. It was a bond that men forge when they live close together and experience joys and laughter, traumas and sadness. No longer would it be Jasper and Robert at each other's side every day. No longer would people look at them as one. Sarah stood quietly in the background; she understood. Both had tears as they gave each other a hug then Jasper broke free and turned to Sarah. He gave her a hug and whispered in her ear "Look after the ol' bugger for me."

Jasper turned and started walking towards to his home. Without looking back he raised his hand and waved. "See you soon, old friend."

Sarah went to Robert as tears streamed down his face. He took a deep breath and looked at Sarah then said suddenly, "I love you" They looked at each other for a few moments then he put his arm around her shoulder and said "Come on, lets meet your new Ma and Pa."

Robert felt comfortable as he walked through the village. All the houses, church, the green where he had played as a child and even The Ship were just as they were four years before. These were places that were part of his life as he had grown up, places that would always be familiar to him and he would think of as home. When they reached the front door of his Ma and Pa's cottage, he paused. He could sense Sarah's nervousness. "Don't worry they won't bite. They'll love you." He gave the door a loud knock. After a minute, it was opened by his father. Joshua stood there for a moment then his jaw dropped, "My God, Robert you're back...... Oh my God, Son how good it is to see you." He then spun round and called out "Martha, come quick the boy has come home."

Martha came hurrying to the door with a confused look on her face. She then saw the son she thought she had lost, standing in the doorway with his arms outstretched She burst into tears and ran over to him and hugged him as hard as she could, "My dear Robert, dear Robert you're home."

Sarah all this time yet again stood silently in the background watching the touching scene unfold in front of her. The first thought that came to her was 'What lovely people'. I just hope that I am worthy of them.'

Robert for the second time that evening had tears rolling down his cheeks. Then he remembered Sarah and spun around, "Oh I'm so sorry dear." Rushing over to her he put his arm around her waist and faced his parents, "Ma, Pa, please meet Sarah, my wife."

This was a cue for Martha to again burst into tears. After a moment's pause she held her arms out, "Sarah, I am so pleased. I am so pleased."

Joshua looked on with love in his eyes. He was so glad that after all his wife had been through she had regained a son she thought she had lost forever. He was also overjoyed that she had also overnight gained a daughter. He frowned though, there was something not quite right that he couldn't put his finger on.

Horatio had been asleep upstairs but was woken by the noise. As he sleepily walked into the room he looked at Robert and Sarah, "Ma, Pa, what's going on?" Martha went to him and put her arms round his shoulders, "Don't you recognise your brother, it's Robert. He's come back from the war."

Horatio looked confused then his eyes opened wide and he ran over and wrapped his arms around Robert's legs. Robert ruffled his hair. "Hello Horatio, I'm home and I've brought you a new sister. This is Sarah." Robert turned to Sarah, "This is my youngest brother, he was just five when I left."

Sarah smiled, "Hello Horatio. I'm sure we are going to be good friends."

Robert looked around. "Where are the others?"

Martha and Joshua glanced at each other but went silent. Robert looked from to the other, "What's up?   What's happened?"

Joshua glanced at Martha, "Dot got married to Bill Tubbs." He hesitated. "The marriage didn't go well.   He hesitated again and then said quickly.   "I'll explain later. Horatio, go and get your brothers and sister."

Robert had a foreboding that something else was wrong and Sarah, sensing this, moved over to his side and linked her arm with his. Joshua cleared his throat, "Peter ......" he stopped as Martha gave a quiet sob.   "Peter was killed in an accident."

Robert closed his eyes and let out a groan,   "Oh no." He turned to look at Sarah with a desperate look in his eyes, "Peter had to take my place when I left. He hated going down the mine. He shouldn't have been there. It's my fault." He looked at his Pa, "What happened?"

"We don't know exactly. It was difficult for him at the quarry and he was very troubled. He left the house one evening and some men found him the next day at the bottom of the cliff at Austell Point." Joshua gave Martha a hug. He looked awkward. "He must have slipped and fallen over the edge."

Sarah looked up at Robert and knew that he felt guilty. "Robert, please don't blame yourself." she said gently.

At this point Walter, Edward, Thomas and Grace came bounding into the room. They descended on Robert but after a few minutes Martha stopped them. "Now wait all of you. You will have plenty of time to talk with Robert. Robert, Sarah come with me outside. I want to have a word with you." She glanced at Joshua as she went giving a look that told her husband that she was alright.

Once outside she held Robert's hand and gave it a squeeze. "Robert dear, I know what you're thinking. Don't." she said firmly. "Your Pa blames himself as well. Peter was a sensitive boy and you and your Pa are strong. Neither of you must dwell on the past. The family needs you both to be strong." She turned to Sarah, "You can't know how much this evening means to me. I am so happy. The past has gone and we have grieved over Peter, we must all now move on."

She took each by the hand and directed them to the door.

Robert stood firm. "What did Pa mean about Dot – 'I'll explain later'"

Martha looked at Robert and Sarah then decided that now was the time to tell them. "Bill Tubbs was not a good husband to Dot and we were very worried about her. She has two gorgeous little girls." She sighed. "The Lord forgive me. - they were the only two good things that Tubbs has produced." She shook her head sadly. "Two lovely little girls that her grandma never sees now."

"Why, what happened?" Robert was alarmed.

"What I'm about to tell you is between us and your Pa."

Sarah squeezed Robert's hand in anticipation. "You probably remember that Ted Edmunds was very keen on Dot. Well, we don't know the details, but Dot left suddenly without telling anyone. Ted says she is happy and living in Winchester. This is our secret, nobody else can know otherwise Tubbs will find her."

Robert was looking at the ground and Sarah could tell that he felt wretched. "You and Pa have gone through so much since I left. I'm sorry I only thought about myself."

"Don't be silly. It's wonderful to have you back – and Sarah here now as well. Both of you go inside. Your brothers and sister are all grown up since you left. Get to know them again and Sarah you're part of the family now, they will all love you." As they turned she said quietly, "God bless you. Thank you Lord."

* * *

Robert and Jasper went to meet Silas Winter the next day at the quarry. After some theatrical hesitation they were given jobs which they had to start immediately.

Robert and Sarah stayed with his Ma and Pa and the following days and weeks were filled with renewed tears, questions and laughter and during this time Martha and Sarah quickly became devoted to each other. Sarah had never known a mother before and she found in Martha all that she had dreamed a mother should be since she was as a little girl.

It was a busy time for the young couple as they set up home in Fig Cottage. Their first night at the Cottage was a nervous time for both of them. Since their departure from London they had virtually no time alone together.

Jasper was there during that first evening helping move the rudimentary furniture and generally helping where possible. When he finally left, Robert gently closed the door behind him and turned to look at Sarah. His love for her had been bottled up, but now as he saw her standing uneasily by the fire he could feel his passion rising. Sarah could sense his desire and she felt a binding commitment she had never experienced before and she shivered in anticipation of the love they were to express to each other.

Robert wanted to hold her, feel her pressed against him and he experienced a physical thrill as she let her body meld against his. They held a kiss that increased in urgency until they led each other upstairs to consummate their lives together.

Neither had experienced such feelings before and it was as if a torrent had been finally released. As their bodies moved together he was rocked to his very soul at the intensity of the feelings that swept through him -- feelings that were by turns gentle, sure, and generous.

Their passion having climaxed, both lay entwined with a feeling of fulfilment, and an emotional bond having been formed between them for life.

June 1817

Charlie was always busy and although he had treated himself to a fine fob watch he was usually late. This was the case yet again on a Monday in the June following his declaration of interest in meeting with Edith on a regular basis.

When Charlie arrived Stephen showed him in to where Ambrose was in a deep conversation with a gentleman that Charlie had seen in Poole several times. Ambrose turned to Charlie immediately and appeared slightly flustered. "Ah, there you are Charlie." He gave the impression of being slightly embarrassed. He put his hand gently on the shoulder of his other guest. "Have you met Francis, eh, Francis Balman?"

"I have seen you in the town. It is good to meet you, sir." Charlie walked over to shake Francis' hand. After a brief handshake Charlie dropped his hand and surreptitiously wiped it on his trousers. Francis' handshake was limp and clammy.

Charlie nonchalantly looked at Ambrose's guest. His round puffy face framed unnaturally red thick lips and was capped by curly brown hair. He wore a dark blue frock coat over a shirt that was frilled at the front and cuffs. His trousers were light brown and tapered down to white spats and low cut shoes. He was a man who took a great deal of care to make sure that he was impeccably dressed.

Ambrose coughed hesitantly. "Charlie, Francis and I have some, eh, business to discuss. Stephen will be in attendance all evening so would it be terribly rude of me to leave you here with Edith?" He looked expectantly at the door. "She should be here any moment now."

As if on cue, the door was opened quickly as Edith hurried into the room. Charlie having just inspected Ambrose's guest he found himself noting how Edith was dressed. She wore a long cream dress with a low fashionable square neckline and puffed sleeves. Her hair was tied up in a casual bun by a wide brown and white band that allowed her face to be framed in feminine curls. She had also obviously dressed carefully, as was natural - for a lady.

"Charlie I am so sorry, have you been waiting long?"

"No, no."   He chuckled. "You know me with my timekeeping."

Ambrose broke into the conversation. "As I just mentioned, Francis and I wish to have a talk and we thought as it was such a fine summer evening we would take in the air. Also a few members of the music society that are friends of Francis are forming a Literary group. We thought we might join them."

Charlie saw Edith's shoulders sag and she gave a gentle sigh. "Ambrose, you and Francis are such good friends. You are almost inseparable." She had started to frown then brightened up and turned to Charlie. "As Stephen is here all evening I was wondering if you would like to stay here for the evening. I can play some music I have just learnt on the piano." She laughed. "I promise not to sing."

"That would be an excellent idea." He quickly added. "Oh sorry, I did not mean that you should refrain from singing." Edith laughed.

Ambrose clapped his hands. "Good that's settled then." He put his hand on Francis' shoulder. "Come along let's leave these two."

Ambrose and Francis left obviously in a good mood. Edith watched them go but her frown had returned. She looked back at Charlie who went to speak. She closed her eyes and shook her head slightly, a gesture that made it plain that no further comment was required.

Edith composed herself. "Charlie, I will ring for Stephen. Would you like tea or some of that excellent brandy that you give to Ambrose?"

"Tea will be fine, thank you."

Their evening progressed with each finding the conversation relaxed and easy-going. After about an hour, during which Edith had played on the piano, Charlie took a deep breath. He was clearly about to broach an important matter. His boyhood friends from Langton Matravers would have been able to empathise with his awkwardness.

"Edith." He felt compelled to make a formal introduction. "Edith, I find your company most pleasing and I look forward to these evenings that I spend in your company." Charlie may have been from humble beginnings but his maturity had taught him the correct way to act.

Edith sat upright in her chair her hands clasped together on her lap She looked quietly expectant. "Charlie that is most kind."

"I have been coming here for some time now."

"Yes quite a long time."

Charlie missed the irony and continued. "May I say that I have reached the point whereby, with your – and Ambrose's permission, I would like our friendship to be more than just a friendship. Charlie thought to himself, 'Why is it so much easier to conclude business than speak of personal affairs?' He realised he was at the point where he had to take the bull by the horns. He moved forward and went to sit on a chair next to hers. He placed a hand on hers. "Edith Tillson, I would like our relationship to be on a more formal understanding."

Edith tittered. "Charlie, I do believe that you want me to sign a contract for some business." The irony was not missed this time and Charlie flushed. Edith instantly regretted she had embarrassed him.

Charlie smiled in self-deprecation. "I am sorry. What I am trying to say is that I would like for us to be betrothed."

Edith smiled. "You are giving me a proposal of marriage?"

"What I am saying is, eh." He stopped, dropped his head briefly, then smiled and finished with a chuckle. "Yes."

"Well Mr Heywood, I do formally accept your proposal." She feigned formality, then relaxed and clapped her hands together. "Charlie, you have made me so happy. Thank you, thank you."

A relieved Charlie stood up. "Edith, would it be rude if I asked you to ring for Stephen. I think I would like that glass of brandy you offered me earlier."

The evening continued with the newly betrothed couple in a more relaxed and comfortable frame of mind as they both saw a happy future ahead. A hurdle had been approached and safely negotiated.

In the month's that followed, little on the surface seemed to have changed with their courtship. They still met for the Music Society evenings; they still took their walks along the harbour and of course they spent evenings having dinner with Edith playing the piano. They were never invited to join Ambrose and Francis at their Literary evenings.

Courtship and Proposal were not Charlie's specialist talents. He had concluded both in manner that was done properly and to all concerned satisfactorily. Charlie was a truly modest fellow, but inside he felt proud of himself. More importantly as he spent more time with Edith he also realised how much he loved her and looked forward to their lives together.

If intimate matters were not his forte, the organising and arranging of the wedding and the future marital home were completed swiftly and competently.

The marriage was held after Christmas at St James' Church in Poole. They did not realise it but their marriage was exactly a year to the day since Charlie had visited in the snow. As was customary, there were just a few guests in attendance. Charlie's mother, who was now becoming quite frail, was delighted for her only son. Ambrose and Francis were also present as was Stephen who stood discreetly in the background.

After the ceremony Ambrose came to shake Charlie's hand. "Congratulations old chap. It's good that we're now brothers-in-law."

"Thank you." He gestured to Francis who was speaking with Edith and his mother. "I hear that Francis will be moving into Edith's rooms now that she is my wife?"

Ambrose hesitated. "That's right. It seems such a waste to have just me rattling around in such a large house."

Charlie didn't speak for a moment and he started to frown. "Have a care, sir. Have a care."

Edith came over to them and linked her arm through Charlie's. "Your Ma, sorry, our Ma says that we are taking her back to the village with us."

"That's right." He turned to Ambrose. "Thank you for your kind wishes. We are about to go. I bid you farewell." After handshakes and kisses on cheeks all round, the newly wedded couple left with Charlie's mother.

Once they were well on their way, Edith looked at Charlie, she was curious,   "What were you and Ambrose talking about in the church?

Charlie glanced at his mother who was now starting to doze off. "It was nothing special."

"Oh." Edith was not convinced but then asked. "I understand that you men have been doing more business together."

"That was it, my dear." Charlie easily slipped into the familiarity of marriage. "As Ambrose's business is increasingly tied to shipping stone from my quarry to London, it makes sense that he should maintain an office over in Swanage."

"That's good news. You have said that business is growing."

"Yes, very much. The Swanage office will be a joint venture and as Stephen is a good smart fellow he will go over there to ensure that all is properly under control. It will not take all his time and he will therefore take up the same duties in our household as he has done in Ambrose's house." Charlie coughed then added. "I understand that he would prefer to look after yourself rather than the two men here in Poole." He added quickly "Of course, we shall employ a housekeeper as well."

Edith sat back and relaxed. Despite her happy mood as it was her wedding day, there was something niggling away in the back of her mind.

Marriage did become a watershed for Charlie. He had always been a confident man, sure of his facts and not afraid to take risks. Despite his gaucheness when courting Edith the surety of marriage dispelled any remaining doubts he may have had about himself. He became more gregarious and with his financial security and self-confidence he became a dominant personality.

He had bought a large house in St George's Lane in Langton Matravers with which Edith was enchanted. Charlie did everything he could to please her and make her life satisfying. They found that their life together was stimulating and Edith was able to support him in business when he needed encouragement or reassurance.

Edith did miss the hustle and bustle of the port of Poole and would frequently go there with Charlie when he had business to conduct. She would visit her brother and her own friends in the Music Society. Charlie and Edith became central to the emerging local bourgeoisie.

As Charlie's business's were thriving it meant that he had to go away frequently to meet with someone in the web of contacts he had established. When in Poole he would occasionally see Ambrose, but he had soon developed a dislike for Francis who had installed himself in Edith's place in the house.

After one such trip he arrived back in Langton Matravers and saw that Edith was looking out of the window obviously watching for him to arrive. As he reigned in, Stephen was quickly on hand to guide his horse and carriage around to the small stable at the rear of the house.

For a serious minded lady conscious of the proper decorum to be displayed at all times, Edith was out of character. It was clear that she had exciting news that dispelled any pretence to proprietary. She almost skipped out to meet Charlie and threw her arms around his neck in a warm embrace.

"Edith, my love, what a lovely welcome."

"I have wondful news. Husband, we will soon be starting your Heywood dynasty." She said playfully.

Charlie paused for only a brief moment before he deduced exactly the reason for Edith's behaviour. He stood back and took Edith's hands and looked at her carefully. "Edith, you're with child?" he said more than asked.

Edith clapped her hands in glee. Yes, you're going to be a father."

Charlie enveloped Edith in his arms and squeezed her tightly as his eyes moistened. He then became full of energy. "First, we'll get a doctor to look after you rather than rely on Ma Salen here in the village, and we'll buy the finest baby clothes and we'll hire a nanny to help you ......"

Edith pressed her fingers to his mouth. "Schh - there's plenty of time to think of all those things."

Charlie's face was wreathed in the broadest of smiles as he took her hands. "No, please, it's just that I know a man who can supply ....." he was stopped again as Edith burst into laughter.

"Charlie Heywood you're incorrigible. I'll wager that you know a man for everything."

Charlie frowned. "It is just that I remember well the terrible times that my mother went through when Pa was killed." His eyes flickered briefly then he broke into a smile again. "My son will want for nothing, I promise."

"I know you will be a fine father. He, *or she,*" Edith emphasised the word, "will be the luckiest child alive." Edith took his hand. "Come, we cannot stay out here all day."

Calvin Seager was passing St. Georges when he saw Charlie coming out of the church. "Good Day to you Charlie. Now that Edith is due to give birth we've seen much more of you here in the village."

"Yes, I know it's a woman's affair, but as I am able to spend as much time here as I wish these days, I am concerned that Edith is properly looked after."

"Is she well?"

"She has not had an easy time these last few months; I have been anxious about her well-being. Without her mother here to support her there is no-one else she can turn to other than myself." He paused. "I'm afraid her brother always seems to be otherwise engaged."

Calvin felt compassion for his old friend. Ever since they had grown up together, Charlie had been the self-assured one who never showed any doubts about how he would handle whatever life would throw at him. "How close is she to the birth?"

Charlie grimaced. "Very close. I have called for Dr Holmes and he has been with her since early this morning. It's not a husband's place to be around at these times, so I was just checking on the church and my, eh, things that I left in there."

Calvin said gently. "Don't worry Charlie I'm sure that Edith will be fine."

Further conversation was interrupted as Stephen came breathlessly hurrying down the hill. "Mr Heywood, Dr Holmes has instructed me to inform you that his work is done."

"What does that mean? God man, is my wife well, is the baby born?"

"Yes I believe so. Dr Holmes says to come quickly as he has to attend to other matters."

"Does he indeed?" He glanced at Calvin but spoke to himself. "What I am paying the man he should be in attendance for as long as I believe is necessary." He turned to dash back home to his wife. "If you will excuse me Calvin."

"Of course, of course, my dear chap."

When Charlie arrived home Dr Holmes was coming down the stairs wiping his hands on his blood stained apron.

"Hell's teeth Doctor, is Edith well? Your clothes are covered in blood."

"Mrs Heywood is sitting up in bed nursing your son." The good doctor frowned, and was dismissive about the condition of his clothes. "Although your wife did not have an easy birth, indeed I had to help your son to enter this world, these are the clothes I wear for attending births. Most of the blood is from previous patients."

"Do you not wash before attending a lady?"

Dr Holmes was clearly irritated by such a question. "What is the point? I consider excessive cleanliness to be next to prudishness. Indeed Mr Heywood, there is no point in being clean. it is out of place at such times." He chuckled. "An executioner might as well manicure his nails before chopping off a head."

Charlie was not listening. "I will go to my wife. I thank you for your time, sir."

When he entered the room it was in darkness with the drapes having been pulled across the windows as was usual at such times. Charlie was alarmed when he saw Edith. She was ashen faced with her hair lank with drying sweat. His son was oblivious to any discomfort around him and was exercising his lungs to his fullest. Edith appeared though to have shrunken from the robust woman he knew and loved. He rushed forward and on one knee took the hand not holding her child. Tears were welling up in Charlie's eyes. "My dearest, are you well? Are you in any pain?"

Edith gently squeezed Charlie's hand and gave him a weak smile "Don't you go worrying, I will be fine." She made a vague gesture in the direction of the bedside table. "Could you please pass that glass of water?" Charlie leapt to carry out her request and she took the slightest of sips then returned the glass to him. She looked tenderly at Charlie. "Come on have a good look at your son."

Charlie did so and tears streamed down his face. "Thank you for my son; we said that if it was a boy we would call him, Jack." He leant forward and gently kissed the bundle on the forehead. "Welcome to the world Jack." Charlie sat by Edith's bedside for a full hour with neither speaking very much. There then came a quiet knock on the bedroom door and Ma Salen appeared. "I am sorry to impose Mr Heywood, but I saw Dr Holmes, and he said that I may be of help to your wife."

She gave Edith a sympathetic look, and Charlie felt guilty that he hadn't asked her to be present at the birth. She smiled and shook her head gently as if to say that she knew what he was thinking but it was of no consequence. "You go and have something to eat. I will sit here with your wife. I will call you if she wants to see you."

Charlie left the bedroom feeling happier now that Ma Salen, who had overseen the birth of half of the village, was with Edith. For a couple of days they took it in turns to be with Edith and she showed signs of gaining back her strength.

However on the third morning when Charlie went in to see Edith it was obvious she was not well. She lay on her back and appeared listless and indifferent. Very soon she complained of a headache and she started to perspire heavily and had a raging thirst. Ma Salen, who had been with her all night looked worried. "How is your stomach pain, my dear?" She asked Edith whilst holding her hand.

Edith nodded. "It seems to be getting worse." She gave an involuntary wince.

Ma Salen turned to Charlie. "Could you get me a fresh bowl of water and flannels. We need to cool her down." She followed Charlie to the door and quietly tugged his arm. "If you believe there is a God then I suggest you pray to Him for your wife's deliverance. She has what is called child-bed fever."

Charlie's alarm increased. "She will be alright won't she? Please tell me she won't die."

Ma Salen did not speak immediately, then quietly whispered encouragingly' "Some of my charges that have had this fever do live to see their child grow up. There is nothing that we can do however, other than to try to cool the fever."

"What about Dr Holmes? Can he help?"

Ma Salen snorted. "There is a firm belief that in these instances the means of carrying the infection is by the person attending the birth. I'm afraid that Dr Holmes' only action would be to bleed and purge her. The poor dear is going through enough without Dr Holmes making it worse." She looked back over to Edith who's fever seemed to be becoming worse. "Can you get Stephen to fetch Sally Gibbs. She had her baby last month and she will be able to act as a wet nurse for your son."

Charlie frowned. "I don't think I know much about her; is she a good girl."

Ma Salen smiled. "Don't worry she has no bad habits that will be passed to your son through her milk. She's a good lass and she could do with the extra money."

Charlie arranged for Sally to attend to Jack but he was devastated by the way that his wife was suffering. The next few days were a living hell for him, as each time he entered Edith's room she appeared to him to be getting weaker. Ma Salen stayed with her at all times only leaving her side briefly to attend to her own needs.

On the third day after the onset of the fever, Charlie went to Edith's room in almost a daze. It was with a heavy heart, and taking a deep breath, he turned the handle and opened the door to the bedroom.

He stopped as soon as he saw the scene in front of him. The drapes had been thrown open and the early morning sunlight was streaming through the window. Edith was perched half upright as Ma Salen helped her take spoonfuls of hot broth.

Edith looked across at Charlie who was frozen to the spot. "My dear husband, I am so sorry to have made such as fuss."

Ma Salen rose from her chair and put her hand on Charlie's shoulder. "Mrs Heywood is a brave lady. She will be alright now." She then quietly slipped out of the room leaving Charlie alone with his wife. He rushed forward, with tears streaming down his cheeks, he sat on the bed holding his beloved wife's hand.

Ignaz Semmelweis, a Hungarian physician demonstrated that the incidence of puerperal fever (also known as childbed fever) could be drastically reduced by appropriate hand washing by medical caregivers. He made this discovery as late as 1847 while working in the Maternity Department of the Vienna Lying-in Hospital.
It was also argued that even if his findings were correct, washing one's hands each time before treating a pregnant woman, as Semmelweis advised, would be too much work. Doctors often wore coats covered with pus, blood and germs and were not eager to admit that they had caused so many deaths!

CHAPTER FOURTEEN
A Women's Place

Tom Wilson was right; life is a series of episodes and events that meld into each other. Barring an unforeseen windfall or tragedy, no-one wakes up one morning and says to themselves 'My life is different today.' This was the case for Jasper and Robert as well as Charlie Heywood, who would each experience situations that would influence and change what would be the next stage in their lives."

As 1817 wore on into 1818 Jasper and Robert re-established themselves in the daily life of Langton Matravers. Although they were now answerable to Silas Winter in the quarry rather than their respective fathers, their way of life quickly resumed to where it had been before they joined the army. The landlord's ale at The Ship was always there to help them to keep in the present, as well as ease the aches and pains from a week spent in the quarry.

At the end of one such evening as they strolled home, Robert paused as they were passing St. George's church. "Jasper, I need to get rid of a couple of ales. I won't be a moment." He vaulted the wall surrounding the graveyard and disappeared down the side of the church.

Jasper eased himself up to sit on the wall and pulled out his clay pipe. As he lit up he gazed around casually taking in the still of night. The dark silhouettes of the stone houses that paraded up Stonehouse Hill were barely discernible apart from the occasional glimmer from the flicker of a candle through a small window. There was a total silence that could almost be touched. Firmly closed doors concealed whatever dramas, emotions or passions that were unfolding within each world.

"Hey, you seem miles away. Are you alright?" Robert re-joined Jasper looking more relaxed than a few minutes beforehand.

Jasper chuckled. "Yes, no problem. I was just taking the night air." He looked at Robert and grinned. "I was just thinking it's all so peaceful. When we were in the army it was never this quiet. There was always something happening, and as you have said before, there was always that gnawing feeling in the stomach about what might happen the next day." He frowned then waved his arm around to encompass all their surroundings. "This is all a sham though."

"What do you mean? The villagers are good folk. Alright some have their problems and there are some that are bad eggs, but they are basically a good bunch."How can you say that?" He thought for a moment. "Anyway as for us, our friends will say that you and I seem content now."

"That's my point they would say that but what we went through in the army, fighting and fear that were part of our lives have left their scars. I don't mean just the physical ones."

Robert interrupted. "They are fading memories."

"Maybe. You tell me that you still have nights where you lay awake in a cold sweat with the visions of Badajoz."

Robert shifted uncomfortably. No-one likes to be reminded of what might be seen as a weakness.

"Don't worry, that's between you and me - and Sarah, of course." He looked at his pipe in annoyance and knocked out the remnants of the tobacco on the wall beneath him. "When I think back I still get riled at how we, and the rest of the regiment, were just thrown out of the army when they decided they didn't need us any more. So much for fighting for your King and country. When it comes to it they don't give a ……" He stopped.

"God, what was in the ale tonight? Look you talk of the army but in the time we were away from the village we had some great times in London." He looked around into the darkness and somewhere a door was slammed but the silence returned immediately. "London was always noisy, busy and full of life." He gave a smug grin. "I also met a very special person there as well."

"Aye you're right. It's a mite different here. The point I'm trying to make though, is that despite outward appearances, not all's well." He took a deep breath and looked at Robert carefully. "Are matters with you and Sarah alright? I saw that she was giving you the silent treatment the other day."

Robert laughed. "It was nothing. A trivial thing, but the joke is that in the morning I will know if Sarah is not speaking to me before she wakes up." He laughed again. "We've never been happier and closer." He eased himself off of the wall. "I can't stay talking all night. I must get home." He looked at Jasper and gave him a slap on the thigh. "Good night you old rogue. I'll see you tomorrow."

Following the winter snow, in early 1818, it had rained constantly and Robert had to make his way carefully through the inevitable resulting mud that it left behind. The talk of Sarah had dispelled any feeling of tiredness and he entered his home with a sense of anticipation for the night ahead.

Robert and Sarah's married life together was like any other. It was not without it's problems, and there were some disagreements, but the bond between them had grown rather than diminished. As soon as Sarah heard him come in she rushed downstairs and threw her arms around his neck. There was a twinkle in her eye.

Robert was rather taken aback by her welcome. "Are you alright dear?" He then recalled that Sarah was being sick when he had left that morning. "You don't seem to have been very well lately."

Sarah gave him a broad smile. "I am as well as could be expected." She guided him over to his seat by the fire and knelt beside him. Before Robert could speak she pressed his hand resting on her thigh and gave it a squeeze. "Would you prefer to be called Pa or father?" She didn't move and fixed him with an enormous grin.

Robert sat still staring at Sarah as the meaning of what she had said struck him. The silence was shattered as he leapt in the air.

"You're with child!" Sarah knew already.

"You're going to be a mother." Sarah had also realised that already.

"Oh God. I'm going to be a father." Now they both knew.

Robert stopped in his tracks and grabbed Sarah's hand. "Oh dear, I wasn't thinking, you have to sit down. You need to rest."

Sarah laughed. "You silly thing. I'm perfectly alright."

"When is it due? Do you have any idea?"

"I've spoken with old Ma Salen in the village. She cannot judge with any great certainty." she gave an impish grin. "It will probably be in November."

Good news has to be shared and Robert went to let Joshua and Martha know as quickly as he could the next day. Joshua shook his hand and with a broad beam said, "Well done, lad."

Martha was more solicitous "I knew it. When I saw her the other day I said to myself she's with child."

Joshua grinned and shook his head. "You women, you always say that you can tell."

Martha laughed. "Well, we can." She gave Robert a loving look. "I think you know how happy this makes us both."

Joshua went and put his arm round Martha's waist. "It is said that the Lord moves in mysterious ways. Just a few years ago there wasn't enough food on our table. Now I have a job that I can do at the quarry and I get regular money. We have you back, Robert, we have Sarah and now we will have another grandchild."

Martha smiled and nestled against her husband but a flicker of a frown crossed her face. "I just worry about Dot. I hope she and the girls are well. I also hope she has seen the last of that man Bill Tubbs."

Joshua gave Martha a squeeze but said nothing.

Robert proudly walked around the village and at the quarry for the next week as if he were a dog with two tails.

Jasper was almost as jubilant as Robert when he heard his news. Suffice it to be said they decided to wet the baby's head in The Ship even though it hadn't been born yet.

The forthcoming addition to the village was suitably toasted and Jasper made his way back home. The cottage was lit only by the flickering light from the dying embers of the fire. His ma was dozing peacefully before joining Isaac upstairs in bed. Jasper looked tenderly at her face lined with the wrinkles earned from a lifetime of honest hard work. The big man's heart reached out to her and he touched her gently on the shoulder.

She stirred quicker than he intended. "What's up?" She reacted. "Oh. It's you Jasper." She stood up slowly. "You've been to The Ship with Robert, haven't you?" She smiled. "How's Sarah?"

"She's fine." Jasper had a notion what was coming next.

Ada put her hand on Jasper's arm and smiled gently. 'How about you son?"

"I'm fine too." Jasper said avoiding the underlying question.

"Do you think you'll find yourself a wife like Robert and Charlie Heywood. Have you thought about it?"

This wasn't the conversation Jasper wanted. "Look Ma, I'm fine." He gave Ada a peck on the cheek. "I've got to get up early tomorrow. I'm off to Swanage early." Another smile and he turned to mount the stairs to his room.

To see Robert with Sarah and Charlie with Edith did in quiet moments give Jasper a slight pang of jealousy, but he did not begrudge them their happiness. With the long hours dictated by the work at the quarry, Jasper's life continued in the routine of work and The Ship. He didn't dwell on his past frustrations but there was growing a feeling of emptiness. It was just that he hadn't met anyone with whom he felt he could share his life.

Jasper's natural leadership of his peers gained him the opportunity to take on more responsibilities at the quarry. To break the tedium he began to ensure that he had the task of checking large shipments of stone out of the quarry and ensuring their safe delivery to Swanage.

Chance can have many consequences: Jasper and Robert being directed to The brewers Tap and Robert meetng Sarah; a misaimed musket ball avoided Lord Serrell and Charles would not meet Emily when she was a widow: If Joshua had gone to work earlier at Crack Lane quarry - Dot would have not married Tubbs and Peter would have found work in Swanage as a solicitors clerk.

Jasper would not have thought that his visits to Swanage would see Chance falling in his favour. On these visits he started to become friendly with Ellen at the stonemasons yard. Ellen had been widowed when her husband was killed at Waterloo. She was a stout and capable woman who did not suffer fools gladly. She was resentful at first of Jasper when she learned that he was a survivor of the Battle but after some time she could see Jasper did not escape the war unscathed. The scar and eye patch were just superficial, other injuries ran much deeper. It became evident that Ellen's no nonsense approach to life, whilst not without sympathy, was good for Jasper. Instead of becoming too introspective he started to look forward to his visits to Swanage. Ellen shared Jasper's outrage about how those of the lower sort were treated, but she was also realistic enough to understand that anger alone was pointless.

It was not long before their relationship started to blossom. One Sunday, after morning church service, Jasper made a special journey into Swanage. Unlike Jasper's normal demeanour, he was nervous as he approached Ellen's house. A similar time where he was unsure whether he went forward or turned back came to mind. He shook his head, strode up and knocked confidently on Ellen's door.

Ellen was delighted to see him. "Why Jasper, what a lovely surprise. What brings you into Swanage on a Sunday? They're not getting you to work on the Lord's day are they?" Jasper's confidence was waning and Ellen noticed the awkwardness. "Come inside." she said gently.

Jasper had prepared for this moment for weeks. He had even practiced out loud the words he was going to use. Ellen smiled for she knew what he wanted to say, and she had hoped that he would. Ellen saw a big man in a unaccustomed situation, and immediately felt compassion for him.

"Eh, Ellen. H'mm, I would like - eh no," He took a deep breath "Ellen we have seen much of each other lately and I have enjoyed your company." he paused, "I thought I should declare my intentions - oh my Lord is that right"

Ellen could not contain herself. She had grown to love the man, but she could not help a snigger. "Oh Lord, Jasper, come on spit it out"

Jasper frowned and then blurted out, "Ellen Bennett, will you consent to be my wife?" Then having said it he leapt forward and went on one knee and took Ellen's hand. "Will you marry me?"

Ellen took both his hands and with a merry laugh said, "Get up you big fool. Of course I will marry you. Thank you." She bent forward and kissed him tenderly. "I love you very much."

His mission accomplished Jasper was at a loss at what to do next. "Thank you." he said lamely and then lurched forward and held Ellen in an awkward embrace.

After a few moments Ellen stood back and taking his hand they went and sat next to the hearth where they spent some hours talking about the future. Jasper had already found a cottage that would be empty in a few months' time. They discussed the actual wedding and decided that they would have the ceremony at St. Mary's parish church in Swanage and as was usual just have a few close friends in attendance.

The marriage took place early December 1818 and much to Sarah's embarrassment, the newly born Jonathon made it difficult for the service to be heard as he exercised his new young lungs.

The newly weds moved into a cottage in Garfield Lane in Langton Matravers. Marriage appeared on the surface to mellow Jasper and they lived happily together. Ellen tried to make each day a journey forward rather than one rooted in the past.

On a misty morning in the New Year following the wedding, Jasper made his weekly delivery of stone to the quayside for loading onto a boat bound for London. Clem Hardman arrived with another load from the quarry as Jasper's part of the job was finishing.

"I'm glad I caught you." Hardman called across to Jasper. "Your Ellen saw me as I was passing through the village. Could you call in home before going back to the quarry."

"Did she say why?"

Hardman shrugged "No." He was not a man to be helpful to others.

Jasper was worried. Ellen had been distracted recently With the naivety of many men he feared that something was wrong and he made his way home as quickly as possible. He burst through the door of the cottage to find Ellen was sitting quietly by the open range fire.

"What's up, my love? I got your message. Are you alright?" his face held a frown as he knelt before Ellen and he took her hand gently.

Ellen looked at her man and smiled, "I saw old Ma Salen this morning. I have missed my last two courses and well, I've got some news for you."

"Oh the Lord save us. What's wrong? Are you badly ill?" He was equal to his friend's innocence at such a time.

Ellen chuckled, "No more than I should be – Jasper Tomes you are going to be a father."

Jasper's jaw dropped, he was speechless. He stood up, eyes wide open, looking round as if expecting to see other people present to hear his momentous news.

At a later date Ellen and Sarah would chuckle at the predictability of their men. Jasper sunk to his knees in front of Ellen, "Are you alright, my dear? Should you not be in bed resting?"

Ellen laughed "Don't be silly, I'm quite well. I'm not the first woman to have a baby. Ma Salen will be round soon to have a talk about what I should do in the next few months. You get back to work now or you won't have work and our little 'un won't have a home to live in."

Jasper was ecstatic but reluctantly went back to the quarry and unable to contain himself, he broadcast his news. Robert seeing his old friend so happy shook his hand warmly and said, "I never thought you had it in you. Well done!." It was as if it had all been Jasper's own work.

The following summer Ellen gave birth to a baby girl that they called Jemima and the big man doted upon his little girl.

* * *

Lord and Lady Wareham decided to spend the Christmas of 1818 at their country house near Corfe. They invited Lord Henry and Henrietta to join them as well as Henry's father the old Lord Olden. Unfortunately Lord Olden was not taken with Lord Wareham's Whig politics and he declined but had readily decided to accept the Duke of Wellington's invitation instead. The Duke was a man after his own heart.

A few days before Christmas, Charles and Henry went out for a ride and they left their wives behind to await their return for lunch. The Ladies were having tea in the Drawing Room that overlooked the gardens. The conversation meandered between various topics until Henrietta remarked upon the gardens. "I must say that Charles did well to employ Humphrey Repton, the garden designer. He has laid out those shrubs, thickets and herbaceous borders in a most pleasing manner. It looked even more beautiful earlier this morning before the frost melted."

"Thank you. I would mention however that it was I that discussed the details with Mr Repton." She chuckled and added ironically. "As if a Lady should know of such things."

Henrietta looked at Emily thoughtfully. "Marriage to Charles has been so good for you. If you don't mind my saying; you have become quite a Lady in - what is it now? - almost two years."

Emily smiled "Yes it is. It has been the best years of my life."

Henrietta looked more serious. "I haven't asked you before now; are you content with the arrangements that Charles set in place for your Estate?"

Emily looked at Henrietta cautiously. "He is my husband Henrietta, it is his Estate now and he will manage it as he sees fit."

Henrietta sighed. "Emily, I understand your loyalty but we are grown women and we should have the choice on how our lives are controlled."

"It is the man's place to take care of those matters. It is our place to be good wives and support our men at all times."

"Do you mean that?"

Emily looked away as if studying the gardens then said quietly, "No." She took a deep breath as if she had decided to speak her mind for the first time. "Women are disadvantaged from childhood. Charles was fortunate to go to Oxford and he had the benefit of studying many things. I would have dearly loved to have had that opportunity. Indeed. It is a simple principle that if women – us – are not prepared by education we cannot be elevated to become true companions to men and more serious - less frivolous in their eyes."

Emily thought for a moment. "Men, and women, are educated, to a large degree, by the opinions and the manners of the society we live in. Until we are allowed to be educated properly, we will not have the tools to assert ourselves."

Henrietta put her cup down emphatically. "My dear Emily, I am so pleased to speak with you like this. I love Henry very much, as I know you love Charles, but receiving trivial attention that men think appropriate to our sex systematically degrades us. In fact, men are insulting by supporting their own superiority.

Emily nodded vigorously then paused and slumped her shoulders. "We may speak in this manner but to what purpose. The law is set, it will be ever thus."

'I'm afraid you are right and I cannot see how it can be changed. I hear Henry talking about the dangers of revolution in the country. However, I do believe that by our actions and behaviour we women can start our own revolution in respect of our condition. We have within our grasp the ability to restore our lost dignity albeit just in our own personal lives." She paused as she realised that she was on her hobbyhorse but these were thoughts that had crowded her mind and she needed to express them.

Emily looked carefully at Henrietta. "I know that you feel strongly about that which we speak, but Henry is not happy when you do so in other people's company." She suddenly got to her feet. "Oh look here they come." After a few moments, Charles and Henry had neared the House and Emily turned to Henrietta. "They look so dashing?"

Henrietta shook her head in resignation. "Yes my dear."

Hugh Lambrick had a most unsatisfactory day.

It had started well with he and Mabel enjoying a leisurely breakfast brought to them by Dot. After they finished their second – no more, always two – cups of tea, Mabel rang for Dot.

Mabel looked benignly at Dot as she started to clear away the crockery. "How are the children, my dear?" Mabel had grown to love having Nancy and Annie around. They brought life and energy to the house.

"They are just fine, Mrs Lambrick." She smiled at her employer who was always so friendly.

Hugh Lambrick gave a polite cough. "That will be all now Dorothy." He stood up and turned to Mabel. "Come my dear, we do not want to be late." They left Dot to finish clearing away the breakfast and went to change into their formal Sunday best clothes appropriate for their attendance at Morning Service.

They left College House to make their way to Winchester Cathedral, which was just a short walk away. It was a bright March day, and all seemed quiet and peaceful. As they neared the Cathedral however the sound of shouting and cheering intruded on the silence of Sunday morning. Upon turning the corner to the square in front of the cathedral, they were confronted by at least fifty men crowded around a farmer's wagon in front of The Old Vine Inn.

Using the wagon as a platform a smartly dressed man was haranguing the crowd, provoking frequent cheers, jeers and catcalls. His attire was not reflected in the throng surrounding him which was fast deteriorating into an aggressive mob. Hugh and Mabel tried to edge pass unobserved as they kept as closely as they could to the walls of the houses. Unfortunately they were noticed by some of those on the fringe of the crowd who started to hurl abuse at them.

"There's two of them toffs."

"I wager they never go hungry."

A few more of the crowd turned to see the object of the abuse. Hugh decided, as in most such circumstances, that discretion was the better part of valour and casting dignity to the wind, he grabbed Mabel's arm firmly and they almost ran to reach the sanctuary of the Cathedral. Once they had reached Curle's Passage near the entrance they paused to catch their breath and composure.

Hugh's brother, Nathaniel, was taking the air when he saw them arrive. He rushed forward to discover the reason for their obvious discomfort. Nathaniel was a man of the cloth and although having heard noise emanating from the square outside the Cathedral grounds he was certain that God's work within the holy precincts was a more pressing matter.

Nathaniel was the younger of the two brothers, and both had the family trait of thin faces, high cheekbones, roman noses and lack of hair. There was a difference in their characters however, which may have been from Nathaniel spending years in the comfort and security of a life within the cloisters of the Cathedral. Close inspection showed that Hugh's eyes would naturally form a squint as if delving into the meaning and motives of the facts before him. In contrast Nathaniel's eyes always had the glint of mirth, which to be fair could develop into a show of compassion, but quite frequently widened into laughter at a calculated witticism.

"Hugh, are you alright? You appear most unsettled."

"Yes, yes we are perfectly well. That is no thanks to that rabble out there. They are being incited again by one of those travelling malcontents."

"I believe it is getting worse. There always seems to be something for people to get angry about these days. If they spent more time in God's house, I would be able to tell them it is God's Will if the harvest should fail. They should come to thank the Lord for his kindness for when the harvest is good."

Hugh he shot a glance at his brother and frowned at his naivety. "He hasn't been very kind for many years lately." As a man of the world, Hugh knew that the poor were in many places getting poorer and he had personally seen much hardship. He shrugged his shoulders he believed the law was sacred and breaking it didn't change the weather and put food on the table.

Nathaniel was not sure whether to rebuke his brother for such a comment about the wisdom of the Lord, but decided against it. They turned to walk towards the Cathedral and Mabel who had recovered from her anxiety linked arms with her husband. It was not long though before she started to listen with alarm at the news that Nathaniel was conveying to them.

Nathaniel grimaced, then spoke reluctantly. "The Reverend Poskit was here a couple of weeks ago. I'm not sure if I've mentioned him before but he is the vicar for most of the parishes on the Isle of Purbeck – including the village of Langton Matravers." He paused and grimaced again. "There are times dear brother, when one feels that one should not talk too much."

Both Hugh and Mabel each had a foreboding. "It has always been a problem for you, Nathaniel. Especially when you have sampled what some may call the devil's liquor."

"Yes, yes that is as may be. That has nothing to do with it but the Reverend and I were having a discussion after dinner, whilst sampling an excellent brandy that Poskit had brought with him. There's a chap down there who seems to have a marvellous supply of the stuff."

"Come on Nathaniel what is you want to tell us?"

"Well, as we were talking, he spoke of Langton Matravers. I remembered that you were concerned at the distress of your housekeeper when she let it slip that she was from that village. The long and short of it is that I mentioned her name and whether he knew her. He became very agitated. Apparently she left the village secretly one morning. She deserted her husband – just like that – with not a word."

Hugh closed his eyes in dismay. Mabel caught her breath.

Nathaniel did not relish the role as the bringer of bad tidings. "I received a message yesterday from Poskit. Apparently he felt it was his duty to inform her husband, a man called Bill Tubbs, that she was here in Winchester." He paused before giving his coup de grace. "Tubbs has said that she is to be sent back to Langton Matravers immediately. She is his wife and she belongs to him." He looked hard at Hugh for guidance. "He says that she has broken the law and that anyone who helps her is an accomplice."

Mabel looked up at Hugh desperate for him to provide an answer but he could only nod, "If they are the facts of the matter, then as she is a married woman, her husband has every right to insist upon her being returned to him."

Nathaniel completed his news. "Apparently this Tubbs fellow is not a very likeable chap. He says that whatever the case may be with the law, if she is not returned without delay he will make the journey to Winchester and drag her back.

"He frowned deeply. "He also added that he would not take too kindly to anyone who tried to stand in his way."

"Poor Dot. Is there nothing we can do?" Mabel looked distraught.

Hugh shook his head sadly. "I am afraid we have to obey the law. If we were to contrive for Dot to avoid going back then we would guilty of aiding and abetting a miscreant." He looked at his wife with compassion. "I know you have become quite fond of her, as indeed have I, but my life has been spent in upholding the law whether I believe it to be just or not."

Nathaniel spoke half-heartedly. "Matthew, one of our vergers is going to Swanage soon, he can take Dot with him. I will stress to him that there is to be no convenient escape by her, and that he deliver her to this man Tubbs."

Hugh shook his head again. "So be it. Please make the arrangements, Nathaniel. We will tell Dot to be ready. Come my dear we will miss the Service if we don't hurry."

As Hugh Lambrick sat in his customary pew inside the cathedral he decided that he was having a most unsatisfactory day.

When Dot was told that she was to be taken back to the arms of her brutal husband she was beside herself with anguish and fear. Mabel Lambrick was upset to see how the news had caused distress not only for Dot but also the way this had transferred to the children.

Hugh was quite firm, although inwardly torn, the law was the law and it had to be upheld. Dot was required to go back forthwith. As it was a week before Matthew was able to leave for Swanage, the ensuing days were unsettling for Hugh and Mabel. Eventually it was arranged for Dot to be taken to Swanage on the following Sunday.

Hugh had made his Brougham carriage available for Matthew. After a miserable journey, as they neared The

Harbour Inn at midday he reined in the horse a short distance away. There was a crowd congregating in front of the Inn and as it was on the previous Sunday in Winchester they were clearly turning nasty. In the midst was Bill Tubbs who could be seen as the main culprit in haranguing the mob. Matthew kindly let Dot remain in the coach and she sat quietly cuddling the sobbing girls as she waited.

Calvin Seagers was also in Swanage that morning with his wife Mary. As they saw the scene in the Square they remained as inconspicuous as possible. When he saw Matthew draw up with Dot he and his wife promptly went over to them.

"Dot, how are you? I never thought we would see you again."

Dot was ashen faced and said nervously, "Bill Tubbs found out I was in Winchester and he sent a message that I was to return immediately."

Mary put her hand gently on Dot's sleeve. Calvin was troubled and frowned, "I am sorry for you. I know it's not easy." There was silence for a few moments as they each watched the other side of the square. Calvin was deep in thought then turned to his wife. "Mary you have said that you need some more help in the house. If Dot is agreeable would you like her to come to us as our housekeeper?" He looked at his wife for her approval making the silent communication that married couples can develop between each other.

Mary gave Calvin an approving smile then turned to Dot. "That is an excellent idea would you be so kind as to do that?"

Dot hesitated. "I don't know. I suppose it's up to my husband."

Calvin had made up his mind. "I will speak with him now." He looked across the square where Tubbs was in full flow. "We shall wait until I can catch his attention."

Calvin thanked Matthew who went on his way. The small group stood in glum silence. It was not long before Tubbs looked in their direction and Calvin summarily gestured for him to come over to them. When Tubbs saw who was waiting he jumped down from the barrel that was serving as his makeshift platform and rushed over to them.

"There you are you bitch. You're back at last." He raised his arm to swipe Dot across the face with the back of his hand.

His hand never reached Dot and he gave a howl of pain as Calvin's riding crop slashed across his forearm. "There won't be any of that." Calvin pulled himself up to register his full authority. He was a considerably larger man than Tubbs and he placed himself in front of Dot

Tubbs stood glowering.

"I want Dot to come into my employ as my housekeeper. I am obliged to ask for your permission but I am sure that it will not be a problem." It was a statement rather than a question.

There was a shout from the crowd. "Come on Bill. What are you doing?"

Tubbs called back over his shoulder. "I'll be there in a minute." He turned back to Calvin and shrugged his shoulders. "Alright she can work for you but I want her wages – they're mine." He looked passed Calvin at Dot and added. "She can earn her and her brats keep."

"One more thing Tubbs. I shall be keeping a watch over Dot and the girls and I will take it as my responsibility that they come to no harm."

Tubbs stared at Calvin, then sneered as he spat out an oath. He shrugged again and turned his back on them to re-join the noisy mob in front of the Inn.

Calvin relaxed and gave a deep sigh.. "God, what an awful man." He spoke to Mary. "We are late, we must carry on to your sister's down the street." He gave a grim smile to Dot and the children. "Come with us and we'll then take you back to the village."

Dot had some relief in her voice. "Thank you so much Mr Seagers. We shall be for ever in your debt."

"Nonsense. Now come along let's get you back – home."

"If a woman was unhappy with her situation there was almost without exception, nothing she could do about it. Except in extremely rare cases, a woman could not obtain a divorce. If she ran away from an intolerable marriage the police could capture and return her to her husband.
A typical case was when Susannah Palmer in Dorset, escaped from her adulterous husband after suffering many years of brutal beatings, and made a new life. She worked, saved and created a new home for her children. Her husband found her, stripped her of all her possessions and left her destitute with the blessing of the law."

CHAPTER FIFTEEN

Catalyst

Catalyst: an agent that speeds up chemical reactions that might take years to interact but with its intervention can now do so in seconds. One event in itself cannot change the status quo without there being underlying reasons for changes.

"Damn his eyes! I hope he rots in hell."

The growled heartfelt curse is spat out by one of four ragged men as the load they are carrying spills onto the ground Each man is covered in stone dust with blood from nicks, scratches and open cuts on exposed skin. A broken and distorted figure they had been carrying on a wooden board is quickly bundled back onto the makeshift stretcher.

"Alright lads get on with it - that's not going to help Sam now."

One glance at the imposing figure of Jasper who barked out the instruction is enough. The other men at the quarry watch the reluctant bearers in silence. The only sound comes from the abandoned ropes and pulleys clicking in the strengthening wind and the crunch of iron-shod boots stumbling on loose stone chippings. The four impromptu pall-bearers quickly finish putting their lifeless charge onto the back of a wagon that is half loaded with stone for carrying down to Swanage.

Jasper stood impassively his feet firmly apart and his arms folded across his chest as he was approached by Bill Tubbs who had spat out the curse. He didn't speak as he looked down at Tubbs, whose face is contorted with unconcealed rage.

"Lord Olden is responsible for this!   The miserly old skinflint should give us chains not those old ropes." he snarls.

The wind drops briefly and there is no sound within the quarry as the men stand awkwardly around with their own thoughts. Tubbs' spleen is not raising a common fury. "Tubbs, you may be right but I - we - wont listen to any of your bile now."

Tubbs opened his mouth to speak but thought better of it and stormed off looking at each man he passed for a glimmer of support, but he is met with none.

Jasper scanned the motionless, dissolute figures for any reaction. Sam's death would not be forgotten or dismissed. Despite the placation of marriage and fatherhood he felt the inner anger that was being excessively expressed by Tubbs and he knew he was not alone. Sam's death could be the catalyst for a backlash that simmered within Jasper and others.

Bill Tubbs was different. He hated the entire system of the ruling class in their fine houses without much thought of the consequences or alternatives. He was determined that at every opportunity he would bring forward the day of their downfall. His head was filled with aggressive action mixed with mindless slogans.

It was just a month since Dot's return that Sam Crocker's senseless death at the Crack Lane Quarry gave Bill Tubbs the opportunity to stir up trouble. He now believed he saw such a chance to use Sam's death to recruit a potential strong ally in Jasper. He knew that Jasper harboured a sense of injustice and Tubbs believed he could use the accident to bring this back to the surface. If Jasper reacted then others would follow. It was Tubbs' chance to get Jasper on his side in what he saw, as the struggle of the lower sort.

The driver of the wagon gave the reins he was patiently holding a flick against the rump of a weary old horse which obediently strained forward against its harness. The wheels creaked as they shattered the stones and small boulders that come under the weight of the wagon's load of stones and the unwelcome addition of the limp figure of Sam Crocker.

As it started to slowly wind its way down Stonehouse Hill Jasper took a deep breath. Despite his dismissal of Tubbs he was attempting to control his own smouldering rage and frustration.

As he watched the scene before him unfold, he pulled out and lit his clay pipe. Like other quarriers digging out the stone he wore a dark grey jacket and moleskin trousers he had bought in Spitalfield Market. These clothes keep out the biting wind on the bleak hilltop and are so hardwearing they would last him for years. He held an essential cloth cap for when he is underground and this had become impregnated with the wet clay that continually dripped from the ceiling of the quarries. As the clay had dried and accumulated it had become very hard and acted as a protective helmet. Around his neck was a simple neckerchief that is used to wipe away sweat and to press onto the many cuts that were part of a day's work. Clogs that are iron shod were a necessary precaution to protect his feet in the stone quarry.

Sam Crocker's fatal accident was senseless. Bill Tubbs was a nasty individual and Jasper had no time for him at all, but maybe he was right. His mind was taken back to his own personal tragedy when his brother Ben was killed when working underground in the family's quarry. Jasper had promised himself that day that he would break free and make his life his own, answerable to no-one. He had tried to escape once - and had failed. Maybe it was time for him and others to stand up against the injustices and rebel against their lot in life.

As Jasper watched the slowly departing crude funeral wagon bearing Sam's body disappear a movement to his right brought him back to the present. He nodded grimly to Robert and shook his head sadly. Unlike many of the other quarriers whose thoughts were on condemning the owner, Lord Olden, Robert's mind went to Sam Crocker's family and how they would now survive. "Poor Mary, she and Sam were devoted to each other." He shook his head sadly.

"Aye, she stood by him. You could say she is – was - a good and proper wife."

Robert shot a glance at Jasper. "What do you mean by that?"

Jasper looked sidelong at Robert and shook his head in exasperation. "Good God Robert, I meant what I said – Mary has been a good wife to Sam and nothing else." He looked back down Stonehouse Hill. "Don't worry about Mary, her children will look after her, although it won't be easy for them with another mouth to feed." He sighed. "I would be more worried about your sister, Dot. Bill Tubbs is a brute; if I can find a reason I will give him some of his own medicine. You can't go between a man and his woman though."

Robert's heart sank, he was Dot's elder brother but Jasper was right no one could stand between a man and his wife. He shivered as the wind started to force leaden clouds across the sky warning of an impending miserable, wet evening. Robert turned up the collar of his moleskin jacket and pulled it close under his chin.

Robert took a deep breath. "Someone had better let Sam's Edith know what's happened." He looked around with a grim smile. "I don't think there will be many volunteers." He shook his head sadly. "I'll do it, though. Better she's told properly rather than by accident. Can you tell Silas where I've gone?" He turned and with no haste followed the wagon taking Sam Crocker's body down the Hill.

Silas Winter the manager at the quarry had started to move amongst the men as the wagon disappeared. "Alright lads. There's nothing more we can do now." He shook his head sadly then looking around at the lounging quarriers. "Come on, get back to work. Ted, check all the ropes in each of the shafts, we don't want anyone else joining Sam. Jasper, whilst he's doing that get the other men to load the stone that's been brought up today onto the other wagons."

Ted Edmunds went about his appointed task, and under Jasper's instructions, begrudgingly the rest of the men resumed their work.

Silas stopped one of the young lads as he hurried passed him. "Sammy, run to catch up with the wagon that's taking Mr Crocker. When you get to Swanage, find Mr Seagers – he will be at the harbour. I want you to tell him that Sam Crocker has been killed. As Lord Olden's Bailiff he can tell his Lordship what has happened. Make sure that you say the reason he's dead is because another of the ropes broke." He looked sternly at the lad. "Make sure you tell him that exactly."

Sammy Nelson nodded eagerly, "Yes sir, Mr Winter." He turned and ran out of the quarry gates pleased to be on an important mission. It also meant he was out of the quarry for the rest of the day.

When Sammy caught up with the wagon, as there was no room at the front he had to sit in the back where he constantly fended off Sam Crocker's body as it jolted back and forth in unison with the lurching of the wagon. It took an hour to reach Swanage and as it stopped outside Mordecai Benfield's undertaker's shop, Sammy jumped down and ran to the harbour. After a few minutes darting around the men loading stones onto the boats he found Calvin Seagers.

To strangers, Calvin Seagers was a fearsome looking man. He was well-built and dressed in breeches, yellow checked waistcoat and a black frock coat. He had a round florid face, which was framed by mutton-chop whiskers and his short top hat was rammed down on his head. He was a no nonsense man and when spoken to by someone he did not know he would fix the speaker with a stare whilst he constantly beat his long leather boots with a riding crop.

"Excuse me Mr Seagers." A timid voice addressed him from behind. He ignored it – if the questioner wished to speak with him he would have to address him from the front. Sammy, who was already trembling at his temerity of speaking to such a broad back moved cautiously around this august figure.

The bearer of the voice came into sight and was in receipt of the full glare of Calvin Seager's frowning attention.

Sammy gulped but persisted on completing his mission. "Excuse me Mr Seagers." He started again.

"What is it boy?" Was the booming reply.

"I'm sorry sir, but I have a message from Mr Winter at the Crack Lane Quarry."

"Well what is it?"

"It's just that I have to tell you that there has been another accident in one of the shafts." Sammy was on the home straight of his appointed task. "Mr Crocker has been killed. Mr Winter has told me to tell you that one of the ropes bringing a quarr to the surface broke and it crushed Mr Crocker." He was now over the line and his assignment was finished.

Calvin's frown deepened. He had already told Lord Olden that the ropes were old and should be replaced. Calvin had sympathy for the men that had to work in the tough conditions at the quarry. Also, as he lived in Langton Matravers he knew Sam Crocker and his wife Mary very well. He looked down again at young Sammy who was waiting to be dismissed his message having been delivered. Calvin's demeanour softened and he reached into his breeches' pocket. "Well done, lad. Here you are here's a penny for a job well done." Then in a more stern voice, " Off you go."

Calvin thought long and hard. Lord Olden had to be persuaded to put chains in place of the old ropes but when Calvin had put it to him before, he was dismissed out of hand. His Lordship had to be told there had been another death and it was Calvin's duty to tell him the reason. He called over to the clerk from the shipping agent. "I have to go to Olden Hall. If there are any problems speak to me tomorrow."

Calvin Seagers was deep in thought as he rode over to see his Lordship. It was not going to be a comfortable meeting.

Lord Olden was at the opposite end of society to the men in his quarry. His life was one of comfort and privilege and could not have been more different to that of his workers whose existence always had been and still continued to be a matter of survival.[21]

Lord Olden's domain covered most of the Isle of Purbeck although he had spent many years at the centre of government in London. At the time of Sam Crocker's death Lord Olden was nearly seventy and he had now retired to his country residence of Olden Hall. He still kept control of his local Estates although Calvin Seagers as the Estate Bailiff, was left to the day to day management.

When Calvin Seagers arrived at Olden Hall, Lord Olden was out on the estate with visitors from London. Age was catching up with him and a single fall had induced him to stop riding, though he was never happier than when on a

---

[21] *"Starting in Kent during the early Spring of 1820 disturbances swept across southern England. The government convinced itself that they were the work of French spies or Methodist ministers. They could not believe that the circumstances of the village labourer had become so unbearable that word of a riot succeeding in forcing an increase in wages or a reduction of rates in one village would be enough to spark a 'copy cat' rising in the next."*

shooting party. When they returned, Calvin went to greet them and help take their guns. Daniel Tomkins, one of Lord Olden's footmen, had been out beating with the party.

"Good afternoon to you Daniel. Did his Lordship have any success?"

Tomkins chuckled. "Unfortunately his Lordship is so poor a shot that I fear that he can only be accused of killing time."

As they followed the party into the house at a discreet distance Daniel glanced over to Calvin and frowned. "What brings you here today, Calvin? You don't seem to be too happy." He looked directly at Calvin. "I fear you bring bad news."

"You're right I have received news from the Crack Lane Quarry which I hope Lord Olden will take seriously." He stopped walking and faced Daniel. "Another of the men has been killed. Did you know Sam Crocker?" Daniel nodded. "I don't know the full story yet but I've been told that one of the old ropes which haul the quarrs to the surface broke, and Sam was crushed. His Lordship is too much of a skinflint to pay for chains to replace the old ropes."

Daniel grimaced. "I'm sorry to hear that but Lord Olden would not have known poor Sam. Why should he be concerned? Working in the quarries is a dangerous business and men do get hurt – and killed."

"Aye, that's right, but this is the third one this year, in this way. You know these are worrying times, and there are those that will take every opportunity to make trouble. Agitators going around the country are stirring up the men. One of them was in Swanage just a week ago. If they now believe that Lord Olden is putting them in danger through greed then they will rebel against him. When I say rebel I use the word for a reason."

"Can't you persuade Lord Olden to listen to the men's complaints?"

"I have tried but he doesn't or won't understand."

"Daniel shook his head sadly, then turned to go downstairs to the servant's rooms. "I have to go, Calvin. I wish you good luck."

Lord Olden followed his aristocratic predecessors as the Lord of the manor and would act the role of protector of his estate workers, as would a father to his family. This was a paternalistic view where each man knew his place in the order of society and a man's status rarely changed. Lord Olden was a traditionalist and he believed that this system had brought stability and from his point of view had created a strong and wealthy country. His wealth and position gave him a closeted life and he was a man used to respect and deferment.

Calvin had to wait for half an hour in the hallway before he was summoned to speak with His Lordship. Lady Olden, and her daughter-in-law, Henrietta together with Lady Wareham passed him as they withdrew from the men and went into the Drawing Room. A maid quickly followed them with a tray bearing tea. The door was left inadvertently slightly ajar when the maid scurried back passed him.

Calvin had no interest in what was being said but could not help overhearing the conversation. After some minutes he heard Lady Wareham say that her husband had mentioned that there were men in Parliament that were wanting changes made that would increase the number and class of men that could vote.

Lord Olden's son Henry appeared exuding the haughty air and confidence that displayed he knew that he was born to lead. He had grown into one the new breed of aristocrats that were products of a public school system. These new men were certain of their own and their country's natural dominant place in the world. He gave Calvin a cursory nod and went into the room.

Calvin heard Henry's wife, Henrietta say, "What brings you in here with us ladies and away from what I'm sure was a very important and interesting discussion?" There was a pause. "However, you have come in just as we were having our own fascinating conversation." Calvin could hear from Henry's tone that he had no interest in what they were talking about but out of politeness enquired, "Really my dear, pray what was the subject?"

"Lady Wareham was telling us that there are plans to let others of a different class the right to vote at elections. I wonder does this also mean that us ladies will be allowed to participate?"

"Are you serious my dear? We have had these conversations before. That would be most unwise. A married woman takes a vow to obey her husband; giving women a vote would amount to giving their husband two votes. Either that, or it would cause arguments within the home, which would change from a place of peace and tranquillity, to a place of strife. Voting would drag women away from their domestic duties and their children."

There was a silence from which Calvin was unable to tell whether his audience was in agreement or were dumbfounded by his remarks. The silence was broken when Henry continued. "I do have some sympathy with changes to whom the vote is given but I fear it will be a few years yet before that happens." He paused "Matters in the country do have to be taken in hand as there are a increasing number of instances of disorder." He then chortled, "As far as women having the right to vote, that will never happen my dear. Now the reason I came to see you is that I require some advice on a matter from your father. Is he in chambers this month because if so I will need to return to London in the morning."

"Calvin." Mr Seagers was not a man to be startled however Daniel Tomkins broke his reverie and was indicating that he was to be followed. "Lord Olden will see you shortly in the Library."

"At last." Calvin said quietly to himself.

Daniel overheard and raised his eyes whilst shaking his head. "Not for the likes of us to question their Lordships." After Daniel had withdrawn Calvin was alone in the Library and he wandered around casually looking at various artefacts and books. The only sound was the steady movement of the clock's pendulum within a rather plain, but nicely proportioned Oak case with a no nonsense flat top. Calvin looked at the brass dial and grunted as he saw the single hand approaching the hour. Two hands were now on all modern clocks but Lord Olden saw no reason to change what had been good enough for his forebears. He considered that life on his country Estate had no need of a more accurate measurement of time.

The clock stirred and steadfastly chimed its news that the day had reached the fifth hour since noon. The door handle suddenly rattled and the doors burst open to reveal an obviously irritated Lord Olden. He brushed passed his Bailiff making straight for the fireplace whereupon he spun around and stood with his chin thrust out and his hands on his hips. No matter what his intention, Lord Olden no longer posed an impressive figure. He was of middle height, had regular features that had become more florid with age and his once sparkling eyes were now watery. He had always considered himself a beau and still wore his white luxuriant hair rather long as if in defiance of the passage of time. He scowled and with no preamble demanded, "I believe you insist on seeing me. What is it man? I am entertaining my guests."

Calvin Seagers was always respectful but he was not a man to be browbeaten. "I'm sorry My Lord but this is a matter I believe is of great importance and it could put you in grave danger if not addressed." He then proceeded to repeat what he had been told and the dangers he had expressed to Daniel Tomkins.

Lord Olden almost without a pause dismissed his warnings. "My good man you have called me away from my guests to tell me of some man who has killed himself on my property. A tragedy I'm sure but it's a dangerous business of which these men are well aware. I trust that the quota of stone being mined has not been affected."

Calvin sighed in exasperation. "My Lord, the men will not accept working in dangerous conditions if they believe that their safety is solely a matter of money."

Lord Olden exploded, "Sir, I have been accused of being reactionary by certain gentlemen in Parliament. We beat the French and their damned revolution but since the end of the war there has been nothing but unrest. There are men with unsettling ideas that are starting to permeate their way through to Parliament. I will not accept a change to a way of life that has made this country what it is today." He moved close to Calvin, albeit this meant him looking up. "The men want me to spend even more money on them? How dare they. There are men with new machines which are challenging the way we manage this estate and I will not have it. If I have to cut costs on equipment – and dare I say on wages then I will damn well do it!" His eyes widened as if in an invitation to be contradicted. "I bid you good day, sir. I have to return to my guests." He then brushed passed a frustrated Calvin Seagers and swept out of the room.

His Lordship re-appeared almost immediately and said in a more conspiratory tone. "I forgot - find that chap Heywood. The way my guests are drinking my brandy I'm sure that we'll need some more very soon. The last shipment was very good, make sure he delivers more from the same place." He then disappeared again.

Calvin stared after him and shook his head. "Bloody fool." He then gave the back of a nearby chair a swipe with his crop and left Olden Hall to his Lordship and his guests.

As Robert neared Sam Crocker's cottage he saw Sarah coming out of the door. Sarah's face lit up and she hurried over to him. "Robert, what brings you home so early?" She stopped and looked at her man and frowned. "What has happened? You look sad." She linked her arm with his and gave it a hug.

"I'm afraid I've got bad news for Mary."

"Oh no. Is it about Sam? I've just left her. She's cooking his meal for when he comes home."

"He won't be coming home. There's been an accident at the quarry. He was underneath a quarr when the rope broke. Mercifully he wouldn't have known anything about it."

"Oh, Lord. Where is he now?"

"He's being taken down to Mordecai's in Swanage. He will prepare Sam to meet his Maker. I've come to tell Mary what has happened."

Sarah gave Robert's arm another squeeze. "Don't worry my love. I know Edith very well – I'll go to tell her." She gave a grim smile. "You go on to The Ship. You could do with a drink, couldn't you?"

"Yes, very much." He gave her a kiss and the tender look in his eyes made any more words unnecessary.

Sarah smiled and then turned to carry on her self appointed task. Robert watched her go into Mary's cottage and then with a deep sigh walked slowly to The Ship.

* * *

Calvin decided that his Lordship's business could fend for itself for the rest of the day and he considered it an opportune time to visit Isaac Butt, the village blacksmith.

Isaac was a young man of just twenty-four years of age who had recently taken over his father's business. Blacksmiths became experienced at avoiding being kicked by a spooked horse but unusually Abraham Butt was careless one morning and he had recently been killed by the back kick of a skittish pony.

Calvin heard Isaac hard at work as he approached Forge Cottage on the edge of Langton Matravers. As he dismounted and led his mount around to the workshop at the rear Isaac was stoking his forge vigorously.

"Good afternoon to you, Isaac. How's business?"

Isaac turned away from the forge his face flushed from the heat and from his labours. "Calvin, 'tis good to see you. Aye, business is good." He left his iron in the fire and went to shake Calvin's hand. "I've had a number of horses from Lord Kenway's stables to re-shoe this week and as you know Lord Olden's horses from his quarries need constant attention. The pulling of the stone wagons over the rocky terrain in the quarries certainly keeps me busy." He took the bridle of Calvin's horse. "Does my beauty here need looking after?"

"Yes, make sure Nugget's well shod," He grunted and shook his head. "I've a feeling I shall be busy in the near future."

Isaac looked at Calvin curiously, "You look worried is there a problem on the estate?"

"Lord Olden is a fool and I don't mind if someone does hear me say that. He will reap what he is sowing."

"I have to sharpen and repair the tools of the men in both of his quarries. I know it's a good part of what he pays them, which is not very much. If I had all their tools or at least half of them at the same time I would be able to charge less." He sighed and shrugged his shoulders. "It has always been that way." He looked at Calvin with a frown. "Ted Edmunds left his tools here earlier and told me about Sam Crocker if that's what you're worried about though?"

Calvin gave his boots a hard slap with his riding crop. "Yes, damn His Lordship! He is asking for trouble and he could avoid the problem immediately with what would be to him a small cost. Probably less than he's spending now entertaining his London friends.

"Calvin take a seat on the bench over there in the garden and I'll get you some tea." He led Nugget to the stable and closed the door and then took a quick look at the forge to make sure it didn't need attention. As he went to join Calvin he called over his shoulder "Florence!"

A young waif of a girl dressed in a simple white, short-sleeved cotton dress with an apron tied just below barely developed breasts came hurrying out to his command.

"Florence, make two teas please, and ask Mrs Butt if she would like some as well."

"Yes Mr Butt, I'll be as quick as I can." Florence then scurried indoors with a look of determination on her face.

Isaac chuckled, "She's doing well. Not the brightest little thing in the world but she's honest and hard working." He chuckled again. "She does drop things though." As if he had been heard there came a crash from the kitchen of pans hitting the floor.

"Did you know that I have taken on Dotty Tubbs – Robert Bollson's sister?" Calvin asked in attempt to clear his mind of Lord Olden.

"Yes I did. Is she alright? Bill Tubbs doesn't treat her very well."

"He doesn't. She's a good cook and Mary and I like her. Bill Tubbs insists that I give her wages directly to him. I don't know how much he gives to her to feed and clothe the children but I do know that much of it goes to George Tupe at The Ship." He shook his head sadly. "What can you do? Her wages belong to him."

"Aye that's right. It was a shame that Tubbs came along at just the time that her father's family quarry was hitting bad times. We know why she married Tubbs, but in the circumstances it was a useless sacrifice." Their conversation was interrupted as Florence came back out into the garden carrying two mugs of tea. "Thank you Florence. If you've finished your daily chores you can go home now."

"Thank you Mr Butt."

Both men casually watched her disappear back into the kitchen and sat drinking their tea in silence. The evening was drawing in. There was no sound aside from the wind as it rustled the trees crowded around the cottage, and the muffled roar from the forge. A wagon slowly wound its way down Stonehouse Hill in the distance as a reminder that they were not alone and that there was a village nearby. It was a scene that had been enacted many times before by the fathers of Calvin and Isaac.

Eventually Calvin stirred. "This country is a fine place to live but there is much that isn't right. Isaac, I fear that we may be in a calm before a storm."

Isaac didn't reply as he studied the ground. His eyes glazed as he recollected that in the past even the death of Sam Crocker would have barely disturbed the peaceful ritual of village life. This was changing and he agreed with Calvin that almost imperceptibly discontent was simmering.

They were both roused from their thoughts when the spots of rain that were in the air very quickly turned into a healthy shower. Calvin drained his mug of tea and put it emphatically down on the bench. "Isaac, I had better make a move, thank you very much for the tea. I'll come back in a couple of days to get Nugget. Let me have your bill for his

Lordship, and I will make sure it's paid promptly." He went to leave then asked, "I have to find Charlie Heywood. Do you know where he might be?"

"I think you may be in luck. Ted mentioned earlier that he walked down from the quarry with him. He said that Charlie had heard about the accident and that he would be calling into The Ship later to have a drink on Sam." He chuckled, "Whatever happens around here, Charlie always knows about it."

"That's for sure. Anyway, thanks very much Isaac, I had better get over to The Ship straightaway." They shook hands warmly and Calvin made the short journey into the centre of the village

The Ship Inn was a cottage that was made into an Inn when the Turnpike Trust changed a country path into a road giving easier access to Swanage. It was ideal for travellers bound for Swanage to pause to slake their thirsts before completing their journey and it had become a focus and meeting place for the village. The landlord and landlady were George and Maude Tupe who brewed and sold their own beer but they also supplied brandy, tea and tobacco amongst many other items that were smuggled ashore nearby.

There was an agreed silence about the smuggling of these goods, which after all had been carried on for as long as any of the oldest inhabitants could remember. Whole communities along the coast connived in the trade, and profited from it. The trade had become increasingly important with the hard times that followed almost twenty-five years of war and for many workers it was paramount for their survival. Charlie Heywood had by now taken over entirely from Isaac Gulliver and all such activity on the Isle of Purbeck was now totally organised and controlled by him.

As Calvin entered The Ship he could feel the sombre mood. He looked around for Charlie and noticed Robert was sat on a wooden settle by the window. He liked Robert and was pleased to have been able to help his father Joshua and his friend, Isaac, when they were in difficulty with their respective family quarries.

"Have you seen Charlie Heywood? I have some business from Lord Olden for him."

Robert grinned "I think I know what that business might be. He will be back soon he's just gone to his Ma's cottage."

Although they had each gone their separate ways, there still remained a bond between Calvin, Jasper, Robert and Charlie Heywood. Calvin called over to George "Bring me a brandy and another ale for Robert." George obliged without delay. "Thanks George." He settled in his seat and drained his glass with two swigs. "After the day I've had today I could do with another drink. How about you?

Robert shook his head. " I had better not. Thanks anyway."

"Another brandy for me please, George." He looked at Robert and chuckled. "Charlie's not only a clever man, he's a good manager and he has ensured that his quarry provides a good profit despite the stiff competition. He has also contacted an increasing number of buyers from the growing towns and London and has nurtured them as prospects for this business. Incidentally, did you know that he has just bought the postal service in Swanage? That's very smart as well. That will keep him in touch with most of what was happening on the Isle of Purbeck."

Ted Edmunds who had been talking with some of the other men from the quarry came over to them when they left. "Do you mind if I join you."

"Of course not." Robert said moving along the settle to make room for Ted to sit down. "It's not Charlie's quarries that make the most money these days is it?"

Calvin was looking through the window where he could see Charlie was at the top of the street hurrying through the rain that was now falling heavily. He quickly finished. "You're right, despite these other interests a large proportion of his income now is the running of contraband. As the old brigade started to find the activity increasingly dangerous, he took over from them. He has always offered a good price for the buying and selling of all landed goods, and all in that business therefore trusts him. He is the only man to be contacted when there is a shipment on offer."

Charlie arrived, and Calvin rose from his seat to go to speak to him as soon as he entered the room. He added in passing to Robert. "I know that most of the men around here work at times for him – including you two and Jasper. It's not my affair though. I run Lord Olden's estate." He looked across the room. "Charlie, good evening to you. Could I speak with you please?"

They both sat down and were soon in quiet conversation in the corner of the room.

Robert and Ted idly chatted about Charlie and the problems in the quarry, when the large figure of Jasper appeared at the doorway. He paused to brush off as much rain as possible as he scanned the drinkers around the room. He saw Calvin and Charlie and gave a nod in their direction. Charlie held Jasper's gaze for a moment but Jasper turned away and went to sit next to Robert. Robert could sense as Jasper made his way over to him that he was still seething about Sam. Jasper called over to his host. "George, three ales please." He didn't bother to ask Robert or Ted if they wanted another drink.

Jasper sat down but didn't speak at first. He sat looking around whilst strumming his fingers on the table. Robert looked at Ted, grimaced, and raised his eyebrows. Ted took the opportunity and said, "I've got to go for a leak." and went out of the back door.

Robert looked at Jasper and frowned.

The mood in the Inn was shattered by a loud crash as the door to the Inn was kicked open and it bounced back on its hinges.

"Bastard! That bastard!"

Bill Tubbs announced his presence with a string of snarled profanities. "What are we going to do about that bastard? Are we going to let him see us all killed whilst he does nothing about it?" He glared about him, his fists clenched, as if he were daring anyone to contradict him.

"Shut up!"

Tubbs spun round to see who was brave enough to disagree.

He had caught Jasper at the wrong time. "Bill Tubbs you will show some respect for Sam Crocker." To emphasise his point he stood up, just being able to reach his full height despite the low ceiling. "Sam is not yet in his grave. What is to be done, will be done but now is not the time." He looked over Tubb's shoulder through the window and saw Dot waiting outside in the pouring rain. "In fact I've had enough of you. Go, take your wife with you, and if I hear tell that there is a single scratch or mark on her…" he moved to within a foot of Tubbs so that the man had to look up. "… then I will personally come calling and you will regret it for the rest of your days."

Tubbs stood his ground for a moment, then his nerve broke and he slowly turned to leave. As he neared the door he muttered to a group that had been reluctantly watching the scene. "She's my wife I will do what I want." Each man in the group looked down. As Tubbs put his hand on the door he turned "We'll not stand for Olden and his kind getting away with treating us like scum. The day will come when they will regret it."

Jasper took a step towards him and he spun around and hurried out into the rain.

The room was silent. Calvin Seagers looked at Charlie and said very quietly "I keep saying that there's going to be trouble."

Charlie nodded grimly then to break the silence that had descended upon the room he called over to George Tupe, "George give everyone another one of your fine ales. We should drink a toast to good ol' Sam."

In relief, everyone breathed out and there were calls of thanks to Charlie and the anticipated raising of tankards in respect to 'good old Sam'.

Jasper looked at Charlie, lowered his head in appreciation and retook his seat. Robert was looking out of the window watching his sister as she was shoved in the direction of her marital home. Without turning he sighed, "I don't know what to do about poor Dot. I've thought about whether I could find her work in London. Sarah says her father could probably help."

Ted was also watching out of the window and said quietly almost to himself. "She has been found once when she tried to get away. Something has to be done about Tubbs."

Robert shot a quick glance at Ted. He chose to ignore the remark and carried on but a worried frown remained on his face. "The trouble is the law is on his side."

Jasper grunted. "I just hope I've put sufficient fear into him for the time being." George came and gave them the drink that had been bought by Charlie and they gestured over to him with their tankards mouthing "To Sam."

Jasper sunk back into a grim silence. He was as angry as Tubbs about what had happened to Sam, but his response was going to be more measured.

Robert said quietly "Tubbs won't let this go. He's becoming a spokesman for the men. Whenever he has the chance to work on any actual or even perceived injustice, he will use it to stir up a ruckus"

Jasper grunted and said simply, "Probably" then remained silent.

Calvin and Charlie had watched as the events had unfolded and after Charlie had called for drinks all round they kept discreetly in the background. Although Calvin had grown up with many of the men in the room he was well aware that they saw him as one of Lord Olden's men. Which of course he was, but he was in the middle. He looked at Charlie "This could turn out to be more than just a local and temporary problem."

Charlie was thoughtful. "This isn't France. I can't see a revolution in England."

Calvin looked sharply at Charlie, "Why not? We have all the ingredients for one. Look, the old order is changing. Lord Olden is of the old guard. He has a concern for the well being of the working poor in his employ as long, and this is important, as they keep within the bounds of what he sees as acceptable behaviour and it doesn't affect his own position and wealth."

"Lord Olden is just one person. I can't see a revolution because of Lord Olden and his actions, or lack of it." Charlie was playing the devil's advocate.

"Many people can be affected by what would appear to be unconnected events. I believe that Sam's death today could be such an event. Look around you; each man in this room has his own aspirations. To many it is just survival. You as a businessman are aware that England has grown richer as a country but ironically it has caused a great deal of hardship as a result." Calvin paused, raising his eyebrows to question whether Charlie was following his point.

Charlie leaned forward. "Gone on."

'The vast majority are like the folks here who years ago would have been happy to survive. Now, here is the paradox; as the country grows richer this stimulates people to want to change the very system that is creating that wealth."

Charlie chuckled. "You've been giving this a great deal of thought, haven't you."

Calvin grunted. "Maybe it's because I'm – you as well – in the middle. Look, imagine a society where all but a very few had homes, food and all the trappings for comfort and pleasure. There would still be those would say 'down with the government' – 'it's not fair the rich have more than me'"

"Well if it's unfair then why shouldn't they?"

"That is a point, yes. What is the second largest source of work on the Isle of Purbeck apart from the quarries? It's the tenant farms where the labourer's livelihoods depend on farming of the land and animals. Who are the largest landowners? Lord Olden and Lord Kenway who rent out farms to tenant farmers. These farmers have had it tough and they always want to reduce the wages of their workers. Discontent – 'it's not fair'."

Charlie didn't respond for a few moments, then in a measured way said, "We have a settled – structured way of life here. We have the landowners like Olden who are the ruling gentry. Then we have the middling sort – tradesmen such as carpenters, builders, bakers and dairymen." He paused and smiled, "Also as you say, people like us businessmen, as well as the professional men of the law and the merchants down in Swanage. Then of course we have those that work on the farms as well as, around these parts, the quarriers." He stopped then added as if playing a trump card. "Then we have the Church. It will always be like this. It will take a great deal to change all that."

Calvin thumped the table with his fist. "I'm sorry to go on about this but you're wrong. That old structure is crumbling. It may be going for a better way – I don't know - I hope so. You mentioned religion; another pillar of our society? Think about it - the local tenant farmers were usually members of the Church of England. This was to keep in with the lords of the manor, around here Olden and Kenway, who grant them their farms. The agricultural labourers are therefore Anglican as well, so as to keep on the right side of the farmers who employed them."

"How is this changing?'

"Look around you at the quarriers in here. Most of them prefer the simpler forms of worship given by the Methodists. As you know, some years ago John Wesley visited the village and since then the Methodists had established a chapel in a barn that is rented from Lord Wareham and there are also chapels for the Presbyterians and Baptists. When did you last go to church? I understand that in the cities there are many churches, but increasingly the worshippers are reducing. The influence of the church will always be with us but it does not control lives as it did in the past."

Charlie shook his head. "You paint a very bad picture. To coin a phrase 'Is England going to hell in a hand cart?' Is there no hope for us?" He laughed.

Calvin relaxed, and then chuckled, "I'm sorry but I am worried. What is happening here is happening all around England. There are radical politicians and agitators that are touring the country holding meetings to promote their factious ideas until they inflame men like Bill Tubbs into open defiance. I believe Tubbs is a very dangerous man." He nodded in the direction of Jasper. "Jasper Tomes is the bedrock of the village but we know he is resentful about a number things. If Tubbs gets him on his side then we are in trouble."

Charlie shook his head in almost mock despair. "Well Calvin, thank you for all that, it's made my day. You will tell me when to jump off Austell Head?"

Calvin laughed. "I certainly will." He stood up to leave. "Look, there are men around who will fight against all these problems. I don't know how, but that's why I'm just an Estate Bailiff." He offered his hand, "I have to go now. Mary will already have my dinner."

Charlie stood as well. "I have to go too. I'll walk with you down the hill." They both left nonchalantly acknowledging various drinkers still in the room.

The next day nothing had changed. A new day broke and the busy village continued to resonate to the sound of the clattering of horses hooves and the grunting of pigs that were kept by many householders. Clucking chickens wandered around the village as they pleased. The pervading smell was of all the livestock melded together but no villager if asked, would notice. The hammering from Isaac's forge continued to give a rhythmical pace to life against this background.

Calvin Seagers' genuine fears of impending turmoil were still very real. However the ordinary villager still went about their daily lives.

"A crowd of about 60,000 people gathered at St.Peter's Field in Manchester to hear a man called Henry Hunt. Although the crowd were unarmed and peaceful, Magistrates panicked and sent in cavalry. As a result 11 people were killed and hundreds were wounded. The event became known as 'The Peterloo Massacre' in a grim mockery of Waterloo."

CHAPTER SIXTEEN
A Little Local Difficulty

On the night of Sam Crocker's funeral the men of the village gathered in The Ship. Many beers were being drunk; "cos Sam would want us to" being the justification.

As Jasper and Robert sat together in their usual seat by the window, they noticed a different mood in the room. Men moved from group to group muttering with an occasional voice raised in anger.

Robert glanced at Jasper, who had hardly said a word all evening, and sensed his pent up anger. "Sam's death has got to you, hasn't it?"

"What do you expect?" Jasper said hoarsely. "We've stood by Sam's grave today; his death was totally unnecessary."

Robert casually put his hand on Jasper's shoulder. "We have got to move on. Sam is not the first to be killed working in the lanes." He bit his lip as he remembered the fate of Jasper's elder brother.

Jasper thumped the table with his fist. "Yes, you're right but ropes instead of chains on the carts killed Sam" He went quiet again, but he was becoming more and more angry, until in a fury he slammed his fist down again. Men around the room started casting nervous looks in his direction. He opened his mouth to speak again but stopped and gave the table another blow and then growled. "We have to do something"

Robert gestured to the room to leave him, and half turning his back to exclude the other drinkers he said quietly. "It has always been this way. What can we do? We don't own the quarries and if we complain we could be out of work." He knew that the truth was not what Jasper wanted to hear, and he wasn't really listening, but he wanted to make his point.

"We've seen places, done things that most of the men in this room would never have dreamt about. God willing we have a good life ahead for us. I have Sarah and you have Ellen and then there are the children."

"What you're saying is that we have to put up with old man Olden's total lack of care, and we have to bend the knee and do nothing." Jasper took a deep breath. "I'm not going to just give in - again."

Robert tried to break Jasper's mood "I remember you getting angry and restless before. I also remember where that got us; nearly being cut to pieces on a battlefield, and then in London, we were nearly on the point of being broke, before you got yourself on the wrong side of the law."

Jasper grunted and then with a rueful grin as he recalled the previous conversation before they joined the army, he said. "Yes, we were much younger then, and were looking for adventure and we wanted to conquer the world. Then, when we were in London we enjoyed ourselves." He paused and sighed, "You and Tom Wilson were right, the likes of us do belong back here in the village." His face darkened, "What happened to Sam Crocker though, is not right - it should not have happened."

"Aye, I agree with you there." Robert looked down and saw that he had almost finished his drink. As George Tupe the landlord went passed he called for fresh ale for himself and Jasper.

Jasper had calmed down but continued on his theme. "When I went to Swanage last week there was another of those strangers by the harbour holding a meeting. There must have been more than fifty listening to him, and there was none there who would disagree with what he was saying. We do all the work, the man said, and what happens when times get hard we suffer. We don't have any say on what happens to us. The likes of Lord Olden pay us a pittance of a wage, we even have to buy and repair our own tools. For his part he spends as little as possible to help us, or even make it safe where we work. He doesn't care about the dangers we have to face to make him money."

Robert nodded. "I was speaking with Calvin Seagers the other day. He said that Lord Olden had been important in parliament when he was younger, and he has always been opposed to every change that would improve the lot of the lower sort. He says that now as Olden gets older, he has become more complacent and resists any change whatsoever." Robert stopped as he realised he wasn't helping the situation and Jasper was bristling again.

Jasper looked hard at Robert. "We left the village to make our fortune away from the likes of him." He paused and snapped "Aye, that will not happen, but we deserve a fair deal!"

Robert looked up to the ceiling in exasperation. "The man in Swanage and others like him are not the answer. They are just feeding off our local problems. Yes, we have a grievance with Lord Olden, but that's just our concern. They are trying to stir up unrest all over the country for their own reasons."

Jasper nodded slowly, "I know, I know, Tom Wilson told us to avoid their schemes. I'm not daft; I can see where they are trying to lead us. I also agree that we should be grateful that we have work ..... and we do have the other ways that we get money from Charlie Heywood." He shrugged his shoulders and looked back at Robert. He felt guilty about the tirade he had been heaping on his friend. As if to justify himself, he added, "I want a better life for Ellen and our little Jemima." A benign smile flickered across his face as he thought of his wife and baby daughter.

Robert was glad that he had been able to placate his friend somewhat but knew that it would not take much to re-ignite his anger. "We are luckier than most, Charlie pays us well for what we bring ashore for him. As you say, we in the village have this other business."

Jasper took a deep breath and nodded, "Aye, but I hear tell that they're bringing in more revenue men. Don't forget as well that during the war they got this fellow, Hardcastle, Bill Hardcastle, who they call a policeman. He has started to poke his nose in everywhere its not wanted. On top of that the Waterguard has one job - to stop smugglers." He frowned. "This part of Charlie's businesses will not last forever, and then where will we be?"

Robert shook his head; he didn't know how to answer. In his usual way, he found that some problems were best left, and hopefully they would solve themselves. Unfortunately this was not always the case but what could he say to Jasper? Robert gave a resigned sigh; he knew there was trouble ahead as Jasper was not alone in his resentment. He noticed that they had emptied their glasses - again. He called out, "Two more ales please George."

The door suddenly burst open to reveal a scowling Bill Tubbs. Robert idly wondered whether Tubbs ever walked into a room without making everyone aware of it. Tubbs stared around until his glare fixed on Jasper who held his stare then turned away dismissively. Tubbs shrugged his shoulders and went to push his way into a large group gathered by the fire.

When the ales had been delivered, Robert nodded in the direction of his brother-in-law, "That man is trouble. We may not like him, he may be a bully, but he's no fool."

Jasper frowned. "He was in Swanage last week as well, and I noticed him having a long talk with the man who held the meeting. I heard him say to Tubbs that other towns and villages were taking action and we should do the same."

Robert didn't really want to hear all this, especially as the ales he had been drinking in memory of Sam were starting to take effect. Blankly he asked, "What for instance?"

Jasper gave Robert a hard look but continued regardless. "He said that in many places threshing machines are becoming more widespread and have been taking away the livelihood of the farm workers. The villagers have started wrecking them. Parsons have been mobbed and forced to sign agreements to take less in tithes from the land." Jasper looked across the room at Bill Tubbs and added. "He told Tubbs that it's up to us to force change where we believe there is injustice."

Jasper looked around the room. The death of Sam Crocker and the others before him had inflamed the passions that were now rising after the consumption of many ales. A few of the men were glancing over to Jasper. 'If anything can be done, then Jasper will know how to do it' was being muttered.

Tubbs was talking louder and louder until finally he addressed everyone in the room "What happened to Sam was not right," he stormed. "and Olden does nothing!" There was general murmur of agreement. "Are we going to sit here and take it?" He saw Jasper staring at him, "What say you Jasper? Are you with us? Olden still lives in his fine house and still has his fine living. What do we do to get rid of a man that rules our lives but does nothing for us? "

"Something terrible is going to happen tonight.' thought Robert, his concern though was being dulled by the intake of ale.

Jasper by now had also had more than his usual quota of ale for a Saturday night. He glared at each man around the room most of whom now were looking at him to see his reaction to Bill Tubbs. He drained his tankard then suddenly his temper snapped. Sam's death, Bill Tubb's rhetoric, the mood in the room and finally the ale brought to the surface his suppressed anger and frustration. He stood up and moved to the centre of the room; all the talking petered out until the room fell silent.

Jasper glared about him. "We are not going to allow Sam's death to be for nothing. We are not going to lie down and take this injustice. The first thing we are going to do, before he allows any more of us to be killed, is to make the old bastard agree to put chains on the quarr carts. By God he is going agree to it." Fixing each man in turn he raised his voice "We are going to make him see that he can't walk all over us."

Robert, seeing Jasper standing alone in the centre of the room, and with the many ales he had by now consumed going to his head, he was stirred to join his old comrade in arms. He rose unsteadily to his feet and went and stood shoulder to shoulder with Jasper. He reached up to put his hand on Jasper's shoulder. Whether this was to keep himself upright or not, was not important. They had faced death together – were they now going let this local tyrant who had made money whilst they were fighting, walk all over them? Waving his tankard which fortunately was again nearly empty he said uncertainly "Aye, lads he's right. It's about time we took action .... and," he hesitated "and ...eh, did something."

Although aware of his companion's state, Jasper was not to be denied and again fixing each man in the room with his one good eye which was now fully bloodshot he roared, "I say we march on Olden Hall. I say we go now. Are you with me?"

A collective spirit moves men to do things that alone they never would dare. This was one of those times. Arms were raised and fists punched the air.

'Time to sort the bastard out!"

"Come on let's go!"

"He won't dare say no"

The room started to empty as the entire assembly to a man followed Jasper through the door. Robert went to sit down for a moment, he wasn't feeling too well.

George Tupe, the landlord was alarmed. He was also dismayed, as he was doing the best business he had done for a long time. With admirable concern for his customers' well-being he called after them "Hold on men. I've got some torches out the back for you to burn."

Robert was dozing in the window seat but as George rushed by with the torches he awoke with a start. Staring around he realised he was now alone. In some confusion he jumped up to make his first steps on the road to freedom for working men everywhere. He went in the wrong direction and tripped on the step down into the Tap Room. Jasper returned to make sure there were no backsliders, and seeing Robert trying to get to his feet guided him to one of the wooden settles. There, Robert was to spend the night of 'The March on Olden Hall' peacefully snoring.

At Olden Hall, His Grace was entertaining for dinner the local Man of the Cloth. Lord Olden enjoyed the company of the Most Reverend Poskit. The man was as opinionated as himself. A thin, bleak man dressed in the customary black of his profession, he had a hooked, purple nose that betrayed the decanters of wine and port that had passed through him. With six parishes within his domain the Tithes gave him a comfortable living without being too arduous. He had his local curates who looked after each of his village flocks and he comforted himself that he was only called in briefly now and again when his weight of office demanded payment of recalcitrant Tithes.

Despite the distance from his flock Poskit was very well aware of the growing discontent that was starting take a grip on their minds. He stirred himself to the maximum of his courage, "Milord, you are aware of the rumblings among the labouring classes around here?" he asked cautiously.

A simple statement he felt, but he did not realise his mistake, the poor Reverend had struck a nerve. Lord Olden leapt out of his seat and fixing Poskit with a penetrating glare he stormed, "These fellows are forgetting who knows best for them. This country trades with the rest of the world, London is the largest city in the world. Who has governed England so we are where we are today?" He paused for breath so as to answer his own question. "The Landed Classes of this country, sir. The Landed Classes. Who runs Parliament, well, sir? Those who own the land. Land is the basis of our greatness" He paused again whilst bringing himself to his full height.

Poskit was about to remind his Lordship that Parliament was run by the landed gentry because it was only they who could vote in the Members. He quickly thought better of educating His Grace with this slice of information. He in fact already wished he had kept quiet in the first place.

Seeing that his audience of one was not to contradict him, his Lordship resumed, "We of the land know how to govern. These new industrial fellows may be making their fortunes but it us that know how to govern. We have to keep the natural order of society – look what happened in Manchester when you let the masses start to agitate. The magistrates had to send in troops to control a crowd of over 60,000. By God, it was lucky for them that only 11 of them were killed when the troops moved against them." He took a pace forward to Poskit who sat back abruptly in his chair. "They are calling it the Peterloo Massacre as if to ridicule our brave Duke of Wellington's actions at Waterloo."

He stopped. He was breathless. All his rooted fears were coming to the surface as he feared his way of life being threatened. He believed however, it was his duty, with the other Members of Parliament, to stand fast. He almost jumped as he remembered one final point. "Before you start to take these people's side." He paused, glaring at the cringing Poskit as his Lordship prepared to deliver his Coup de Grace. "I have received notice that there was a plot to kill the entire Cabinet. Yes, sir, that's the sort of revolution that we have to deal with. It must be crushed immediately. I have been informed that a chap called Thistlewood and four of his fellow conspirators were found in Cato Street in London. They were hanged from the gallows without delay."

Having ensured that his point was well made, and that he was not to be denied, he went to pour himself a further large brandy. After a moment of two there came a pang of guilt that his poor guest had received a full broadside of what were his own fears. He said in a quiet voice as if to reassure Poskit that he was quite safe. "What is it these chaps around here are worried about."

Poskit started nervously, "Well Milord, a few of their number have been killed in the quarry and they believe that you to do not care for their well-being" He took another gulp of Port, but kept his eyes peering over the top of his glass at his host.

His Lordship looked surprised, "These fellows are forgetting themselves. Have I not provided for them to send their children to your Sunday Bible school?"

"Oh yes, and very good it is for these young urchins to read the Lord's Word."

Lord Olden shot a quick look at Poskit, "You are just teaching them to *read* the Bible? You are not teaching them writing or arithmetic or any other such dangerous subjects?" He demanded.

The Reverend reacted quickly, "Of course not – that would be totally unnecessary." Both men stared at each other; one his florid face lit up even further by the roaring fire, the other's face though seemingly paled even despite the efforts of the flames.

There was a full minute's silence as each digested the conversation that Poskit for one had wished had never happened. It was not a good idea to get on the wrong side of this man who also held his Living within his gift.

The silence was broken as the door flew open. It was Lady Olden in a state of high anxiety. "Your Grace, there is a mob outside and they look dangerous." For the moment Lord Olden was aghast, but he had always been a man of impetuous action and strode passed her to the front entrance whilst calling for his footmen to follow him. At the opening of the door his jaw dropped. There confronting him was a mob of some twenty or more men, most of whom looked familar but who were not now showing their usual deference and humility before him. All the years of fear of the mob and revolution confronted him. This was it – the time had come – was he to be dragged to his knees and beaten to death in his own home?

He heard his wife behind him sobbing, "What do we do? They look so angry" she said. Lord Olden was no coward but he had never had to face such anger and rage targeted at himself. He spun around, "Milady, control yourself. Barker, Tomkins, see what these fellows want" At which he retreated back to the drawing room at the rear of house, leaving his confused wife staring at the mob.

Lady Olden was indeed upset at the commotion, they were shattering her peaceful existence. She went to the window and peeked through the curtains. The burning torches being held high in the night air caused long shadows to be cast towards the Hall. She recoiled at the sight of this chanting mob but she was drawn to a huge man, who appeared to be their leader, who had a vicious scar that ran across his scull to a black eye patch. His appearance was made even more frightening by him being silhouetted by the burning torches that the men were brandishing.

It had taken over an hour for the band of villagers to reach the carriageway leading to Olden Hall. Jasper had by this time ,collected his thoughts. He looked around at the men he had known all his life. As they left The Ship, it had started as a drunken caper with much shouting, jeering and pointless threats aimed at Lord Olden, a man most of the quarriers had seldom seen. After a while, spirits were dampened as repetitive chants dried up and the men became subdued.

Some men, who had taken too much of George Tupes ale, were left behind as they lent over the undergrowth, clearing both heads and stomachs. Others, more sober or timid, silently drifted off home.

There were still about twenty men left and as Jasper looked from face to face he could see, although heads had cleared, they were in earnest and their anger was genuine. Although these men were not troublemakers, they nevertheless believed their cause was real and just.

Jasper sensed there was also an underlying tension. He shared their disquiet as he was leading his friends and fellow villagers into a situation he recognised could be creating a great deal of difficulty for them all.

He looked ahead of him to the snarling Bill Tubbs who spat out another oath. In contrast he turned to see the determined but apprehensive face of Ted Edmunds.

Jasper recalled the words of George Fitzherbert and Tom Wilson. Does he let Bill Tubbs take the path that will lead to upheaval and violence and what will be the end result. Or, was Ted the silent majority in the village who wanted common sense and a proper consideration for their working conditions.

The way these options crystallised in his mind, Jasper knew what he had to do.

Josiah Tomkins, Lord Olden's head footman, was not a big man. He was of medium height and build, with mouse coloured hair that framed a chubby face. He was happy being a footman in a rural country house where the biggest trauma was when cook was late with preparing dinner. He certainly did not have any argument with these fellows and was very nervous as he hesitantly left the front door. He quickly realised he was alone as Barker hadn't moved and was still standing on his toes as if trying to see what was happening over Tomkins head. Tomkins muttered under his breath "Thanks, friend"

As he came closer to the jeering mob he started to recognise familiar faces. He looked from one to another "'Joseph - Thomas - Ted, what do you men want." He looked back over his shoulder, "If his Lordship recognises any of you it will mean big trouble."

Bill Tubb's voice boomed out above the rest, "We want Olden. Where is he?"

Tomkins jumped, but then he recognised Jasper Tomes. Whilst Tomkins was at Lord Olden's command, he was frightened stiff of Jasper. "Oh dear, oh Mr Tomes I'm so sorry," he stammered, "It's just that his Lordship wants to know why you are here and what you intend to do." 'This isn't fair, why was he piggy in the middle?' he thought.

Jasper looked sternly at Tomkins, but said gently, "Don't worry lad, we have no quarrel with you. Sam Crocker was killed this week because his Lordship still won't replace the old pulley ropes with chains. His quarry is the only one not to have changed."

Behind Jasper a few of the men encouraged by the dark night and the remaining alcohol in their veins were getting restless. Bill Tubbs who was not going to waste this opportunity to get at the hated Lord Olden, hurled a rock at the nearest window. This was followed by one of the burning torches being tossed and landing at Barker's feet. The crash of glass and the roar of the thrown torch caused four simultaneous events. A squeal escaped from Tomkins lips, Barker spun around and ran down to the basement kitchen where he sat shaking and strumming his fingers on the kitchen table, on hearing the noise the Reverend Poskit fell to his knees and started praying, and Lady Olden spun around, gently swooned and settled onto a conveniently sited chair.

Jasper turned and stormed at his fellow protestors "Stop that you numbskulls! Any more nonsense and we will all land up in jail or hanging from the hangman's gibbet. Bill Tubbs you will be first if I have any say in the matter." He caught hold of Tomkins arm and led him towards the house. "Look Josiah, tell his Lordship that all we want is his promise to put chains on the quarr carts. Tell him that if he does nothing, the deaths of Sam Crocker and those who will surely follow him, will be on his head." He pulled Tomkins to face him "Tell him that the men are angry and I can't promise I can keep them back unless they get the right answer." He then gently pushed the bewildered Tomkins in the direction of the still open front door.

Tomkins' first thought when he was free of Jasper's grasp was to flee as far away from Olden Hall as his legs would carry him. Whether it was a resolve that was well hidden within him, or the knowledge that he had no where to go, but he slowly went back into the house to deliver the message. After peering into a few of the rooms, gathering an ashen Lady Olden in his wake, he eventually found Lord Olden and reverend Poskit. Poskit was still on his knees praying whilst Lord Olden was sitting at his desk nervously fingering an old musket pistol that hadn't been fired for thirty years, and to which there were no musket balls for its use.   He fixed Tomkins with an uncertain gaze. "Well, man."

'Why am I in the middle of all this?' Tomkins thought again before speaking. "Excuse me, Milord" he started "I think you may be able to turn them away. I believe Mr Seagers had to inform you last week that one of their number was killed because one of the old ropes broke on a quarr cart. They are very upset 'cos this is the third time this year this has happened. If you could promise that chains will be brought in without delay, then I'm sure they will disperse and go to their homes." Tomkins was warming to his task.

"Damn their eyes! How dare they try to blackmail me. I'll have them all hanged.'   he blustered without much conviction. "I will not give in to the demands of a mob - of a rabble." he glared up at Tomkins and then at Poskit and his wife in turn.

There was a polite cough from the Reverend Poskit. "Excuse me milord. I know its not my business and well, I totally agree with you of course, but I think it would probably be better to keep the men happy." he glanced nervously at Lord Olden trying to judge his reaction.   There being no immediate onslaught, he continued,   "Remember all those riots and other goings on there have been around the country. We don't want any of that around here if we can help it."

Lady Olden saw his lordship wavering. She quietly went to stand behind him putting her hand on his shoulder. "Your Grace, I know you will do the right thing. You must not give in to these bullies but the Reverend does have a point." She stopped and looked at the Reverend who was relieved to have support.   She addressed him, "His Lordship is not insensitive to the wellbeing of his men. He is no doubt very saddened to hear of the death of that poor man." She looked down at his Lordship who gave a reluctant grunt which produced a smart tap on the shoulder from his wife.

Tomkins, a bystander as was his place, hesitantly said. "If it please your Lordship. The last time I was on my way to Swanage on errands for you, I remember taking an order for the very chains in question to Jacob Butt the blacksmith." He paused and shot a glance at Lady Olden.

She frowned, then nodded quickly. "Yes, quite so. Carry on Tomkins."

Tomkins took a deep breath. "I will go to tell those men outside to be off and to leave immediately. I shall say 'How dare you make demands above your station'. I shall then tell them that you look upon all your employees as part of your family. However, if they misbehave, you, as their father figure, has to be stern sometimes for their own good." He paused again expecting to be dismissed on the spot, but as there was no response he added, "I will then tell them about the order that I took myself to Mr Butt and repeat that your Lordship will not have demands placed upon you and in any case the matter is in hand."

There was complete silence as Tomkins finally finished. He was sure he had gone too far. The silence was broken as Lord Olden jumped to his feet "Go on tell them" he roared, "Tell them how dare they come here like this. Especially for a matter I had already settled. Go tell them - or I'll be out there to deal with them myself." With that he went to pour himself a further large French brandy supplied by that excellent fellow Heywood. He turned his back on the room and stared steadfastly out to the rear of the house which was all peace and quiet.

Lady Olden flapped her hand at Tomkins "Go on, you heard. Tell them to go to their homes and the matter, as his Lordship has said, is in hand."

Tomkins, the hero of the hour, almost ran back to Jasper and the men who were starting to get restless again.

"Well?" Jasper demanded, sure that he would be bringing bad news.

"All has been settled" Tomkins began smugly, "His Lordship did not want to hear of it. He said no immediately. Lady Olden and the Reverend Poskit were on his side but I stood my ground. I told him to see sense and order the chains or he would be sorry for the outcome. In the end he saw that I would not take no for an answer. As I persevered, you will get your chains."

Jasper squinted at the messenger, "Are you sure? I don't care what was said, but will we definitely get the chains?"

"Yes." Tomkins replied simply.

"Right." He turned and addressed the men still waiting. Some had already drifted off as sobriety and doubt cleared the minds. Those remaining were the ones whose anger was most genuine and who wanted an answer to their demands. "Its time to go home, men. He looked back at Tubbs. "That means you as well Tubbs. Lord Olden has agreed, we will be getting a safer quarry." Jasper turned and shook Tomkins' hand, "Well done Josiah. I know that wasn't easy" he paused and added with a grin "whatever was said. Next time you are in The Ship you will not have to pay for your drink." He laughed, "Be sure to bring a thirst with you."

"Thank you Mr Tomes." Tomkins then returned a much relieved man to his quarters in the roof of the house. There he consumed almost the entire bottle of brandy that Charlie Heywood had brought but which had been separated from the rest of the shipment.

So ended, a little local difficulty, that was settled without recourse to events that could have escalated out of control.

The next day The Reverend Poskit decided to visit his brother, the Dean at Salisbury Cathedral. A period of quiet reflection in cloisters would overcome the awful traumas that can be experienced in the secular world.

As far as Lord Olden was concerned the whole episode was now closed. Lady Olden quietly told Calvin Seagers the next morning to order the chains for urgent delivery to Crack Quarry. She then also decided a vacation away from Olden House would be appropriate. By mid morning she had decided to visit her dear friends Sir William and Lady Fairfax in Hanover Square, a most agreeable new area to the west of London. She had received only the previous week a letter from Lady Fairfax telling of her new-born taste for astronomical and other sciences, by attending lectures at the Royal Institution. Such a stimulation of the mind would be such a refreshing change from the stultifying routine of Olden House. She called for her maid, Flora, who was still on the verge of hyperventilating at any moment after the events of the previous evening. After assuring her that the world was now safe again for her to participate in its continuance, she told the quivering maid to pack items essential for an extended stay in London.

Next she called for Tomkins. He entered her drawing room looking rather the worse for wear. When he came to stand next to her to receive his instructions she caught the unmistakable odour of stale brandy, reminiscent of that emanating from His Grace on a regular basis. She looked up hard at Tomkins for a moment, then softened her gaze. "You did well last night, Tomkins. I think the whole affair would have been that more severe without your intervention."

Tomkins response was an exhalation of breath in relief. The brandy was still battling to re-emerge but he managed a brief "Thanks, milady." through clenched teeth.

Lady Olden gave a little smile, "I have an errand for you. " She paused and smiled again, "Which will mean you being in the fresh air. I want you to take a letter down to Swanage for delivering post haste to London." Tomkins nodded gratefully, "It is to be sent to my friend Lady Fairfax," she added rather unnecessarily. "Oh, and book a passage for myself and Flora on the market boat to Poole tomorrow morning."

She looked at Tomkins' ashen face. "I also have one other errand which can be done tomorrow. I believe that the trip to Swanage will be sufficient for you today." She decided that she should finish giving her instructions as swiftly and without delay. "I want you to go to Lord Wareham's Estate where I understand Lord Henry is visiting." She paused then added dismissively. "They are discussing some political matters." She finished, much to Tomkins relief. "Please inform them exactly what happened here last night. Right you may go."

Tomkins replied quickly as the brandy and he were soon to part company "Certainly milady, Right away, milady." and turned on his heel to carry out all that was essential for himself and his employer.

Lady Olden called after him "And you may take the rest of the day off afterwards." Then said quietly to herself "I think there would be no other point."

The rest of her day was spent supervising Flora and speaking with the rest of staff to ensure that His Grace was properly attended to in her absence. The following morning came, and as she bade farewell to her husband, she felt a pang of sympathy for this once great man who would be now living a more lonely existence. Remembering the poor men who had lost their lives, and the suffering of their families because of his intransigence, such thoughts were soon ameliorated.

The carriage ladened with her Ladyship, maid and luggage wound its way down to Swanage and drew up on the quayside next to the waiting market boat. Captain Jenkins rushed forward to assist her on-board. She gave the other passengers a cursory glance as her baggage was embarked for the brief trip across Studland Bay into Poole. There were few passengers on board on that particular day. There was just her Ladyship and her maid, a quarry manager and a man of middle years with a young lady who he introduced to the other passengers as his niece. A couple of local businessmen sat in quiet confidential discussion with each other.

The crew prepared to cast off when there was an urgent call from the quayside, "Hold fast my man, a servant of the King wishes to come on-board." There stood an immaculately dressed man in his mid twenties wearing a red frock coat, cream coloured waistcoat and black trousers which met with immaculately polished leather boots at the knee. He introduced himself as Officer Keziah Wilmot of the King's Waterguard. His look of disdain was framed by long sideburns and a stove pipe hat. Although he appeared to be bored with all about him, his eyes travelled from passenger to passenger as he filed each away on the chance that it may be of future use to him. He grandly explained to the Captain that he had been appointed to Swanage on a mission to curtail the practice, and apprehend the perpetrators, of smuggling. "I have been informed that you and the fishing folk around here may be able to assist me in my task." he added darkly.

Captain Jenkins assured him that he would, of course, be at his service at any time. At which he turned his back upon this most important gentleman and set sail for Poole.

Lady Olden was relaxed as the scene of recent anxiety slowly slipped behind her into the distance. The water gently lapping against the side of the boat as it eased its way across the Bay was soporific, but she maintained her decorum as she sat upright in her seat with hands resting on her lap. The other passengers spoke in hushed tones so as not to disturb the fine lady.

It was Lady Olden that broke the peace. "Captain Jenkins, what is the purpose of all those buoys?" she asked casually.

The good Captain who had been making this journey for over forty years, man and boy, jumped out of his reverie. "Where? What? Oh those they're fishing pots milady." he said quickly. He tried not to look in the direction of Officer Wilmot, but failed.

"What do they catch?" her ladyship persisted.

"Fish milady." Then realising his insubordination, he added "Lobsters."

"Oh how interesting. I love lobster. I would be fascinated to see how they are caught."

What Lady Olden did not realise was that many of these buoys marked the barrels of contraband waiting collection by Charlie Heywood's men in the time honoured practice. Attached to a plank, so weighted that the barrel would be kept clear of the mud, it would be ready to be collected when it was safe from the revenue men - or any of the new breed of enforcers. They mingled with the countless fishing buoys and with the fishermen constantly sailing back and forth to harvest their catch.

Captain Jenkins was well aware of this practice. "I'm not sure that I want to disturb the men's catch." he hesitated, "It's a man's livelihood, milady." He glanced in the direction of Officer Wilmot who had risen from his repose and was curious to see what was happening.

"What is the problem, Captain?" he asked with as much authority he could muster.

"No problem, sir. I was just explaining to her Ladyship that the local fishermen catch lobsters and that their pots are marked by the buoys."

Lady Olden was starting to become irritated. "I have just asked the man to pull one of them in so I could see how a lobster is caught. I do not understand the problem."

Wilmot, seeing his position was to uphold the demands of the better sort, turned to the hapless Captain, "My good man, pull one on board now, and look lively."

Jenkins looked from one to the other, went to say something and stopped. He shrugged his shoulders, 'It wasn't his problem'. He nodded to one of his crew who had loyally joined his Captain. "Thomas, do as the man says. Pull a pot on board." He looked hard at his crewman in an effort to relay his meaning, "See if you can find one that is weighed down with a big 'un." he said.

Wilmot, a look of triumph on his face, turned to Lady Olden expecting a compliment on his swift action on her behalf. She in turn thought, what a pompous little man, and turned to watch Thomas.

Thomas meanwhile, understood exactly what his Captain was meaning. Pull out a lobster, not a barrel of brandy. This was easier to say than to do, as he did not know how each buoy was marked. He leant over the side and pulled at one of the buoys - it felt heavy, too heavy for just a lobster pot. He let it go. "There's nothing in that one, Cap'n." He repeated this a couple more times.

As each buoy was released Lady Olden became increasingly bored with the whole episode. "Heavens, why is such a small task such a problem." Thomas surrendered his loyalty and seized hold of the nearest buoy and started to haul it to the surface. Whether it was his fearing the wrath of such a noble Lady, or the knowledge that a rope bearing a large barrel would require his maximum strength, he used all his might in giving the rope a final pull. It was his lucky day, and it could be said his unlucky day. It was his lucky day because he had chosen a buoy that was indeed marking a lobster pot. It was his unlucky day as the effort he applied was far in excess of that required. The lobster pot exploded from the sea and continued in an arc that went over Thomas's head ending accurately on the centre of Officer Keziah Willmot's stovepipe hat.   As the good Officer was still wearing his hat a look of alarm changed to daze as he sunk backwards onto his rear end.

Lady Olden could not help herself. All breeding deserted her as she gave a quiet snigger. She quickly remembered her station and waved her hand dismissively to the entire assembly and airily said, "Please God, just forget what I said and get us to Poole with no further ado." At this she turned to face her destination.   Facing away from all other passengers and the crew of the Pride of the Bay, she could not help a smile that refused to leave her lips until she disembarked.

CHAPTER SEVENTEEN

Tubbs Meets Ted

Life may have felt uncomfortable in Olden Hall for Lady Olden, but she was able to escape from her country Estate and take up residence at her house in Mayfair, London; Dot had no such choice. She was trapped in Hollow Cottage under the power of her malevolent husband. To her relief Tubbs was too drunk, or had been with his whore in Swanage, to make many marital demands upon her. She always felt that she was walking on eggshells and feared that he could snap at any moment and she dreaded the extent of the violence he would mete out to her or the children. She was almost relieved that the occasional slap across the face was the limit so far of what she'd had to endure. Whatever he may do there was no escape for her, and no one was allowed to stop him.

Dot's absence in Winchester had been heart-rending for Ted Edmunds, but he was relieved that she was safe whilst away from the grasp of her husband. When Ted found out that she had been brought back to the village he was desperate to help her. The sight of her standing forlornly in the rain when Tubbs came storming into The Ship after Sam's death almost broke his heart. He desperately wished an opportunity would come along for him to help a person he had long realised that he loved.

The week after the villagers march to Olden Hall, Ted saw Tubbs stagger out of The Ship. Ted wanted to confront him about his treatment of Dot but realised such action would be fruitless, and would probably make matters worse. Ted decided to ignore the man, but Tubbs noticed him and called across the road. "How's our love sick wimp?" He sneered followed by a stream of crude insults.

Ted did not want to provoke Tubbs when he was in this state, and attempted to walk on the other side of the road. Tubbs was not to be denied and he swayed across the road to antagonise his unfortunate victim. "You weren't man enough to take my woman were you?" Tubbs moved closer. "I know you were the one to helped her go to Winchester. You little…"

Ted stopped him. "Look, just leave me alone. I will have nothing to do with you."

"You are a total weakling aren't you? You and that bitch of mine would have been good for each other."

Ted could take insults on himself but abuse of Dot he could not accept. "Now you watch your tongue, Tubbs. That is a lady you are talking about and I will not stand for her to be spoken about in that way."

Tubbs gave a loud, coarse laugh. "And what are you going to do about it?" He stepped right in front of Ted and gave him a hard push in the chest that caused Ted to stagger backwards against the church graveyard wall.

Ted scrambled up again. "Keep your hands to yourself."

"Or what?" Tubbs lurched forward again and raised his fist to launch a swinging blow to Ted's head.

Ted was sober and more agile than his attacker. He stepped aside, and with pent up anger he gave the man he hated a firm shove. Tubbs missed his target and pitched forward with his momentum for a few steps then tumbled over to the ground. If he had just fallen, then he would have been up with no more than bruised knees and hands. Unfortunately for Tubbs as he fell to the ground his face hit the graveyard wall and his head snapped back. He lay there not moving and Ted stood, mouth wide open, in horror.

"Bad luck Ted. You almost saved him from tripping over his own feet." A voice made him spin around to see Silas Winter and two others from the village that had been watching the whole scene from the doorway of The Ship.

Walter, the curate, had also seen the whole affair as he was leaving the church. He hurried forward to see what damage Tubbs had suffered. On his way passed Ted he confirmed Silas's comment, "If the Lord is my witness you nearly saved him from falling over." Walter knelt beside Tubbs and Ted was sure he heard the good curate mutter. "Pity." Walter then turned to look up at the crowd that had gathered. "He's still breathing." He rolled Tubbs over roughly.

Tubbs face was covered in blood. His nose was at an angle, obviously broken, and he was bleeding from the gashes all over his face. His eyes flickered open and as he tried to speak several yellow teeth were dislodged. He winced from the concentration of trying to move but his attempt failed. Nobody was quite sure what to do next. After a few moments, during which Tubbs' soft moaning developed into loud, strangled sobs, he was finally able to cough out. "I can't move."

Silas looked at Walter. "I've seen this type of injury before in the quarry. Looks like his neck is broken."

Walter got to his feet, leaving the broken figure on the ground, he put his hand on Ted's shoulder to console him. "Don't upset yourself, Ted."

"I can't believe it can be so serious - he just fell forward. All I did was ….."

Walter stopped him. "We all saw that you tried to stop him tripping over. Now you go on home and leave him to us."

Ted protested. "Can't I help?"

"No, no. You go." Walter gently turned Ted around in the direction of his home and nudged him to get him moving. Then he addressed the other men. "Give me some help. A couple of you take his arms around your shoulders and we'll drag him back to Hollow Cottage." Tubbs was a heavy man and it took much effort to bundle him along. He croaked out a constant stream of invective to those supporting him as well as cries of pain as his neck lolled back and forth.

Dot was shocked when she saw Tubbs being brought in and laid on his bed. After being told what had happened she thanked Silas and Walter and assured them that she could cope. To her credit she did what she could for him in the next few days, albeit she was tight lipped and was incapable of giving any love and tenderness. The children were sent to stay with Joshua and Martha. It was apparent from the start that Tubbs was paralysed from the neck down, and she had to tend to all his bodily needs. She tried to minimise his pain and fever by cold cloths on his face, but after a week the cuts had become discoloured and were seeping and would not heal. He was also slipping in and out of consciousness.

When Robert heard about Tubbs he went to see his sister to offer his help. His heart was cold to the man, but he was proud of the way Dot bravely carried out her duties as a caring person.

A week after Tubbs had fallen, Robert made his daily visit to Dot and went straight up to the bedroom where she was sitting on a chair by the invalid's bed. Dot looked up as he came in the room and quickly replaced a cold cloth across Tubbs' forehead. This provoked a small cry of pain and single worded oath but received no thanks for her efforts.

Robert frowned in distaste. "Is there any improvement yet?"

Dot shook her head and indicated that they should go back downstairs before she spoke. "I'm afraid he seems to be getting worse. I sent a message to Ma Salen asking if she could help in the way she always does for people not well in the village. She said she couldn't as one of her grandchildren had a cold and she was worried about her."

Robert shook his head sadly. "I understand how people feel." He sighed. "It's not right though."

Dot shrugged. "He isn't able to eat much. He has no feeling below his neck, cannot move his body and the gashes on his face are giving him a great deal of pain."

"I haven't had a look at him properly yet.   As you know, I was in a hospital after the battle at Waterloo and the look of him reminds me of many of the men who were there with open cuts and gashes. I'll go and have a good look at him." He entered the bedroom and quietly leaned forward over the bed so as not to disturb Tubbs, who had his eyes closed. After a moment or two he stood back, shook his head and returned downstairs. Grim faced he answered Dot's silent question. "I don't think that there is anything that can be done for him."

Dot remained still and then asked simply. "What do you mean?"

"He won't get better."

They both looked at each other without speaking for a few moments before Dot turned away. Robert saw her shoulders sag as she gave a long sigh. He went and put his arms around her as she turned to bury her face into his chest. She stood sobbing silently for some time.

Bill Tubbs' pain got worse until one night he died. Dot had spent another night in a chair in front of the range, and when she came into the bedroom she found him lying perfectly still. She sat by the bedside for some hours, sometimes quietly weeping and then just staring at the bed.

Tubbs funeral was a brief ceremony with just Dot supported by Robert at the graveside. Tubbs' two daughters stayed with their grandparents.

CHAPTER EIGHTEEN

Realism at the Top

Excuse me my Lord, there is a footman by the name of Tomkins from Olden Hall who insists that he speaks with Lord Henry." Lord Wareham looked across to his guest and raised his eyebrows in surprise. Lord Henry frowned, he was displeased that a footman should be so bold. Stott, the butler, continued "He says he has a message from her Ladyship, Countess Olden."

Lord Henry still irked, reluctantly acquiesced . "If that is the case, with your permission Charles, send him in."

"By all means Henry." He gestured for Stott to summon Tomkins. "I trust he is not the bringer of bad news." He thought for a moment. "We must continue our discussion. Your friends on your side of the Chamber must be aware that there are urgent issues to be addressed."

Lord Henry was about to speak when Tomkins appeared nervously in the doorway. Lord Wareham waved for him to come forward and immediately it was apparent he was on serious business. Lord Henry became alarmed. "What is it man? Are his Grace and the Countess well? Come on man, spit it out."

"Yes my Lord they are quite well." he paused. "Now."

"Now? Now? What do you mean? For God's sake man what has happened?"

Tomkins inwardly was pleased that he had the complete attention of such illustrious gentlemen. "Two days ago a group of about fifty men from the village of Langton Matravers attacked Olden Hall. I'm afraid they were in an ugly mood. Windows were broken and they made certain threats."

"My God. You say His Grace and the Countess are unharmed?"

"Yes my Lord."

"Well what was it all about? What happened?"

"A man was killed at the Crack Lane Quarry and the men blamed certain tools that they have to use which they think are now dangerous. They demanded that His Grace make changes."

"How dare they!"

"Quite so, my Lord. His Grace was most displeased but I.." Tomkins hesitated realising he was on the threshold of impertinence. "His Lordship was persuaded as all matters had been considered, he was able to tell the villagers that their complaints were groundless. The new equipment was about to be delivered."

"Good. And then."

"The mob dispersed and that was the end of the matter although it was distressing for all concerned." Tomkins couldn't help adding. "Lady Olden instructed me to go the very next day to ensure the delivery of chains to replace the old ropes was not delayed."

Lord Wareham coughed but remained looking out of the window; a smile flitted across his face.

Tomkins had finished his errand but was able to add. "I visited the Quarry on my way here My Lord. I told the men the chains would be delivered within the week."

Lord Henry was impressed with Tomkins initiative. "Well done, Tomkins. What was their reaction."

"Thank you, My Lord. The majority are feeling rather sheepish about what happened although their anger was very real on the night. For the time being they are satisfied, but life is very hard for them and it's not like it used to be before the war. Since the war there have been a number of bad harvests and the price of food keeps going up."

'Don't they realise they are Acts of God; there have always been bad harvests."

"Aye, My Lord but there are strangers who tell them that it is unfair that they are the only ones to suffer. They tell them stories of men around the country that are taking matters into their own hands."

Lord Henry was outraged. "Well Tomkins, you can tell them that the government is not taking kindly to troublemakers who spread malicious ideas. Laws will be passed that will clamp down on these damn radicals. We will start here and now. Who were the ringleaders of that infernal mob?"

Tomkins was aghast; he could not reveal the names of friends and the good men of his village who just wanted some justice. It would mean for them at best prison or transportation and at worst, the hangman's rope.

"Well Tomkins? Who were they?"

Tomkins flustered. "My Lord it was dark, I couldn't see their faces."

"Really? I think you had better start remembering or do we have to arrest all those in the quarry?"

Lord Wareham cleared his throat. Lord Henry frowned and turned to look at him, then understood his meaning and gestured with an outstretched arm for Tomkins to leave. "Thank you, Tomkins. That will be all. You may return to Olden Hall, but we will speak further on this matter."

After Tomkins had left Lord Henry shook his head. "The scoundrels!"

Silence followed during which Lord Wareham walked around the room deep in thought. Some minutes passed until he finally spoke. "Whilst I believe strong action has to be taken against anyone promoting or indulging in any form of unrest, there is a danger that any precipitous action will in itself cause more problems."

"The Government must take a lead. It cannot stand aside."

"Henry, we both believe that action has to be taken, however we appear to agree to disagree on what that action should be."

Lord Henry grunted and said dryly, "I agree." Lord Wareham smiled and nodded in recognition of the paradox. Lord Henry continued. "We have to have strong government otherwise there will be anarchy."

"Quite so. However, there are real grievances. There are machines that are doing the work of many men."

"Yes, but new large works are being opened which employ sometimes hundreds of men."

"Yes I agree; to a point. However, many are still without work. We must do something to help those poor devils that are destitute and not just react with draconian measures. I fear there will be trouble here as there has been up in the north. Mob rule has taken over in a number of cities, Derby and Sheffield I believe, have had troops sent to restore order. We don't want that to happen here." Charles turned and looked out of the window once again in deep thought. He took a deep breath and exhaled. "Henry, we have had a generation of war. I believe that we will now have a generation of upheaval. It is beholden to the leaders of this country to respond carefully to events. An uprising cannot be advanced softly, gradually, carefully, considerately, respectfully, or politely. A revolution is an insurrection, and act of violence by which one class overthrows another."

"That is why we must be firm."

After a moment's pause Charles took a deep breath. 'I am not talking about some vague speculation, but how day to day life and conditions throughout the country can create a series of events that become unstoppable."

"I have said already Charles, we must be firm."

"Henry, we are both men of the world. I have been wanting to come to a course of action that I believe, if taken, will be paramount in preventing our country taking a voyage into the unknown. We are fortunate that although there are those that agitate and travel the country, there is not yet a populist leader." He paused, "Yet"

Lord Henry looked alarmed, "Thank god."

"There is an alternative, and may I say, I think an English way. We are men of the world and we know that although we in Parliament make the laws and lead the country there are others that we must satisfy, may I say appease."

Henry looked uncomfortable.

Charles raised his eyebrows and grimaced. "You know of whom I speak. The circumstances I have just described cause uncertainty. These people in London financed our armies during the war and are men of vast wealth and therefore power. Men of finance will not allow the markets to be unpredictable and thereby jeopardise their wealth. They have made it quite clear that if this country was to slip further into disorder then they will move their wealth elsewhere which would be devastating for England."

Henry slumped in his chair. "I do understand, but what is this alternative."

"It has been suggested that matters be dealt with on a local basis. I am travelling to London tomorrow. I understand that preferential loans will be available to carry out whatever is necessary to control the population in each area of the country. When I return I suggest we meet again to discuss in detail what has to be done."

"Is this such an urgent matter?"

"Yes. I believe the incident at Olden hall proves that matters are reaching a crisis point."

They were interrupted when Stott entered the room bearing a silver tray with glasses and a decanter of brandy.

"You paint a very sorry picture Charles, and I look forward to our next meeting. However, I am still incensed with those scoundrels who have attacked His Grace and the Countess. I will forgo any action until we speak further but that does not mean that I will not respond as I deem appropriate in the future."

Charles sighed, "Thank you Henry." Then as a good host, he tried to brightened the mood. "I consider that now we should have a glass of the excellent brandy I have been able to acquire.

"That's an admirable idea."

The brandy was brought to them and each man studied their glass, sniffed the aroma then let the amber nectar warm its way down their throats. Charles eventually smiled and said. "The French certainly make a damn fine brandy."

'Yes they do. Do you get this from that chap Heywood?"

"Yes, he seems to run most of such trade around here. If you know what I mean?"

"He's a very shrewd fellow from what I hear. This is not his only, eh, venture."

Charles paused and thought for a moment. "Heywood provides money for our workers when they help him. That income will not last for ever, since the war the government are now making more effective efforts to stem the loss of revenue as a result of this trade."

Henry sat back in his chair and took another draught of brandy. "Yes, I know, I suppose you have heard the Waterguards are being provided with more men and resources. It won't stop smuggling straight away. Men like Charlie Heywood will realise they just have to become more ingenious in their activities. Eventually though, it will become too dangerous for them."

Charles drained his glass and grinned. "Pity in a way." He then spoke in a more business-like manner. "Henry, I made my point just now, and I believe that we should both give the matter some attention. However, I think that is sufficient talk for today."

CHAPTER NINETEEN

Smuggling

If you wake at midnight, and hear horse's feet,
Don't go drawing back the blind, or looking in the street,
Them that ask no questions isn't told a lie.
Watch the wall my darling while the Gentlemen go by.
(A Smuggler's Song by Rudyard Kipling)

Since being open for business some thirty years before The Ship Inn had been unlucky with its landlords as three husbands had died, the trade being taken over by their wives. The current landlord was George Tupe. Poor George, being a nervous man, the knowledge of the fate of his predecessors could only have further stressed him as he was married to Maude a very strong minded woman - and they didn't get on. George would never see bad in anyone and could easily be persuaded in most matters. Maude however ruled her empire with a rod of iron.

Despite being able to supply items which were not easily available by buying from Charlie Heywood, business at the Inn was not good. This had put further strain on the marital relationship. Maud had dictated that it was cash on every sale, whilst George would give a nod and a wink when asked for credit.

A few months after Sam's funeral, George was sitting quietly in the tap room out of harms way as was his habit. An inner warmth was growing as he sampled the brandy from a new cask delivered the previous night. His revelry was shattered when Maude, a wide and capable women nearly broke the door off its hinges as she charged in causing George to topple to the floor. George was so startled that he bit the glass that was raised to his lips and blood started oozing from the wound.

"In God's name, why have you been giving credit to that drunken old sot Gabriel Wooley?" Maude stormed.

George didn't know if he was more frightened of his wife or that his blood was now dripping onto the tap room floor. He spat out a shard of glass, "Oh dear, oh dear, oh no," he spluttered. "I'm bleeding." he added pointlessly.

"Look, I have told you we can't afford for old soaks like Wooley to get free drinks." She ignored George's predicament. "How in God's name is he going to pay for all those drinks that you've given to him?"

George grabbed a rag that had been tied to the tap on a nearby barrel of ale. He dabbed his split lip and looked up at his enraged spouse. His eyes widened and his mouth gaped as if he had only just seen her. Blood drained to the back of his throat and he started choking uncontrollably.

Maude still oblivious to his plight, carried on haranguing the poor man, "Well, come on. How are you going to get the money he owes us?"

It is said that in moments of extreme fright men do things they would not normally contemplate. Such a moment hit George. He leapt to his feet and thrust his bleeding face into Maude's. "Can't you see woman, I might be bleeding to death here," Blood splattered over his wife. He stopped. It was only a brief moment of valour, as his bravery deserted him as quickly as it surprisingly arrived.

He spun around in an attempt to put as much distance between him and the object of his terror. In his haste, he tripped over the upturned chair he had just knocked over, and promptly collapsed in a heap again on the sanded floor. He lay there helpless with his hands trying to protect himself from a whicker broom his better half had seized and was using to good effect.

Maude stopped as she ran out of breath, and stared at her hapless husband. She decided that she'd had enough. "I'm not putting up with this anymore." Then, without explaining what her ultimate sanction was to be, she left like a ship in full sail.

George remained sprawled on the floor dabbing his wound. He had lost the will to move.

It was a Saturday night, and Jasper and Robert had left the quarry late so they decided to go straight to The Ship Inn. As they reached the village they saw Maude Tupe looking as though she was about to breath fire. Without looking to the right or left she stormed passed them and reaching her mother's cottage, burst through the door and it crashed shut behind her.

"My God, I wouldn't want to get on the wrong side of that woman. Poor ol' George." Robert chuckled. As they reached The Ship he turned to Jasper with a grin, "It seems like it's been a long week, they're going to go down well this evening." he said enthusiastically. It had been like any other week, but Jasper nodded and allowed Robert to open the door with a flourish to allow Jasper to be the first to order the drinks.

A short dark, panelled, corridor led to the doorway of a crowded room. Wooden settles lined three of the walls with a large log fire dominating the other. The ceiling was so low that the fog of tobacco from a multitude of clay pipes, and the smoke from the fire, hung over the heads of the drinkers. The light that came through the one small window was reduced to a minimum and the main illumination was from the roaring fire. The smell of old ale, smoke and many bodies that had been working hard all day pervaded the entire room.

An especially noisy group of drinkers were gathered around the fire. Jasper glanced over to them and saw that they were hanging on every word of Charlie Heywood.

Charlie was in an excellent mood. He was expansively telling a tale that held his group's attention and caused them to burst into repeated laughter.

Charlie caught Jasper's eye who returned his look with a nod. After a few more minutes Charlie looked again across the smoke filled room at Jasper and raised a quizzical eyebrow as if asking a question that only he and Jasper knew. Jasper response was a scowl and he turned his back. Charlie shrugged and seeing the glasses of his audience were emptying, shouted in the direction of the tap room, "George, get your backside in here."

Nobody had seen George since Maude had thrust all aside earlier as she disappeared out of the front door. Charlie shouted again, "George where are you? You've got customers waiting."

George appeared still holding the rag to his mouth. He looked desperately around to see if his erstwhile attacker was still in the room.

"Come on George, look lively ..... good God Man. What's happened to you?"

"It... it's ..... it's alright, just a small problem" he stammered. The poor man tried to gather himself. His voice was trembling as he asked the room in general, "Who's next, what do you want?"

Charlie was the first to respond, "The same again for myself and these gentlemen here," then looking in the direction of Jasper and Robert, added, "as well as my good friends over there." He looked at Jasper and gave a friendly nod and wink.

George disappeared to return minutes later expertly holding three tankards in each hand. Robert grasped two of them passing one on to Jasper. He gave him a quick glance and then at Charlie. "I saw the look he gave you. Do you think you'll change your mind?"

Jasper responded gruffly, "He can go to hell - it's getting too dangerous."

Robert frowned and hesitantly said, "Charlie is alright. Don't forget when we were in London it was him who helped Tom Wilson to get us back to the village." He stopped, then added with a grin, "Which got you out of trouble." He hurried to continue, "Look, we need the money we get from Charlie."

Jasper just grunted. He agreed with Robert, but he hated the fact that his life was still not his own. This resentment was worse now that he was increasingly dependent on Charlie Heywood.

Robert continued, "He says there is a shipment of just eight barrels coming into Chapman's Cove. All we have to do is unload the boats when they come ashore then use a large one of the stone carts to bring them to the church here in Langton Matravers."

"Is that all!" Jasper snorted. "Alright, I know we will do it. It's just that I don't want Charlie to think that he can snap his fingers and we dance to his tune." He paused, "Oh whatever, I'll speak to him later. It will do him good to wait."

The evening went on in much the same way as most Saturday evenings. Voices became louder and problems much clearer, as memories and senses dulled. Conversations were more emphatic, whilst teller and listeners made less and less contact with each other. Laughter increased and the occasional argument stopped before becoming serious.

Two men stayed in contact with reality. One was Jasper because his large frame could consume the same as his compatriots with less effect. The other was Charlie Heywood who kept his glass in his hand at all times but consumed far less without anyone noticing.

Midway through the evening Charlie caught Jaspers eye again and gestured towards the door and moved in that direction. Jasper took a deep breath, nodded, and followed him outside.

Once in the night air Charlie started without hesitating. "Jasper, I know you seem to have a problem with me lately, but haven't I looked after you well? You wouldn't be able to spend all evening in there if it wasn't for the work I give to you." He looked Jasper directly in the eye, "You get well paid, especially with the extra I give you for organising the others."

Jasper shrugged, "Look, let's get on with it. Yes, I appreciate the work and yes, you do look after us all well. It's just that...." he grimaced, "...first my father, then a sergeant, a quarry manager now you as well."

There was a moments compassion within Charlie. He respected the man in front of him, he was different to the others. After a short pause he stirred himself, "Let's get on with business." he said abruptly. "Chapman's Cove will have visitors tomorrow night about an hour after sunset. There will be a cargo of only eight barrels of brandy which are needed urgently by one of my important customers. The rest of the ship's cargo will have to be buoyed in the bay. The ship's crew will take care of that, we can get them another time."

He looked at Jasper. He was satisfied that this man knew his stuff and knew what to do. Jasper wouldn't let him down. Nevertheless he added, "You'll need one of the larger stone carts so that you only have to make the one journey. Take them to the church; it should all be very simple."

Jasper nodded. Charlie had ignored the facts that it would be in complete darkness and that the barrels would have to be man-handled up the cliff face. Thankfully the men he would use from the quarry were tough and skilled enough to complete the job in double quick time. "Shouldn't be too difficult. Are you sure about the church though? How much have you hidden in the roof. The place will collapse if you're not careful."

Charlie dismissed his point, "Don't worry, I know what I'm doing."

Jasper was still not completely happy, "One more thing. Have you checked whether the revenue men and Willmot's Waterguards are in Poole tomorrow?" He stared at Charlie aggressively, "The men are worried that this work is getting too dangerous. I don't want another shambles like last month."

Jasper recalled the last shipment was a disaster for all concerned. A dozen of his men went to Tilly Whim Caves in the early hours of the morning at low tide. A shipment of wine and brandy were to be moved from their temporary storage in the Caves. As soon as they started to load the barrels and chests onto carts they were surrounded by Revenue Men. They fought like demons with their flails and clubs. Fortunately no-one was killed, and eventually Jasper's men were able to slip away into the darkness.

Every cloud has a silver lining as the following day local people waited for the next tide and were grateful for a few of the barrels that were unscathed.

Charlie looked somewhat sheepish. "They were tipped off. That fellow who told them has disappeared .... if ever I get my hands on him..." he stopped, shaking his head. "I have some men in Poole keeping a lookout for Willmot and the others. If they start to move in this direction I have runners that will get here well ahead of them. You will have to take care of that Riding Officer in Swanage though. It shouldn't be too difficult, he's not the brightest I'm told."

After a few more minutes discussion their business was done and they returned to re-join the drinkers inside.

* * *

The next day saw the revellers bleary eyed but present at St. Georges church for the weekly Sunday Morning Service. Adherence to the church was natural, each man, woman and eventually child having been instilled with their parent's faith, would attend every Sunday. They were all God-fearing folk, as had been their forebears before them, and they devoutly stuck to the church as their central authority. In such a country village it was not like in some of the cities where dissenters were becoming more numerous.

Jasper, with Ellen who had Jemima on her lap, sat near the front as was right and proper for his standing in the congregation. Robert and Sarah sat across the aisle with young Jonathan sitting proudly next to his mother.

The Reverend Poskit had never seen much of his flock, and since the incident at Olden Hall had not been seen at all. Matters were left in the hands of local curates. Walter Godbert had been taking services at St George's for as long as most could remember He decided this Sunday to use the passage from St Peter 2 verse 18 as his text:

Servants, be subject to your masters, with all fear:
not only to the good and gentle, but also to the unjust.

His sermon on obedience to one's betters was met in silence and mainly with blank stares. After some time Walter started to drift. His voice eventually dropped becoming inaudible but for the front few rows. His audience continued to stare blankly up at him. They had alternated between standing for the hymns and kneeling for the prayers and now just waited for Walter to finish.

Jasper idly looked to his right at the vestry wall His gaze was suddenly fixed on a crack that went all the way up to the ceiling where he was sure he saw a movement in the wooden boards.

'Good God' he irreverently thought. 'How much has Charlie got up there?' He glanced over to Robert and noticed that he was also looking and frowning.

Jasper returned his attention to Walter and gave a loud cough. Walter jumped and peered around. He collected himself and brought an end to the service reminding all to mark his words carefully.

The congregation slowly filed out of the church shaking hands with Walter on their way through the doorway. The feeling was mostly not of inspiration but that they had acted properly as good Christians. Having thanked him for the service Jasper asked, "Walter, have you looked around the church lately."

Walter replied slowly. "Eh, no not lately." Then with a frown, "Should I? Have I missed something?" Although he had been at St George's for years, he could be dismissed at anytime, he had no security in his position as a curate. If anything went wrong he would be in trouble. Reverend Poskit was a hard man and was very conscious of money coming in from the Tithes and certainly the maximum that could be spent.

"What's the problem?" he asked, his concern rising by the second "What should I look at?"

Seeing that he was frightening the poor man, Jasper replied casually, "It's alright, don't worry. I was just curious." He looked down at the hapless curate. "I will get a couple men to have a look around just to see if everything is as it should be."

Walters attention was diverted to two young villagers that were waiting patiently at his elbow "Curate, we would like to arrange the baptism of our little Eva" the father proudly said, as he touched a shawl covering the bundle in his wife's arms.

Jasper moved away and seeing Robert walking ahead of him, called him back "Don't forget I did have a talk in the end with Charlie Heywood last night. I've agreed that we will run some barrels ashore tonight.   You were right, they will be landed at Chapman's Cove. We have to be there about an hour after sunset."

Robert nodded, "How many men will we need. They're a bit nervous after last month."

Jasper grunted. "I don't blame them, but we'll need about six of them. Tell them not to worry the revenue men are over in Poole today. Get Bert to borrow a horse from the blacksmith's stables and send him over there to make sure they're too busy to worry about us. Charlie said he's got a man there already but I would rather be safe than sorry. Also I want a watch kept on that Riding Officer in Swanage. I want him kept busy for the night."

Robert chuckled. "I've heard that Bill Hardcastle likes a drink I will get one of the men to go into Swanage and, shall we say, keep him well supplied.

Ellen had moved on and after a gossip with a group of the other women of the village, she turned back. "Jasper, are you coming. Let's get on home "

Jasper turned back to Robert, "Get the men to meet at Austell Point above Chapman's Cove just after sunset." He then added with a grin. "Tell them there's a bit extra in it for them tonight as this run is a last minute job. Charlie can afford it." After a further thought. "Right, that's it.   I'll see you here a little while before sunset, we can then get the carts and meet the rest of them."

At that Jasper, turned around to catch up with Ellen. Although she was a good, dutiful wife he did not want to upset her.

Charlie Heywood was standing the other side of the lane from St George's and had watched the exchange between Jasper and Robert. He knew their part of tonight's job was in good hands For now, he had to organise for the shipment to be carried to his customer, who in this case, was in Salisbury some fifty miles away.

The night came, and Jasper and Robert having taken a cart from the quarry, met the other men at Austell Point As the men were scrambling down the cliffs to the beach Jasper turned to Robert. "Bert has just come back from Poole. He said that the revenue men were too busy inspecting the boats of the local fishermen over there. They won't be able to be anywhere near here tonight   Did you got someone to took after Bill Hardcastle in Swanage?"

"Yes." Robert replied chuckling. "I've sent Amos to meet him at The Harbour Inn. He's Hardcastle's nephew and they know each other quite well.   They should have met a couple of hours ago."

"Are you sure? Amos is young and he likes his beer a bit too much. Will he keep his head clear enough to make sure that Hardcastle doesn't leave?"

"Yes,   he will." Robert answered quickly, but a frown crossed his face. There was a call from the men down on the beach.   Robert cast all other thoughts out of his mind and turned to join them.

The cliff face was covered with loose shale and ridges of hard limestone rock. As youngsters, Jasper and Robert had raced each other down the cliff face. By digging their heels into the shale they were able to slip down at high speed. Robert used his old skills to good effect and was on the beach in minutes. After what seemed an age the soft sound of oars gently stroking water could be heard. Then out of the darkness two small boats emerged with their crew slowly pulling its way onto the beach. Instructions, unnecessarily whispered, were given for the barrels to be manhandled out of the boats to the foot of the cliff face.

The barrels were heavy and it took a great deal of effort to winch them up the cliff with the rope and pulley - also borrowed from the quarry. Robert was overseeing the operations from below whilst Jasper was at the top to help roll the barrels and lift them onto the carts. He returned to the cliff's edge in time to see the last barrel starting its journey upwards as Robert followed behind and beneath it. Jasper gave a sudden intake of breath. The rope had started to slip from around the barrel. If it broke free it would career downwards and it would not be possible for Robert to get out of the way. The barrel would take Robert to the bottom of the cliff and he would certainly be crushed to death.

Without a thought for his own safety. Jasper hurtled down the cliff face digging his heels into the gravel to stop falling face first to the bottom. He reached the barrel just in time and grabbed the rope and the barrel. Holding onto them was such an effort that it would have torn most men's muscles from the bone. Jasper held on but the rope kept slipping through the palms of his hands until they were raw. Robert crawled up slowly until he struggled to reach level with the barrel and was able to tie the rope securely back in place.

Robert looked at Jasper whose face was streaked with sweat and dirt, and blood streamed from his hands. "Guess we're even now."

Jasper grunted and gave a brief wry smile. "Come on, lets get moving and finish this damn job."

Without any further mishaps, but still with much effort, all the barrels were loaded onto the carts. Sacks and small stones were scattered on top in a casual effort to mask the real shipment. As the tiring eight men neared Langton Matravers a breathless Amos came running to meet them.

"What in God's name are you doing here" demanded Jasper "You're supposed to be looking after Hardcastle."

"Oh God, I'm sorry." Amos said desperately.

"Well?" Jasper demanded again without stopping his small convoy making its way down the hill.

Amos started nervously, "It's just that he was late for when we were supposed to have met. That money you gave to me from Mr Heywood .. well I started without him."

Jasper was exasperated "Alright forget that for now. Where is Hardcastle."

"He said something about not getting any sense from me." Amos looked down embarrassed. "He said that he might as well have a look around as he had heard that there might he something afoot tonight." Amos looked up at Jasper and the other men innocently, "l don't know what he meant by that."

Jasper shook his head despairingly, "You are a complete numbskull. He probably guessed that you were trying to keep him busy." Jasper looked in the direction of Robert who stared steadfastly at the ground. "He knows that you're from the village, but there's nothing we can do about it now." Jasper thought for a moment then continued, "Go ahead of us to the church and have a look around to make sure he isn't about. If he isn't there, go to the start of the road to Swanage and wait. Make sure we can see you from the church. If he then comes into sight, raise your hat and scratch your head." He thought and added "Whatever you do don't shout or try to attract our attention in any other way. One of us will be watching you all the time from the Church"

Amos nodded even more nervously than before. He was frightened of Jasper Tomes. He scuttled off as quickly as he could to wait at the church.

Some minutes later Jasper and his men drew up outside the vestry door. Without a moments delay they unloaded the carts and rolled the barrels inside the church. There was a small, winding stone staircase behind the altar which led up to a large room above the knave. Jasper ran up them but stopped when he reached the top and gave a gasp. The room was completely crammed full of barrels of brandy and tea chests. This was Charlie Heywood's main stock room

Robert joined Jasper at the top of the stairs and his eyes widened "'No wonder the roofs creaking and the wall is cracking." Robert looked around at the piled up contraband. "This church will collapse in on itself before long."

Jasper shook his head and expelled a sigh. "Come on men. There's nothing we can do about it now" He lowered the rope via the pulley through the trap door to the knave below. The barrels were slowly and painstakingly winched up to the room and stored the best that they could evenly across the creaking floor. As the last barrel was rolled into place there was a large crack and the floor timbers sunk another few inches. The three men left in the room froze, and then on tip toe, as if this would lighten them, gingerly made their way back to the staircase. Running down the stairs they met the rest of the crew assembled around the carts waiting to be told they could disperse to their homes.

Robert suddenly grasped Jasper sleeve. "Oh no, look at that cretin."

They all turned to see what he meant. There was Amos innocently humming to himself oblivious to a large figure on horseback approaching him from behind. He was startled out of his reverie as a booming voice demanded. "And what are you doing here, lad?"

Amos spun around to be confronted by the august figure of the His Royal Majesty's Chief Riding Officer for the Isle of Purbeck, Mr William Benjamin Hardcastle. With all the dignity he could summon, he looked down at the distraught Amos. "It's a bit late for you, isn't it lad?"

Amos's eyes bulged, he opened his mouth to speak, then remembering in a blur his instructions he raised his hat and turned to face the church. He was again confronted, this time by a group of eight angry looking men, staring at him. In total confusion he went to scratch his head, realised the futility of the action, dropped his hat and descended into noiseless confusion.

Jasper was the first to recover from everyone's surprise. He walked forward to Hardcastle who had dismounted and in the friendliest tone he could muster, "Oh, it's you Bill, how are you? I thought it was only us poor quarrymen who had to work such long hours." He looked at Hardcastle and added confidentially, "Now please, don't you go telling our foreman that we got caught in the Ship again and had to take Saturday's last delivery of stone to the store tonight."

He walked around a confused looking constable and put his arm around his shoulder, "We don't see enough of you up here in the village. Is it because those scoundrels in Swanage are keeping you so busy?"

Hardcastle jumped, he didn't want it to get back to his employers that he had been insulting the good people of their town. "No. of course not. It's just that ...anyway may I see what is in the cart." he said pulling himself up straight to recover his authority.

"Of course, of course. Help yourself" Jasper said casually. He then turned to his men. "Get on home now to your womenfolk, lads   We will take these last stones to the store first thing in the morning."   With his back to the good constable he added, "Thanks for your work tonight, well done."

Returning to Hardcastle, "Have a good look wherever you want . Do you mind if we leave you to it? It's been a long day and I must get back to my good woman before she starts to worry."

At that he left Hardcastle absently giving a cursory look at the stones piled on the back of the cart. Seeing nothing unusual, he shrugged and rode off to Swanage.

Jasper had caught up with Robert, who sighed, "I'm glad that's over We used to think these jobs were fun."

Jasper's grunted his agreement and bade Robert good night.

It was a rare, hot but breezy summer's day at the Crack Lane quarry when Charlie Heywood met with Jasper a couple of days later. The stiff sea breeze was sufficient to blow the stone dust around forcing the men to pull their neckerchiefs over their mouths and noses . The grit in their eyes meant they all kept a permanent squint

Charlie looked around for the quarry manager and spying him outside his wooden shack, called him over, "Silas, could you spare me a moment." Silas Winter jumped quickly to his feet, Charlie Heywood was the coming man and it would be best to be in his good books "Yes sir, Mr Heywood, how can I help?"

"I need to speak with Jasper Tomes, can you spare him for a few moments?" Charlie asked casually.

Silas was well aware what his business with Jasper would be about. He had earned needed cash carrying out runs for Charlie himself "Of course, sir." He turned and saw that Jasper had seen Charlie and was already making his way towards them. As Jasper reached them Silas looked stern "Now do your business with Mr Heywood, Tomes, and get back to work as quick as you can."

"Of course, Mr Winter" Jasper responded with a grin. "Gooday Charlie. Let's go over there out this wind" he said nodding towards the entry to one of the shafts.

Silas gave a grunt and by shouting "Come on, put more effort into it." across to a group of men already straining to lift stone onto one of the carts, he resumed an unwelcome and unnecessary supervision.

Jasper chuckled, "There's no harm in him." then addressing Charlie he frowned. "I'm not happy"

Charlie quickly interrupted before Jasper could continue. "Yes, yes I know. You had problems at Chapman's Cove but there's not much I can do about your men if I'm not there. You have hauled barrels up that cliff many, many times" he smiled and added, "I hear that you were able to save the day." he said in a congratulatory tone.

"It's not that, I can handle that part of the job." Jasper said dismissively "It's other matters that I'm not happy about. The revenue men and waterguards with their Riding Officers are becoming more persistent. The time was when even milords knew that a village depended on the running of merchandise " He snorted ."I well remember what happened at Snodbury."[22]

Jasper looked hard at Charlie. "Times are changing. The government are properly trying to stop the business now. Whatever the consequences, there are more revenue men who are being encouraged to carry out their duties to the full."

Charlie listened to all of this and could not totally disagree. "I know, I know. What we have to do is to get smarter. Remember, for the time being, if Hardcastle is in Swanage how is he to know what we are doing in the village, what is happening at Chapman's Cove and whether our friends in Worth Matravers are busy. These places are miles apart. He is one man and it takes him time to get from one place to another. Just think, we're standing here at the quarry, we could be anywhere for all Hardcastle knows." Charlie

---

[22] Snodbury was a village on the coast in west Dorset. The local revenue men decided they were going to stop the trade of illegal running completely in their area Their success destroyed the village as there was not enough work around to keep the community going. Villagers were starving and the menfolk moved their families away and joined the destitute in the burgeoning cities. The local magistrates had to quickly tell the revenue men to revert to the occasional raid and turn a blind eye to the trade.

stopped.   He knew what he said was true but he also knew Jasper was right as well - times were changing.

Jasper was staring down at Swanage in the distance deep in thought. He appeared to come to a conclusion and turned to face Charlie, "Alright, we have to be smarter. When we have a job, all the government's men will have to be properly watched, we will need to know where they are when we are busy." He made a mental note to speak with Robert about not using Amos in future. He gave Charlie a wry smile, "Which will cost money."

Charlie nodded   He had been successful in his business enterprises by being fair and paying a fair price for a job well done. "Yes, I quite understand. You and I have to sit down together to set up a lookout system for the area. If we get it right then there is still much money to be made for a good few years yet. In hard times there are always opportunities, if you're clever enough." He looked again at Jasper, "There's something else that's worrying you. What's that?"

At this, Jasper demeanour changed to frustration. He shook he head. "What are you doing to the church?" he asked "St George's is over five hundred years old. I know it is showing its age now, but what you have crammed into the room under the roof will bring the whole building down "

Charlie winced "Yes, I have been looking at that and I've arranged for most of the goods to be taken over to one of the old lanes in my Gully Quarry." He added quickly, "You may think that money is my only concern." he grinned, "and it is important but I do have loyalty to the village....and St.George's."

Jasper looked doubtful. Charlie carried on regardless of his scepticism. "I have spoken with some men in Swanage who I have worked with quite a bit. They are arranging for a rebuild of much of the structure. An architect from over in Weymouth has already drawn up the plans."   Charlie warmed to his explanation. "I won't be able to provide all the money needed, Lord Olden and some other businessmen in Swanage will all contribute." he paused and chuckled, "If there's more needed along the way it will be provided thanks to the revenue."

CHAPTER TWENTY

Partnership and Wilmott Humbugged

"The Reverend Dafdd is worse than that old skinflint Poskit."

Charlie smiled inwardly. Jasper had come to Charlie's house to discuss the latest shipments from France. Eight months had passed since Jasper's inner rage had spilled over into his leading of the march on Olden Hall.   The natural rebelliousness of youth was giving way to the maturity of a reasonable man but the temper of his youth was still on a short fuse whenever he felt there was injustice. After no more than a peremptory greeting, he let rip. "Poskit left matters with old Walter and the other curates around here. They had sympathy for anyone who was struggling to pay their Tithes to the Church."[23]

Edith was about to enter the room, but hearing Jasper's raised voice, she decided to come back later.

Charlie was used to Jasper when he was in full cry. "I know what you mean, but I'm sure the Reverend Dafdd will be less, shall we say, enthusiastic about collecting his Tithes when he settles in."

"I hope you're right. When he arrived fresh from Wales, I'll grant you, he did a tour of the parishes within his domain

---

[23] *"Tithes were paid by parishioners to the local Rector as a proportion of the produce extracted from the land or their other activities.   The fluctuations between good and lean years meant that Tithes increasingly became fixed as a sum of money.   After a number of bad harvests, tithe-holders still had to hand over the same amount of money as in a good year, even though they had less produce to pay it.   There were a succession of bad harvests. in the years following the Napoleonic war."*

and he appeared keen to ensure that his flock were prepared for the next world. That's all changed. Now as a true minister of his church, he sees the prompt collection of his Tithes as more important to him than any spiritual needs of his congregations."

Jasper was in full flow. "He hasn't been very sympathetic to the needs of this world. Look what has happened to Cole Hulbert and Bert Adlard and their families. Cole and Bert's farms were like my Pa's quarry; their families had always owned them. The church's Tithes were kept at a level they couldn't afford. After the bad harvests they have had to uproot their lives here and go to one of the big towns up North. God knows if there is work for them. Dafdd has become remote from the day to day life of his flock and oblivious to the problems of bad harvests."

Charlie grimaced. "I agree. In a very short time, the Reverend has become unloved and is thought of as unapproachable and arrogant by those who should be looking to him for guidance." "Did you know that his vestry meet in The Anchor Inn. They know he won't go there because he has fallen out with Matthew Gibbs, the landlord?" Charlie shook is head in resignation. "There will be a backlash if he is not careful. It can easily happen."

Jasper grinned at Charlie "He's allowed you to keep some control on church affairs though. Now as the Church Warden you're legally responsible for all the property and movable goods belonging to a parish church aren't you?"

"That's right. I've persuaded Dafdd to leave the day-to-day maintenance of church buildings and contents to myself." Charlie replied casually.

"There can't be many pies you haven't got your fingers in these days."

Charlie paused and looked at Jasper thoughtfully. "You say that and alright its true but what about yourself? If it wasn't against the law to form groups or unions, you would be a good leader for the men in the village. You hate injustice, you're not like that awful man Tubbs who had wanted to change everything and you could represent them."

Jasper grunted. "Getting back to Dafdd, as you are now the Church Warden, is there anything you can do about him? "

Charlie shook his head. "No unfortunately. Well not immediately anyway."

"Do you know why Poskit left? He was here for quite a few years."

Charlie laughed, and peering at Jasper, raised his eyebrows. "Straight after the unfortunate business at Olden Hall, he went to see his brother in Winchester. Life there was less stressful for him and he decided to remain within the sanctuary of Winchester Cathedral shut away from the trials and tribulations of the outside world."

"The church is meant to administer support and solace wherever possible, I can't say that I can remember him being in the village very much at all, anyway. I don't think many around here miss him."

"The new curate, Benedict, will be here shortly. As I am now the Church Warden to St. George's, I like to speak with him occasionally away from the church."

"Yes a pity about poor old Walter, the previous curate. He was well liked and he did try to help those in the village as much as he could. It was a surprise to us all when he died suddenly."

"God Bless him." Charlie shook his head in genuine sadness. "As I promised, we will be virtually rebuilding the church over the next couple of years. Unfortunately Walter won't be here to enjoy the improvements." He tried to brighten Jasper's mood. He grinned. "You frightened poor old Walter when you said you were concerned about the state of the Church."

Jasper shrugged apologetically. "Yes, shame, I was only trying to help."

They both turned towards the door as Stephen politely knocked and announced that Benedict had arrived. Jasper made a sign as to whether Charlie wanted him to leave. "No please stay, this won't take long. When I'm finished, we need to speak about Officer Wilmot. I do take on board everything that you say about the Reverend. It's just that I'm not sure exactly what to do about him yet."

Jasper studied Benedict as he nervously came into the room. He was young and obviously shy. He was tall and slightly built, with a pale complexion and his blond hair was prematurely thinning. Forever unsure of himself because of his height he had developed a slight stoop, as if he did not want to stand out in a crowd.

Stephen asked politely "Is there anything that you will require, sir?"

Charlie hesitated, then said. "No, that will be all Stephen. Benedict won't be here for long." Benedict looked relieved. Although he had already developed a fear of his employer, the incumbent Vicar, he had also soon realised that not very much went on in Langton Matravers without Mr Heywood being involved. To cap this he was also in the company of the fearsome Jasper Tomes whose very presence made him tremble.

Charlie casually perched on the edge of a small desk and indicated for Benedict to take a seat.

Charlie then proceeded to discuss the collection of Tithes, who was in arrears and whether Reverend Dafdd was aware of those tardy in their payments. He then spoke briefly about the Church, and the on-going refurbishments. After about fifteen minutes or so Charlie brought their meeting to an end.

"Well done Benedict you're doing a good job. Please keep me informed if any of the villagers come to the attention of The Reverend regarding their Tithes." With that he bowed his head briefly in a dismissive gesture.

The grateful Curate responded. "Thank you sir, Mr Heywood." He looked nervously in the direction of Jasper unsure whether he should bid him Good Day. He decided a swift exit was called for and quickly left.

Jasper and Charlie smiled at each other in the way of two men who were in control of events.

Charlie coughed and put on a serious air. "Officer - sorry, Chief Officer Wilmot wants to meet us."

Jasper looked surprised. "Oh really? Why?"

"Over the last few months Wilmot has become very good at getting information about the our activities in this area. So good in fact, he has become highly thought of and that's why they have just appointed him as Chief Officer of the Coastguards as they are now called."

"I'm pleased for him." Jasper said flatly, he was not impressed.

Charlie frowned. "That is as it may be, but we can't afford to get too complacent."

"Alright, sorry, you're right. No matter what they call themselves he will struggle to do much better than before."

"In certain respects, yes. He is frustrated by two major problems. One: He is not a local man and therefore is not trusted or taken into the confidence of anyone in the area."

Jasper chuckled. "I'm not surprised, whatever the government may do, smuggling is rife all along the coast. Almost everyone in the coastal towns and villages of Dorset knows someone involved in smuggling."

"Yes he has a problem. He's in enemy territory so to speak. Also his second problem is that if they were to catch anyone they would have to be in possession of contraband otherwise prosecution is impossible."

"So why should we worry then?"

"Smuggling is still a lucrative business for those willing and clever enough to prepare and plan properly, but we have to stay one step ahead."

Jasper smiled with some pride. "Aye. As soon as you tell me a shipment is due the entire area of the Isle of Purbeck is covered by men watching for the movement of any officials. We've a group of youngsters with good speed in their legs or the beacons are lit on the hilltops. Either way, we can avoid any confrontation."

"Yes, I appreciate all the work you've done. You're doing a great job and I don't want to interfere with your side of the business." He paused. "We have to be prepared though, for even more interference from the better organised bodies of Coastguards, Revenue and Excise men and ultimately the Police. One of Wilmot's men was here a couple of days ago, he says that Wilmot wants to meet both of us. He must have a reason for wanting to see us. I'm just not sure what he has up his sleeve."

He stopped and went to the door and called out. "Stephen could you bring in some brandy, there's a good chap." He turned back to Jasper and grinned. "The time was Jasper when we would never have thought of sitting here waiting to be served some brandy. We are going up in the world."

Jasper felt slightly uneasy which Charlie sensed.

"Jasper relax. This is what you wanted isn't it?"

"Yes, but…."

"Yes, and no buts. You now work in my Gully Quarry but you spend less time in the quarry and more on the 'import' business. We work together and each have a share in the business. Come on, you have never been more comfortable, financially."

Jasper nodded appreciatively. "I can't argue with that. I just feel awkward about it."

Charlie waved his arm in a dismissive manner, then warmed to his theme. "I won't deny that I have become quite wealthy myself. Smuggling is very profitable and I now own or rent three quarries in the area. I also have an interest in a company in Poole that sells the stone as well as a share in my dear wife's brother's shipping business." He stopped and frowned.

"What's the problem?

"Oh nothing. It's just I worry about Edith's brother, Ambrose. Now is not the time to speak of that, though." Charlie quickly carried on. "I wanted to meet you today because we have now much to lose by being careless. I don't know what Wilmot wants but I want to emphasise that when we meet him we have to be on our guard."

Stephen had by now brought in the brandy and Jasper raised his glass. "Here's to the future."

Charlie responded. "The future but we must be wary when we meet Willmot. "

Ted Edmunds was a sensitive man, but whenever he saw Dot he was reminded of, and still felt uncomfortable about Bill Tubbs' death. On her way to her work at Calvin Seager's house one morning she saw Ted hurrying towards her. He was obviously late for his work at the quarry, but hesitated when he saw Dot.

Dot saw his hesitation but nevertheless she wanted to speak with him. "Ted, I've been trying to contact you but you seem to be avoiding me."

"No, not at all." Ted was flustered.

Dot looked him directly in the eye. "Yes you have, and I know why." Ted looked away not knowing what to say.

"Ted, I know you think you were responsible for what happened."

"I pushed him and he fell into the wall. If I had not touched him he would be alive today."

"The Curate saw everything. He was drunk - again - he tried to hit you and he tripped."

Ted hesitated again. "I still feel guilty."

"Well don't."

"I see people in the village look at me and I know they think I pushed him because of the way I feel about you." He stopped he had already said too much.

Dot smiled. "No-one in the village thinks any such thing." She put her hand gently on Ted's forearm. "We spoke before I went to Winchester, and yes we both have feelings that probably now in the circumstances we feel are wrong."

"There is no way we could ever…"

"Ted stop. It is said that we should not speak ill of the dead, but Bill Tubbs was not a good man. The only thing he ever did which I will thank him for, is my two daughters. Ted, he was ruining my and their lives. I will not let him ruin the rest of it."

"That is as may be, but because of what happened I could never take his place."

"Look I am a widow, but that is not the end of my life. What will happen in the future will happen."

Ted looked uncertain of what to say next. Dot brightened up. "The reason I have tried to contact you is that Ma and Pa are having the family around next Sunday for tea. They want to have a small celebration for the birth of another son for Robert and Sarah." She chuckled. "Ma Salen is certainly kept busy these days. They have said that they would like you to join us."

"Alright, but I must be going I'm late for work."

"No Ted, I know you. You are definitely coming on Sunday aren't you? Ma and Pa will be very disappointed if you don't turn up."

Ted paused then smiled. "Yes, I will be there. Please thank them for their kindness."

He then turned and started to jog up the hill. Dot sighed and watched him until he was out of sight.

Keziah Wilmot's meeting with Charlie and Jasper took place at The Harbour Inn on a Sunday. Wilmot was on official business and as he entered the room he was determined to carry out his duties honestly and meticulously. He was expecting an aggressive or defensive attitude from the two men who he knew were the perpetrators of the smuggling that took place locally. He was immediately disconcerted by the greeting he received. Charlie, relaxed and smiling got up and gave Wilmot a warm, welcoming handshake.

"Good Day to you Keziah, let me take your hat. A drink I'm sure would be most welcome?" Charlie said as he guided him to their table.

Before Wilmot could answer a large measure of brandy was set before him. Jasper smiled and said "you'll like that, it has been specially brought in by the landlord for his best customers."

Wilmot was confused as to what to do as he knew very well who had supplied the landlord. He looked at his hosts who raised their glasses of similar brandy and both said "Cheers!" and with broad smiles waited for Wilmot to drink. He did not want to be churlish so he raised his glass and took a long gratifying draught. Charlie and Jasper, smiling, looked at him with raised eyebrows, "Well?"

Wilmot was furious as he found himself on the defensive, "Yes, it's certainly a fine drink." He put his glass down hard on the table, "Now look here, I know what you're at. I know very well where this brandy came from" he stared accusingly at Charlie and Jasper.

They looked surprised and after a moment Charlie responded innocently, "France, I believe."

"No, no that's not what I meant. I meant how it came to be here." He was not going to let these rogues make fun of him.

"Oh, I see" said Charlie, "I understand it came by boat," then after a pause, "There would be no other way could there?"

Wilmot became redder and redder as he became incandescent with rage at these two villains who were not only making fun of him but also the King's Uniform that he proudly wore.

Charlie relented. It was not a good idea to totally alienate this man, who was after all an Officer of the Crown. "Oh, I'm sorry. You think that this brandy might have been smuggled ashore." He stopped and looked at Jasper. After some thought he carried on, "Mr Wilmot, we all know that smuggling has been carried on along this coast for as long as anyone can remember. Most folks around here are aware of this and I include all sorts of people, from Milords, the church as well as ordinary folk." He looked to see the effect he was having on Wilmot. "I also recognise that the government are now trying to put an end to it. It is my opinion that it won't truly stop until the duty is not so high for bringing goods legitimately into the country"

He studied Wilmot for his reaction on what was undeniably the truth. Wilmot may have agreed with Charlie's words but it was not his place to condone the activities that he was specifically employed to stop. He then remembered the success that he was about to achieve. He sat up and with a look of triumph said, "You may well justify yourselves, but you will be stopped from carrying out these crimes. In fact, the reason I wanted to meet you today is that my men will be arresting a certain Amos Paine.

Jasper was taken aback although he was able to keep his face passive. Since Amos had almost caused the whole operation at Chapman's Cove to be exposed to Officer Hardcastle he had not been trusted with anything important. He carried out the odd errand but was generally told to keep out of the way when a landing was being carried out. The trouble was he talked too much.

Charlie asked casually, "Amos? What has the poor chap done?"

Wilmot warmed to his point. "He was overheard by one of the excise men from Poole talking about how he had organised for a shipment of brandy to be landed at Dancing Ledge." He looked from Charlie and Jasper triumphantly. "My man, being a stranger around here, found out his name through Mr Hardcastle."

Charlie chuckled "Have you met Amos Paine. Do you think he could organise such a thing?"

Wilmot hesitated, "No, I don't know the man. It appears though that he has talked his way into jail ... or worse." Wilmot regained his composure, "My men left Poole this morning to arrest Paine at his home in Langton Matravers this very afternoon." He sat back in his seat with satisfaction. Without realising what he was doing, he raised his glass and took another long draught of brandy.

Charlie studied the table for a few moments, then looking at Wilmot's glass "You're in need of a refill." Waving away Wilmot's protest he went over to the landlord. Sam Cobbald was sitting in the far corner of the room but had heard every word. After a brief whispered conversation Jasper returned with glasses re-charged.

Wilmot was frowning "I hope you weren't discussing our conversation with the landlord"

Charlie responded quickly "Oh no, Sam was just worried that you weren't happy with the drink he was serving." Wilmot just grunted and turning back to Charlie and Jasper, missed Sam slipping out of the back door.

There followed an uneasy silence which Jasper broke, looking hard at Charlie, "I'm worried that Officer Wilmot's men are going to arrest Amos. What is to be done?"

Wilmot interrupted "There's nothing for you to do. The King's Justice will take its course." He was starting to enjoy himself. "The man has admitted his guilt in front of witnesses."

Charlie nodded "Aye, it seems he did speak too much. I can save your men some trouble though." He glanced sideways at Jasper, then continued, "Amos came down to Swanage this morning. Your men will find him at a Mr Benfield's establishment." Jasper choked on his drink.

Wilmot seemed not to notice and addressed his hosts smugly, "If that is the case then I'm afraid gentlemen with the power invested in me as a servant of the King, I am going to require you to remain in my company. I have instructed my men to meet me here as soon as they have been to Langton Matravers. When they arrive we will all go to Mr Benfield and I will personally make the arrest." Wilmot had not had such a good day since first arriving in Dorset.

There followed another awkward silence, Wilmot refused more alcohol, and no one was sure what to say or do. Finally, Wilmot stirred remembering some intelligence he had gleaned. "Mr Heywood, I understand that you have an interest in a small lugger that is moored in the harbour. My men will not be here for an hour yet, what a splendid opportunity for me to make an inspection. I trust that there will not be anything there that you would not wish me to find?" Life was getting better by the minute.

Charlie casually looked at Jasper who shrugged his shoulders and shook his head. Charlie turned back to Wilmot, "Keziah, what a splendid idea." He got to his feet and made straight for the door. Whilst Wilmot scrambled to recover his hat Sam Cobbald returned and as he walked passed Charlie he gave him the faintest of nods. The three then made their way along Shore Road to the harbour.

Cobbald had told his cellar boy, Thomas, to run to Langton Matravers and get Amos into Swanage as quickly as possible. Amos was not to argue, he was to do as he was told. Cobbald added "Tell him Mr Heywood and Mr Tomes had said so."

Thomas ran the two miles to Langton Matravers as fast as his legs could carry him. As soon as he reached Amos's cottage he burst through the door unannounced.

Amos was dozing in front of the fire. It being the Sabbath Day and with a few extra coins in his pocket for running an errand for Mr Tomes he was quite relaxed. He nearly leapt out of his chair as the silence was broken by Thomas bursting through the door.

"Mr Paine. Mr Paine. You've got to come quick." Thomas spluttered, trying to catch his breath.

Amos looked in total surprise at his unwelcome guest. "What are you talking about?" he demanded. "It's the Lord's Day and I'm resting."

Thomas was not to be denied, he was on a mission. "The Coastguards are on their way here to arrest you."

"What?" Amos gasped, " What for?"

"They are going to arrest you for smuggling." Thomas spurted this out whilst at the same time tugging Amos's arm in an attempt to pull him to the door. "Mr Tomes says you're to come with me."

Amos was totally aghast. "But I was only ….. I haven't really …. Oh God! What have I done?" He was on the point of panic.

Thomas persisted "Please Mr Paine come with me. Mr Heywood and Mr Tomes say you must." He said pulling again on Amos's arm.

Amos was already in a daze when the names of Heywood and Tomes struck fresh fear into him. "Mr Tomes said I was to ….. Oh God what have I done?"

At last Thomas's efforts were rewarded. The combination of fear of arrest by the Coastguards and not doing what Mr Tomes said, prompted him into action. As they went outside they saw a group of about half a dozen men in uniforms asking questions outside The Ship. As they started to sprint down the hill Amos looked briefly over his shoulder and saw gratefully that those being questioned were looking doubtful and were shaking their heads.

Half way down the hill Thomas had to stop, and putting his hands on his knees he gulped in air. Amos had by this time grasped the full seriousness of his position and he turned and started to drag Thomas into another scamper into Swanage. They arrived at Mr Benfield's totally breathless and bedraggled.

Mr Mordecai Benfield was a tall, thin and dour man dressed in the customary black of his profession. He had a large beak nose, long face with long sideburns and a hairless dome. His natural expression could not be called anything other than grim. He was the undertaker to the town of Swanage.

He looked Amos up and down with professional expertise then turned to go into a room at the back of the shop. He came back with suit and collarless shirt. "Here, take these and put them on. The last person to wear these is in no need of them anymore. You look a mess at the moment, most unbecoming of any client of mine."

Amos guessed the condition of the previous wearer and started to protest. "Put them on!" Benfield snapped. "..and be quick, you have to compose yourself.   When you've got dressed cover your face with this chalk "

By the time that Amos was in Mr Benfield's establishment the Coastguards had given up trying to find their fugitive. Their leader, Jack Harden, was an ex marine sergeant and now held the rank of Chief Boatman in the Coastguards. Harden was a burly honest chap but none too bright. Anyone that his men asked in the village denied knowing who they were talking about. In the end Harden decided that the best course of action was to meet with Mr Wilmot, as arranged, to await further instructions. They dutifully made their way down to Swanage and The Harbour Inn where after some time Wilmot returned looking both disappointed and irritated.

Forgetting what Charlie had said earlier he looked to Harden and brusquely demanded "Well, where is he? Where's this Paine fellow?"

Harden was nonplussed "Mr Wilmot, sir. They have never heard of him in the village. Are you sure Paine is the person we're looking for?"

Wilmot was about to explode when there was polite cough at his elbow, "I'm sure you will remember, Keziah.   I was trying to be helpful when I said that Amos Paine came down earlier today and is at Mr Benfields's place."

"Right, yes of course, I remember."   Turning to his troop, he pompously announced "You'll see that good intelligence saves much wasted time. I will take you to him now and I will arrest the blackguard myself." He turned to Charlie and lowering his voice said, "Mr Heywood, if you would be so kind to lead the way".

"Of course, Keziah" Charlie said and moved off in the direction of the High Street.   Jasper, scarcely concealing a smile took a pace backwards and with an extravagant sweep of the hand, gestured for them all to lead whilst he brought up the rear.

Wilmot started to feel worried. When they reached Mordecai Benfield's shop, Charlie stopped to allow Keziah and Harden to enter. Wilmot hesitantly said, "But this an undertakers. Why are we here?"

"Please, go in. Mr Benfield will explain." said Charlie encouragingly.

When they entered the Funeral Parlour, Mr Benfield came solemnly forward. "I believe you have come here to pay your respects to Amos Paine He gestured towards the other side of the room to where there was a coffin perched on two triangular stands. The lid was open and displayed the figure of Amos, hands clasped on his chest in prayer and his face a deathly white mask.

Wilmot was by now completely confused. He squared up to Charlie and demanded "What's this all about Heywood?"

Charlie looked down at the floor and solemnly said, "You were so desperate to find Amos I thought I had better bring you here without delay."

Wilmot looked back and forth between the coffin and Charlie. "Are you trying to tell me the man is dead?"

Charlie faked surprise, "Well, yes."

"Are you sure? You are not trying to lie to me are you? This seems very convenient. What did he die of?"

Charlie showed helpful concern, "Yes I'm afraid he's very dead. As dead as one could be." There was a stifled cough from Jasper at the back of the group. "I'm sure Mr Benfield will be only to pleased to let you examine the corpse." He said with emphasis on the word 'corpse'

Benfield respectfully came forward and tilted his head for Wilmot to proceed with his inspection . Wilmot slowly edged forward. When he neared the coffin, Charlie announced "He died from a fever." Shaking his head slowly he added, "The same fever that has taken away many good folk around here recently." Wilmot jumped back in alarm and pulled out a kerchief from his pocket and clasped it to his nose and mouth. His eyes were wide open as he looked around at the ensemble in the room.

He fixed upon Harden and taking a pace towards the door gestured with his thumb "Go check that the body is truly dead."

Harden looked at Wilmot in similar alarm, "Pardon, sir?"

"Mr Harden, Do as you're told, check the body."

Harden stammered, "Yes sir. Certainly sir. Thank you sir." He edged sideways towards the coffin, mouth and nose similarly covered. When still some distance away and with no more than a very cursory glance he stepped back quickly and stated "Yes, sir. The body is dead, sir."

Wilmot took charge again. Marching out of Mr Benfield's shop he quickly rejoined his men. Charlie and Jasper stood dutifully awaiting instructions. Wilmot glared at them both, "That man is damned lucky."

Charlie raised his eyebrows in surprise. "Yes, sir."

Wilmot continued unabashed, "Damned lucky, he could have been arrested and could well have been hanged from the gallows."

Charlie frowned and shook his head slowly as if trying to grasp the sense in that last remark.

Wilmot was feeling under pressure and decided that he had had enough. Staring again at Charlie and Jasper he decided upon a closing threat, "I hope that the time we have spent today has made you realise the danger you are now in if you continue with illegal activities." He looked from one to another. "I will leave it at that for now, but be warned, and remember what happened to Paine or you will suffer the same way."

Charlie nodded wisely, "Yes absolutely – don't catch a fever."

Wilmot's eye's nearly popped out of his head. There was a snigger from the troop behind him. He spun round "Right Harden, get your men in pairs" he waited for them to obey, then shouted "QUICK MARCH" As he passed Charlie and Jasper he gave a snapped salute and disappeared on the road to Poole.

Charlie and Jasper watched them march up the High Street until they disappeared over the brow of the hill. Charlie turned to Jasper "He's no fool and there are more of them being sent" He grimaced "We've said it before, there will come a time when bringing-in shipments will become too dangerous." He shrugged and turned towards Mr Benfield's parlour putting his arm around Jasper's shoulders as they walked. "We've still got a few years yet. We had better make the most of them."

They re-entered Benfield's shop and were greeted by Mordecai with a most uncustomary smile on his face. Jasper shook him warmly by hand. "Thank you, Mordecai. We appreciate your help and I'm sure that Charlie will be generous."

He looked at Charlie who responded immediately, "Of course, I will be back in the next few days." he said then added with a broad wink. "Incidentally, how is our corpse getting on?"

Mordecai smiled again and nodded towards the coffin "See for your self" he chuckled.

Jasper and Charlie approached Amos's resting place and were greeted by the temporary corpse lying peaceably and snoring loudly. Resisting the temptation of giving Amos a rude awakening, Charlie said "It would be better to leave him there until Wilmot and his men have completely cleared the area." Then as an afterthought to Benfield he added "Tell him when he does wake up that Mr Tomes would like an urgent word with him."

Jasper smiled, "Yes I think he needs to realise that we're not playing games here. His stupidity could cause problems for us all. I'll make sure he is aware of that." He turned once more to Mordecai, "Thank you again."

As they stepped out into the gathering dusk Charlie muttered "What a complete waste of time."

He walked on for some time in silence then turned to Jasper, "I have had a message from Lord Henry Olden - he wants to see me. He wants you to come with me as well." Charlie chuckled and asked, "Have you been to Olden Hall since your visit that night?"

Jasper stopped walking, "Why would he want me there? And no, I've not been near the place since then. I thought it best not to."

Charlie smiled, "Don't worry about that. The old guy now lives in London. Lord Henry wouldn't know who was there that night or who wasn't." He changed tack, "Ive heard that there's much talk in Parliament about reforms." He looked at Jasper who showed immediate interest as it was his pet subject. "Look, we'll have a proper talk before we go. To give you an idea of what they are thinking about though; they are worried about any possible consequences of the doing away with the law that makes it a crime for men like us getting together in a meeting to discuss any of our grievances."

Jasper laughed, "I wouldn't think that you would have many complaints. Life is pretty good for you now isn't it?"

Charlie's eyes narrowed, "I'm still like you and all the rest from the village. My roots are still here." he snapped.

Jasper put his hands up "I'm sorry Charlie, I didn't mean to be insulting. Thanks be to the Lord, I'm really pleased that

at least someone from the village has broken the shackles."
He smiled and raised his eyebrow, "No hard feelings?"

Charlie relaxed "No, of course not." As they started to
walk back towards the High Street he put his arm around
Jasper's shoulder "It's been a long day. I've got one small
piece of business to finish here in Swanage. You go back to
the village. He paused then added, "There are no shipments
due for a couple of weeks. I'll meet you in The Ship next
Saturday evening and we'll talk about the meeting with Lord
Henry.

Jasper nodded in agreement but frowned "I'll see you
there, but I'm not sure that me and Lord Henry will see eye to
eye."

Charlie laughed, "Don't worry. Anyway, see you next
week." he ambled off in the direction of the harbour and
Jasper started to trudge back up the hill to Langton Matravers
and his dear wife.

Jasper spent the next week working in the quarry. He met
Amos Paine on the Wednesday evening and it was a meeting
that Amos would not forget in a hurry. He had been
frightened of Mr Tomes before, but by the end of the evening
he was terrified of him. It would have the desired effect and
Amos was very careful what he spoke about in the future.

A stark message was delivered on the Friday to Jasper
from Charlie which was "Don't forget our meeting.
Important!" Thomas, the young lad from the Harbour Inn
was sent to deliver the message. He had been told the exact
words to say and Jasper smiled to himself as the lad
squirmed as he repeated it word for word as Jasper towered
over him.

The pair met as arranged and after a few pleasantries,
Jasper confirmed that he had spoken with Amos. Charlie
could imagine the scene but was not amused, "Well done.
With the government's men getting more active the last thing

we want is a buffoon like Paine causing more problems." Jasper took a sideways look at Charlie. Despite his usual affable manner there was a hard edge to Charlie Heywood when it came to business.

Charlie carried on in a business-like manner. "Lord Henry is in London at the moment but he returns to Dorset this week. He sent his own personal man, a chap called Tomkins who says he knows you. I understand he was at Olden Hall when you made your previous visit."

Jasper laughed, "Tomkins, Josiah Tomkins. Yes I know him. I'm not surprised he's moved up in the world. I've learned since that it was him, with some quick thinking and a silver tongue, that stopped the night turning ugly." Jasper looked hard at Charlie and cautiously carried on "Look, Charlie are you sure about this. I don't fit in with the gentry at Olden Hall."

Charlie responded dismissively, "I've already said, don't worry. When we get there just let Lord Henry talk. Let him tell us why he wants to see us. If he asks you a question just answer directly don't add anything else." Jasper nodded and Charlie continued, "I suspect that he wants to talk to me about the goods that we bring into the country. He will probably know that as far as this part of the country is concerned, this business goes through me."

Jasper looked worried, "Won't he have Revenue men or Coastguards there then?"

Charlie grunted, "Definitely not. He is one of my biggest customers. I know too much and have kept records of his,… and his father's, involvement."

Jasper nodded slowly, "Alright, but you've said before that he is starting to become an important man in London. If the government are properly trying to stop smuggling then this must put him in a difficult position."

"Exactly!" Charlie looked at Jasper, eyebrows raised with a look of almost triumph. "We can't try to be too clever though, he's no fool, but I want to know what he has in mind."

Jasper was calculating the meaning of what Charlie was saying. He then looked at Charlie quizzically, "Alright, but why me? You don't need me there you do this side of the business."

"Jasper, come on, don't put yourself down. The folks around here look to you for leadership. They respect you, are even frightened of you." Charlie shook his head, "You must know that what you say, happens." He paused then continued. "Lord Henry must be worried about the response of the people around here if the Coastguards start to catch some of our men."

Jasper agreed, "I can see that. It's been something that folks believe is their right to carry out."

Charlie continued "It's not just folks around here's reaction to smuggling being stopped. Revolution is in the air. We've had a Prime Minister assassinated. Alright that was during the war. Since then though there has been a plot to kill the entire cabinet. We've had the English army riding over English people and killing women and children. Agitators are touring the country and whipping up dissent and unrest." Charlie smiled, "You stormed Olden Hall and you've also recently been to some of the meetings by these men that are trying to stir up trouble. The Government are worried."

Jasper was confused "I think I understand, but what can we …. I do? I feel I'm out of my depth."

Charlie smiled "We shall see what it's all about next Tuesday." Charlie, having finished their business, sat back. He drained his glass of brandy and inspected the empty glass with satisfaction, "Whatever we may think of the French they do make a fine drop of brandy." He put his glass down firmly and called to the open Tap Room door, "George, two more brandies, please."

The drinks came quickly as George knew who to look after. Charlie nodded in appreciation, took a sip, then rose from his seat. "I'll get word to the quarry manager to let him know that you won't be there next week. I'll meet you at the church at the middle of the day and we'll go over to Olden Hall together." He gave Jasper a friendly wink. "I have some business to complete with George. He doesn't take much these days but I always keep my local customers happy." He looked across the room "I see Robert has arrived. By all means mention that we going to Olden Hall but don't go into any detail. The less said the better until we know exactly what's afoot."

Jasper watched Charlie as he went, and in his familiar way, put his arm round George's shoulder.

Robert came and sat in the seat just vacated by Charlie. "That looked important." He waited, expecting an answer.

Jasper hesitated, then said simply, "It could be. To be honest I don't know myself yet. Charlie is certainly starting to move in high places these days" He shrugged, he'd had enough of serious talk for one night and changed the subject, "How are Sarah and the young 'uns."

The conversation then returned to that of life in the village and the evening passed like so many others.

CHAPTER TWENTY-ONE

Planning for the Future

Charlie and Jasper made their way to Olden Hall with Charlie seemingly in a good mood. Jasper was more circumspect. He had frequently walked along the ridge overlooking the mansion nestling in the valley without taking much notice. When he and the villagers made their demands on the old Lord Olden he did not at that time take much notice of the place.

The road wound its way down in a long arc through trees to finally skirt around a large lake and finally spread itself into a large expanse in front of the impressive façade of the country seat of His Grace, the Earl of Purbeck. The area in front was large enough to allow a number of coaches to dispatch their grand passengers and then for the horses to turn and make their way to the stables at the side. The crunching of their footsteps on the gravel stopped as Charlie and Jasper paused to fully appreciate the grandeur of the country seat of His Grace. The front of the house was inset with two wings on either side creating three sides to a square. Four columns stood guard on the entrance that was through two large eight foot high ornately carved wooden doors. They looked at each other and Charlie grinned, "It's a mite different to Garfield Lane, isn't it?" With that he strode forward, "Come on, he wants to see us, don't forget. I will not be overawed by a pile of stones which you probably helped to dig out of the quarry when they rebuilt this place a little while back."

As Jasper neared the firmly shut double doors he wondered how they were to inform someone inside that they had arrived. Suddenly the doors were swept back and a very tall, thin and haughty individual dressed in gaiters and red frock coat peered down his nose at what it seemed he saw as unwelcome intruders. The three stood in silence for some moments before the reluctant doorman cleared his throat and enquired, "I assume you, " he paused then continued, as if having decided that the word had to be applied, "gentlemen, are Heywood and Tomes?"

From the lack of a local dialect Charlie assumed the man was from Lord Henry's London household. He strode forward and passed the erstwhile barrier into the Hall then turning around said crisply "It's Mister Heywood and Mister Tomes. Please inform Lord Henry that his guests have arrived." At which he turned his back and chuckling at his friend's unease he put his arm around Jasper's shoulder in his characteristic manner. He gestured towards a large portrait of the old Lord Olden that dominated the Hall from the break in the stairs as they divided towards the East and West Wings. Grinning, Charlie gave Jasper a wink, "A good likeness I believe? Oh sorry, you never did meet him, did you."

The footman was left staring at their backs and saw no alternative but to carry out Charlie's instructions. As he walked passed them he heard Charlie, who continued to study the painting, say "Pompous sod."

The footman, whose name was Siddings, pushed open the door to the Library where he waited for the assembled company to acknowledge his presence. Lord Henry stood in front of the fireplace and was addressing the other members of the party. His younger brother by just a year, George was lounging in a chair with his legs crossed in the relaxed pose of a gentleman. The vicar the Reverend David Dafdd scowled in the direction of Siddings but sat respectfully upright waiting to be addressed. Lady Henrietta was seated in a window seat calmly sewing. The group was completed by Tomkins, who stood discretely in the background.

Since his conversation with Lord Wareham after the attack on Olden Hall, Lord Henry had tried to ensure wherever possible that safety for the workers in his quarries was improved. This helped the discontent to subside locally but tales of the outbreaks of the rising of disorder elsewhere were a matter of constant discussion.

Lord Henry had been summarising his reasons for calling the meeting and the actions that he was to propose.

When he finished his point George was obviously irritated. "I'm damned if I can see why we should cowtail to these men.

"It's no good George, pretending that there isn't a problem. The number of unsavoury incidents are still growing and they are becoming more organised. Lord Wareham has met with certain men in London who have pointed out that it is in everyone's interests to make sure that this country does not drift into a situation that becomes out of control." He paused and looked in the direction of Siddings with a frown, "Yes, Siddings, what is it?"

Siddings took a deep breath and with due respect to his employer announced, "Mister Heywood and Mister Tomes have arrived, sir. Shall I tell them to wait in the kitchen until you are ready to receive them, sir."

Lord Henry responded immediately, "No, not at all. Show them straight in, Siddings." He then turned to his brother as Siddings left the room. "Now George, I want you on my side in this matter. Remember we are not alone, Lord Wareham is meeting in a similar fashion on his Estate at Furzebrook. These meetings are taking place across the country at the direction of this very well connected group in London. If I say that even His Grace the Duke of Wellington takes heed of those people, I think you will appreciate my point."

George raised his eyebrows, grimaced and replied "If you insist, I will support you entirely."

Charlie and Jasper were taken to the door of the library and were told to wait outside. Charlie turned and whispered quickly to Jasper "Now relax. You survived a Frenchies cavalry sword – you can survive an English milord's tongue."

The entire company turned as Charlie and Jasper were ushered into the room. "Mister Heywood and Mister Tomes." Siddings announced and then withdrew.

Lord Henry took stock of his visitors. Charlie Heywood who he had met briefly several times, was dressed casually in a dark suit and waistcoat with an open collarless shirt. He looked confident as if he was aware what the meeting entailed. Lord Henry was instantly impressed when he looked at Jasper. Jasper had his usual grey moleskin suit and his Lordship had noticed him rub his boots on the backs of his trousers as he was about to enter the room. He was obviously nervous but it was clear that he was a man to be respected. His size, scar and eye patch would be intimidating and there was a no nonsense air about him.

Lord Henry grunted in satisfaction. Tomkins, from his local knowledge had chosen well. He indicated for them to be seated at a highly polished mahogany table. "Gentlemen, thank you for coming today." he began. "I will get straight down to the point at issue. This country spent a generation at war with our nearest neighbour, France. There were many reasons for these hostilities not the least of which was the revolution in that country and the awful reign of terror that ensued."

Jasper shifted in his seat 'What has this got to do with us' he thought. Charlie could sense that Lord Henry was not finding the conversation easy.

Lord Henry continued "Now, I'm sure that you gentlemen will agree that situation must not happen here." There was no reaction from his guests.   Lord Henry frowned,   "As Englishmen we see ourselves as a cut above those neighbours of ours. However, to ensure that revolution did not spread across the English Channel a great number of laws were passed that, I'm afraid went against our traditional freedoms. Some of these are now being abolished but dissent and outbreaks of violence are still increasing."

Lord Henry felt he was losing his audience. "Let me just remind you of an incident that occurred here in Dorset. My Lord Kenway was put into a position where the wages he was paying to his labourers on Creake Farm were too high to be sustained. This farm is not rented to a tenant so he quite rightly decided himself to reduce their wages." he paused and scanned his audience but was met with blank stares. "Unbelievably six of his workers saw fit to remonstrate with him on the matter They petitioned him and quite rightly he had them arrested. Their ringleader, Elward by name, was sentenced to be transported and the rest put in jail. Elward tried to escape and was shot."

Jasper shook his head, "Poor Stephen. How his wife and four children will survive, I don't know."

Lord Henry ignored the sympathy, "Yes, that's right a Stephen Elward. Very regrettable I'm sure. However you are no doubt aware of what happened at the inquest. The jury found that Elward had been 'most unjustly and fouly murdered'."

His Lordship paused for effect, he then strode to the table and thumped it hard with his fist, "This is the start of the breakdown of law and order. When the properly appointed officers of His Majesty cannot carry out their duties with at least the tacit support of the population," he paused again "then this can only lead to revolution." he thundered.

He took out a kerchief tucked in his sleeve so as to dab sweat that had appeared on his top lip. He turned to take his place again in front of the fireplace.

Charlie and Jasper had completely different reactions to his Lordship's outburst. Jasper was thinking about Stephen Elward and thought it typical of these people to only see it as a threat to their power and comfort. Charlie meanwhile was trying to work out the angle. What did his Lordship want? What was the bait to Charlie and Jasper for them to help him - and how?

George and Lady Henrietta looked at Lord Henry anxiously. Lord Henry took a deep breath and quietly continued. "All around the country there are separate issues. Each of these will be addressed by people like myself. On the Isle of Purbeck we have work from the quarries and with the increase in building in the new cities there will be work for probably our lifetimes. However, along the south coast there is another industry which, I'm afraid, gentlemen has a much shorter life." Stopping, he looked directly at Charlie and said, "I, of course, mean smuggling."

Charlie tried to maintain a look of injured innocence.

"There are two main reasons why this practice will be stopped. Firstly, the Waterguards have been reformed and will be recruiting in large numbers. The new force will be called the Coastguards. You may have noticed just outside Swanage the building of a row of cottages. These will house the new Coastguards brought from other places in the country so they will not have sympathies with the local people. They will be well trained and although the smuggling in this area seems very well organised," he was sure a smug look flit across Charlie's face "- they will win in the end."

Charlie appeared calm and then after a short pause, politely asked, "You said that there were two main reasons…."

Lord Henry responded, "There will be no need for smuggling."

Charlie was at last confused. He still could not work out what offer Lord Henry was to put on the table.

Lord Henry was almost triumphant as he felt he had unsettled his guest. "The activity of smuggling has been with us for many years but it was at an exceptional level when we were at war with France. Duties have still remained high so it is still profitable. These Duties are now being reduced. On top of this, England is the most powerful trading nation in the world. No foreign ship sails anywhere without our navy's approval. If we can produce more and cheaper goods than anyone else why would we want to have duties to protect our industries? It's called Free Trade and the idea is growing in support."

Charlie had gone quiet and his mind was racing. Jasper also remained quiet his only thought being that it would seem that he would soon be back working full time in the quarry.

The room was silent. George looked at Charlie with an expression that read 'you're out of your depth.' The Reverend was making a quick calculation as to whether anything he had just heard would affect his Tithes. Lady Henrietta had stopped sewing and was deep in thought.

Charlie finally stirred. "I assume that you are worried that what happened at Snodbury some years ago when smuggling was stopped effectively, will happen on a large scale here on the Isle of Purbeck. I also assume that you believe that Jasper and myself could have some influence on the people around here. You think that we would be able to stop matters getting out of hand when the money from smuggling dries up?" He looked round the room at all those present. He then turned to Lord Henry "Alright what's the deal. Good business doesn't happen unless everyone gets something and everyone goes away happy."

Lord Henry's eyebrows shot up. He was not used to be spoken to in such a manner. However he realised he was not dealing with a fool. His respect grew as he understood he was dealing with a real man of business.

Charlie continued before his Lordship could speak. "As far as I can tell we all have our own different interests in our discussion today -

Firstly, and I make no apologies, myself as a man of business" he paused and with a frown added, "of the middling sort."

Secondly, my good friend here Jasper Tomes is here for the people of the Isle of Purbeck,

Thirdly, our silent vicar here who is responsible for our souls. - and the collection of his Tithes" The reverend went to speak but was silenced by Lord Henry putting his finger to his lips.

Charlie continued, "and finally yourselves, the people in power – the government."

All concerned digested what had just been said. There was then a polite cough from the window seat. Lady Henrietta addressing her husband, enquired, "Are you not forgetting a great number of people who may have some concerns? I am talking dear husband of approximately half of the population." All the gentlemen present looked confused except for Charlie who grinned to himself in appreciation of her Ladyship's courage. Lady Henrietta rose to leave, placing her sewing on her seat. Everyone scrambled to their feet as she swept passed them. She turned at the door that Tomkins had rushed to open, and announced, "I am gentlemen, talking about women." She then disappeared to leave an embarrassed Lord Henry and an awkward group not knowing what to say.

The Reverend Dafdd studied his fingernails and said quietly, "Corinthians 14 : Verse 34 "Let your women remain silent."

Lord Henry frowned then collected himself, "I do apologise gentlemen. Such nonsense."

Charlie, ever the man of action broke the mood, "Well, shall we get down to business?"

Lord Henry looked at Charlie and thought, 'I like this man, what we have in mind will work'. He quickly looked at all present in the room. "Shall we start with what could be the biggest problem – that of ensuring that local people around these parts do not take heed of the dissenters and troublemakers?" he began.

Charlie interrupted, "That's really down to you.   Jasper and me can talk until we're blue in the face, but if they are starving or working under dangerous conditions then no matter what we say - you have a problem." Jasper was alarmed as here was Charlie talking to Lord Henry Olden as if he was an equal. Charlie however was unabashed. "What have you in mind, sir." He said holding Lord Henry's gaze.

Lord Henry was glad to get down to brass tacks. "First of all, I will promise that I will invest the latest equipment in the quarries that will make their work safer. You can tell them that does not mean that these machines will do their work instead of them. This country is becoming more and more wealthy, and cities are growing which need Purbeck Stone and Marble. If we can meet these orders at better prices, then their jobs are safe and I can look at the wages that they earn."

Charlie nodded. "I agree in this respect as I have, as you probably know, interests in some quarries myself."

Lord Henry continued. "I will also promise that I will use all the influence at my disposal to push through new laws that will directly benefit the working man. His Grace, my Lord Wellington ,is a reactionary on these matters, but myself and others in parliament," he paused not sure whether he should add anything more, but then said, "as well as a powerful group of men, who prefer to remain anonymous, will hold the day. Wellington cannot hold the tide back forever without risking the revolution we all fear."

Charlie nodded, "That's fine. That is the future, but mouths have to be fed every day. As the money from," he coughed, "other sources, starts to dry up who feeds the baby tomorrow?"

Lord Henry smiled, "Quite right 'free ale tomorrow' what about bread today? At the moment, what is one of the biggest expenses the men incur just to keep working?" He continued without waiting for an answer. "Their tools, their repair and the replacement. To a lesser extent also their footwear in the stone quarries. There are a number of blacksmiths in the area all of which have plenty of work. My Bailiff, Seagers, has spoken to Jacob Butt in Langton Matravers and he will do all this work and I will pay him." He looked triumphantly at Charlie who it was obvious was impressed. "Of course, the price per job he will charge me for all of this work will be less than individual orders, but he will have all the business and will benefit."

Jasper cleared his throat and cautiously he asked, "Do you mean My Lord that in effect the workers will be getting their wages increased because they can keep it all for their families."

Lord Henry nodded then continued, "Also I will commit, " he paused, "all matters remaining equal, to maintain the wages on my farms. I will also speak with my tenants and I'm sure that they will agree to do likewise on their farms." He grimaced and then added, " I will also speak to My Lord Kenway and I hope that I may persuade him that this course of action will be beneficial to both of us." he then added quickly, "I cannot of course, make any promises in that matter."

Charlie asked thoughtfully "If you don't mind me asking how will you find the money."

Lord Henry was waiting for this, "Ah-ah, eventually it will pay for itself as I will be able to expand the business. In the meantime, the gentlemen in London have agreed to fund these costs at very preferential terms over a long enough period of time." He then added darkly, "That is their business."

Charlie got up and paced the room, his impertinence again surprising Jasper. Charlie turned to Lord Henry. "Right that's the workers looked after for now, and hopefully the future. You have the security of your business expanding, and" he grunted, "your friends in London are reassured that if this area of England at least, was to revolt it could be to the detriment of all." His gaze caught the Reverend Dafdd and he added, "If my dear Reverend's flock are happy they will not continue to drift away to the cities. His Tithes will be safe." He added with a grin "I understand that the heathen word is gaining ground in the cities – their souls around here though will remain in your safe keeping. I would mention bye the bye that your Reverend's Tithes are higher than most."

Jasper's head was spinning. He looked at Charlie marvelling how he seemed to be able to hold his own with his Lordship.

Charlie was not finished yet, "That just leaves two people in the cold. Your Lordship, and your father before you, have been steady customers of mine for many years. Now, as I have said, I have other interests but the import business still at this time is the bedrock." He turned to Jasper, "My friend here's income will be much diminished if this business," he paused searching for the right phrase, "closes down."

Lord Henry was not to be defeated. "You two are a major part of this discussion. Yourself, Mr Heywood, is one of a growing breed which are called entrepreneurs. You have the business sense and expertise to see an opportunity and see the profit potential." Lord Henry paused to see the effect he was having on his audience. He was pleased to note that Charlie seemed to show genuine pride. However Charlie wanted detail. "How do you propose that I gain money and influence to benefit from these opportunities?"

"I don't." Lord Henry said flatly. "Well not immediately. My brother George here, has influence and the men of great wealth are desperate to invest. Working together, with care there is a great future in a country that is bursting with ideas and inventions."

Charlie turned to Jasper, "Sorry dear friend for leaving you to last." Then returned his question to Lord Henry, "How does Mr Tomes here become part of this grand plan?"

"He is a most important part of it. He is the natural leader of men in this parish. They all look to him for advice and if they are in trouble, what they should do." Jasper looked to the floor slightly embarrassed. Lord Henry continued, "What we have said here today will not happen overnight and there will be some who will need to be convinced." He looked directly at Jasper, "I understand that you can read and write, is that correct?"

Jasper was taken aback, "Yes sir, I can read and write after a fashion. I learnt whilst in the army."

"Good, that helps. Mr Tomes it is within my gift to fill the position of the Mayor of Swanage. Mr Cattle who currently fulfils this role is now old and will be retiring. You will become the new Mayor of Swanage and you will be in the perfect position to see a situation before it becomes a problem and deal with it." He looked at Jasper who's mouth had dropped. "Of course, there is a Living and accommodation in Swanage that goes with the position and I am sure that you and your family will be very comfortable."

Lord Henry returned to his position in front of the fireplace so as to address the entire room. "Gentlemen, there is a very real threat that England could be destroyed by a revolution. This country is at a time in history where we could lead the world for the next hundred years. We must not let this opportunity be lost because of old prejudices - we must use plain English common sense. As I said earlier, our meeting is being repeated throughout the land and with God's grace we will come back from the brink of disaster." His voice had risen to an orators pitch but he stopped abruptly to face the fireplace to regain his composure.

The room fell silent for some minutes as each had their own thoughts. Finally Lord Henry turned back and looking at Charlie and Jasper he smiled openly, "There is still much to be discussed, but I think that is enough for today. I bid you gentlemen good day and no doubt we will meet again very soon." He turned to Tomkins who had respectively stood by the door since Lady Henrietta had left. "Tomkins, arrange for our guests to be taken in a carriage back to Langton Matravers or wherever they wish to go." He turned to his brother, "George, a quiet word if you please." George rose and joined his brother at the fireplace their backs to the rest of the room.

Charlie and Jasper left and waited for their carriage to arrive. They stood in silence, their minds racing. Eventually as they left the grounds of Olden Hall Jasper turned and said, "Just one thing who is this powerful group of men."

Charlie chuckled, "One thing you must always remember – money talks."

* * *

When Jasper returned home, Ellen was anxious to know if it meant trouble for them as well as their friends in the village. As Jasper entered the house her first questions were "Well, have you still got work? Is his Lordship reducing everyone's wages?

Jasper was still in a state of some bewilderment. "No, far from it." he said cautiously as if working out what he said was correct. "His Lordship is keen to help us, - us, I mean, all of us." He went and sat in his chair next to the fire and gazed at the flames deep in thought.

Ellen was exasperated "His Lordship is keen to help us, is he? Oh yes, I'm sure. What's in it for him? Whatever he says, it's him that will come out on top." Ellen did not take her eyes off her husband. "Well?" she demanded.

"Ellen, we have to take what he says on face value. He will be able to increase the money his workers will have to spend and he will improve their working conditions in the quarries." Jasper then briefly went through the plans that Lord Henry was to put into place. Ellen looked doubtful.

"What can we lose?" Jasper said finally. "If he doesn't do what he said then he will have broken his word. Whatever we may think, whatever his father has done – or not done in the past, I believe he is a man of honour. In any case, we would be where we are now if he did break his word."

He stood up and went and put his arm round Ellen's shoulder. "Listen Ellen, it's in his interest for his workers to be happy. It's not in his interest for people to start rioting and withdrawing their labour." He gave her a hug. "I'm not saying that there will not still be troubles and there will not still be people who are unhappy." He thought for a moment and then said with a frown, "In fact I am convinced that there is a very real danger of big trouble ahead."

Ellen faced Jasper, "So, where do you fit in with all of this? Why did you get called to Olden Hall?"

Jasper looked down obviously embarrassed. "Well, he wants me to talk with people and try to answer their problems if I can, or go back to Lord Henry if I can't. He explained how Charlie's smuggling will become more difficult and he wants me to convince people around here that although they will very soon lose the money from Charlie's business, in the end they and their families will be better off."

Ellen frowned, "Why would you do that? You have to work in the quarry and you have enough problems of your own."

Jasper coughed and looked down again, "Well, I am to become the Mayor of Swanage and in that position will have the time to go round and meet with people and act as their spokesman, if necessary." He hesitated, "It will also provide a Living and a house in Swanage."

Ellen's mouth dropped. She started to speak then stopped. Finally she burst out "You….. you – you've sold out!"

Jasper's embarrassment dissolved into anger, "No I have not! " he shouted, "In the Lord's name when we met you said that you wanted me to look forward not dwell in the past . For God's sake woman that's what I'm doing." Jasper's eye glared and he took a step towards Ellen. For the first time she felt the power that her man exuded.

Ellen was a strong woman herself but no woman or man would defy Jasper Tomes when he was roused. Uncharacteristically she broke down in tears. Jasper continued to glare at Ellen, then he relented and he moved to comfort her. "Look dear, let's not talk about this anymore now." He kissed her gently on the forehead and took her into his arms. "We'll talk again tomorrow if you wish. "

The evening passed with very little conversation and when morning came although Jasper was prepared to discuss the matter again, Ellen never raised the subject. Whatever she may think she loved her man. He was the master in his own house, and her upbringing told her that she had to be content for her husband to act in the way he saw fit.

Jasper spent a number of days deep in thought. He had to speak to the men in both Lord Olden's quarries; Crack Lane quarry and the Eidibury. He finally decided that he should take the bull by the horns and face the men without any more delay.

A few days later, as he made his way up Stonehouse Hill, he met Robert on his way to work. "Morning to you, Jasper. What brings you up here today?"

"I have to speak with the men." He looked at Robert with a frown. "As you know I was at Olden Hall with Charlie and I have to let those working in his quarries know what his Lordship has planned."

Robert looked worried. "Oh dear. The men here at Crack Lane depend on this work. Some have moved away with the hope of finding work in the cities. The majority though are tied to the village through age, family and for many, fear of the unknown in a large city.

"Yes, I know. I've thought hard about what I have to say to them and it is good news - eventually."

"Eventually? They're fearful for their work. If they just think they will be out of work, with all their pent up grievances, out of desperation they will cause trouble."

"I have not been a regular quarryman lately and that was at Charlie's Gully Lane. I just hope they will still see me as a friend and fellow villager."

As they turned from the track into the quarry Robert clapped Jasper on the shoulder "Best of luck. You know you will have one friendly face in the crowd." As he made his way to the shaft head he was passed by Silas Winter.

Jasper gave him a broad smile. "Hello Silas, how are you? I've heard that you've not been too well lately."

Silas winced and massaged his left breast, "Not so good, Jasper. Not so good. I keep getting these pains in the chest. I'm sure that they will pass, though." He looked at Jasper and smiled "Are you not working at Gully Lane today?" He chuckled, "What it is to have friends in high places."

Jasper looked at Silas and was about to speak but stopped and shrugged his shoulders. Ignoring Silas' comments he said, "Can you get everybody together. I want to speak to all of them."

Silas frowned, "Why?" Although he would always defer to Jasper he still liked to think of himself as the boss in the quarry. He continued without waiting for a reply, "Do you mean all of them, even those down in the lanes?"

"Yes, all of them. I have something to tell them on behalf of Lord Henry Olden." Jasper turned away and went to lean against the same wall he had used so many times. Jasper was uneasy.

He watched as the workforce slowly assembled at the head of the main shaft. There was murmuring and some worried faces that portrayed their fears of what was about to be announced. Finally those in the deepest lanes covered in dust and blinking in the daylight joined their mates. Silas scanned the crowd, then turned to Jasper, "That's about everybody. They are all yours." Silas then went and stood at the front and turned to face Jasper.

Jasper approached his fellow workers and hopped up onto a stone so that he could see everyone.

"What's it all about Jasper?" called out Bill Coombes one of the older men.

"I can't support my brood on the wages His Lordship pays now. He will hear from me and a few of us lads if he tries to cut our money." This was greeted by growls of agreement.

One of the young boys nervously spoke up from the front, "We still have work do we, Mr Tomes?"

Jasper waited until they all fell silent, then started, "I have spoken with Lord Olden and he has told me that he is worried that other quarries have put in new machines and their stone is being bought instead of ours because it's cheaper. His Lordship says he will have to close the quarry if things carry on as they are at the moment."

There were gasps and one voice shouted from the back, "I'll wager he will still be able to feed his family."

"The bastard. I say we go and make him keep the quarry open."

Jasper raised his arms and pressing his palms down, his authority amongst his peers regained silence. "Hear me out." He glared in the direction of the dissenting voice. "Lord Olden will be buying some of those machines so that we can sell our stone at a good price which means that you keep your jobs." He raised his hands again to maintain the silence, "He will not be paying for them by cutting your wages." This was greeted by a lone voice "Thank the Lord."

Another voice called out "The cost of food is going up. Unless we get more money I might as well have no work."

Jasper turned in the direction of that voice. "His Lordship can't afford to pay all of you more at the moment but he can make it so that we can keep more of the money you're already paid." He paused for effect. "Lord Olden is proposing to buy your tools and pay for them to be re-sharpened and repaired each month by Jacob Butt."

Jasper was dismayed by the reaction.

"Aye we've had good news before and nothing happens."

"He's in with the toffs now. Do we believe him?" This was greeted with some shouts of agreement whilst others called out, "Jasper won't let us down." The meeting seemed to be breaking up into separate arguments.

Jasper feared that matters were getting out of control.

Robert had remained silent until now. He looked around and then pushed his way to the front and jumped onto the stone alongside Jasper. He shouted across the increasing noise, "Men, what have we got to lose? I believe that if Jasper Tomes is happy then I'm happy. Jasper will look after our interests." he paused as the noise lessened. Robert saw his chance and with real anger in his voice he shouted above the din, "Trust Jasper. What is the alternative? If we agree to stop work then we break the law and we'll end in jail ….. or worse. If we all march over to Olden Hall it won't be like last time. The young Lord Henry Olden will bring in the troops and we will be in jail or probably shot on the spot." He had won their attention. "There are others in the village who are worse off than us. I say trust Jasper to speak for us." There was a roar of approval from the majority of the crowd and the remaining negative voices were howled down. He had won the day.

Jasper looked across to Robert and nodded his thanks. He turned back to the workers in front of him as the meeting was breaking up into individual conversations. "Right men, get back to work or you'll have Silas on your tails." He looked round at Silas and noticed with concern he was wincing and rubbing his left breast. He roared at the remaining workers still talking in groups, "Get on with your work or there won't be a quarry for you to worry about." That was enough for the quarry to return to its customary hive of industry.

Jasper walked over to Silas "Come on Silas you're not well. I'll take you home in one of the carts and let your Betty look after you."

Silas winced, "Thanks Jasper. I don't feel good at all at the moment."

The journey to Silas's cottage took place in silence with Jasper's concern for Silas mingled with some relief that the day had been carried with Robert's help. This was tempered by his fear that trouble had not gone away.

Three months after the meeting at Olden Hall Lord and Lady Wareham hosted a private dinner for Lord and Lady Olden. It was an occasion that happened quite frequently when the four childhood friends were both back in the county.

The two Ladies were seated on a red and cream stripped silk damask settee with Lord Olden sitting back on a mahogany side chair.

Lord Wareham was standing with his hands clasped behind his back in front of a white marble carved fireplace holding court as the host. The conversation had spanned some of the many events in London including a recent Ball held by the erstwhile Prince Regent, now King George.

Charles cleared his throat in that manner that announced a change of subject. "Henry, now that you have had time to digest your meeting with that chap Heywood, what do you think will come of it?"

"To be quite frank, I'm not sure. " He chuckled. "Whatever may happen, Heywood will be alright. The other one Tomes is a fearsome looking man. Do you remember him when he was in your regiment?

Wareham grunted. "Once seen, never forgotten although he didn't suffer his wound until right at the end of the war." He patted his empty sleeve. "We have that in common, but no, he was just one of the other ranks."

Such matters would not normally be the concern of the Ladies but being such old friends the four spoke quite freely together. Lady Olden who had been present for some of the meeting with Charlie and Jasper said playfully. "He certainly is quite a commanding figure." Lady Wareham stifled a giggle which all tried to ignore but Lord Olden gave a momentary frown. "I am told that a man of such physical stature commands the respect of others of the lower sort."

Lord Wareham nodded in agreement to her Ladyship's comment. "I understand that you have arranged for his appointment as the Mayor in Swanage, is that right Henry?"

"Yes, and he will be moving into a larger house in the town befitting of a man of that station. I understand that his wife is a bit of a firebrand and she was not entirely happy with her new position in Swanage society, but I'm sure that she will of course support her man at all times."

"Good, I think that appointing him as Mayor may be the key factor in keeping the lid on any trouble that may occur here on Purbeck. His natural authority will now be re-enforced amongst his kind."

Lord Olden laughed "It did not take long for Tomes to use his new power. The quarry manager at Crack Lane died last month of a seizure and Tomes spoke with me to ask that his friend, Bollson be appointed to the post."

"That's good. I have been told that those two are inseparable and they, by and large, have the ear of most of the villagers. If Bollson has more money to support his wife and family then he won't want the boat to be rocked."

Lady Wareham showed concern. "Do you think there will still be trouble?"

Lord Wareham grimaced. "I'm afraid there could be a flash-point. I just hope that the improvements in the lot of the local people around here together with the authority given to Tomes will stop it going too far."

Lady Olden shook her head sadly. "It seems so wrong that all this talk is about this peaceful country being so close to what happened in France."

Lord Olden put on an solemn tone. "We do not have the benefit of hindsight. Chaps like Heywood will be making this country wealthy but that wealth comes at a price. Change of any sort causes uncertainty.

Lady Olden scoffed. "There are some changes that should be made.

"Lord Olden sighed. "I do not think we need to discuss your pet ideas today."

"Why not?" She responded indignantly. "We are all friends here so, when can my pet ideas, as you put it, be discussed?"

Lord Wareham was conciliatory. "I suppose you are referring to the status of women?"

"Yes she was…."

"I can speak for myself….."

"Yes, but my dear, women naturally indulge in such silliness. How can your ideas be given credence when women are visiting mediums and fortune tellers; reading trivial novels; engaging in rivalries with other women and immoderately caring about dress and manners."

"Women's faults, and yes we do have them as do men, are mainly as a result of their low status in society and insufficient education.   I am not alone when I say that granting additional rights to women will, in fact, improve society by turning women into equal participants in all aspects of life."

Lord Wareham looked at his wife and raised his eyebrows indicating embarrassment but she shook her head. "Henrietta makes a very reasonable point.   I have read the book, Vindication of the Rights of Women by Mary Wollstonecraft. Whether you men like it or not, women will achieve equal status eventually,"

Lord Wareham was a little surprised by his wife's reaction and looked at her thoughtfully for a moment. He then sighed. "There are many parts of our society that may seem unfair and we ignore them at out peril. I do believe that there will be changes very soon but I'm afraid a change in the position of women will not happen in our lifetime."

Lady Olden sat back. "I fear that you are right." There was silence in the room for some minutes then she rallied her spirits. "We owe it to ourselves to start changing opinions even if it be in the beginning in a small way." She looked at her husband and smiled. "Do not fear I will not embarrass you my dear, but I will devote my life to creating a momentum whereby women attain power over themselves. As I said: I am not alone."

Charlie wasted no time in meeting Lord Henry's brother George to discuss possible business ventures. George's major, and probably only asset, was that he had a number of contacts in London and from one of these he learnt that Parliament intended to create large cemeteries outside of the precincts of the city. There was a growing concern that with the ever increasing population of London the churchyards within the city were fast filling up. Two sites had been identified away from the city. One was to the north of London on the hill that led down from the small village of Highgate and the other in the south on the commons at Norwood. It will be some years before these projects came to a conclusion but Charlie could see the opportunities. The supply of Purbeck stone for the mausoleums and gravestones could be used as a cornerstone of the expansion of his business into London.

Charlie spent months working through the various issues and hurdles that would have to be overcome. Eventually he was ready and realised that the scheme he had devised would require some initial financial support. Lord Henry was always kept informed of the conversations between Charlie and George. When he was told that they would need finance he said that Rosenfeld's, the group that were backing him on the quarry, were keen on other investment opportunities. The Rosenfeld's knew of George, but were unsure of him. He gave the impression of being a typical aristocratic second son who had been born with a silver spoon in his mouth, and they were not convinced of his business abilities.

Their agents had already advised them that in Dorset a certain Charlie Heywood had impressed all that had dealt with him.

Despite Charlie's plans for expansion being of minor investment interest for them, they decided that they would like to meet him. There were a number of much larger projects that would be surfacing in the future and they would need men ready to manage these enterprises.

They told Lord Henry to arrange a meeting and so both Charlie and George were invited to the offices of the Rosenfeld's in the City of London.

Charlie was given an address in Old Jewery next to the Bank of England. When he arrived he was escorted by a bewigged and gartered usher into a vast wood panelled room. Six foot high portraits adorned two walls, a third wall contained an enormous fireplace whilst on the remaining wall the window was firmly shut.. Lord Henry and George were already there and were in conversation with three gentlemen dressed in sombre frock coats. As Charlie entered the chamber he was immediately put at ease by his hosts each of whom rose and walked forward to shake his hand. Lord Henry and George remained seated and nodded their welcome

The eldest banker, which is what they were, spoke first, "My dear Mr Heywood we are delighted that you have taken the time to meet us. My name is Amit Rosenfeld and these are my brothers Solomon and Mikael. May we call you Charlie?*

Charlie warmed to these men who were in a completely different class to himself, but welcomed him so generously. "Of course, sir." Charlie replied.

"No please - Charlie, we are all businessmen here. By name please." Amit gestured to a chair next to Lord Henry at the large rectangular table that stretched almost the length of the room. He regained his seat on the opposite side of the table and then adopted a more brisk manner. "I understand that you wish to invest in a business opportunity, and you would like to give us the chance to join in this venture. If I understand correctly from your proposed partner," he said nodding in the direction of George who shifted uncomfortably in his seat, "you wish to invest in the forthcoming creation of cemeteries."

Charlie smiled to himself and made a mental note to remember this professional way of conducting such meetings. He then took a deep breath and started. "These cemeteries will require large quantities of stone and marble which can be supplied from Purbeck. Whilst Lord Henry has the large Crack Lane Quarry and I now have full ownership of a number of smaller quarries we always have to compete with other quarry owners to supply to the London wholesale merchants. Which means prices for our stone are suppressed."

Charlie paused for a reaction from the assembled company. He was given an encouraging open palmed gesture by Amit. Charlie continued, "By just supplying the stone we are sacrificing the major profit to be made at the London end of the business. In the case of the cemeteries, that is the sale of the end product to the mourners. What I am proposing is that this venture would entail buying out the largest London merchant, so that in effect we would control the entire business chain from the quarrying of raw material - stone and

417

marble - selling it to our own London based company, and then the end product on to the customers."

Charlie sat back for a moment to take a breath, and there was a momentary silence before Solomon spoke, "Do you know who is the largest wholesaler in London? Would he be prepared to sell his business to you? It seems to me that if he is the largest then he knows good business when he sees it."

Charlie warmed to his point, "Yes, the company is Samuel Tyler and Company, although its now run by Sam's son, James. I know James from my first business of selling consignments of my stone to his company. James is getting old now and hasn't been very well. He has no family now; his wife died last year and his two sons were carried off by the big outbreak of cholera three years ago. He can see the profit to be made but has lost the will to carry on since his wife died." Charlie stopped and shook his head sadly.

Mikael tut tutted grimly, 'That is indeed sad, the poor man." he stopped to show due respect, then continued, "So what do you propose?"

"I may have acted too quickly but I have spoken with James about the future. He has agreed in principle to accept a modest sum for his company which would be followed by a generous annuity to be paid for the rest of his life. This annuity would be based on a percentage of the profit made by that part of the business that he once owned. I have given my word that this profit would be fairly shown."

When Charlie stopped again, there was another pause which lasted for a full minute. The silence was broken by Amit who nodded his head slowly. "So please Charlie, summarise this venture for my brothers and I."

Charlie looked in turn at each person sat around the table before he started "I believe this venture has all the requirements to be an excellent business. First, Lord Henry and myself will have a secure outlet for our stone from the quarries which we will sell at a good but fair price to my own company in London; Sam Tyler's old company. In the case of the cemeteries, by the employment of good stone masons from Purbeck we will be able to sell directly to the mourners. The cemeteries are just a part of the total business for Purbeck Stone. London and other cities are expanding fast and there will be an increased demand for Sam Tyler's merchandise."

Charlie paused to take a breath. "Finally, you gentlemen here in London will receive interest on your initial loan plus, I suggest, a percentage of the profit from the London based part of the business."

"Why do you need a loan? This will be a profitable business apart from the initial payment to Samuel Tyler why can't you pay for all your costs out the profit?" Solomon asked directly fixing Charlie with a steady gaze.

Charlie stood his ground, "If we do not have any capital behind the business we will be depending on using the credit of the people that supply us with whatever we may need. That is like borrowing from our creditors and the slightest downturn in business means that we will be late in paying them. They will then withhold supplies." He looked at each of the Rosenfeld brothers and finished simply by saying, "Then we go bankrupt."

Solomon nodded slowly and said 'The problem is that we are therefore taking all the risk, we always want commitment from the people to whom we lend money. Are you prepared - are you able, to invest yourself?"

Charlie looked across to Lord Henry and George "Lord Olden has said that he will match whatever money I am able to put into the business. I have calculated the amount that we will need from you gentlemen." He paused, looked down for a moment then looked again at each brother. "Gentlemen, I will be concluding some business next week which will enable me to meet my part of the investment.'"

Mikael nodded with raised eyebrows, "This is indeed good news. Pray, it is your affair, but may I ask what this business is next week?"

Charlie looked straight ahead, "It is from the import side of my activities and I will receive a large shipment that has committed customers and will provide me with a substantial profit"

Lord Henry spluttered a cough and studied the floor.

A quick smile crossed Amit's face then disappeared immediately. He then looked at his brothers. Mikael nodded and Solomon closed his eyes both giving their approval. He addressed Lord Henry, "Sir, you have indeed brought an astute businessman to meet us. We are very impressed with his grasp of a very promising business opportunity. He has satisfied us that as long as he, Mr Heywood, is the major force behind this venture then we thank you for the chance to join you in this enterprise." He then rose and approached Lord Olden with an outstretched hand. "My Lord, I very much appreciate your time this morning. If you would now pray excuse us I wish to conclude a minor detail with Mr Heywood." The gartered usher had already entered the room and despite a momentary frown from Lord Olden, he and his brother were ushered out."

Amit came and sat in the chair just vacated by Lord Olden and indicated to Charlie to resume his seat next to him. "The cemetery business and the sales of Purbeck Stone will indeed eventually create fine profits. However when we have a conclusion to the arrangements for this venture and you have the time, I would like to introduce you to another gentleman who has some interesting ideas. One of which, shall we say just for now, is that there would appear to be opportunities in the area of travel. You have no doubt heard about the invention of an engine that moves by steam upon rails. A service that will run between two towns in the north of the country is being built as we speak. It is our belief that the potential profits in this area are vast and could make us all very wealthy men."

Charlie thought to himself 'Even more wealthy.'

Amit continued. "I will say no more at this time but think about what I have said. I would like to think that you would look at any proposals we may present in a favourable light."

It had taken Charlie only a brief moment to realise the enormity of what could lay ahead of him. "Of course, Sir. I will be available whenever you deem it appropriate"

"We are most grateful." Amit then rose and proffered his hand which Charlie shook as well as those of his two brothers.

Charlie hesitated and was slightly confused "I thank you sir. I can assure you that I will give much thought to what you have said. I am however concerned that we have not discussed the sums involved and your terms of business for the quarry stone enterprise."

Amit smiled, "My dear Charlie. When you are ready with the details I would like you to arrange to meet my Chief Clerk and let him know the sums that you require. I am sure that when he reports back to us we will be in a position to draw up an Agreement. My good sir, we agree with you, good business is where all parties benefit. I am confident that there will be no problems." He again smiled warmly, "I wish you good day and we look forward to a mutually beneficial partnership. I have a feeling that this could be the start of many business ventures in which we may work together."

Charlie was ushered to the door. He found Lord Henry and his brother still outside. As if he could not care less, George casually asked, "What did they want to speak with you about?"

"Oh, they wanted to know where they could contact me and other such personal details."

George frowned but Lord Henry dismissed any further conversation. He waved his hand and a coach quickly drew alongside, Lord Henry turned to Charlie, "Well done I'm sure we will meet again soon. Come George, Lady Henrietta awaits us." They then climbed into their carriage and disappeared in a cloud of dust in the direction of the west end of London leaving Charlie standing alone in the street.

Charlie was momentarily dazed with the speed of events then realised that all that he could ever wish for was within his grasp. He clenched his fist and punched the air and shouted, "Yes!"

Charlie spent the next few days concluding preparations for the London side of his new business enterprise then returned home still flushed with his success. He would reflect later that life seems to counter its highs with a fair share of lows.

As soon as Edith met him at his front door she burst into tears. "My dear, whatever is the matter?" He embraced her and looked at her closely to see any signs of sickness. There were none. "Is young Jack alright. He has not been taken ill has he?"

"No, no he is quite well. It is Ambrose. He has been arrested."

Charlie's face fell. Over time he had become less charmed by his brother-in-law. The fact that Ambrose shared a house with Francis was unusual and many in Poole had soon started to mutter about what took place behind their front door.

"The Reverend Dafdd has seen the work of the devil in his parishes and has announced that he will clean up any decadence. He has sent in spies to a number of clubs in Poole and they are the ones that Ambrose and.." she paused then added with distaste "…Francis frequent."

'What crime has he supposed to have committed?"

"They are both accused of lewd conduct and committing unnatural acts. The Magistrate says the penalty is for them to be hanged." She burst into another torrent of tears.

Charlie feared that this may happen, but he was torn; he still dealt occasionally with Ambrose on business but he did not understand how a man that he had at one time liked, could change so much. He knew exactly what the crime of unnatural acts meant but could not understand what could bring men to indulge in such behaviour. He also realised that he felt some guilt for the fact that he was concerned that people could connect him with Ambrose and Francis.

"Where is Ambrose now?"

"They've taken him to the prison in Winchester."

"What a mess." Charlie walked towards the window and stared out with his mind racing. He was in a quandary; he had no animosity towards Ambrose because as far as he was concerned what the man did in his private life was no business of Charlie's. However, now was the worst time, if there could ever be a worst time, for this to blow up. Charlie was on the brink of achieving what he had dreamt of when he first started running errands around the village as a lad. Nothing could be allowed to interfere with his ambitions but Ambrose was his brother-in-law and there was a family commitment.

He turned back and faced Edith. "I will speak with Jasper who as the Mayor may be able to persuade the Magistrate over in Poole to deal leniently with Ambrose."

"Oh thank you - thank you." Edith rushed forward and hugged Charlie.

Charlie took her by the shoulders and spoke softly. "I can't make any promises but I promise I will do what I can." He paused for a moment then added, "I think that if I can help him then it would be for his own benefit if he went to

London. There will be work for him to do there when my business starts to expand."

Edith hugged him again. "Thank you my love."

Charlie was not seen very much in Langton Matravers or Swanage for some time after his meeting in London. So it was with surprise that Robert received an urgent message in the middle of July for him to meet Charlie at The Harbour Inn the following day. The message also said that he was not to worry about leaving his work at the quarry.

Robert made his way straight home that evening deciding not to visit The Ship on his way. The door of his cottage was open and as he entered Sarah had her back to him tending to a pot on the range.

She was wearing her simple ankle length red skirt and dark grey blouse. As usual she wore a white apron over the skirt that was tied high just above her navel. Her hair was back in a bun but the day's chores had loosened several strands that now hung down over the side of her face.

Robert coughed gently but the noise still made Sarah jump "Bless me, Robert, you near frightened the life out of me." She smiled sheepishly as if sorry to be such a fool. She casually tucked the errant strands of hair behind her ear and met Robert with a kiss on the cheek.

Robert looked at her with concern. "How are you, my love? You've been very pale lately. Are you still feeling faint - are you alright".

Sarah put down the pot she was still holding and looked at Robert nervously, "Yes, I'm as well as I should be. Robert, " she hesitated, "Robert, I fear we will have another little mouth to feed." she hesitated again, "Are you cross?"

Robert quickly moved to her and put his arms around her. "Of course I'm not cross. The Lord has smiled on us again" he said happily.

"I wish he would smile on someone else." She took a sharp intake of breath. "Please forgive me, Lord." she whispered heavenward. "It is just that life is difficult enough and now with another little 'un on the way I don't know how I'll cope. I'm already fair worn out at the end of each day." She sighed then after a moment wiping the back of her hand across her eyes and forehead she said, "I'm sorry Robert I'm being all weak and thoughtless."

"Don't be silly dear." There was nothing else he could think of to say. He understood Sarah's feelings but what could he do? He had to work and Sarah had to look after the house, him and the children. He couldn't do anything about that - it was the way of life.

Sarah straightened up, brushed her apron down and tucked her hair behind her ear again. Then glancing over her shoulder at the fire, "Your meal is ready. There's me going on about my day and you've been in that quarry.   You'll be hungry no doubt. Sit down my love and I'll bring you your dinner."

Robert felt he should say or do something but in the end said simply, "Thank you" He paused then added,   "I do understand." Then looking around. "Where's that young scamp, Jonathan?"

"He's already eaten. He's playing with some of the other children." She put down a tin plate with Robert's dinner of potatoes, bacon and onions.

Robert started eating then looking up said with a smite, "Oh yes, I nearly forgot,   what with hearing your news. I won't be at the quarry tomorrow. I have to meet Charlie Heywood in Swanage." He chuckled, "That Charlie, he has already organised for me not to be at work for the day." He stopped as he saw Sarah was frowning. He knew why.

"Robert you know we've talked about this, it"s not like it used to be when you first started to do jobs for Charlie. You could get yourself killed, or be caught, very easily now." She paused waiting for a reaction, but Robert kept staring down at his food. She slammed down a loaf of bread onto the table in front of him. "Who would look after the children then?' She patted her stomach, "All of them."

Robert was irritated He wasn't irritated with Sarah, it was the irritation of hearing something he did not want to hear. Sarah had the bit between her teeth, "Now you're the quarry manager we've got a little extra to get by on - especially as you don't have to pay for your work tools anymore. That money would all end. With you gone your family would have to go on the parish, would you want your family to live on charity?"

Robert sat in silence just looking at Sarah. Before he could speak, Sarah relented. She squatted down alongside him and held his hand. "You're my man and I will always support you whatever you do" She gave his hand a squeeze, "Please tell Charlie you don't want to do his work anymore."

After a few more moments of silence Robert took a deep breath, "Alright my love. I have already said to Jasper that this work has to stop. He agrees with me that it is now getting too dangerous. I'll tell Charlie when I meet him tomorrow."

Sarah looked hard at Robert then said simply. "You promise?"

"I promise."   Robert added with a grunt,   "Whatever Charlie says."

Sarah stood up and turned to the fire, when she was facing away from Robert she grimaced, raising her eyebrows. She knew that Charlie was very persuasive and Robert was too nice to deny anyone.

After a moment she spun round with a large smile and said in a confidential whisper, Jonathan won't be back for a good while yet." She walked back to Robert and pulled him to his feet "We have some time alone." Rubbing her stomach she added, "The damage is done now. You're a big man at the quarry, show me you are still one at home."

Robert needed no further invitation.

The next day Robert was at The Harbour Inn early for his meeting and watched through the window as Charlie arrived in a single-seat Berlin carriage. Robert smiled to himself as he realised that Charlie was starting to look quite distinguished. Under a dark serge suit a waistcoat strained to contain a midriff that was evidence of a diet of good food and 'imported' Port. His hair had now receded and as if to compensate, his round face was framed by bushy whiskers which disdained to progress to his chin.

Charlie's manner hadn't changed, as soon as he threw the door of the Inn open and saw Robert his face broke into a broad smile. As Robert rose to greet him he strode across the room and placed his arm around Robert's shoulder and with a booming voice proclaimed, "Robert, dear old friend, how good it is to see you again" Robert was immediately overwhelmed by the warmth of his greeting. Charlie made him feel that he was indeed his closest friend. "Robert where have you been hiding? It's been a long time." Charlie discounted the fact that Robert had never left Langton Matravers or Swanage for months and that Charlie had been everywhere but back to the village.

With some confusion, Robert started, "Well I've not been anywhere......." but was cut short as Charlie noticed Ben Mellor the landlord who was standing respectfully at the door to the tap room. Charlie turned his head away from his host and whispered to Robert. "Since Seth sold up, I've not met this fellow before, what is his name?"

Robert instinctively replied in a similar discrete manner, "Ben."

Charlie strode across the room and grasped the hand of a slightly bewildered Ben, "My good man - it's Ben I believe. Yes? Good " Charlie continued before a reply came "I hear you run a good house here. I've been looking forward to meeting you."

"Eh, thank you, sir" Ben stuttered.

"Good. Good. Now Ben, I have some business to discuss with my dear friend here, would you be so good as to bring two large glasses of that excellent brandy I understand that you recently acquired." Charlie lowered his head whilst raising his eyebrows giving Ben a look as if they both shared a secret. Charlie always kept an eye on where his shipments were delivered locally. Moving towards the door he noticed two old regulars who hadn't uttered a word since Charlie had made his entrance. "Bring the drinks to the bench outside, Ben, and give the same to those two fine gentlemen in the comer." Without further ado he put his arm back around Robert's shoulder and guided him outside to the old wooden bench leaning against the front wall of the Inn.

They had no sooner sat down than Ben brought their glasses of brandy. He was assured that there was nothing else he could do for them at the moment and he left them alone. Charlie waited for Ben to disappear inside then turned to Robert and his smile disappeared and was replaced with a frown that expressed concern. "Robert, I have been able to trust you to do a good job for me in the past. So, next week I have a large, important shipment being delivered and I need you to make sure it's landed and stored without any problems." He paused tilting his head and squinting his eyes whilst holding Robert's direct attention, "The problem is that I hear tell from Jasper that you want to stop this work. You think that it's getting too dangerous. Is that right?"

Robert's face reddened, they had both grown up together, albeit they had gone their separate ways, but they had never been really close friends. Charlie now made Robert feel nervous. He was flustered that Charlie should have heard of his misgivings, "Erm .... Yes I have mentioned that to Jasper." He paused for a moment and taking a deep breath continued, "Charlie, I have a wife and young 'uns who depend on me. My boy Jonathan wouldn't be able to support the rest of the family if I was not here." Charlie grunted to himself, remembering how he had to support himself and his mother at a very early age.

Robert was anxious to continue, "I thank you very much for the money that you have been able to give me in the past. The Good Lord only knows how we would have managed without it" He hesitated again but his worries had to be said, "Keziah Willmot and his Coastguards are making our business more and more difficult. As I think you probably know, those cottages they are building on the edge of town overlooking the harbour and bay means that he will have his men around all the time. Willmot is no fool but fortunately none of our men have fallen foul of him yet but our luck will run out soon."

Charlie held up his hand to acknowledge Robert's point and nodded his head slowly. He suddenly stood up and took a few paces towards the harbour and stopped deep in thought. After some minutes he turned, went to the door of the Inn and called out, "Ben, two more glasses of that brandy. My friend and I have a thirst." He then returned to sit next to Robert. "I understand your worries and I knew that this would come one day"

He paused as Ben re-appeared with their drinks and continued when they were alone again. "I am already making plans that will mean that this business will be able to stop. I need this one last job to be carried out without any mistakes. Robert, I need a man I can rely upon and you are that man. I really do appreciate your worries. I am asking you for one more time and there's a bonus in it for you." He put his hand forward onto Robert's shoulder, gently shook it and made a gesture that had worked so many times for him. He raised his eyebrows and lowered his head and gave a reassuring wink.

Despite himself Robert was won over. Later he would softly curse to himself for being so weak but Charlie was hard to refuse. Sarah would not be pleased! "Alright just this last time." he said reluctantly.

"Good man - Good man. I knew I could rely upon you. Thank you Robert you won't regret it." A frown crossed Charlie's face. There was a brief pause he then abruptly changed the subject, "How are you getting on now that you are the manager up at Crack Lane?"

Robert was not sure why he asked at this point, "Well, yes, good, the extra money is very useful."

"What about the other men? Are they happier now because they will be keeping more of their money for themselves?"

"Yes, but you can still feel that at the slightest sense of injustice, trouble will boil over. Remember as well that there are many men in the village that work on the farms around here. Lord Kenway has threatened to reduce the wages of a number of them and they are not happy. A few have been meeting and some of our men have joined them. They have been talking about marching to Kenway's Studland House. Lord Kenway is the biggest landowner this side of Poole and he's being blamed for everything from the weather, to bad harvests or even the price of bread"

Charlie looked alarmed, "Is it serious?"

"It could be." Robert sighed. "Jasper suggested that I give the more outspoken of their men some of your work." He smiled and added, "They're not daft. They would see the reason why they should suddenly be included." He stopped smiling and with a frown, "In any case from what you are saying that won't be possible for very much longer."

Charlie nodded. "Good point. Robert, you must keep Jasper informed if it looks as if trouble will break out."

"I will" Robert replied simply.

"Good man. It's to the benefit of the men around here that matters don't get out of hand." Charlie resumed a more business-like manner. "To the immediate future, next week's shipment. I understand your concerns that's why we need to get Willmot and his men out of the way."

"Yes - but how?" Robert said cautiously.

"I've spoken with old Captain Jenkins. As you know, he has his boat The Pride of the Bay. He doesn't do much work these days but some extra money is always welcome. I want him to act as a diversion." Charlie chuckled, "I've arranged for the good Captain to set sail at dusk with a couple of men. At that time he wouldn't be taking people across to Poole and fishermen around these parts don't fish at night"

Robert was intrigued, "I see, I think. Where does Willmot come into the plan?"

Charlie chuckled again, he was pleased with himself. "His men drink in the Anchor on the quayside, Jasper has arranged for Bill and George Saunders who work for Captain Jenkins to go there on Saturday night They will have a few drinks and talk about having to work next Wednesday night. They will make sure that the Coastguards overhear them and they are bound to tell Willmot."

"Are you sure Willmot will do something?" Robert asked.

"I'm certain. Especially as I understand a while ago when Willmot first arrived in Swanage he made a bit of a fool of himself in front of Jenkins, his crew and the old Lady Olden." Charlie looked at Robert grinning, "He wouldn't want to miss the opportunity of making arrests of smugglers caught red-handed. You know how difficult it still is for him to get a conviction and on top of which he would get his own back on Jenkins."

Robert nodded, "I see and where will I and my men take the landing?"

"The crew of the East India Company's ship the Albemarle, will drop anchor in the Channel off Chapman's Cove. When they get your signal they will then bring the shipment alongside In the years since the quarry has been worked the path down to it has become too dangerous to use. The large caves under the lea of the cliffs at that point though are perfect for storing the shipment until we're ready to move it on. It can only be approached from the sea now, and only when the tide is right and the tide will be right next Wednesday night.   Alf Simpson's lad Billy is a good runner, when Alf sees Willmot off in hot pursuit of Captain Jenkins he will send Billy over Ansell Head to let you know," he paused to smile, "the coast is clear."

"It takes a while to get down to the beach at that point, I will have to be down there ready to row across to Dancing Ledge. How will the lad let us know Willmot's busy chasing the good Captain?"

Charlie was ready for the question, "He will take the message to Tom Bridles cottage at the top of the cliff. Tom will draw his curtains to mask his light inside. He'll open them three times in quick succession." Charlie chuckled, "I heard tell that Willmot asked once why Tom's cottage had been built in such a bleak spot. He was told that only smugglers would want to live there.   I understand he didn't appreciate the joke."

Robert thought through carefully the plans that Charlie had detailed. He marvelled at the attention to detail. Eventually he said "I can't think of anything that may have been missed. How many men will I need?"

"It's a big delivery you will need at least a dozen good men."

Their thoughts were interrupted as they heard Jasper call out a greeting as he rounded the corner from the harbour. He made his way across to them and was greeted with warm handshakes. Jasper looked from one to the other and said to Robert "I take it that Charlie has been talking to you about next Wednesday? Are you happy with the arrangements?"

"Yes I think so. I can't think of anything that's been missed."

"Good." Jasper turned to Charlie, "I will make sure that Bill and George understand their part on Saturday night in the Anchor."

Charlie nodded in appreciation of a job well done then called out to Ben Mellor, "Ben, be a good man and bring more drinks for my two friends here." He reached into his pocket and produced a silver crown," That should cover all the drinks and a little something for yourself."

Ben was very grateful, touched his forelock and disappeared inside to do Charlie's bidding.

Jasper shook his head, "You're incorrigible, Charlie. You've probably made another friend for life."

Charlie chuckled "You never know when that might come in handy, in any case he seems a good man." He smiled looking in the direction of the door to the Inn. "Right, I will have to go now. I don't think there is anything else to discuss. If you do think of anything, Robert, speak with Jasper. I'll bid you farewell and the best of luck for next Wednesday - not that you'll need luck."

He then turned and climbed into his carriage where his horse had been patiently waiting pawing the ground. They sat down, and after their drinks had been delivered, Jasper tapped Robert on the knee, "Don't worry. I know your concerns but I believe Charlie has covered everything."

Robert shook his head, "That Charlie is unbelievable. There I was ready to say that I wanted to stop working for him and I end up agreeing to do probably the biggest job he's had in years. He did mention a bonus though but not how much."

Jasper laughed, "From what Charlie has told me, there is enough profit from this shipment for all concerned to be paid handsomely. Don't worry, I think that you can tell Sarah that if there is anything that the children need then it will not be a problem."

Robert nodded but deep down there was the slight churning in the stomach; a feeling of foreboding.

As Charlie's horse pulled his carriage leisurely along the High Street he was very pleased with his day. He now felt that, baring accidents, the shipment would be secured. He made his way to the offices of a firm of solicitors where he met James Tyler. Charlie felt confident enough for provisional Agreements to be drawn up; what could go wrong?

The Anchor, which was favoured mainly by the local fishermen, was a whitewashed stone building on the harbour front facing the bay. The line of high backed wooden settles were laid out in a line creating a corridor from the front door that protected against any strong draughts from the sea winds. It being summer, many drinkers were outside. Some sat astride wooden benches or casually leant against the front of the building unconcerned about any residue whitewash brushing off on their backs.

Charlie's plan started out even better than expected. Keziah Willmot being a bachelor decided not to spend the evening at home alone and went to join some of his men at the Anchor. He wasn't a particularly welcome addition to their group but after all he was the officer in charge. The conversation was stilted as Keziah had little to contribute and his men were not relaxed by his presence.

After several drinks Willmot went to relieve himself outside. Seeing through the window when he was about to return Bill and George, followed their instructions. They started talking loud enough that when Willmot was the other side of the settle he could overhear their conversation.

"Captain Jenkins says he has some work for us in the Bay on Wednesday night. He says it's to bring in something that's urgently needed." Willmot stopped in his tracks and wide eyed, he strained to listen to the rest of the conversation. "I'm not sure what he wants to bring ashore, but it seems important." Willmot was beside himself and carried on listening intently. "Captain said not to tell anyone."

Willmot breathed to himself. 'Yesss got them. That can only mean that smug Captain Jenkins will bring contraband ashore and I, Keziah Willmot, will catch him red-handed.'

The conversation then moved on to the attributes of the comely new serving girl, Isabella, brought in that evening by the landlord, Matthew Gibbs. This was of no interest to Willmot and he re-joined his rather reluctant colleagues. He immediately whispered to them that all leave was cancelled on Wednesday as there was an important mission that he would lead personally. He then sat in the bar room looking casually around but trying not to look at the table who's conversation he had just overheard. After a while he became bored. He could never see the enjoyment of sitting in an Inn drinking all evening. He finished his drink and said farewell for the evening much to the relief of his companions.

He could not help himself from glancing at the table he had overheard when he passed them. Bill nodded in his direction and bade him innocently, "Good evening, Mr Willmot." As soon as he had gone through the door he was sure he heard them explode into laughter.

"Life is what happens to us while we are making other plans."

At dusk on Wednesday Captain Jenkins sat on the capstan that tethered his boat, The Pride of the Bay, and puffed slowly on his pipe. Jenkins had taken a great deal of convincing to act as a decoy but Charlie had been as persuasive as ever. He was of the same mind as Robert as he mused that this would definitely be the last job he would do for Charlie. Jenkins had already reduced his fishing and the ferrying of passengers across the Bay to the point where he had virtually retired. He had been prudent and with much hard effort over the years and with the potential sale of his boat he had saved enough money to be able to sit back to enjoy a life free of work.

As he bent down to knock his pipe on the capstan he saw a movement in the corner of his eye. He carried on clearing his pipe but as he sat upright he could see Keziah Willmot behind the corner of Bay Street Willmot and his men had flattened themselves against the wall but had failed to realise their reflection was there to be seen in a window of Bill Thorpe's chandlers shop. Jenkins chuckled, it would appear that Charlie's plan was starting to work.

All it needed now was for Bill and George Saunders to arrive. They were not the most reliable, punctual or sober crew he had ever used, but this was a short and easy sail out into the Bay and back again.

Jenkins grunted with satisfaction when his intrepid crew arrived almost on time. However Jenkins almost immediately closed his eyes in frustration and said softly to himself. "Oh no."

"Good evening, Cap'n. We're ready to do this important job for you." Sam called out loudly.

George theatrically remonstrated with a loud "Ssssch." as if they were trying to keep quiet.

"In God's name, get on board." Jenkins could do without any such nonsense.

The two brothers jumped on board and whilst casting off made as much noise as they could with the dropping of chains together with loud curses. They made sure anyone near the harbour knew that they were about to set sail.

Jenkins had already started to get a bad feeling about the whole business. Also he did not know that Willmot was about to throw a spanner in the works with tragic consequences. Willmot had originally decided that he would follow Jenkins out into the Bay in one of his new Coastguard vessels and catch him in the act of loading the contraband.

Unfortunately it was a cold, overcast night and the Bay was in total darkness. There was only the odd light shining from the windows of the houses in Swanage and they reached no more than a few hundred yards from shore. The wind was also increasing, and although Willmot was an ex naval officer and his men were good seamen, the thought of tossing about in complete darkness in the middle of the Bay did not seem an attractive idea to Keziah. He could brave the elements, but even then the most skilful of sailors could lose track of another vessel in the pitch dark of the night. He decided to stay on the quayside waiting for Jenkins to return. After all it would be much easier to arrest the crew on land than steering alongside a pitching vessel in the middle of the Bay.

Alf Simpson was standing at a discreet distance holding the shoulder of his lad; watching the watchers. Billy saw Captain Jenkin's boat cast off and he looked up at his father. "Do I run to Mr Bridle's now pa?"

Alf Simpson was worried as he watched Willmot let Captain Jenkins set sail with no attempt to follow him. Why was Willmot not moving? Had he got wind that the real landing was at Dancing Ledge? Charlie had made it very clear that the night's shipment was very important. Alf dare not jeopardise the whole affair. If he sent his lad with the message that all was going to plan and Willmot then made a move on Robert and his men, then it would be a disaster for everyone. Alf hesitated "No, wait lad I'll tell you when." He stood and waited for Willmot to make his move.

Robert meanwhile had rowed around Egmont Point into Chapman's Cove. He and his men sat in two boats quietly rocking on the waves with oars shipped staring up in the direction of Tom Bridles cottage. After a time the signal was made from The Albemarle's boats that they were ready to make their move. Ted Edmonds sat with a lantern that had already been lit and he was protecting it from being washed out and as well as making sure that it could not be seen by mistake by The Albemarle. Robert sat tight waiting until he could see Tom's light on the top of the cliff. Time passed and the cottage remained obstinately dark and lifeless.

The Albemarle signalled again. Robert waited. Half an hour passed and his men were starting to get restless as the wind increased, as did the rocking of their boats. "Something must have gone wrong" one man murmured. "Come on, let's get moving Billy Simpson probably got lost in the dark when he was running from Swanage." Came from another.

Water was now starting to blow over the crews as they sat still, waiting.   A particularly large wave crashed against Robert's boat soaking all aboard. Clem Hardman always an impatient man called across to Robert from the other boat. "Come on Robert, let's get moving one way or another, we're getting bloody cold and wet sitting here."

Robert made a decision. Although there was no sign of life at all coming from the cliff top, he decided to press on. "Light the lantern and make the signal for The Albemarle to follow us." Ted Edmunds swung his lantern and an acknowledgement came back immediately and within minutes the two boats from the Albemarle emerged through the darkness. "In God's name, it's about time." Were the first words called across the waves.

Robert ignored them and shouted his reply over the noise of the wind. "Follow us, Dancing Ledge is about 50 yards away. My men will get onto the Ledge and when you get alongside we'll throw a double rope for you to put around each of the barrels and chests." He then turned to his own crews "Now pull as hard as you can lads. The sooner this job is finished the better." A very bumpy 15 minutes saw them reach Dancing ledge. "Ted, stay in one of the boats. Keep the other boat seaward and use an oar to make sure that neither crash into the rocks. Right, the rest of you onto the Ledge as quick as possible."

By the time they had all scrambled up onto Dancing Ledge the first of the Albemarle's boats was ready to unload. Two ropes were tied around each barrel then joined so that they could then be dragged up onto the Ledge, The cargo of one boat was discharged, and the crew pulled away to allow the second to take its place. The now empty boat did not wait around but made its way back immediately to it's mother ship.

The coxswain of the second boat was not happy. He had been waiting at the mouth of the Cove for what seemed ages. He was getting increasingly more wet and uncomfortable as each minute passed. He then had to wait for the first boat to unload before him. He called up to those on the Ledge, "Ahoy there, get this lot up as quick as you can, I'm ticked off with this job." His men needed no invitation to carry out their task as quickly as they could.

All the chests and all but one of the barrels were unloaded. The ropes were by now soaking wet and when looped around the final barrel this time they slipped. The whole crew desperately rushed to re-tie the barrel accompanied by a string of curses from their boat's coxswain. The moment the final barrel was hauled up a large wave crashed the boat against the rocks and threw the crew across to the opposite side. With the entire weight on one side the next wave caused it to capsize and all the six men on board were thrown into the foaming sea.

Four men including the coxswain were dashed against the rocks within seconds. Three of their bodies were washed ashore over the next week. One was never seen again. Ted Edmonds seeing the tragedy thrust the oar he was holding towards the figures thrashing about just yards from him. One was lucky when a wave caught hold of him and dumped him onto a secondary ledge just below Robert and his men. He was quickly hauled up to them. The last man grabbed hold of Ted's proffered oar and pulled on it in his panic. It was snatched fromTed's hand and he staggered back but fortunately landed on the floor of the boat.

The man still in the water was caught by yet another wave and luck was on his side. He was thrown into the side of Ted's boat giving him a large gash across his cheek. The luck was that he was able to keep a hold of the side of the boat.

Robert had watched in horror the events below him. To his great relief he saw Ted stagger back to his knees on the bottom of his boat. He shouted as loud as he could, "Are you alright Ted?"

Ted waved indicating that he was still alive. He then called back "I couldn't hold onto the other boat. I'm afraid it's been carried away." He then turned to the poor soul hanging on the side of the boat. Look mate, I'm going to pull you on board. Don't make any sudden move or you'll drown us both." With that, Ted grabbed hold of the waistband of the man's trousers and with all his might pulled him up to the lip of the boat. When he was able, the sodden individual hooked his leg over the side and collapsed on board. To his credit his first words were, "Where are my shipmates? Are the safe?"

Ted shook his head, "One is up on the Ledge. The others ...." He stopped and shook his head.

He was then distracted as he heard Robert shout again. "Ted, we need to get away from here before the storm worsens. We will get to the lower ledge one at a time and when a wave pushes the boat high enough we will jump on board." He then turned to his men behind "Right, first one tie a rope around you and I will hold the other end. Get down to that ledge there and when you hear me shout - jump - go for it." He looked at each of them, "Men, it's tough in the quarries. Let's see how tough you are now." The first man took a deep breath and did as he was told. It was a slow operation as each man picked his way down to the bottom ledge. Clem Hardman was the last man before Robert. Seeing his mates make the boat, Clem got overconfident and miss-timed his jump. He caught the edge of the boat but fortunately bounced on board. He gave a howl of pain. His shin bone was at an angle that indicated a clean break.

Robert was the last to go. He coiled the rope around a rock and made his way down to the lower ledge. Half way he slipped and at that moment a huge wave lifted him up to the height of Dancing Ledge. The rope rose above the rock which it was looped around and Robert was swept into the sea. He didn't surface.

The fury of the storm carried on unabated. The men in the boat looked on in horror and fell silent, Each man desperately searched the foaming waves for any sight of Robert.

Ted Edmunds could be heard "Oh God. No, please." he breathed in anguish.

"The waves continued to crash against the rocks but did not reveal any sign of their victim. Ted continued to plead, "Please, please, please - no."

Another huge wave crashed into the boat nearly capsizing it. Everyone was tossed into each other. Clem Hardman's leg bounced onto the side of the boat provoking another loud curse. "I'm in agony here. My leg's killing me. Can't we go back to shore now."

"Shut up." was the response from most of the men who did not bother to look round but kept searching the waves,

"Hey! Come on lads, in the Lord's name help me on board." Everyone spun round to the opposite side of the boat. There was Robert's head, his hair plastered down on his forehead and his hands gripping the side of the boat. Ted was the first to react as he scrambled over the still cursing Clem Hardman and grabbed hold of one of Robert's hands. Another man quicker than the others rushed forward to take hold of Robert's other hand and with all their strength they hauled the bedraggled and exhausted Robert on board.

Robert lay in the bottom of the boat as he gasped to recover his breath. He lay panting looking at the crowd of soaked figures huddled together in the boat. Nobody spoke as they stared at him waiting for him give directions. Robert gathered his wits as fast as he could. "Right, is everyone here?"

Ted answered. "Aye, all our lads are here."

Robert took stock of the situation and then took command.

"There's not much room with all of us in one boat Those of you who feel most able, take an oar and when I say pull, take us away from this God forsaken rock. We are going onto the beach, it's too rough now to go around Egmont Point and its only about half a mile to the land." He looked at Ted Edmonds who was now crouched at the front of the boat. "It's going to be a long haul as we won't be able to climb the cliffs, we will have to go the longer way round back to the village." He looked down at the wincing, forlorn figure of Clem Hardman, "We have also got to take it in turns to carry Clem with his broken leg."

As they slowly pulled their way to the beach Robert mumbled under his breath, "God preserve us, what a night. Four men lost and one broken leg. Never again."

Before Robert returned home he made sure that Clem Hardman had been delivered back to his wife, Ethel. She showed little surprise and sympathy when told it was mainly Clem's own carelessness that had caused his injury.

"Damed fool." Was her immediate response. She helped Ted Edmunds get Clem into his bed, then she confronted Robert. "How in the Lord's name will we survive with no money coming in until he can work again?" Without waiting for a response she continued, "He can't go down in the lanes with a broken leg and his Lordship is not going to pay him for laying in bed."

Robert was irked and fed up and could do without Ethel's tirade. He walked over to the window and peered into the darkness. After some minutes he turned and held his hand up to stop Ethel firing another volley. "Clem works in the Crack Lane Quarry, as the manager I will give him duties which he can do sitting on his backside. He can take the carts down to Swanage until his leg heals." He looked hard at Ethel, "Just make sure that he gets to the quarry on time and I'll make sure he does a full day's work." He turned to leave but then faced Ethel again and added angrily, "I know it won't be easy but it's his own bloody fault."

With that parting shot they left and bidding Ted goodnight Robert returned to a waiting and anxious Sarah. When he appeared at the door she made sure that he was in one piece and there were no officers of the law with him. She sighed and said a quiet "Thank the Lord."

Sarah took his arm and walked him to his chair by the fire that she had kept alight. She knew her man and kneeling at his feet she asked with concern, "You've had some problems, haven't you?"

The warmth of the fire, the trials of the night and the loving comfort of Sarah suddenly made Robert overcome with tiredness. With a deep breath he said, "Yes, my dear, but not from the Coastguards. We lost some men in the Bay." Sarah took a sharp intake of breath. She knew all the men that had gone with Robert that night and their wives were close friends in the village.

"No, none of our men." Robert said quickly. "We lost four poor souls from the main ship out in The Channel. The weather turned bad and after their boat had off-loaded their cargo it was caught by the heavy seas and they perished on the rocks." He closed his eyes with his head in his hands and then gave out an enormous yawn. He looked at Sarah the tiredness showing on his face, "Sarah, I will tell you all that happened in the morning but right now I would love a large mug of tea. Can you use what's left from Charlie's last shipment?"

Sarah jumped to her feet, "Of course, " she said, "and there's water near boiling in the kettle." By the time she returned just a few minutes later Robert was fast asleep in his chair with his head thrown back, mouth open and snoring loudly. She smiled and went to fetch a blanket which she put over him. After raking the fire down for the night she went to bed with a sense of relief. This relief was mixed with a determination in her heart that her husband was not the next to perish on one of Charlie Heywood's missions.

The storm that raged in Chapman's Cove would subside overnight as Robert slept. However it was to be more than matched by the man-made storm that was brewing in Swanage. All the plans that had been put together by the Lords Olden and Wareham, Charlie Heywood and Jasper were in danger of being dashed by a rash act of folly. Calvin

444

Seagers fears expressed to Charlie in The Ship looked as though they were about to materialise.

CHAPTER TWENTY-TWO

Rhetoric or Revolution

Rhetoric is the art of persuasion that is indifferent to right and
wrong: its only concern is to convince. (Plato: Republic)

Captain Jenkins wasn't sure if he had done the right thing.
As he cast off and reached the open sea he was expecting to
see the dim outline of Wilmot's boat trailing him. As time
passed it was obvious he was alone. A storm was brewing
and experience told him that it was going to be an
uncomfortable night for anyone off shore. There was not
much for his crew to do. A straightforward trip out into the
Bay a couple of circles, then a pause as if picking something
out of the water, was meat and drink to himself and his crew.
Charlie had given them a flagon of brandy as comfort against
a cold night on the open sea. Once clear of the shore he
retrieved two tin mugs from the wheelhouse and filled each
to give to his men.

The next hour passed without incident but there was no
sign of Wilmot. It became boring and his crew of two
consumed the brandy with a relish to pass the time. The wind
was starting to increase and whilst there was no problem
weathering the gathering storm it seemed as though he was
wasting his time. He was also getting concerned that Bill and
George had almost finished the flagon of brandy and were
now not at their sharpest, in fact, they had got to the stage
where they could hardly stand. Jenkins could sail his vessel
single handed if needed but he felt it was time to go back to
Swanage. He just hoped that he had not let Charlie down.

The thick blue tunics of Wilmot and his men only just kept
the cold wind at bay. Wilmot had moved to Wash Lane just
thirty yards away from Jenkins mooring position. The

command of silence to his men was broken by the stamping of feet which belied their discomfort.

As Captain Jenkins approached the harbour he saw that the Wilmott's boat had not moved. He tied up on the quayside and told his men to get on home. George tripped as he tried to jump ashore and fell awkwardly and landed heavily on both knees. His brother theatrically tried to get him back on his feet.

Wilmot saw his chance to what he thought would be to catch them red-handed with contraband. Striding from out of the darkness he called over his shoulder, "Right Coastguards, do your duty, arrest these men."

George was totally confused and forgot that he hadn't committed any crime. Staggering to his feet he shouted, "Come on Bill let's leg it." He started to career down the quayside with Bill unsteadily following.

Wilmot summoning his most authoritative tone shouted after them, "Stop in the name of the King. Stop or my men will fire."

Captain Jenkins could see matters were getting out of hand and he leapt forward with his hands on the air, "Look they've not done anything wrong."

Wilmot not to be denied, called back, "Out of the way sir, or my men will fire."

Corporal Stills behind him had his rifle raised said, "Pardon Mr Wilmot what did you say?"

He turned and shouted from a distance of just a few feet, "You buffoon, I said if he does not stand aside - Fire, "

Corporal Stills jumped in alarm – and fired.

Captain Jenkins who was moving towards them, jolted backwards and crumpled in a heap with a jagged hole shattering his forehead.

Everyone on the quayside froze. Wilmot's mouth gaped open.

The silence was broken by a voice from the direction of the doorway of the Anchor Inn. Matthew Gibbs, the landlord, had seen the whole episode, "You bloody murderers. You've shot poor old Captain Jenkins. You bastards." he snarled.

Wilmot swung round and with his face inches from Stills' bawled out, "You damned fool. Why did you fire."

Stills stuttered and spluttered, "Oh God, Oh no. I'm sorry sir. You made me jump and I thought you said 'Fire'"

"You idiot" Wilmot shouted.

By now there was a crowd gathering.

"What's happened?"

"Good God, is that old Captain Jenkins lying there?"

Several men rushed forward to the body that hadn't moved. Kneeling by the prone figure, after a moment Matthew looked up at Wilmot, and with tears of rage in his eyes muttered, "He's dead. You bloody murderer!" He then started to move towards Wilmot.

Wilmot could see the situation was turning nasty and definitely getting out of hand. He faced the growing crowd who were moving towards him with their fists clenched. He started to panic and decided to beat a hasty retreat in the direction of the High Street and out of Swanage. He called out a breathless command, "Men, you're dismissed." He then sprinted at full speed putting as much distance as he could to the scene behind him, closely followed by his men.

A small, angry posse started to pursue them but stopped when Matthew raised his arm to stop the chase. "Come on, we know where to find him. Someone had better go to let poor Martha Jenkins know what's happened. The poor woman" He looked in the direction of the departed Wilmot "The bastards."

The group then despondently walked back to the quayside where Mordachai Benfield was already taking care of business.

* * *

The following morning broke with clear skies and a watery sun but the biting wind persisted. Matthew Gibbs woke with that gnawing feeling in the stomach that something was wrong. His first thought was for his eldest lad George who had recently had the fever. Many in the town had succumbed to the latest outbreak but as Matthew stirred he could hear George talking excitedly to his younger brother William.

As Matthew swung his legs over the side of the bed he heard the sound of voices being raised outside on the quayside. Looking out of the window he saw that there were about a dozen men who he recognised as all being fishermen of the town. As he watched whilst getting slowly dressed the crew of four men from the lugger Fair Maid joined the animated group.   It was then that the tragedy from the previous night rushed back to mind.   He saw the jaw of a young man that had just arrived drop in surprise. His face then turned to anger and spinning around he aimed a heft kick at an empty crab pot which was propelled into the sea.

Matthew hurriedly pulled on his moleskin trousers and as he descended the stairs he buttoned his collarless shirt which still had the sleeves rolled up above the elbow from the previous day. He paused at the door and quickly inspected himself in the mirror whilst putting his feet into his boots. He, as usual, sported several days growth of beard and with a grunt licked his fingers so as to slick down the errant hairs from his thick dark mop that were sticking up from a night's sleep.

Matthew was an intelligent man, now in his early thirties, and was of a larger than average stature.   His family had owned the small Seacombe Quarry and he started working for his father, Mike Gibbs, in the same way as Jasper and Robert.

Matthew was the eldest sibling and he became the owner of Seacombe Quarry when he was twenty three years old. Tragedy had struck when at the end of another long day working for most of the time in pitch darkness, he started to crawl along one of the lanes to make his way to the surface. His way was blocked and after groping in the dark realised it was the lifeless body of his father. He had to crawl over the top of the prone figure and with much effort, and tears streaking the grime down his face, he dragged his father to the bottom of the shaft. Calling out for help to his two younger brothers who were on the surface, the three of them were able to pull the lifeless form of Mike Gibbs to the surface.

. He was determined that he would not spend the rest of his days crawling along underground in pitch darkness only for his worn out body to be found in the same way as his father's. Not without difficulty he found work for his younger brothers at the larger Crack Lane Quarry. He then sold Seacombe Quarry and used the money to put a down payment on the Anchor Inn on the quayside in Swanage.

He soon built a reputation as a good host but not one with which to cross swords.

Having witnessed the previous night's drama, his wife, Milly, caught his arm as he was about to leave. She knew Matthew "Be careful." She whispered.

As he approached the group which was fast growing into a sizeable crowd he heard someone say "Look, here's Matthew now. He saw what happened."

All the faces turned to look at Matthew. "Who killed poor old Captain Jenkins? We heard it was that bastard Wilmott?" Matthew looked around. Fishermen were different from other men of the lower sort. They owned their boats and were governed by the tides so they made their own judgements as to when to set sail to bring in a catch. He judged that not a boat had left Swanage harbour on this morning.

Matthew jumped up onto a capstan so that he could be seen. The crowd was still growing. The fishermen were incensed at the killing of one of their own and Captain Jenkins was a man who was loved and respected. As the commotion built the crowd started to grow. He could feel that it was not just the Captain's fate that was igniting a general mood of anger.

Matthew was not a troublemaker, his problem was that he could get carried away on emotion. He held his hands up so that he could be heard. "Listen men, Captain Jenkins was killed for no good reason. We all knew him, he was well-liked by virtually everyone in the town – wasn't he?"

"Aye, you're right." Was a chorus from the crowd.

"He had plied his trade in the Bay all his life. He never have a bad word to say about anyone and you could always rely on his help if needed."

Jed Williams the captain of the Fair Maid called out, "When my boat was out of action, he let me use his boat so that I could still bring in a catch. The Lord knows what I would have done without his help. Aye, he was a good man" This brought another round of growled approval.

Matthew continued, "Captain Jenkins was not doing anything wrong. He was trying to help those goddam Coastguards." He paused for effect to let his words sink in, "What did he get for his help? I'll tell you what he got. He was shot down – killed – in cold blood!" As Matthew's version of the shooting gave no hint of the misunderstanding between Wilmot and his man the mood was further stoked by incredulity and then to fury.

Matthew was warming to his theme. "What are we going to do about it? Are we going to let Wilmot get away with his murder?" Matthew paused again, then continued, "What

451

will happen about this pointless killing? I'll tell you what –
nothing! If Wilmot was to be put before the Magistrate he
would get off scot free. Magistrate Bothroyd is in the pocket
of Lord Kenway. His Lordship has only one thing on his mind
– and that's making as much money as he can from the hard
work of you who work for him."

One man pushed his way to the front, "Aye, you're right.
I work on one of his farms and he has told us that he will be
cutting our wages by a shilling a week."

There was another roar of anger. Matthew knew he had
touched a nerve. Joseph Budden called out, "It's not just the
Coastguards and Lord Kenway. That Reverend Dafdd, he's
put up his Tithes again. I'm a tenant on one of Kenway's
farms and these have been hard times in recent years. But
Dafdd, that arrogant son of a bitch, cares nothing for any of
us. It seems to me that if Lord Kenway or Reverend Dafdd
don't starve us out then the King's men will shoot us!"

The action of Wilmot and his men was in danger of
blowing the cap off the volcano.

"Kenway's at his Studland House now" Matthew shouted
across the heads of the crowd which was fast degenerating
into a mob. "I say we go there now. I say we tell him that
Wilmot must be brought to justice."

The farm labourer turned round and waving his fist
shouted "We're with you aren't we lads?"

"Yes!!" was again roared back.

Joseph Budden did not want to miss the chance of
rectifying his own pet grievance. "I also say that we get
Dafdd and take him to Studland House and get Kenway to
make him promise to reduce his Tithes."

"Right! We'll do it." Matthew assumed full command.
"Joseph you take a dozen men and collect Dafdd from his
rectory and meet us at Corfe. Alf, Jim and Mike, you're good
horsemen go tell Bob Richards you want to borrow three of

his best mounts. Tell him what's happening here, I'm sure he will agree. If not take them anyway. Go around as many of the farms as you can and get the lads on the land to meet the rest of us at Corfe Castle. They'll be only too glad to join us. We've had bad harvests since the war and Kenway is going to reduce their wages so that he still makes his money. I tell you it would be better to be a dog than work on the land next winter if he gets his way."

Matthew stopped, looked around catching as many eyes as he could. He noted several unfamiliar faces in the crowd who were nudging the men around them and angrily making gestures with their clenched fists. Matthew was too inflamed himself to care so he raised his own fist in the air and shouted "Come on, men. Now is our time. We are going to fight back."

A tremendous cheer drowned all opinions and reservations. Those detailed for tasks went to their business and the rest, now about two hundred strong, started the trek to Studland House eight miles away.

Matthew had certainly got carried away this time. Unlike the march by Jasper Tomes and the workers from the Crack Lane Quarry there was now a general mood throughout the area for rebellion. This was not a single issue, this was going to be an attack on the three pillars of English society. Now under threat were the government as they were the landowners, the church and the rule of law.

Milly Gibbs had watched her husband throughout his tirade. She was fearful of where this would end. There was no point in her trying to stop him. Matthew's passions were inflamed and he had a temper. She had felt the back of his hand in the past. She loved him but she knew he was not to be stopped when the mood took him.

As Milly saw the crowd fall in behind her husband, Ellen Tomes came and stood alongside her. "What's happening? I heard that poor old Captain Jenkins is dead."

"Aye that's right. The coastguards killed him." Gesturing to the disappearing crowd she added, "They're all off to make sure that Officer Wilmot is brought to justice."

Ellen studied those filing passed her, "There seems to be more than the fishermen in that crowd."

"Yes, all the old sores have come out. I'm frightened for where it might all end." Milly turned to Ellen, "Your man should know about this. He's the only one they will listen to."

Ellen frowned, "Yes he should know what's happening. He's up at Langton Matravers, I'll get a message to him." She looked round and seeing George Gibbs watching with his brother, she asked, "Could you get your George to run up to the village. He's certainly quicker than me."

Milly hesitated, then realising her husband needed to be reigned in, she called George over to her. "George, I want you to give a message to Mr Tomes He's up in the village." She paused and said to Ellen, "Where will he find him?"

Ellen thought quickly. Jasper did not usually tell his wife his business but she remembered him mentioning Jacob Butt before leaving the house early that morning. "I'm sure you'll find him at the blacksmith's cottage."

Milly spoke to her boy, "Run as fast as you can, George. Tell Mr Tomes that Captain Jenkins was killed last night and most of the town are on their way to storm Studland House. Also tell him that some of them are going to get Reverend Dafdd on their way." She looked hard at her boy, "Have you got all that George?"

"Yes, ma. I saw what happened." At that he spun round and ran as fast as his young legs could carry him.

* * *

The road to Studland House passes through the village of Corfe which is dominated by the ruined Castle. When the throng arrived at the village, Matthew turned and held his arms aloft. "Take a rest here lads. We'll wait for the others from the farms to join us. Get yourselves ready to deal with his Lordship." After a thought he added, "Aye lads, we'll also wait here for Joseph. He will have to come this way after getting his Reverence."

After the previous night's storm the road was muddy and the steep hill out of Corfe was very slippery. The hard slog strengthened the resolve of most of Matthew's ardent followers. There were a few of the older and the less convinced about their mission, seeing the slippery road ahead, they turned back.

Matthew looked around and found a large stone to sit on under the ruined walls. He was joined by Jed Williams who gave Matthew a careful look then said, "Are you sure about this Matthew? The good Captain was a lovely man and I owed him much for when my boat was laid up." He paused and looked around at the assembled townspeople which were now being joined by a steady stream of men from the farms in the area. "This could get out of hand and there would be big trouble. Lord Kenway is not the kindest of milords. He'll want his revenge if we harm him or his property."

Jed thought that he had persuaded Matthew to have second thoughts. There was a moment's pause but any further talk was cut short by a shout "Here comes Joseph and he's got Dafdd with him" There was a short pause then laughter followed by another voice calling out, "His reverence doesn't look happy." The Reverend Dafdd was walking in front of Joseph's men and every few yards he was given a shove in the back almost causing him to stumble each time. He was finally brought before Matthew.

On seeing Matthew, Dafdd' eyes widened and he spat out, "So it's you Gibbs is it? You're the ringleader of this rabble are you?"

Matthew snapped and leapt to his feet, "Rabble are we? What does the Good Book say *"The Lord is my shepherd. I shall not want........he restores my soul"*. You are supposed to look after our souls but all you *WANT* is to increase the money you take from us so that you can sit on your fat backside and wine and dine with the fine Lords and Ladies." He turned away and frowned, not sure if had said that right. He shrugged, then spun back and put his face inches from that of the unfortunate Dafdd. "When was the last time you took a service? In fact when was the last time you were in one of your churches?" Matthew turned away and added to no-one in particular "Man of God? He's no better than a leech."

Alf, one of the riders sent to the farms came galloping up. He reigned in his horse and in turning it round to face Matthew managed to get its rear end to knock Dafdd off his feet. Ignoring what had happened he spoke to Matthew, "I've told as many as I could to go on to Studland House if we've left here. They didn't need to be told twice."

Matthew looked around him quickly taking in the growing horde of angry men. The unfamiliar faces in the crowd seemed to have increased and they were very animated in their conversations with those about them who would listen. Matthew started to worry but events already had a momentum of their own. Riding on the wave of his own rhetoric he called to all about him. "Right, come on men let's go and sort out that bastard Kenway"

Amid much cheering and waving of fists the host moved onward resolute in believing that this time they would get justice.

* * *

456

Jasper met with Jacob Butt whilst he was at his forge. There may be many folk around and about that were unhappy but Jacob was not among them. He now had a regular supply of business from the quarries which was increasing as more stone was being extracted. This was on top of the work that was brought in from the local gentry.

On seeing Jasper, Jacob downed tools and told his eldest son who was learning his trade to keep the fire on heat until he returned. "Gooday to you, Jasper. How is Ellen and Jemima or is there another Tomes in the world yet?"

Jasper shook his head, "It's only Jemima, unless there's another on the way that I don't know about." he said laughing. "I haven't seen you lately and I thought I would see that all was well with yourself." He paused and added smiling, "I thought I would also get up to date with what's been happening in the village. If you don't know about something then it's not worth knowing about."

Jacob responded, "Couldn't be better for myself, or for most of the stonemen in the village." Then he added with a grimace, "It's not too good for many of the others around here, though." He stopped and asked, "Would you like some tea or I've got some of Charlie Heywood's brew?" He grinned and gave a wink. Getting a 'Yes' he called out to his wife for two mugs.

They then spent some time talking about the village. There was good news of a couple of successful births and the impending marriage of one of the village girls to a farmer over at Worth Matravers. Jacob's mood changed when he related the problems facing many villagers who worked on the land following the last two harvests that had been very bad.

After a while Jasper thanked Jacob and rose to walk in the direction of The Ship Inn. He was anxious to get news of George Tupe who he had been told was finding it increasingly difficult to cope since his wife Maud had gone back to live with her mother. He had just reached StoneHouse Hill when a breathless George Gibbs saw him and came running over.

"Mr Tomes. Mr Tomes. I've got a message from Mrs Tomes."

"Alright lad get your breath" Jasper was immediately alarmed that there must be a problem with Ellen or Jemima.

George blurted out "Mrs Tomes said to tell you that Captain Jenkins has been murdered and all the town and other people around here are marching to Studland House and they say they are going to kill Lord Kenway and the Reverend Dafdd." Poor George confirmed that a message repeated is never quite the same as the original.

Jasper's eye took on a steely glint, "Are you sure, boy?"

"Yes Mr Tomes. That's exactly what I was told to tell you." George was, like many, in awe of Jasper and having delivered his message he wanted to go home.

"Alright off you go. Just tell -" he was interrupted by the sight of a galloping horse ridden by Mike one of the three mounted messengers despatched by Matthew Gibbs.

Jasper called for him to stop and grabbed the bridle as the sweating mount came alongside him. "What's the rush?" he asked at the same time as avoiding being knocked to the ground.

Mike repeated the message he had now given a dozen times. "We're all going to Studland House to get justice for Captain Jenkins and stop Lord Kenway cutting everybody's wages." Another message that ignored the whole truth as a great number of the marching horde did not get paid by Lord Kenway.

Once having delivered his piece to Jasper he pulled the reigns hard to the side and before Jasper could react he was gone to continue on his mission.

Jasper was momentarily dumbstruck. What had started as a quiet day with a comfortable walk of two miles to his home village had been changed by two messages that portended the disaster that Lord Henry had feared.

He ran back to Jacob's forge. "Jacob, have you a horse that's fully ready for a hard ride?"

Jacob initially frowned. He had not seen Jasper so animated but then looking around he nodded in the direction of a chestnut mare calmly munching on the grass. "Aye take that one. I've just finished re-shoeing her and she's ready saddled to take back to Lord Wareham." He looked at Jasper and added, "She's a strong one, she will be able to take a man like yourself with no problem."

"Thanks very much, Jacob." As he quickly mounted Jacob heard him mutter "In God's name I hope I'm in time." At which he dug in his heels and he disappeared in the direction of Corfe Castle.

At the junction with the track running between Corfe Castle and Wareham the half mile long driveway to Kenway House has two Lodges either side.

When the dissident army had reached the entrance to the Estate they were confronted by Gabriel Hammond the gatekeeper. Although a retired military man he was initially unnerved by the sight of two to three hundred shouting and gesticulating local citizenry bearing down upon him. However, as he had faced the columns of the French, he would confront this force of mainly local men.

There was a pause in the momentum of the mass and Matthew taking his cue approached Gabriel. "Stand aside Gabriel, we have no quarrel with you."

Gabriel stood his ground, "This is Lord Kenway's private Estate and nobody goes passed me without my permission."

Before either could speak again the Reverend Dafdd broke free of his captors and stumbled forward "This rabble have come to do mischief. I am a prisoner and I fear for my life," he stopped seeing no concern on Gabriel's face. He added quickly in the hope of more sympathy, "...and I fear for the lives of Lord and Lady Kenway."

Gabriel looked back at Matthew "Is this right. Are you here to do harm to his Lordship?" Matthew was not going to engage in conversation but simply stated, "We are here for justice. We will not be denied, Stand aside."

Those near enough to hear this exchange took up Matthew's demand, "Make way. We will not waste time here on his Lordship's flunky." The mass now started to press forward.

Matthew, albeit resolute in his mission, was starting to worry. The tempers and passions were exceeding even his own. One of the men that he recognised as one of the newcomers in the town, rushed forward and grabbing Gabriel by his jacket spun him round and threw against his own front door where he lay spreadeagled and stunned. The man, then gesturing for all to follow him, called out, "Come on men! It's time for Kenway to get a taste of our justice."

Matthew looked on as the throng pushed passed him. Seeing Gabriel struggling to regain his feet he went over and helped him stand, "Are you alright?" he asked with concern.

"Aye, I'll be fine.' He looked to the front of the crowd. "That man is not from these parts. I'll warrant he's not interested in your problems. He is here for his own reasons."

Matthew nodded and seeing that Gabriel was only shaken he left him and ran through the press of men so that he could be at the head when they reached the House. He reached the side of Gabriel's attacker and still walking, addressed him, "Sir, I don't recognise you. What's your name? What's your business here?"

460

Without breaking step and not turning to look at Matthew he responded, "The name is Bert Cato. I'm here to see that Lord Kenway and his kind receive their just deserts." There was a snarl of hatred across his face as he spat the words out. As if he felt that it needed further emphasis he growled, "Kenway and all them fat aristos live off the backs of us, the working masses." Again for further emphasis he addressed those nearest him, "Are we going to let this bloodsucker keep us down under his heel? I say we throw him out of his fine house and burn it down."

Matthew was now truly frightened as men that he had known all his life were taken on a wave of hatred as they snarled their approval of Cato's rallying calls. Matters were fast getting totally out of control.

Studland House was a large square mansion that had finished being built just ten years previously. It portrayed the image of the Establishment - it was permanent - it would be there when the mob before it were gone. It was a plain straightforward red bricked building without too much superfluous ornamentation. It was a building suitable for a man without pretensions. There were long windows all around so that every side could view the surrounding landscape. Rectangular bays at the front guarded double doors of black oak panelling. When shut they firmly repelled all visitors but when opened they displayed a wide welcoming entrance.

The crowd went quiet as the house stood defiantly before them. This calm was broken when Matthew watched in horror as a number of men rushed to pick up ornamental stones which were then hurled through one of the ground floor windows.

Matthew leapt forward and faced what was now a mob. Holding his arms up he shouted, "Men, this isn't what we came here for. We're here to get justice for Captain Jenkins.

Lord Kenway won't pay wages to those who destroy his house and threaten his family."

Cato was intent on making the most of the situation. Pushing Matthew aside he moved forward to the front door and started kicking his heel into the woodwork. "Come on help break this down and we'll drag Kenway out here." Three men joined Cato and started to batter the door. The mob was now in Cato's control.

At this point, men at the back of the throng spun round to the noise of horse's hooves at full gallop. They spread out to allow a way through for the awesome figure of Jasper Tomes. The rage on his face was unlike any had seen from their neighbour and now Mayor. Jasper charged his mount in between Cato and the three others who were at the door and the rest of the mob. Jerking the reigns round the rear of the horse bowled over two men at the door. Leaping from the saddle he grabbed hold of Cato by the collar of his jacket and the seat of his trousers and flung him into the crowd. Cato and about six men landed in a heap. The remaining man at the door ran at full pelt back into the crowd.

A hush fell over the scene. Jasper stood in front of them his legs apart and his hands on his hips. "Any man who wants to kick the door down goes through me." His face was flushed and the deep scar across his head was a livid cleft. The steely glint in his eye diverted the look from any that was caught by it. Who was going to risk it? The mob paused, uncertain to what would happen next. Three hundred men against one is not a contest but these men, with the exception of Cato and his cohort, were not soldiers or revolutionaries. They were farmers, fishermen and tradespeople. All they wanted was justice and a fair deal.

Matthew had recovered his composure and approached Jasper. Cato had struggled to his feet and called across to Matthew, "Are you going to let one man stop us?" Matthew spun round and said with an even tone, "Look you, shut up." Cato opened his mouth to speak but was cut off. "I said shut up." He looked over to the men close to him, "Bill, Tom, Harry - take him over to that field over there. There's a big pool of water from the rain last night. Sit him in it to cool him down."

There was a cheer. To most the sudden realisation of what had been about to happen shocked them into silence when Cato was dragged away.

Matthew faced Jasper and spoke softy, "Jasper, Lord Kenway has a lot to answer." There was a murmur from those nearest to him. A look from Jasper and they went silent again. Matthew continued, "Poor Captain Jenkins was shot down in cold blood last night and we want justice."

A farm labourer growled quietly, "Aye, I work on one of his Lordship's farm and I want justice as well. We can barely keep our families clothed and fed on our wages and now he wants to cut them by a shilling to nine shillings a week. If he does that all his tenants on their farms will do the same." This provoked a louder murmur of anger.

Joseph Budden was not to be denied and by now had made his way to the front pushing the unfortunate Reverend Dafdd in front of him. "This dog has put up his Tithes although there's not much coming off the land from the last two harvests. Why is it only those who work that suffer?" The murmurs of agreement were getting louder again.

Matthew turned to Jasper, "These men have real grievances. If something's not done then, it may not be now, but one spark of injustice will see that man Cato and his type win the day."

Jasper nodded. He could see that Matthew spoke the truth. He raised his hands for silence. This was the moment of decision that George Herbert and Tom Wilson had prophesied he would have to face. It was as though his whole life had come as a preparation for this time. He looked back at Studland House then back at the mob.

He took a deep breath and then spoke briskly, "Right. Matthew you come with me and we will speak with his Lordship. When we get in there keep quiet and let me do the talking. You lads there," he said gesturing to a number of men he knew from the town, "Keep that man in the field, and don't let him anywhere near the House." He then turned to the rest of the crowd and called over their heads "The rest of you go back towards the lodge at least a hundred yards. I promise you that I will speak on your behalf and I will come back to you to report what happens." There was the start of a drift back up the driveway. To emphasise his message Jasper called out again, "Please, I promise I will do what I can, but go back from the House" This achieved his aim and the crowd as a whole started to move away. There were many who had had enough and started to leave to go back to Swanage or their farms.

He spoke quietly to Matthew. "Jed Williams stayed with Gabriel at the gatehouse and has told me exactly what has happened.

He turned towards the House when a plaintiff voice called out "What about me?" The Reverend Dafdd was still shaking.

Jasper gestured to Joseph. "Let him go. Your Reverence come with me. I strongly suggest that when we get inside if you know what's good for you, say nothing." He looked at Joseph then back to Dafdd, "or I'll send you back out here to be looked after by Mr Budden again." Dafdd gave a yelp of thanks and scurried to stand alongside Jasper and Matthew.

Jasper turned and seeing faces at a window he called out "Please advise his Lordship that I wish to avoid any bloodshed and further damage. I would be honoured if he would allow me to meet with him to this end."

One of the faces disappeared and there was a long wait until Jasper feared that his request was to be denied. Eventually the front door was opened slowly by a footman who stood aside to let pass a large shaven headed man. As the man strode forward he was tapping one hand with a heavy cudgel held in the other. His face was one of malevolent aggression. The man spoke, "I am Lord Kenway's Bailiff anything you have to say can be said to me."

Jasper was unabashed. He said nothing for a full minute and Matthew started to fidget uncomfortably. Finally Jasper spoke in a quiet even tone, "Please pass to his Lordship my respects. Can you also tell him that it is very important that I speak with him personally. If this is not possible please advise him that I will re-mount and make my way back to Swanage. I will advise the men you see behind me of his refusal and I will also have released that man in the field who has his own reasons to be here. Please advise Lord Kenway that his reasons are certainly not in his Lordship's best interests."

Jasper's eye did not blink as he held the Bailiff's stare. Jasper then finished by saying, "I will wait for what I consider a reasonable time to pass on my request. If there is no response to grant me permission to meet Lord Kenway personally then I shall leave." With that he turned abruptly and holding the Reverend Dafdd' arm in a vice-like grip marched him back to the start of the Driveway some thirty yards away.

The Bailiff hesitated then shaking his head, grimacing he disappeared inside.

Matthew looked at Jasper, "My God. You move in high places to be able to make demands on his Lordship in such a manner."

Jasper shook his head "No. I know my place as do you and the rest of the men from around these parts. It's him and his kind who want to change our way of life." he gestured to

Cato who was still under close guard. "His Lordship though needs to know the danger he is in if he ignores my request." He turned to observe Studland House for any sign that an answer was forthcoming. After a few moments a round chubby, bespectacled face appeared in an upstairs window then quickly disappeared. Again Jasper felt he had failed, then the door was thrown open and the Bailiff came forward to stand on the top step. He waved his hand to call Jasper to him. Jasper stood his ground and returned the Bailiff's glare.

After a few moments the Bailiff shrugged and strode forward to stand in front of Jasper, "I'm a local man like yourself, Tomes and this play acting is all nonsense."

Jasper who knew the man as John Meagen grunted in reply, "I agree. His Lordship I'm sure is watching us, he has to know that these men behind me are not to be taken lightly."

Meagen nodded, "Yes I have told his Lordship exactly the position and that he could not afford to ignore your request to meet him." He went to turn back to the House and added "Follow me, his Lordship will see you now - alone."

Jasper had taken a pace then stopped, "Mr Gibbs here will join me. I'm also sure that he will not deny an entrance to the Reverend Dafdd." Having made his point he walked passed Meagen up to the House. He then stood aside to let the pursuing Bailiff take the lead and direct him to Lord Kenway.

Through the large Entrance Hall the door to the library was open. As the visiting party approached the doorway a pinched faced Lady scurried passed them without glancing in their direction. They entered the room and Lord Kenway was standing behind a large desk flanked on either side by two very nervous looking footmen.

Lord Kenway a short rotund man was dressed in a brown frock coat under which was a yellow waistcoat and fussily tied cravat. The waistcoat barely covered the stomach before reaching a pair of tight breeches which met knee length leather boots. His clothes gave the impression of being slightly dated and old fashioned. Lord Kenway had a round smooth almost shiny face with no trace of any whiskers; any hair was limited to a slight fringe at the side and back of the head. Perched on the bridge of his nose was a pair of pince nez over which he peered at the intruders.

The Reverend Dafdd rushed forward proffering his hand. Lord Kenway's hands remained steadfastly behind his back and with a flick of the head gestured for Dafdd to be seated in a chair at the foot of an imposing wall of books.

When his Lordship spoke, his voice was of a high note and a slight quaver belied his underlying nervousness which at this moment was bordering on fear. He pursed his lips and with all the authority he could muster expostulated, "What do you rogues and that rabble outside want from me, what, what?" The sentence ended with a mannerism picked up in the Court of the late King George 111 and surfaced when in a state of anxiety.

Jasper ignored his Lordship's question. "My Lord you are in great peril today. Outside there are many men good and true but they are sorely aggrieved. Among them are outsiders who are presently roaming the country with the one aim of provoking rebellion and a break down of law and order."

Lord Kenway interrupted before Jasper could continue, "Yes, yes quite so.. His Grace the Duke of Wellington has warned against the mood that is afoot. He has vowed to stand firm and to keep our traditional rights and laws. He will not allow the country to be bowed by revolutionary ideas."

Jasper responded quickly, "I know not of the politics in London. I do know that there are many opposed to his Grace's ideas and that they should win the day." He looked sideways at Matthew who showed his confusion to what was being said. Jasper nodded towards Matthew and continued, "Mr Gibbs here represents those men," he pointed out of the window, "who have certain grievances that must be settled. We cannot answer the problems for the rest of the country but we can satisfy those good men outside. If we do not then I fear that yourself and your property are gravely at risk."

Lord Kenway was alarmed and his resolution was waning but he continued to bluster, "I have already sent one of my men in all urgency to Poole. There will be troops here before the end of the day."

Jasper shook his head sadly "I fear if that is the case and we have no satisfactory resolution then they will be too late for yourself." He paused for effect, "..and there is your family and Studland House to consider. My Lord this affair may end with much bloodshed. I fear for the men outside as well as yourself. It may end there but it could be the spark that ignites the fire across the country. Remember France."

Lord Kenway sunk into the chair behind his desk. He pulled a silk from the pocket of his coat and wiped his face which was now sweating profusely. "What is to be done? What is to be done?" he trembled.

Jasper gave a great sigh of relief. He had driven his message home. He took a pace forward which drew no movement from His Lordship's guards. To take the moment he spoke quickly, "The matter can be settled without delay. Firstly, Chief Officer Wilmot would have been trying to do his duty. He may have been over zealous and clumsy but he is an honest man. I would suggest that you let it be known that you condemn his action but then arrange for him to be transferred immediately, possibly to Hasting or Ramsgate. I would strongly suggest that he leaves tonight."

Jasper looked back at Matthew and added, "I believe that if he is not seen around here again he will be soon forgotten. Is that not the case, Matthew?"

Matthew was still in awe of all that was being spoken and nodded hastily. He was not going to challenge his Lordship and especially Jasper.

Jasper turned back to Lord Kenway, "Secondly, the shilling a week you are proposing to take from your labourers' wages is to be dropped. You will continue to pay them nine shillings a week which is only just a living wage for these poor men. I would add, sir, that over at Selbourne where their farms are very much the same as your own, they are paying eleven shillings a week." Jasper stopped to wait for a reaction to his proposals.

Lord Kenway stared at Jasper, then after a few moments peering over his Pince Nez he asked cautiously, "Is that all that is required?"

"Yes, my Lord." Jasper responded simply. He then noticed Dafdd who had been sat as commanded, in silence, "Oh, there is one other matter. This man of God has in successive years increased his Tithes with no regard to what has been produced from the land. He now lives in luxury whilst his flock, after many bad harvests, are on the point of ruin. His Tithes must be halved. This will likewise be similar to other parishes."

Dafdd leapt from his chair, "How dare you! I will do no such thing."

Lord Kenway was recovering his composure and also rose to his feet and spoke abruptly to his Reverence, "Dammit sir! You will be quiet. You will also do as you are instructed. I may add, sir, if I hear any more from you then I shall speak with His Grace, the Earl of Purbeck, who holds your Living and have you replaced. "

Dafdd slumped back into his chair. This was a battle he could not win. It had been a terrible day for his Reverence.

Lord Kenway addressed Jasper again, "I agree with your proposals. Wilmot will be transferred forthwith. The labourers wages will remain at nine shillings. Oh," he glanced in the direction of the deflated man of God, "- and the Reverend Dafdd will halve his Tithes with immediate effect." He looked at Jasper with a frown, "Is that all it will take to end this affair?"

Jasper slowly nodded his head in agreement. "Yes, my Lord. Times are changing and men just want simple justice." He then finished by saying, "I hope this affair is totally at an end and there will be no reprisals." Lord Kenway dismissively waved his hand. "Thank you my Lord. I will let the men know of your understanding and they will no doubt disperse to their homes immediately."

With no more to be said Jasper and Matthew turned and walked quickly to the front door where they passed John Meagen. He offered his hand which Jasper took and Meagen said a quiet "Well done."

When outside and they were clear of the House Jasper stopped and spoke firmly to Matthew. "Your nonsense back in Swanage nearly caused a disaster. I suggest, Matthew, that you think first before you start preaching revolution."

"I didn't. I was just....." Jasper cut him short.

"You may not have meant it but that is what you nearly caused. You would have had blood on your hands and you would have landed up swinging from the hangman's gibbet." He softened his tone, "What is done, is done. As it happens, good has come out of today."

"Thanks to you, Jasper." Matthew said quickly.

"Aye, that is as it may be. It's just a pity that to get any change there has to be a threat of some sort. Trouble is, I don't think that will change any time soon." He paused, then brightening up he continued. "Now go tell the men the good news and tell them to go home. Tell them to be quick about it as the troops will be here before long. We don't want any misunderstandings. Jasper thought for a moment then added, "Get a few of the big lads to grab hold of Cato's mates. It's obvious which ones they are, then frogmarch them all back to Swanage. There's always a boat soon to be sailing for France. Put them on one of them and Charlie Heywood will pay their Captain to dump them on a French beach. They like revolutions in France, they'll feel at home.

Matthew laughed, "That will be a pleasure. I will see to that myself.

Jasper then waved across for his horse to be brought over to him. "I had better take Lord Wareham's horse back to Jacob Butt else I'll be in trouble." he said with a chuckle.

As he rode off Matthew said under his breath, "I don't think so somehow."

Printed in Great Britain
by Amazon